CU00484792

About the Author

The author is a full-time doctor and medical writer who has seen first-hand the impact technology and bureaucracy has had on patients over a thirty-year career.

Flick of a Switch
A Neurosurgeon's Tale

Tim Jacobsen

Flick of a Switch
A Neurosurgeon's Tale

Olympia Publishers
London

www.olympiapublishers.com
OLYMPIA PAPERBACK EDITION

Copyright © Tim Jacobsen 2022

The right of Tim Jacobsen to be identified as author of
this work has been asserted in accordance with sections 77 and 78
of the Copyright, Designs and Patents Act 1988.

All Rights Reserved

No reproduction, copy or transmission of this publication
may be made without written permission.
No paragraph of this publication may be reproduced,
copied or transmitted save with the written permission of the
publisher, or in accordance with the provisions
of the Copyright Act 1956 (as amended).

Any person who commits any unauthorised act in relation to
this publication may be liable to criminal
prosecution and civil claims for damage.

A CIP catalogue record for this title is
available from the British Library.

ISBN: 978-1-80074-127-0

This is a work of fiction.
Names, characters, places and incidents originate from the writer's
imagination. Any resemblance to actual persons, living or dead, is
purely coincidental.

First Published in 2022

Olympia Publishers
Tallis House
2 Tallis Street
London
EC4Y 0AB

Printed in Great Britain

When a middle-aged couple dies in a mysterious cliffside accident, Lewis Thomas, neurosurgeon by day and wine connoisseur/ functioning alcoholic by night, is asked by police to assist with their investigation. The post-mortem uncovers a chilling mystery: one of the victims has a stimulator planted in his brain. With no clues as to its origins, who made it, who implanted it, Lewis' curiosity is piqued. As he becomes more and more deeply involved in the police investigation, unimaginably sinister corporate deception is exposed. Will Lewis live to regret it?

Dedicated to the front line medical and nursing staff around the world frustrated by politics and bureaucracy.

CHAPTER 1

So, you're about to retire. You've probably worked your whole life. You've had a few holidays, maybe spent a lot of time and effort on your children who, by now, are getting on with their own lives. So, just when you think you may have a chance to relax and spend your pension on holidays to places you have always wanted to go, or maybe tick a few things off that bucket list people always talk about, you start getting hip or knee pain in the mornings, or worse still, diagnosed with a terminal disease, develop heart problems or have a stroke. Mike had that stroke.

Mike Taylor was a salesman for a US medical device company. He had worked for them for years. He liked his job, but was certainly ready to give up the long trips and the constant necessity of meeting sales targets. Sales is a stressful job. Lots of early starts, long-distance driving and, of course, the obligatory wining and dining of clients. Turning 60, he had a rugged face with an equally unkempt brown and grey beard to match his messy hair. Mike always wanted to interact with his clients. He liked to wear his red and white chequered shirt to meetings, the buttons gripping to the fabric for dear life as his belly fat and hair poked out from the spaces between them. For some reason, it made him think he would be more approachable. Mike was overweight due to his love of high carb foods and beer, and he was looking forward to retiring in a year. Indeed, he would have time to work out, get fit and be the man he'd always wanted to be.

After a satisfying breakfast consisting of two fried eggs, sausages, bacon, waffles with maple syrup and two cups of strong coffee, Mike kissed his wife goodbye and squeezed himself into his car. Just shuffling himself into the driving seat caused him to wheeze. He took a few moments to catch his breath before stretching out to fasten his seatbelt. While driving his car to his next sales appointment, Mike detected a faint headache across the right side of his head. He had continued to drive without giving the sensation much thought, but before long, became slightly disorientated. Mike swallowed, shook his head and tried to blink a few times. Snap out of it, he thought. The pain didn't subside and his ability to see straight began to wane. As his vision blurred, he lost any sense of direction. The car weaved across the road. Mike, trying to take control of his vehicle, suddenly lost the feeling in his left arm and leg. "What the fuck!" He began to say, but the words tumbled out of his mouth, heavy and incomprehensible. He tried to speak again, but once more, the words came unruly and disobedient like boulders crashing and crumbling down a hillside cliff. With his right arm, Mike had just enough strength to manoeuvre his car onto the sidewalk before causing any accidents. Thank God for his automatic Chevrolet Sedan! A clutch pedal would have seen him to his deathbed. Mike sat in a daze, his mind befuddled and frightened, unable to understand what was going on. Fortunately for him, a lady walking by discovered him in this state and called an ambulance straight away.

The neurons in the motor cortex on the right side of his brain had lost their blood supply due to a blocked cerebral artery. He could not move his left arm and leg and only time would tell how much function he would recover, if at all. The stroke came as a real blow to both him and his family. Mike Taylor had taken his health for granted his entire life. Only when he fell ill did he realise he should have celebrated life, his loved ones and being able to do what he wanted to do without pain or heartache. Humans will always abuse their body until it's too late to do anything about it. Smoking, drinking and unhealthy diets will all take their toll eventually, but until that time comes, we eat, drink and get merry. At least, that's the philosophy Mike Taylor lived by before he had his stroke.

After six months of intense rehabilitation and frustration, Mike's left side was still useless. There was a flicker of movement but nothing else. Understandably, he was angry. Like most people who are incapacitated by illness in later life, he questioned why he had worked so hard for other people and waited too long to enjoy life after retirement. He wished he could go back in time and spend more quality time with his wife and work less when he was younger, but you don't think like that when you're on the conveyer belt of life, do you?

Working hard for the majority of his adult-life did turn out to be quite advantageous, though. Mike had gained some useful medical knowledge from his position at the sales company which, ironically, sold rehabilitation devices for spinal cord injury patients. Unable to work and with a lot of extra time on his hands, he dedicated his days to researching the latest advances in the management of stroke patients. His research revealed to him that stem cell treatment was going to be the next medical breakthrough. From what he understood, scientists can take what are called pluripotent cells and grow these cells in laboratories using any tissue, be they from the heart, muscles or from neurons. In the labs, scientists regulate the environment so the cells have enough food and oxygen necessary for growth. Another thing he came across was deep brain stimulation, also known as DBS. This technology has transformed the lives of people with epilepsy or Parkinson's disease. It is a procedure where a surgeon drills a small hole into the skull and a wire is used to target a specific area of the brain. The wire is attached to a small battery under the skin which releases a current of electricity which evens out the abnormal electrical signals that occur in epilepsy or movement disorders. Mike watched videos on the internet of a patient with Parkinson's disease. Some of the patients had severely exaggerated movements of the hand, so much so that the patients couldn't even drink a glass of water without spilling it all over themselves. After activating the stimulator, though, the abnormal movement appeared to stop. Mike's mind was blown... in a good way this time. After a bit of digging and falling into a few Wikipedia wormholes, Mike discovered that there was a Neurosurgeon in the UK who was also implanting these special devices into people with epilepsy. Bingo. He went by the name of Mr Crispin Humphries.

Mike was somewhat puzzled to find out that someone who wasn't a doctor could be transplanting devices into people's brains. He discovered that surgeons in the UK are prefixed with 'Mr' rather than 'Dr' and that surgery in the UK actually developed from 'barbers'. What an odd bunch of people, he thought, imagining his own barber starting to do brain surgery on him at the shop. He was, however, reassured after reading the many flattering testimonials on Mr Crispin Humphries' website. It didn't take long for Mike and his wife

Beverly to hop on a plane over the Atlantic.

Mr Humphries' clinic was on the prestigious Harley Street in London. From the moment they stepped foot in the building, the two received five-star treatment. Humphries' clinic wasn't like any old clinic. In fact, from the chandelier in the lobby and the courteous doorman who led them in, the clinic seemed more like a luxurious hotel than a place to receive any form of medical treatment. A young receptionist led the two into Mr Humphries' office which also seemed more like a lavish hotel suite than a room in a doctor's practice. Crispin greeted Mike and Beverley with an exaggerated show of hospitality.

"Welcome, welcome, welcome… please, sit!" He said, presenting the two with a grin so wide that each of his perfectly sculpted, snow white teeth shone on full display. Crispin ushered them to sit down on a plush purple chaise longue. "You've come a long way, it seems." He remarked, and then, despite neither Mike nor Beverly having had the chance to respond, added, "good… good." Clearly this was not going to be an open conversation.

Crispin explained what the process would be if Mike decided to go forward with the surgery. His voice was assured and his spiel well-rehearsed. As he spoke, Crispin paced around his office like a shark circling his prey. Though she didn't want to admit it, he reminded Beverly of an overly enthusiastic TV presenter. Humphries' air of superiority matched the glamourous interior of his office. His desk was an enormous mahogany table, so thoroughly polished Mike could make out his reflection on its surface. A variety of high-tech gadgets were arranged on top, alongside an open box of cigars wrapped in gold ribbon and an enlarged photograph of himself receiving an award. This was presented in a gold-encrusted frame to match the cigars which, Mike assumed, were just for display.

"And so!" Crispin announced excitedly, making Mike and Beverly jump. "What will it be?" he asked, intentionally drawing out the 'be' for theatrical effect. The two felt more like guests on a chat show than patients at a medical appointment.

"Well, I… err…" Mike stuttered.

Crispin interrupted. "Do you want to live, Mr Taylor? Or do you want to live?"

"I guess I want to live," responded Mike.

"Well, what are we waiting for? We can put you in for surgery next week." And that was that. Mike's fate was sealed.

The surgery went well. With no complications nor hiccups to contend with, Mike and Beverly made a prompt return to America where Mike was able to recover in the comfort of his own home. Nothing seemed to change initially, but within a few months, Mike slowly regained the use of his left arm. Within six months, Mike was able to walk independently. At last, retirement was beginning to look like the paradise the two had both dreamt of. At least, it was for a while. After around a year had passed since the DBS had been implanted, Mike's memory began to falter. As well as that, every so often he would have an aggressive episode. Nothing too out of the ordinary for a cantankerous old man, but for Mike, someone normally so docile, sudden angry outbursts seemed out of character. Beverly was afraid for her husband, so they decided to revisit their neurosurgeon in the UK.

Back in Mr Humphries' sumptuous Harley Street Clinic,

Crispin told them both he did not see any connection with Mike's mental deterioration and the insertion of the DBS. A CT scan of the brain confirmed that there were no apparent abnormalities. Crispin reassured them both that it would settle down but later took Beverly to one side and privately explained that Mike may be developing early signs of dementia and that, as a stroke victim, had a higher risk of dementia in any case. Crispin apologised and said that, unfortunately, he could help no further and discharged them. This was deeply disappointing. The two of them felt completely at a loss. To have come so far just to be told that there was nothing more to be done was devastating.

Beverly decided that while they were in the UK, they should pass by the coast and travel to Dover. It could be their last chance to appreciate a small break together before Mike's condition worsened. They went to a very traditional English pub and reminisced about the good old times over wine coupled with pie and mash. Although Mike was convinced that he was still in America, they were able to have a giggle and look back at all the wonderful things they had done. After dinner, a light stroll along the coast was in order. Beverly greedily breathed in the fresh sea air, drawing out each inhale as if to soak up and prolong what she believed may be the last time they would be able to do this together. They held hands as they walked along the top of the white, Dover cliffs. The sun had almost been extinguished by the sea; the finals rays, a haunting, blood red tableau on the horizon. Beverly caressed Mike's hand as she held it in hers, a hand which, before the procedure, had been a limp, useless appendage. No longer like a bird's broken wing, Mike's grasp strengthened. Palm to palm they walked closer towards the cliff edge. The remaining light cast a final shadow behind the couple, a ghostly dark trail reaching back towards the mainland. "I know I am not right, Beverley, but thank you for putting up with me. When do we go to England?"

"Mike, I love you. I'd do anything for you. And we are in England, silly."

"I know, yes, I know. Don't call me silly." His tone became aggravated, as it often did before an episode, which frightened Beverley.

"Sorry, darling." She said in an attempt to comfort him. A tear began to form in the corner of her eye. "Yes, I know. Let's try to enjoy the sunset, shall we?"

Mike lunged forwards. Beverley had no choice but to grab his hand and be in unison with him, fearing something may happen if she let him go. He was looking straight ahead. Beverley smiled awkwardly, slightly stumbling as Mike quickened the tempo.

"Mike, darling. Be careful." Beverly's voice wavered as she spoke, not wanting to provoke Mike into a fit but equally worried about the approaching cliff edge. Heights made her stomach churn. Mike was beginning to stumble too and, Beverly noticed, he had a strange, detached look in his eye, like he wasn't all there.

"Mike?" Beverly spoke again, more insistent this time. "What are you doing?" Mike pressed on, locking his fingers around Beverly's hands. Beverley, still afraid of distressing Mike by showing she was panicked, tried to wriggle free but to no avail. She instinctively began to tug him back. Mike showed no sign of stopping, though. If anything, he was gathering pace. Unable to totally match his stride, she whipped in front of him, placing both of her hands on his chest. Mike stopped in his tracks. A quick glance over her shoulder confirmed her fears. They were heading straight towards the edge of the cliff.

She was now in front of Mike who was looking out towards the sea. They were both balanced leaning into each other at the edge of the cliff. Beverley had her arms outstretched on Mike's shoulders. Her head bent forward looking at Mike's feet while she caught her breath. Both silent and still. She was just about to talk when Mike pushed forward again forcing Beverley backwards.

Suddenly, she lost her footing. There was a pause. Everything came to a standstill. It seemed as if she was moving in slow motion. And then there was only air and space and gravity pulling her down. She had spoken too late. As time began to spiral, so did she. But not without grabbing Mike's coat, in some vain attempt to grab onto something solid. The last thing she saw before the collision was the vacant look in Mike's eyes, as if his soul had already departed. Beverley felt the thud of the rocks on the side of her head, searing pain and then... darkness. They say your life flashes before your eyes before you die, but there was no flashback, no floating down a tunnel towards a bright light. Just darkness and expiry of consciousness. A flickering candle flame blown out. In the black void, only the quivering silhouette of the flame remained, but even this gradually faded away into nothingness. The brain understood that this must be death and ceased to function.

CHAPTER 2

It was evening, and Lewis Thomas was at home when his mobile phone rang. It was the on-call neurosurgical registrar, David. Registrars are trainees aiming to become consultants and, although not experts, they have enough knowledge to perform basic operations. When appointed as a consultant, you are supposed to be an independent medical practitioner. It can take about eight years to become a consultant, though surgery is, of course, a life-long learning experience. Lewis hated being on call with David. David was one of those irritating militant doctors who bask in the glory of being a junior neurosurgeon without actually having any of the skills.

"Mr Thomas? David here. We have a twenty-two-year-old foreign male who has crashed a stolen vehicle. No seatbelt and utterly intoxicated. He has sustained severe facial injuries, and the CT scan shows a large subdural haematoma. Glasgow Coma Scale is 4, extending to pain and a fixed dilated right pupil."

"So, what's the plan?"

"I think he needs an urgent craniotomy and evacuation of the subdural."

"You okay to crack on with it?"

"Absolutely," said David.

"By the way, what does it matter that he's foreign?"

"Nothing, I was just trying to be accurate."

Lewis was being pedantic. David was always trying to get above his station. That wasn't really the issue though. Lewis just didn't have any faith in David. David could probably do the operation, but Lewis knew that it would take David twice as long and that he would provoke the theatre staff with his dickhead comments.

"Right, better get on with it then! It doesn't sound like we have much time if he has a fixed pupil." If the pupil is fixed and dilated, this usually means that there's a large clot of blood causing the brain to press on the nerve which controls pupillary dilatation. Hopefully you'll never need to check, but for future reference, dead people typically have both pupils fixed and dilated.

Anyway, Lewis now found himself in a slight predicament. You see, he'd opened a bottle of his favourite red and, although on-call, had convinced himself that a couple of glasses would be all right. Just like the night before. And the night before that. The bottle was a blend of four grapes, and without any tannins, it was so smooth and delicious. How could he resist? One glass became most of the bottle, save a mouthful that remained at the bottom. He felt better if he left a small amount. In his mind, this meant that he had not drunk a whole bottle by himself. If only that were the only obstacle though. Having had his fill of the wine, he couldn't say no to half a packet of cigarettes, could he? He hated the fact that he smoked, if only for it signalling his inability to stop. He had tried everything: hypnosis, nicotine patches, the Allan Carr book, acupuncture and electronic cigarettes, but all without any success. He cleared the mound of cigarettes from the ashtray into the bin which, having built up over the last few evenings, appeared to be evolving into a colony of empty bottles, cigarette butts and take-away boxes threatening to consume the bin itself. Lewis eyed the packet of cigarettes on the countertop where two remaining orange snouts poked out. I suppose, he said to himself, if I leave one, it's not like I finished the whole packet... Restraint was not one of his strong points.

With a sigh of resignation, he lit what he promised would be his final cigarette and contemplated what would happen if he left David to do the operation alone. Nope. Not a good idea. He stubbed the cigarette out, put his leathers on and made off to the hospital on his motorbike.

In theatre, unaware of Lewis who was watching him through the shutters, David was wasting time prancing about and ordering the theatre staff around. What a dick, Lewis thought to himself.

"I don't use these theatre drapes, go get me the ones I normally use!" David barked.

"These are the ones Mr Thomas uses," said Patience.

Patience was a large Afro-Caribbean theatre nurse who didn't take bullshit from anyone. As she moved around the theatre, her buttocks seemed to sway from side to side independently of her body. Two imperfectly round globes hypnotically swinging to and fro like pendulums. Any sane person wouldn't risk upsetting Patience. It was easy to imagine those globes doing some good damage. David, however, was a fool.

"I don't care, they're not the ones that I use!" David whined. He was making quite the performance. Patience, knowing better than to waste energy on such childish displays, appeared to swallow down her response. Patient she was, and intuitive. Patience knew what the surgeon needed before he even asked for it. She was well known for helping junior surgeons who were out of their depth but afraid to call for help. You would be forgiven for disbelieving that this woman was in fact one of the 'behind the scenes' staff, a fact which often puzzled many patients at the hospital. You would also be forgiven for thinking she loathed her profession when faced with her signature abruptness and bullish demeaner, but Patience loved the job and was proud to be involved in saving people's lives, even if she never got the credit. She certainly didn't do it for the money, that's for sure, as the money for what she did was a pittance. Having been raised by the most humble and selfless of parents, money had never been a priority for Patience. Her family had come from the Caribbean in the '50s and, following in her mother's footsteps, Patience had always dreamt of becoming a nurse. While the likes of David did not make her job any easier, Patience was used to dealing with such incompetency. Lewis, who was still enjoying this little sitcom from beyond the theatre shutters, debated how long he should wait before intervening.

The patient had been placed in headpins to stop the head from moving when drilling into it. Lewis could see that David had made the rookie error of puncturing the patient's ear lobe with one of the pins, a classic mistake when someone is rushing through an operation. Some doctors are naturals. Their hand movements are gracefully coordinated, advancing through the operation as if in an expertly choreographed dance. They can make even the most complex of surgeries look easy. David, however, was rough. His hand movements were less like a dance and more like a bumbling drunk skating on ice. Slightly concerning, as you can imagine. This was an emergency, and David was skating on very thin ice. The routine checks, despite the theatre staff protesting, were being ignored by David. Have the antibiotics been administered yet? Is he even going to operate on the correct side of the brain? Lewis was beginning to worry. Time was critical for the patient's survival. He edged ever closer to stepping in, but part of him held back still hoping that David could figure this one out for himself.

David stood at the patient's head and, with unmerited authority, proudly commanded the room. "Okay, everyone pay attention to me. This patient will die unless I take this clot out of his brain, so I need you all to keep focused." Everyone rolled their eyes in unison. Of course, everyone had seen this infantile behaviour before, but David was an extreme case. He loved to be the star of the show.

"Knife." Patience handed David the instrument which, with a few uncertain strokes, he used to make a semi-circular incision in the skin. A trail of scarlet red arterial blood began to seep out the incision. David just stood there, watching the blood flow from the wound. He quietly asked for suction as if unsure of his next steps and then, with a panicked flap of his arms, squawked several octaves higher, "suction, now!"

"Hold your horses, sunshine." Patience said. "Look, if you press on the skin edges as you cut, it will reduce the blood loss." David did this, and indeed, it controlled the bleeding. He looked at the anaesthetist.

"Can you reduce the blood pressure please? I think it's too high. That's what's causing the bleeding."

The anaesthetist looked over the newspaper that he was reading and, with a slight nod of his head, pretended to fiddle with a few knobs before returning to reading his paper. He knew there was nothing wrong with the blood pressure. It was David's technique and inexperience that was lacking. David had spent almost ten minutes just making the incision. Lewis was pacing outside. On the one hand, he wanted to believe that anyone could be a good surgeon, but in his heart of hearts, he knew it would take a lot more training and mentoring before he could leave David alone in the operating theatre. Maybe David would be better off training to be a sexually transmitted disease physician. Yes… for the elderly in the Outer Hebrides. That would be safer for the rest of humanity. Patience had already prepared the electric drill in anticipation of the next move, but David was still trying to stop every tiny bleeding capillary.

"Drill, quickly boy! We are not trying to make it as dry as the Sahara Desert, we are trying to save this boy's life."

David grabbed the drill out of Patience's hand and placed it over the skull, visibly angry that a nurse was telling him what to do. The drill slipped off of the bone.

"Can you hold the head still?" he snarled.

Lewis had had enough. As he entered, there was a unified sigh of relief in the theatre. "Hi, David, how's it going? Was a bit bored at home so I thought I'd pop in."

"Excellent, Mr Thomas. In fact, everything is going splendidly well. Right, Patience?" Patience just stared at David. "Right," he gulped. "Well, we're just about to crack open the skull." Worryingly, crack seemed like the appropriate word to use with the drill still in David's hands.

"Grand. I'm just going to get scrubbed in. I'll try not to take over." Lewis was going to take over. The water hardly touched his hands before he put his gown and gloves on. Bollocks to theatre protocol! Lewis knew that there was little evidence to suggest that thoroughly scrubbing the hands made any difference, anyway.

David attempted to drill into the skull for the second time, but again, the drill slipped off the head.

"Excuse me," Lewis said calmly as he took the drill out of David's hands. Within minutes, Lewis had drilled three holes into the skull. Lewis wasn't even thinking that much about what he was doing. After so much practice, it came automatically to him now. He could probably do this kind of surgery with his eyes closed. Patience changed the attachment and Lewis lifted a flap of bone to reveal a bulging layer of dura, the tough layer of tissue separating the delicate brain from the inside of the skull. The dura normally protects the brain; however, it was as tight as a drum skin here.

"Knife, please." Patience already had the knife in her hands. She passed it to Lewis. Lewis punctured the dura and with a pair of scissors, opening it up. This sudden relief of pressure caused an explosion of blood to erupt through the fleshy crater. The brain bulged and swelled, a red mass boiling over the side of the skull. Using bipolar cautery, Lewis stopped a few of the bleeding vessels on the surface of the brain.

"Let's leave the bone flap off and close up." The brain had become so inflamed that the sharp edges of the skull were cutting it. Lewis could not replace the bone. He knew that if he tried to squeeze the bone flap back on with a swollen brain, he would almost certainly increase the brain pressure further and damage the patient even more. If the patient survived, he could have a plastic insert placed into the defect. David, frustrated that he didn't, or rather, couldn't do the operation himself, sulked. The corners of his mouth slightly downturned, resembling a small child who has just been scolded.

Lewis closed the wound himself, leaving in a drain to prevent excess blood accumulating postoperatively. He then put a metal staple into the pierced ear, damaged by David's poorly placed headpins. Patience cleaned and dressed the wound with a bandage. She could smell the wine behind Lewis's mask, but she didn't say anything. There was no point in jeopardising his position. He was a great surgeon and the NHS needed him. Lewis quickly checked the pupils under the drape and discovered that the right pupil was still fixed and dilated. A bad sign. The left pupil had started to dilate too, an even worse sign.

"David, can you do the operation note and organise to rescan the patient? Let me know if there is a clot on the other side."

"Yes, Mr Thomas. You know I could have done this operation, don't you?"

"Yes, I'm sure you could." Lewis didn't want to add any salt to David's wound by telling him the truth. While it wasn't a particularly tricky operation to do, he doubted anything more complicated would be in the remit of David's skills.

With clots on the brain, time is everything. Unfortunately for this patient, it was probably too late by the time the patient was transferred to the neurosurgical unit. The damage to the brain had already been done. Yet another young life, full of potential, full of promise, expired.

As soon as Lewis felt that he was no longer needed, he got on his motorbike and headed back home. On arrival, he opened another bottle of wine, reached for his last smoke — once again, promising himself that this would be the last — and listened to Wild Horses by the Rolling Stones. Just as Lewis had predicted, David phoned him later that night to say that the patient had fixed dilated pupils and that they were going to perform brainstem death tests in the morning. It wasn't unusual for patients to die after severe brain injury. Perhaps surprisingly, what he did worry about were the ones who did survive, often with behavioural problems, memory loss, volatile moods and permanent headaches. Sadly, many were not even aware of their new bizarre, unfamiliar behaviour.

It tends to be the families who have to bear the burden of their loved one's disability. Sometimes, though, the patients were happy in their confusion.

Lewis used to see the survivors in his outpatient clinic. He would pat himself on the back thinking what a hero he was for saving so many lives. The families were always so grateful. As he became more senior, though, it dawned on him that ironically survival wasn't always the best outcome. He hated to admit it, but sometimes, he wondered whether it would have been better for his patients to have died. This is something Lewis especially felt whenever he caught up with outpatients at the clinic who understood their plight. They would chastise him and tell him that he shouldn't have saved their lives. One patient said that his life had become unbearable. With tears in his eyes, he announced that his wife had left him, he couldn't do his job, and that he had ended up alcohol dependent and on the verge of homelessness. Lewis realised from that moment on, that saving lives, wasn't the aim. No, if you want to be a real hero, Lewis thought, improving the quality of someone's life is what every surgeon should aspire to.

Lewis kept himself to himself. Most of his time was spent worrying about the patients he had operated on, or the ones he was going to. He had had girlfriends since graduating from medical school, with the longest relationship lasting for three years. They had moved in together and even talked about having a family. Lewis knew all along that it wasn't right, though. He didn't have the balls to end it, so instead, ran the relationship into the ground by spending every waking hour in the hospital, even when he didn't need to be there. The relationship eventually died, as expected, and she left him. He often thought of the words of his former cardiothoracic surgical boss, Mr Charles. He believed that "surgery and marriage are not compatible".

"Did you ever get married, Sir?"

"Did I ever get married. Did I ever get married?" replied the surgeon, who had a habit of intentionally repeating any question for dramatic effect. "Yes, I did. I saw her recently. She turned out to be a right old hag. Thank the Lord, I divorced her after a week! Surgery and marriage are simply not compatible."

Mr Charles went on to pursue a series of noncommittal relationships and developed a reputation as a bit of a philanderer. He wasn't much of a Casanova, though. Lewis befriended the scrub nurse who the cardiac surgeon happened to be seeing. At a social gathering, she confided in Lewis that she was upset by Mr Charles and wanted some advice.

"I do love him, but when he wants sex, he rings a bell and insists I bring him chilled champagne before we make love." Lewis paused to think. Lucky bastard.

"So, you don't want to shag him?"

"Well, yes, but it's not romantic, is it?"

"Well, I suppose it depends on your idea of romance." Lewis wondered what attracted the young scrub nurse to a prominent, multimillionaire cardiac surgeon with a four-storey house in Kensington.

It wasn't that Lewis did not want to have a girlfriend or

even a wife, it was that he knew he was too selfish to dedicate his time to a single person and neurosurgery at the same time. Or rather, he could dedicate himself to one person, but he wanted this person to be himself. At least, that's what he told himself. It's easier to not feel bitter about being alone, if you convince yourself it's an active choice you've made. You see, Lewis had a penchant for the finer things in life and simply preferred to keep them for himself. Both at home and at work, he was immaculately dressed. He could be found sporting classy, vintage English suits. Sometimes, he would go for the whole shebang, flaunting a bespoke tailored waistcoat, tweed jacket and shiny, silver cufflinks — the lot. At one stage, he even had a pocket watch. He later discarded it, though, as his colleagues made fun of him by buying him a monocle, pipe and deerstalker hat.

Lewis didn't know he was handsome. He was blessed with full, shiny brown hair which he parted to one side, flopping it over his forehead. He had enviably strong cheekbones, oaky brown eyes and just enough stubble to pass as cool and insouciant but still look soberly polished. For all his dignified good looks and flashy attire, Lewis remained very softly spoken and never raised his voice unless totally necessary. He did not feel the need to be in the spotlight, nor did he enjoy too much attention being on him at any one time. While he loved the perceived glamour of being a neurosurgeon, in reality, it was not as wonderful as he imagined it would be when he started training to be one. This was partly because he hated the hospital management. The National Health Service was increasingly cash strapped, making it difficult for him, or anyone else for that matter, to prosper. He was not able to pioneer any new treatments any more. His waiting lists had become unmanageable, and each new day brought with it a tidal wave of complaints. Regardless of the havoc being wreaked by the hospital management, Lewis did still feel terribly grateful to be a neurosurgeon. Quite frankly, he wasn't even entirely sure how he wangled his way into the position.

He only got two B grades and a D in his high school examinations, and with these relatively mediocre results, he got a place at Bangor University to study oceanography. He had no idea what this entailed, but it had connotations of sea, sun and sex. His headmaster persuaded him to retake his A-levels, and the second time around, Lewis was awarded three B grades in total. His reward was an unconditional offer to study medicine at a prominent London medical school. Every so often, Lewis would fantasise about what life could have been like had he pursued oceanography. Perhaps analysing fish scales would have been a more fulfilling profession… who knows?

During his first year at medical school, Lewis spent most of his time drinking, eating, shagging and failing exams. He didn't take the curriculum seriously and failed to take useful notes, instead opting to photocopy those written by the more diligent students in his residency which he then went onto share with his fellow med chums. His exam technique was appalling, and he was no stranger to last-minute cramming before tests. He would spend hours desperately consuming notes and textbooks which he didn't really understand because he never listened in lectures to later find out he had been reading the wrong section. He was a master of bucket-memory — pack it all in, try to remember it, and then throw it all out once the exam has finished. It didn't serve him well though. It came has no surprise when he flunked all his exams and had to spend his entire summer retaking them. Fortunately, he didn't have to retake the whole year.

In his second year, Lewis had broken his jaw at a school rugby tournament. He went into a tackle head-on, and the knee of his opponent crashed right into his jaw. Lewis felt a crack but foolishly carried on. After a second and conclusive tumble, Lewis collapsed on the pitch as blood began to pour out of his mouth. An ambulance came and carted him off to the nearest A&E department.

"Open your mouth, please," said the casualty officer.

"I can't." Lewis had mumbled through his clamped-shut jaw, the words just a whisper escaping out of the small gap between his unyielding lips. The casualty officer tried to force it open himself causing Lewis to shriek out in pain.

"Okay, best get an x-ray," said the casualty officer. No shit Sherlock, Lewis had thought. It was this early experience as a patient, exposed to the sometimes harsh and unempathetic attitude of some medical staff, that made him vow to never end up like that if he ever qualified.

Sure enough, he had broken his jaw in two places. He was transferred to the ward and had his jaw wired up for eight weeks. On a diet of protein drinks, Lewis lost a lot of weight. He was warned to go to A&E if he ever felt sick so as not to choke on his vomit. Well, of course he played it to his advantage during his second-year anatomy exam. Lewis put his hand up and told the invigilator that he felt sick.

"If I don't go to casualty now, I could choke on my vomit and die!"

Miraculously, he felt better when he arrived in A&E. The dean of the medical school was obviously informed about

Lewis' absence, and though not stupid, gave him the benefit of the doubt. He warned him that despite breaking his jaw playing for the medical school, he was on a tightrope with regards to being kicked out. It became a bit of an in-joke that Lewis Thomas was going to be the one to surely drop out, so everybody was pretty astonished when he passed his final medical examination and qualified to be a doctor. Maybe it was what the dean had said, or maybe it was due to the quota (a specific number of doctors must qualify each year otherwise there would not be enough graduates available to fill much needed junior doctor positions). Whatever it was, it certainly had nothing to do with his study skills.

When Lewis took up his position as a house officer in the South of England, he was worked like a dog. He was young, though, so the long hours, binge drinking and shagging when not on duty — sometimes on duty — didn't take a massive toll on him. This was before the European Directive imposed limits on doctor's working hours, now, apparently, a maximum of 48 hours a week. He took the Oxford Handbook of Medicine around with him everywhere, stuffing it into his oversized white coat. His pockets used to bulge with the amount he shoved in there; local anaesthetics, tourniquets, pens, foldable tendon hammers and condoms, just in case.

The moment which cemented his career in medicine came one night when Lewis saw a very aggressive patient arriving in A&E. The casualty officer was particularly useless and referred every patient to the medical and surgical team, rather than making a decision and discharging the patients. She saw the aggravated patient stagger in, high on drugs and half held up by the police, and instead of admitting him, sedating him and sectioning him under the Mental Care Act, she told the officers to take him back to the prison cell. In his state of severe psychosis, after being reincarcerated, he managed to smash his head repeatedly on the cell wall. When he arrived back at the hospital less than a few hours later, his face had been totally distorted by the damage. The head injury was so severe that it had sent him into cardiac arrest.

"Mayday, mayday, casualty department!" bellowed from the hospital tannoy. While the on-call medical team would race across to the relevant area in the hospital, you could always tell who was in charge as he or she would be seen sauntering, never in any haste to get to their destination. Newly qualified doctors tended to sprint as fast as they could, foolishly believing that they could make a difference by arriving a few seconds earlier. In reality, they would arrive sweaty, flustered and out of breath. When Lewis was a medical student, there was a cardiac arrest during a consultant ward round. The junior team shot off. Before Lewis was about to join them, his then consultant grabbed his shoulder.

"Never run to a cardiac arrest," he whispered. "In fact, never run anywhere in a hospital. It's not worth it."

They walked calmly together, and he was right. The junior doctors were flustered and unsteady, while Lewis and his consultant arrived cool and collected just moments later.

Lewis arrived in the resuscitation department. The area where the most serious of medical traumas occur. The same chap that Lewis saw passing through earlier that evening was on the resuscitation trolley, his Picasso-esque face mutilated by his relentless pounding on the police cell wall. The paramedics rushed him in with one of the police officers still handcuffed to the poor bastard. A Senior House Officer, Steve, suggested uncuffing him.

"It's unlikely he'll be going anywhere…"

He had bilateral, fixed dilated pupils, only just detectable from within his bruised and swollen face. A bevy of people surrounded the patient as Steve started the resuscitation procedure. Adrenaline. Shock. More adrenalin. Increased shock. Lewis didn't have a clue what to do but was thankful that someone more senior was there. Suddenly, another message came from the tannoy. "Mayday, mayday, Jefferson ward."

Steve looked apologetically at Lewis. "I'd better stay here; can you go to that one?"

"Sure, Steve."

Lewis's heart was pounding as he ran to the cardiac ward. He was trying to find the chapter in the Oxford Handbook of Medicine under the chapter 'Cardiac Arrest for Dummies' but found it hard to find the page while running. He couldn't resist the temptation to run, despite what his old consultant had told him. Lewis had skidded into the cardiac ward, almost crashing into the nurses who were surrounding the patient. The patient had gone into ventricular fibrillation, where the heart goes into an uncoordinated rhythm and so failing to pump blood to the brain.

"Lewis," said one of the nurses, ushering him over. "Mr Brown is a 66-year-old man who had a heart attack last night. He was stable, but has suddenly gone into VF."

Lewis ordered the nurses to get the drugs trolley out. "Yep, the trolley is here…" replied one of them. "Good, okay, let's get venous access."

"Yep, he's already got a Venflon in."

Lewis started looking at the drug trolley. There was a vast array of drugs there, adrenaline, noradrenaline, potassium

33

chloride, calcium chloride, atropine, naloxone. He was studying all of them, thinking how cool it was that they all had different coloured tops to identify them in an emergency. Unfortunately, he still didn't have a clue which one to give. The cardiac night sister was observing Lewis as he stood there, realising he was another junior doctor with little hands-on experience. During his moment of indecisiveness, the patient, fortunately, reverted to normal sinus rhythm and started to wake up. The emergency was over. Lewis glanced sheepishly over to the cardiac nurse.

"Phew, a crisis over, thank goodness for that. I thought he was going to revert to a normal rhythm, anyway... but, err, thanks for your help!" He scuttled off back to the resuscitation area of the hospital.

Back in the resuscitation ward, there was a feeling of failure. The casualty consultant knew she had made a wrong call. The patient from the police cell was dead. Steve, who was jotting down some notes, saw Lewis come in.

"How did it go with your patient, Lewis?"

"Yeah, touch and go, but I think he's going to be okay." He replied, knowing he didn't do anything. Lewis felt like a fraud.

"Well done, Lewis, your first life saved! Unfortunately, this poor sod didn't make it. The police are shitting themselves at the moment, so there's a bit of paperwork to do here, I'm afraid." It was the first time that Lewis had felt like he could be responsible for someone dying.

This life was to be a far cry from oceanography. From that point on, he committed himself, as if he'd taken an oath, to work as hard as he possibly could in his career to help save lives. Fast forward twenty years, and Mr Lewis Thomas is a well-respected neurosurgeon in a top London hospital. Over the years, he has seen the NHS engulfed by bureaucracy, unnecessary policies, reduction in hospital staff and a massive increase in so-called managers. He has seen the morale of medical workers dwindle down from mountainous heights to sub-zero levels. People no longer come to work with a spring in their step. They come to work wondering how long it will be until they finish their shift. But that was Lewis Thomas' life, for now. Single. Neurosurgeon by day, borderline alcoholic by night.

CHAPTER 3

Detective Sergeant Steven Smyth was in charge of an alleged suicide case. He was in his mid-40's and a divorced father of two children. Never seen without a tie and perfectly ironed shirt, never trusting anyone. He was pale, probably vitamin D deficient due to all his time spent beavering away at his desk, had a noticeably receding hairline, and a friendly, round face. His dark brown eyes matched his bushy black beard which he grew in an attempt to make himself look tougher than he was. It didn't work. DS Smyth was slightly more obsessive than his colleagues when it came to investigative cases. His colleagues sighed when he was in charge as they knew 'Detective Goody-Two-Shoes' would prolong any case until all loose ends had been tied up.

The story was on the local BBC news and in the local papers. Two American tourists had jumped to their deaths from some cliffs in Dover. The location was a suicide hot spot, so this wasn't entirely unusual. The involvement of the American Embassy complicated it, however. The Embassy had to be informed of all developments and DS Smyth needed to be completely satisfied before closing the case. DS Smyth was chosen, despite being stationed in London, as his chiefs knew he would do a thorough job, and this was destined to be a high-profile case.

It took him just two hours by car to reach the site of the suicide. As he pulled up, he could make out the blue and white tape cordoning off the area. He got out of the car and squinted to make out the edge of the cliff through the sea haze. He walked to the edge, the wet grass dampening the ends of his trouser leg, and, careful not to step too close, peered over the side. Crimson stains coloured the rocks beneath him where the Americans had fallen to their deaths. He took a few steps back and wiped his brow with the back of his hand. There weren't any clues in the immediate area to suggest foul play. The locals, who had gathered around the cordoned zone, told DS Smyth that the Americans had been seen in a nearby pub just before their supposed suicide. DS Smyth felt it necessary to question the landlord of the pub about this. Interestingly, the landlord had said that there was nothing abnormal about their behaviour whilst he served them. They were seen in high spirits, celebrating how well Mr Taylor was following his massive stroke and the fact he could walk again, laughing and joking.

Something didn't add up. Both bodies were taken to the local hospital morgue until the post mortem could be performed. If anything even slightly suspicious was in their system, like excessive alcohol or drugs, he would be informed. The bodies were severely mangled, though, and perhaps too distorted to reveal any new information regarding a struggle before plunging into oblivion. The pathologist was Dr Davies, a portly, ruddy-faced doctor, who had seen many a late evening in the local pub, reading Greek text with his usual pint of ale. A local eccentric. Dr Davies' secretary undertook the task of obtaining the couple's medical history. The information was hard to come by. Other than revealing Mike's recent stroke, there was little in the files to suggest any other health concerns. The family of the Taylors' were notified by the American Embassy of their parents' deaths. As suicide was an unnatural cause of death, they would do the post mortem in the UK rather than America.

When the pathologist examined the bodies, he had noticed the surgical scar on Mike Taylor's head. He cut through the scar and found a metal disc attached to a wire. Puzzled by his findings, he attempted to remove the disc which had become embedded in the brain. The surrounding area was much denser than usual, and although the head had been damaged by the fall, this seemed unconnected. After a slight tug, the wire came free.

"What in the world?" he said aloud. A deep brain stimulator…

He had never seen anything like this before. The device had a peculiar logo imprinted onto the main body. There was a tiny lightning strike insignia engraved over a small letter 'B'. He thumbed the small metal disc which glinted under the bright surgical lab light. On further inspection, he could see that the name of the manufacturer was non-existent. There wasn't a serial number on the device either to locate its place of origin. When he looked back down at the brain, he also noticed that there were lots of little black deposits in the brain tissues, speckled around the wire's track. Dr Davies frowned.

He informed DS Smyth immediately and suggested that it would be wise to have the opinion of a neurosurgeon. He gave him a list of names of surgeons who may be able to help as he had no experience with this kind of technology. He balanced the stimulator and wire on top of the face and wrapped the body back in the shroud for further inspection later. He then turned to examine Mr Taylor's wife, Beverley, who was lying next to her husband on the mortuary slab. There were no abnormal findings in Beverley Taylor. She was, or rather, used to be a perfectly healthy 45-year-old with no health concerns. A small amount of alcohol was detected in her system but nothing else.

Dr Davies was used to seeing dead bodies, but this was a gruesome sight. Both bodies were severely disfigured. The bones of limbs had torn through the skin, cracked white matter protruding through once perfectly encased forms. The skin, now an amalgam of lacerations, lesions and darkened bumps, seemed more alien than human. The skin of the head was peeled forward over the eyes from the pathologist's dissection. They did not represent the good lives that Mike and Beverley Taylor had not long ago led. They were lumps of broken flesh. The mortuary technicians wrapped the bodies up and transferred them from the examination table to their new temporary homes; two of the twenty refrigerated cubicles that were available. The tomblike doors closed with a resounding clang and the lights went off. The technicians sometimes thought they could hear spirit sounds as they locked the doors of the hospital morgue. Occasionally, dead patients that are not actually, ahem, dead are transferred to the mortuary. In the past, technicians have found the poor buggers making ghoulish noises from within the morgue.

Dr Davies knew he should have put the stimulator in a sealed bag, labelled and stored securely for further examination, but he was dying for a pint and thought he thoroughly deserved it after such an exhausting day. So, off he went, leaving the bodies and their tales behind him.

Top of the neurosurgical list that the pathologist had given to DS Smyth was Mr Lewis Thomas. So, the following day, he travelled across London and went to Mr Thomas' secretary's office.

"Are you the secretary of Lewis Thomas?" DS Smyth asked.

"Yes, how can I help?" she answered.

"I'm looking for him on an urgent police matter."

"Oh, gosh! I know he's in theatre, but he normally pops up between cases for a coffee. Are you okay to wait? I'll phone down and see how he's getting on."

"Sure, I'm happy to wait."

DS Smyth promptly sat down on a chair in the secretary's office. He looked around the office, eyeing the various untidy stacks of clinical notes scattered across the floor, an erratically annotated calendar pinned to the wall and an endless line of A4 folders dominating the shelves. The folders were labelled: 'Thank You Letters', 'Complaints' and 'Mortality and Complications' respectively. It was a simple space, though a tad disorganised and in need of a little sprucing up. DS Smyth hoped that Mr Thomas' surgical technique was tidier than the state of his secretary's office. Sure enough, Lewis Thomas entered a few moments later in his blue scrubs.

"DS Smyth," Lewis hovered in the doorway uneasily. "What can I do for you?"

He racked his brain to remember what he could have possibly done to be put under investigation. As far as he was aware none of his patients had died so it couldn't be manslaughter. Surely illegally downloading porn didn't merit a visit from a detective?! Perhaps it was the young man that Lewis had operated on with David the other day. Maybe they just wanted a medical statement?

"Mr Thomas, my name is Detective Sergeant Steven Smyth. I wonder if you could help us with our enquiries?"

Oh, for Christ's sake. I'm going to go to prison for a crime I have no idea I committed.

DS Smyth continued. "There was an apparent suicide in Dover, and the patient had a brain stimulator inserted. I confess that I didn't even know you could put these things in people's brains, but the pathologist hasn't got much experience with these matters and suggested we contact yourself as an expert."

Lewis suddenly relaxed. He realised that they wanted his expertise, not to jail him! His body language changed instantly from that of a hunted animal to a pretentious peacock.

"DS Smyth, lovely to meet you! Yes, I guess I do know a thing or two about brain surgery. Tell me more. How can I help?" he announced confidently.

DS Smyth proceeded to fill him in. If Lewis was going to examine the body, he needed to get permission from his clinical director. These days you have to get permission even to pass wind. Consultants used to get paid by the NHS then bugger off and play golf, but those days are now long gone. Which is a good thing, of course. Lewis was awful at golf.

He made a phone call to his clinical director who was, coincidentally, in his office writing a new annual leave policy. The clinical director was not happy about the prospect of Lewis missing a clinic. It would impact a large number of patients on the waiting list. However, since it was a police matter, he decided it would be less hassle to argue and approved the leave, provided Lewis took it as annual leave or did an extra clinic to make up for his absence. As Lewis didn't go on many holidays, this wasn't a problem. Lewis was elated to have been recommended to help with a police investigation. Finally, a bit of excitement to liven up the drudgery of regular clinical duties...

That night, two figures entered the hospital morgue. Both were dressed in black and wore balaclavas. One was tall and well-built, the other far shorter in stature and thinner by comparison. The smaller figure managed to pick the lock with a device which had a small needle-like probe at the end. They inserted it into the keyhole and, after pressing a button, a little whirring noise began. The mortuary door opened with an almost inaudible creak. It was disconcertingly dark inside. The taller one walked straight into a trolley. CRASH! It screeched as the wheels, obstructed by a safety brake, scraped along the ground. The smaller one punched the figure in the chest in annoyance. Under torchlight, they opened the large refrigerator doors. Each one housed four bodies. They proceeded to systematically open and close the doors. They unwrapped and rewrapped several bodies, exposing the faces of old, gaunt-looking cadavers, until they finally uncovered the mangled bodies of Mr and Mrs Taylor.

The torchlight exposed the stimulator displayed in full view on Mr Taylor's face, as if it had been expecting them. The short one swiped the device and gently placed it in a plastic bag. The same pilferer then replaced it with a similar stimulator in the exact same position. Something grabbed their attention. The sound of distant footsteps echoed towards them, a rhythmic tap, tap, tapping getting louder with each step. Someone was coming to the mortuary door. They exchanged a quick glance before silently agreeing to lay on top of the stiff, contorted bodies and hide. There was a slightly acidic smell of slowly decomposing bodies mixed with a metallic aroma of congealed blood. They held their breath, trying to inhibit their gag reflex, as they lay in silence. The smaller one managed to keep the refrigerator door ajar with one hand and maintain a steady hold on a gun in the other.

Outside the entrance of the mortuary, a hospital porter stood. There was a jangling of keys and then a puzzled gasp when the porter discovered the door was already unlocked. The taller figure was cramped and struggling to breath. He turned to free up some space but, in doing so, accidentally knocked the replacement stimulator off of Mr Taylors head. Time stood still. The moment between flight and collision seemed to last a lifetime. A single shrill clang could be heard on impact as the device made contact with the refrigerator floor. The sound pricked the porter's ears, and he froze. Another excruciatingly drawn-out pause, ensued.

"I can hear you!" The porter finally said, voice trembling. "I'm going to call security; they are on their way!" He dashed off, spluttering something about the spirit sounds being true.

The two figures quickly removed themselves from the refrigerator. The smaller one pointed to where the replacement stimulator should have been, whispering aggressively and frenziedly gesticulating. The taller person pushed the smaller one away. They heard several distant footsteps come from beyond the door. Assuming it was security, they pulled themselves together and escaped to the hospital grounds undetected. Switching the stimulators didn't really go to plan, but at least they had removed the evidence.

The following morning, the mortuary technicians were preparing the bodies for examination by Mr Thomas. They had taken out Mike Taylor's body and exposed the head. As soon as Dr Davies entered the room, he noticed that the stimulator had gone. He looked around the body, in the shroud and under the trolley. He couldn't find it anywhere and started to panic.

"Where's the stimulator that I placed on this man?" he demanded accusatorily.

"No idea, I never saw it when I took the body out." Replied one of the mortuary technicians defensively.

"Oh, bother." Dr Davies was baffled.

The policy meant that he should have kept it sealed in an evidence bag and locked away; he would now have some explaining to do. He had no choice but to inform DS Smyth.

"How can such an essential piece of information just be lost?" questioned DS Smyth, confused.

"I have no idea where it has gone, and I have no reason to suspect the technicians... I simply don't understand. I placed it right there..."

"Is there a possibility that someone broke in?" asked the detective. Dr Davies had not yet been informed about security being called the previous night.

"I suppose we have had 'break ins' before. We found a man in here a couple of years ago. He was naked, intoxicated and sleeping next to a corpse. It later transpired that he was one of the hospital porters. When they arrested him, they found a lot of photographs of himself and different corpses at his home. We had to keep it quiet as we feared a major public outcry. We tightened up the security with a new fancy lock. The only way in is this door here, and only security and the technicians have a key."

DS Smyth examined the hospital CCTV, but it didn't cover the mortuary as it was located in the basement of the hospital. The police interviewed the porter who was sure that he heard something. However, on speaking to the hospital security officer, it was clear there was no evidence of any suspicious activity apart from what the porter had said on the night. There were no prints nor clues. It was a total mystery where the stimulator had gone. There was no sign of a break-in, but since the stimulator was a critical piece of evidence, they had no choice but to treat this as suspicious and as theft. DS Smyth informed his superiors, and due to the American connection, they advised the mortuary should be made a crime scene. Lewis had been picked up by the police and was already on his way to Dover. He was unaware of the latest developments. When he arrived, Lewis put on a forensic overall given to him by one of the attending police constables.

Dr Davies thanked him for coming down. "I'm sorry but this may be a wasted journey for you. I wanted you to look at the stimulator which was embedded in Mr Taylor's head, but as of last night, it seems to have disappeared."

"What did it look like?" asked Lewis.

"It was a disc with a lightning bolt logo on it, and it had a wire attached to it. Look at the track where the wire was. They both inspected the brain. Lewis saw the black deposits in the brain tissue.

"Very strange," said Lewis. "I've only seen this sort of thing with hip replacements when I did my junior orthopaedic placement. It's called metallosis. It's where the metal-on-metal joints rub together and cause deposition of debris in the tissues. It can lead to a lot of health problems. But I've never seen this in the brain."

"I agree," replied the pathologist.

"The only other person who may know about this kind of thing is my neurosurgical colleague, Mr Humphries. He puts in stimulators for epilepsy patients. It may be worth asking him."

The pathologist didn't want to tell Lewis he was number two on the list and maybe this Crispin fellow should have been number one.

DS Smyth thanked Lewis for coming down and apologised for any inconvenience, especially on his annual leave day, and drove him back to his home in Notting Hill Gate, London.

CHAPTER 4

On the other side of the world, Professor Santos was a world-renowned neurosurgeon based in San Paulo. He travelled all over the world presenting at international neurosurgical meetings. Other neurosurgeons would greet him as groupies would a rock star. And a rock star he was in the eyes of many of his patients. They too would travel the world just to have him, the mighty Santos, perform surgery on them. Sadly, he wasn't blessed with rock star looks. Man, he was ugly. His face had been scarred by acne as a child, leaving unalluring pockmarks engraved across his cheeks and forehead. He had a large bulbous nose, heavy eyebrows which drooped over eyes and seemed to pop out of his head. He was also terribly short. From behind, the professor could be mistaken for a child. Often, when he turned around, he would frighten people expecting to see an infant and not a painfully unattractive man. What he lost in looks, he certainly gained in brains. He was a polymath. A genius even. A world class inventor and, at heart, a neurosurgeon. He was married with three daughters — to his disappointment, he couldn't spawn a neurosurgical male heir. In his spare time, he liked to play the violin. However, he didn't have the liberty of enjoying much of his wealth as he was in such high demand. He was inundated with patients who wanted to come to see him.

Professor Santos felt the only way to curb the influx of

patients seeking his care was to increase the price of his operations. The total amount included his fee, the anaesthetic fee, the hospital and the implants which, altogether, came to over half a million US dollars. People paid deposits of thousands of US dollars just to be on his waiting list. It wasn't like the NHS where the British people took the health system for granted. Here, money was king. If you didn't have it, your health suffered.

Professor Pedro Santos was fabulously wealthy. What made him stand out from other surgeons was that Santos was putting in stimulators for patients with paralysis. Nobody else was doing this. He was using none other than the proprietary Brainionics stimulator, the only one of its kind on the market. Since at the time it was experimental, only Professor Pedro Santos was licensed by the company to use the technology on human subjects. His road to success was a tough one, and this didn't happen by magic or by being nice.

He spent his formative years doing his PhD in a laboratory using rat models. He simulated brain ischaemia, when brain tissue dies or is about to die following a stroke. He worked out how to re-perfuse, or feed, the cells of the brain, after clipping a cerebral artery, simulating a stroke. During his experiments, he placed a tiny metal clip on the artery to stop the blood flow, mimicking a stroke. He worked out that after two minutes, there was irreversible damage to some of the neurons. The function of that part of the brain was lost. Once the damage occurred, supplying this area with more blood by removing the clip made things worse — opposite to what people thought. He tested every factor he could think of to improve or save the dying brain cells. He changed the blood sugar level, the temperature, and even the dilution of the blood with saline, but none of these factors seemed to make any difference.

A colleague, Matheus, had also worked in his laboratory. He was a neuroscientist, not a surgeon. His PhD focused on the effect of electric stimulation on the brain. The stimulus was achieved by placing a tiny electrode into the rat brain and passing microvolts through it. Pedro thought it was a complete waste of time but was impressed that Matheus didn't instantly fry the poor rat's brain. On the rare occasion, he did, and the smell of barbequed rat tissue would fill the lab. Matheus had asked Pedro to use his surgical skills to make a tiny hole in the rat's skull so he could feed a small electrode through it. The rat's head isn't particularly thick, and one can penetrate it using a short, sharp instrument a little bigger than a needle. Pedro had used the same techniques on his rats.

On one occasion, while cleaning the cages, a domestic had left the cage door open and both sets of rats escaped. He managed to gather them up and placed them in the cages not knowing which ones were which. The next day, Matheus inadvertently placed an electrode in Pedro's partially paralysed rat. When Pedro discovered there was a mix-up, it was too late. Pedro was furious that this had ruined his batch of rats and jeopardized his experiments. He was about to cull all the rats in his group when he noticed that his partially paralysed, limping rat was no longer limping. How curious, he had thought. Pedro asked Matheus to turn the current off. The limping returned almost immediately. The two looked at each other. In a cartoon, lightbulbs would have flashed bright above their heads. Without saying a word, they both knew that this could be the medical breakthrough the world had been waiting for. Never in history had applying an electrical current to dying or dead tissue reversed paralysis.

Over the next two years, they repeated the same painstaking experiments over and over again, refining them and developing them to be totally sure of their discovery. It certainly wasn't a fluke. Unbeknownst to Matheus, however, Pedro had patented the technique. Once the patent was in place, he developed the company Cerebrostim. From then on, Pedro shunned Matheus, keeping all his efforts and contributions to the discovery away from the public eye. Matheus watched Pedro rocket to stardom from afar. He did not fight to have his share of the limelight nor his share of the wealth merited from their discovery. Betrayed, depressed and hopeless, he became a professor and now works at a university in town trying to make ends meet.

Meanwhile, Cerebrostim grew fairly quickly. Pedro Santos was not stupid, and although many surgeons do not have a business brain, he did. However, Pedro could not find any investors among the big US medical technology companies. As the procedure was still experimental and had not been used clinically in humans, investors were apprehensive to get involved. Overseas, however, there was Brainionics. Brainionics was an Israeli company interested in remote monitoring and new technologies. The company is home to some of the world's most brilliant scientists and funded by global venture capitalists and a relatively small contribution by the Israeli government. It didn't take long to strike a deal with them. Pedro sold his patents to the company for an undisclosed amount. Not enough to retire, but enough for him to have the freedom to work when he wanted.

Brainionics worked with the military and developed remote medical applications such as robotics and wireless monitoring. It would be a massive advantage if you could observe the vital signs of the patient on the battlefield and decide whether evacuation of the casualty to a major trauma centre was necessary or not. It was relatively easy to review blood pressure and pulse rate remotely but monitoring the raised pressure in the brain was at the time impossible. The bony skull protects the jelly-like control centre of the body. They say the eyes are the windows to the soul but, in actual fact, the only connection from the eyes to the brain is the optic nerve. The optic nerve passes through a small hole in the skull, so you cannot monitor the brain with any detail by looking through the eyes. Assessing brain pathology is performed by visualising the engorged veins at the back of the eye, indicating some degree of raised intracranial pressure. However, this can still be fairly unreliable. The only real way to visualise the brain is a computerised tomography (CT) or Magnetic Resonance Imaging (MRI) scan. These are large pieces of equipment which need a lot of maintenance and skill to operate but are mostly impractical on the battlefield. There have been numerous attempts to monitor pressure in the skull in the field, or at least assess potential developing blood clots, however, until then, nothing had been successful.

Working with Professor Santos, Brainionics succeeded in developing a portable drill which housed a biodegradable wireless transmitter. The initial prototypes looked very impressive, as to be expected from the amount of money Brainionics invested in building it. The first tests were on cadaveric heads sourced from prisons. There was an agreement that if a prisoner died, they would have no choice but to surrender their bodies to further medical science. The bodies were beheaded, with just the head being purchased for the cause. It was cheaper to ask for the head rather than the whole body. Dead body parts are an expanding business. Dead bodies actually have many uses. In some cases, the bones are demineralised, sterilised and used in surgery for bone grafts. As you can imagine, it is rare for surgeons to tell recipient patients that some of the bone graft they use for fusion surgery may have come from a dead person. Not to alarm you but you've just had part of a dead mass murderer sprinkled into you. Delightful.

In one of the experiments, there were three decapitated heads pinned down to the top of the table in one of the labs. It looked like something out of a horror film. One of the faces on the heads was grimacing as if it were in pain. Pipes attached to a pump containing normal saline cannulated both the carotid arteries and jugular veins. One head at a time, Professor Santos made an incision over the right frontal part of the skull. As the heads were still fresh at the time, blood oozed and trickled down from the slit in the flesh when he cut into the bone. He used a small self-retaining retractor which he carefully gripped with both hands to drill down into the skull. He removed the drill bit from the device and then replaced the device over the hole. A silver disc followed the path of the drill with a soft whirring sound. It embedded itself into the small burr hole. After removing the hand-held device, Pedro then closed the skin with metal staples. He was testing three devices on three heads. All of them worked perfectly. There was a round of applause from the engineers and, most importantly, the corporate heads of Brainionics. The speed of delivering a device into the brain was astounding.

"Wait, gentlemen, let's see if we can pick up the pressures remotely," Pedro said.

One of the engineers turned on the pump. Another

engineer was holding a small black box. Suddenly, a LED display lit up. It was a green display showing the numbers from 1 to 10 mmHg oscillating in time with the pump.

"Turn the pump up!" Pedro demanded.

Saline fluid pumped through the cannulated arteries to the brain, which in turn, increased the pressure and volume of the brain in the skull. The display lit up in amber and then red as the numbers jumped from 18 to 35 mmHg, 35 being the higher limit of intracranial pressure. Another rapturous round of applause.

The CEO of Brainionics, Gad Dayan, came up to shake Pedro's hand. Gad Dayan used to be in the Israeli army, and from there progressed to the secret service. When he decided to leave Mossad, he had the necessary contacts and money to set up various businesses. He was appointed the CEO of Brainionics and, from his station, oversaw the integration of remote medical monitoring for the Israeli army. He later expanded its use globally, though still mainly providing for military services. Brainionics started to make a profit and reinvested said profit into stimulation devices, including the work of Professor Santos. It was time they received something in return.

"Professor Santos! What an innovation! Now that we have proof that this technology works, we want to go global. We need your help though." What he actually meant to say was: we have invested in this, so we need to see some sales. Of course, Professor Santos was all in.

Five years later, and the Brainionics headquarters in Tel Aviv had quadrupled in size. It was enormous. There were hundreds of computer terminals and even more workers. All personnel had to dress in black, largely to keep up professional appearances and ostensibly to intimidate any outsiders. All employees had a certain number of silver lightning strikes on their lapels. The number of strikes determined their status within the organisation. For example, technicians who controlled the patient forums — handling and censoring content written by or produced for patients — have a single lightning strike. These technicians were responsible for maintaining the stellar reputation of key surgeons spearheading the company, such as Crispin Humphries. Those who partook in programming the top-secret devices usually bore two to three strikes, as did the guards protecting the building and the invaluable data and devices within. Gad Dayan, when in uniform, also had one strike. His, however, was enlarged and in a dazzling golden colour.

The building inside resembled a large call centre, but the actual construction of the building was cleverly assembled in the shape of a brain. The architect had erected the various departments of the building to align with the related areas of the brain. For example, the marketing group were based in the left frontal wing of the building, the centre for creativity. The communications officers were adjacent. The building's main hard drives and storage were located in the left temporal area, where the brain stores memories, and the basement housed the control centre where the brainstem would be. Finally, large windows at the front of the building represented the headquarters eyes. There were, of course, restricted areas only accessible to senior technicians, Gad Dayan and, if necessary, the military too. Most of the scientific work that took place here was entirely confidential. If any significant technological breakthroughs were leaked, it could be devastating for the company and, depending on whose hands it got into, for the world. The intellectual property on site could change the course of human evolution.

Year on year, the company released new and innovative products. The share prices reflected this, steadily rising annually. The Remote Intracranial Pressure Transducer and Intravascular Detection Enabler (RIP-TiDE) was in every US and Israeli medical military base. Sales of RIP-TiDE were increasing exponentially, especially in the Middle East and China. The technology was fool proof; any Tom, Dick or Harry with any surgical training could insert it through the skull.

For all the architectural prowess and technological grandeur of Brainionics, their website was terribly modest. The homepage only contained a brief description of the company's patented RIP-TiDE technology and a link to an online training video. When clicked, a short-film appears guiding viewers through the insertion of a RIP-TiDE device.

"Hey, folks! Gather around! My name is Rob! Welcome to the Brainionics' online training video!" The screen shows a basic first aider in scrubs standing against a sterile, white background. "This is Jodie. Jodie is a twenty-two-year-old student who attended one of the Brainionics RIP-TiDE insertion courses. Jodie has absolutely no medical training. Jodie, how's it going?"

"Well, you know what? Anyone would think I'm a brain surgeon! This kit is so simple to insert. Anyone can do it! I'm going to demonstrate how to insert the monitoring system on my colleague, Jane. Poor Jane has been suffering from headaches and thinks that raised intracranial pressure is causing her headaches. Jane is probably mad…" Jodie looks to Jane and smiles sympathetically. "But hey! That ain't going to stop us! She will benefit perfectly from RIP-TIDE! Right, Rob?"

"Right!"

"Rob, here, is going to inject a little local anaesthetic into Jane. Jane, are you ready?" Jodie announces blithely.

"Go for it, Jodie!" Jane announces with an unnaturally large grin painted across her face.

Jodie preps the head, shaves a tiny bit of hair and puts the device over the right frontal lobe. Within seconds the machine engages onto the skull and automatically drills through the bone. A small disc penetrates through the layers of the scalp and bone resting on the dura. Jane tries to smile through the procedure but cannot hide the obvious pain she is experiencing. The small incision is closed using staples to the skin. The insertion of the RIP-TiDE took precisely 3 minutes.

"Jane, how are you feeling?"

"Jodie, I didn't feel a thing."

The camera pans to a monitor displaying a series of readings in different colours. Rob continues to narrate.

"Jodie, let's look over here and see what we have. Okay, here in red, is Jane's blood pressure. Here in green, is the pulse. Here in blue, we have the oxygenation of the brain. And, finally, here in yellow, we have the intracranial pressure. Jane, do us a favour and cough would ya?" Jane gives an exaggerated, fake cough. The pressure jumps from 10 mmHg to 85 mmHg in one quick spike on the yellow dial. "Did y'all see that? We can remotely measure Jane's parameters from all over the world. And, with our unique encryption coding, it's completely secure too. I hope this demonstration gives you confidence in RIP-TiDE, the only remotely operated wireless intracranial monitoring system in the world. Be safe folks!"

The video times out.

This particular video went viral and, before long, Jane became somewhat of a celebrity. There would be live streams of her movements using a split-screen; one side showing her activities and the other side showing her intracranial pressure. Scientists watching were able to gauge the changing state of her intracranial pressure in relation to external factors such as the weather or even moon cycles. Anyone who tuned in could see what Jane was getting up to and the subsequent impact on her brain whenever and wherever. Her pressure would undulate depending on what she did. Fans would send in special requests and watch in awe as the science unfolded. Sadly, it did also attract some attention from unwanted perverts, so the live streams were eventually taken down. Ultimately, broadcasting Jane's life online had served a marketing purpose for Brainionics; not only were the general public now aware of their technology, but the attention of wealthy investors was also aroused.

Jane was not the only person to be analysed by the company, though. Brainionics were paranoid about protecting their assets and would guard their precious technology no matter what the cost. Gad Dayan asked for the staff, including any external consultants involved in their products, to be tracked and monitored. This was done with their own proprietary GPS tracking devices, drones and hidden cameras. Of course, Gad understood that this was wholly unethical, despite telling them all it was for their own safety. He simply chose to prioritise the secure development of his company's technology over the privacy of his personnel. With the ongoing Israeli-Palestine unrest, as well as with espionage abroad, it was in everyone's best interests to avoid any of his devices being used unwisely for military application. At least, when it wasn't his call.

From within his office, Gad Dayan could be heard shouting. By the tone of his voice, it was clear that he was furious about something.

"You are stupid!" he bellowed. "It was a straightforward request! All you needed to do was exchange the damn thing." He had received information that one of his company's stimulators was under investigation in the UK. He had instructed one of his operatives there to ensure that there was no link to the company. His instructions were clear: remove the stimulator and replace it with a competitor's so that Brainionics would not be under scrutiny. The stimulator did not have the correct regulatory approval for surgery in England yet. It should never have been implanted.

He paused and responded to the voice down the telephone line. "Well, at least that is something. What happened to the replacement stimulator?" There was another pause as he listened. "Don't blame him, you fool. He is a true idiot, but I thought you had this under control!" He paused and became slightly more passive. "Okay, okay, let's see how this pans out. You need to keep close to the investigation. Do what you need to do, agent." He slammed the phone down and ran his hands through his hair. He knew that finding one of their stimulators in a high-profile case could have serious implications for the company. If the stimulator caused the suicide, they could go under. At least planting a competitor device there would throw them off the scent. He poured himself a small shot of whiskey, took a gulp and sighed. The good news was that they had their stimulator back.

CHAPTER 5

It was a miserable Monday morning in London. The heavy rain hammering against the window woke Lewis before his alarm had a chance to. Lewis hated mornings. The worst Mondays were the grey ones, where an unwelcome, grainy fog seemed to suffocate the city's soul. He rolled out of bed, put some coffee on and sat down to watch the news.

On Mondays, he liked to hum to himself, *Tell me why, I don't like Mondays*, a hit by the Boomtown Rats from the 70s and 80s. It was about a girl who shot her teachers with a gun. When asked why, she said she didn't like Mondays. Sometimes, Lewis would imagine himself as the girl and the teachers as the hospital management. He lit another cigarette. Lewis caught sight of his reflection in the mirror and grimaced. He was aware his dislike of the hospital management was becoming pathological.

"One more," he promised himself, with a sly wink. Lewis was fatalistic. He was well aware of the damage that smoking could do to his body and mind, but he was also aware that humans were vulnerable whether they smoked or not. His job was surrounded by death and disability in otherwise fit and well individuals. You know, the ones that go to the gym, the vegans, the teetotallers, the most dedicated, health-fanatics you could think of. You can do everything 'right', and yet one day, still be struck down with fatal brain pathology. Whether by accident or from a sudden brain bleed or tumour, nobody is immune. Nobody is invincible. Everyone knows someone who knows someone who has experienced this. Maybe a healthy young mother who develops breast cancer, or a young athlete who finds a tumour. In Lewis' eyes, the day you die is written in the stars. So, he justified his habit with this outlook. Smoking gave him the time to reflect on life, anyway. It was meditational. He would light the cigarette, inhale the nicotine and get that instant hit. Then he would mull over life. In the morning, processing what the day would entail, or in the evening, reflecting on what the day had offered up to him. During working hours, he didn't have the chance to smoke, not that he had the time to think about it anyway. There used to be smoking rooms in hospitals, but they're long gone now. He still remembered when you could smoke on aeroplanes. He thought it was funny that the non-smoking signs still alight every time you take a flight. Really, shouldn't they have been replaced with something more... current? Imagine reading in the safety information leaflet: NO GETTING DRUNK AND OPENING THE EXIT DOORS. You are probably more at risk of encountering that than someone smoking on a plane now. They could do a sign of a small figure holding a bottle while falling out a plane door. At least that would add a little humour to the journey.

Anyway, no one knew that he smoked. Aside from Patience, that is, but Lewis was oblivious to her knowledge. There was no hiding anything from dear Patience. He hated the smell on his hands and the taste in his mouth, so he fastidiously brushed his teeth and sprayed aftershave on himself after a smoke. He knew he should probably take up yoga or something mindful instead, but he didn't feel ready to give it up. Despite the shame attached to doctors smoking, it was something he just liked to do alone. It is slightly hypocritical, after all, to smoke like a chimney then lead a sermon about the risks of lung cancer. To be fair to him, he rarely lectured patients. Who was he to do this anyway? He always advised and sometimes even encouraged bad habits, especially to the terminally ill patients.

He had purchased a property in Notting Hill Gate as a medical student with help from his now deceased parents around twenty-five years ago. It was now worth ten times as much. It was a Victorian house set over three floors. It had a basement, a ground floor and a first floor. The basement was what he liked to call his den. He would smoke and drink and listen to music there. It was also home to his fabulous wine collection. Lewis had meticulously labelled all the reds on racks according to origin and dates. The whites he kept in a cooler. His Japanese whiskey collection was equally impressive. On the ground floor could be found his kitchen. A spacious, high-ceilinged arrangement with little furniture, though fitted with an Aga and complete with an old battered island. His fridge also lacked provisions. It was empty apart from a few beers, on the off chance a few friends came around, some out of date milk and a half dozen eggs.

The property came with a washing machine and tumble dryer, though Lewis wasn't sure how to work them. Instead, he elected to take his laundry for a service wash. On the same floor was his living room which had a little more character. A battered chesterfield sofa took its place in the centre of the room, boasting classic rolled arms, a deep buttoned back tufting and a low seat base. Worn patterned rugs adorned the floors, hiding cracked, unpolished wooden floorboards. The lumpy, textured wallpaper was embellished with old pictures and portraits of family and friends whom he never saw but kept hung on the walls, as well as impressionistic watercolour paintings which he inherited from his parents when they died. Lewis wasn't a big fan, but at least they added some colour to the room. There was a display cabinet revealing a smooth, life-size skull and some old surgical textbooks. The room's centrepiece was a large, stone fireplace which, though still functioning, he rarely used. On the mantlepiece sat an array of taxidermy; stuffed squirrels, ducks and other birds were met with uneasy stares whenever guests came around. One in particular had a lopsided, beady eye which seemed to follow you with its gaze wherever you walked. The décor was, indeed, quirky and eclectic. But it was his home, and it suited him.

His bedroom was on the top floor, and he would watch the morning proceedings from his bedroom window with a coffee. On this particular day, while he sat surveying the city below, Lewis ran over the events from Dover. What if it was one of Humphries' patients? Where had the stimulator disappeared to? Could he find out? Why, on second thoughts, was he bothered? He shook his head and turned around to face his home. He should probably spend more time cleaning this mess up than worrying about sorting out the detective's shit.

Although he wasn't a hoarder, he was starting to gather a lot of junk. He wasn't much of a cleaner. About once a year he would attempt a clear out, throwing away items which he hadn't used over the last year. He always stopped short, though, keeping things for sentimental reasons or thinking that it may come in useful one day. It never did. Intrinsically, he was lazy and didn't have the patience to spend his time on the everyday events in life such as cooking, cleaning and travelling in the London traffic — hence his motorbike. Glancing at the clock, he realised he must have got carried away with his thoughts about Dover. After a quick shower and a final smoke, he shot off on his bike to work.

Lewis used to feel a buzz on his way into work. When he first started, bright-eyed and bushy-tailed, he couldn't wait to be on shift. A lot had changed in the NHS since he first became a consultant, though. He now used his ride to the hospital to rant to himself about the state of the NHS and his hatred for unnecessary and unsustainable managerial systems. His internal dialogue on this morning was particularly frenzied.

Due to an increasingly politicised and bureaucratic health care system, the NHS is inundated with hospital managers. The problem is, they don't seem to 'manage' anything particularly well. In Lewis' eyes, managers are like parasites, spawned by unbalanced and misguided political decisions, feeding off the UK health service.

Getting rid of some of these managers would save the NHS a lot of money. Lewis had seen managers, one by one, come into the department and try to change things without listening to the front line medical and nursing staff. And then, after a couple of years, they would move jobs, taking zero responsibility for any of the mess they had made. Chief Executives and Medical Directors come and go, each getting OBE's, even Knighthoods on the odd occasion, for being political puppets. Most clinical managers begin as regular anaesthetists, surgeons or physicians, but give up their regular job to sit in umpteen meetings and bully doctors. Why? Aside from a hefty pay rise, in Lewis' opinion, they were probably just no good at their original calling.

When Lewis was a junior doctor, he never once came across a manager. Senior medics and matrons ran the hospital. Now, this new breed of tyrant is everywhere. Deputy this and deputy that, hurling abuse at real doctors and surgeons without the foggiest idea what they're talking about. Get rid of them, save the NHS money and improve efficiency, thought Lewis. It wasn't exactly brain surgery, and he should know.

Hospital protocol has turned into one enormous shitshow. As an example, take the handling of Mr Blogs. Eighty-four-year-old Mr Blogs is admitted to the emergency department with a fractured hip. There is probably a delay whilst the orthopaedic team take time to assess him and decide what further treatment he needs. You see, they need to ensure he goes to the correct ward and the logistics behind this are quite a task. Mr Blogs, therefore, spends ages (this length of time is, of course, relative. Some might find ten minutes unjustifiable) in the emergency department — the family, understandably, kick-off and contact the papers. The press, of course, goes wild for it: MR BLOGS LEFT FOR DEAD IN WAITING ROOM and MR BLOGS POPS HIS CLOGS. The Minister of Health sticks his nose in, demanding the chief executives get their medical managers in shape. This mania funnels down to the administrative staff who, after sending a slew of emails and edicts to the masses, trigger a knee jerk response to impose a limit of four hours in the emergency department on all patients.

On the surface, this makes it look like the government are doing something good for patients. Beneath the surface, though, all hell breaks loose… Emergency nurses admit the patients directly to the ward after a rushed and incorrect assessment. This makes the definitive treatment even more delayed. Meanwhile, ambulances hover outside the emergency department so patients can wait inside the vehicle rather than in the building where the clock will start ticking. Lewis remembered one particular occasion where emergency consultant colleagues started screaming at him to admit someone with a bit of back pain to the neurosurgical ward before they missed their targets. Regardless of the unnecessary screaming, you cannot get rid of these poor patients. They are relentless. They demand pain relief and physiotherapy for days. They want to be 'pain-free', as if that is their right. What they really need is to get off their arses more, so their backs don't seize up. Because of these otherwise perfectly well individuals, there are no beds for urgent tumours or routine work left. Remember the patients' charter? No. Neither does anyone else, political bullshit. Of course, there are other factors. There are too many to list them all.

If Lewis were the Minister of Health, he would send a bill to every patient letting them know how much their 'free' treatment would be if they had to pay for it: "So, Mrs Blogs, not happy with your treatment, eh? That is fine. Why don't you pay £20,000 and we can get your scan today and operate on you tomorrow? Sorry, what was that? Did you say you haven't got any money or insurance? Right then, you have to wait like everyone else. Goodbye."

Lewis parked up outside the front entrance on his motorbike. He used to come in by car but since they started charging everyone who used the car park, he decided against it. How happy he was for the hospital managers and executives who had their lovely and free barrier-protected car park. He used his security badge to access the building and headed straight to his office on the sixth floor where he dumped his gear. Luckily, he still had an office to himself. The management were planning to have open office space for all consultants, just like the hospital canteen staff, switchboard operators, porters and volunteers. Obviously, all the above are vital for a hospital to properly function, but consultants have to make complex decisions and keep discussions with patients confidential. They have a greater need for space and quiet to think, don't you think? Lewis certainly did. His daily managerial tirade was one day going to be his downfall both physically and professionally, but the smallest of things were now winding him up.

Lewis fired up his computer to look at the patient scans that were on his list that day. Some irritating screensaver popped up about the dangers of MRSA infections and a reminder that it was 'SAFE HAND-WASHING WEEK'. What utter bollocks. The screensavers were centrally programmed by the hospital IT department so they could only be changed by those with administrator privileges. They were programmed to pop up after ten seconds of inactivity. Give me a break, Lewis thought. Lewis once gave the department a telephone call to reset it. It went a little bit like this:

"Hi there, is this the IT department? Great. I was wondering if you could do me a favour? We have important meetings where we discuss patients' scans, and the hospital screensaver keeps popping up. I know how vitally important these messages are to you, but do you think it would be possible to change the settings? Maybe to 5 minutes of inactivity?"

"Sorry, buddy, but it's a no. If you need to change the settings, we need a letter from your directorate manager, countersigned by the clinical manager. If it's a reasonable request, we should be able to do it."

"Okay, thank you, you absolute wanker." He didn't actually finish the call like that, but that's what he imagined saying.

Lewis waggled the mouse to re-access the patient's scans. He looked at the brain tumour on the screen and considered his approach. It was a frontal lobe tumour which, if you are going to have a brain tumour, is probably the best place to have one. We still don't know what all the functions of the right frontal lobe are, at least in any detail, which can make operating there riskier. Several regions in the brain control language function, but the left hemisphere is dominant in language in about 92% of people. Unless you are left-handed — in which case, in 50% of left- handers — the right frontal lobe can control speech. The patient was right-handed, though.

In his mind, he went through all the steps of the operation and, more importantly, any potential complications which could occur. There are lots. The screen saver popped up again. Satisfied with the approach and preparation, he called his registrar, Amal. The junior neurosurgeons rotated every six months, so they got to see lots of different neurosurgical specialities such as paediatric, vascular, tumour and spinal. Lewis was glad it wasn't David.

"Hi, Amal, are you free to go around and see the patients for today's list?"

"Mr Thomas, I'm sorry, but I have to do my mandatory fire lecture this morning. I've tried to put it off for the last three months, but the business manager said she would report me to the clinical director if I missed it again. I'm sorry, but I should be out by midday."

"Okay, no worries. I'll see you later then."

Any other registrar and Lewis would have got quite irritated, but Amal was a hard-working, empathetic doctor already. She would, one day, be a fantastic surgeon. In a small way, it was easier for Lewis to do the operation himself anyway; he knew he could do it faster and didn't have to spend the time teaching.

Lewis took the stairs to the level below where he arrived onto the preadmissions ward. It was a holding bay for patients — a new idea from one of the recently appointed managers. Previously, the patient came into the hospital bed the night before. You could discuss in detail with them and their family about the scans and what to expect from the surgery. More importantly, they would have a bed for the list the next day. Nowadays, there is no guarantee that there will be a bed as the preadmission ward closes at 5 pm due to staff shortages. Lewis found a nurse and proceeded to hunt down his patient. All the patients are huddled together in one room, like frightened animals about to go to slaughter.

"Hello, Mr Dykes, I'm Mr Thomas. Hopefully, you recognise me from when we met a couple of weeks ago at the clinic."

"Yes, of course, Mr Thomas. I can't say I'm pleased to see you, but I will be glad when the operation is over." Lewis had developed the ability and confidence to make the patients feel at ease. They trusted him with their lives.

"As you know, we are going to make an incision over here." He touched the top right side of his forehead. "Then, we will remove a flap of bone and get on with removing the tumour. I can't tell you I can remove all the tumour and we will have to wait for about a week to find out what kind of tumour it is. It could be a non-cancerous one. If so, provided the operation goes well, hopefully that will be the end of it. If it comes back as a cancerous tumour, you may need further treatment with radiotherapy."

Just by looking at the scans Lewis knew that it wasn't cancerous, but having been caught out before, he thought he best mention that it might be, just in case. Also, if you remove all the tumour and it is non-cancerous you are going to be a hero. If you don't mention that it may be cancerous, and it is, their trust in you is lost. "You know there is a small risk to your life; paralysis, infection, cerebrospinal fluid leak…"

Ever since a recent ruling by the English courts, surgeons must discuss the potential risks with patients in detail. Lewis didn't always. He would weigh up the patient's personality in the outpatient clinic and, if he thought they were inquisitive, go into a lot more detail. Most of the time, however, he would just discuss the most common complications. He didn't like reeling off a list of complications just to please the courts or defence solicitors. Half the patients had no idea what he was talking about. The only thing it achieved was scaring them shitless with a load of alien medical jargon before the op. Patients want to know whether the doctor can do the job, and that if there were to be any complications, the doctor would be able to deal with them.

Time is forever an issue. More factors to contend with include severe overbooking combined with the fact that patients are no longer admitted overnight. This means there is less and less time available for patients to discuss their concerns with their consultants. Worse still, they might only have the chance to discuss their worries with registrars like David who would likely put them off surgery for life.

Like other countries, the cost of patients suing the NHS

has run into billions. Solicitor firms are making an absolute mint from the misadventure of patients. Medico-legal affairs were unsettling for Lewis. If a patient has terrible care, of course, they should have some reimbursement to compensate for their change in lifestyle. They may need rehabilitation, further surgery or even house modifications. The problem was, patients simply set the bar too high. Surgeons and doctors are heroic, but they are not magicians. You can do everything right but still have complications to contend with. That's just life. Some of the best medical professionals in the world have been faced with legal proceedings because of ungrateful, unsatisfied patients with too high expectations.

It wasn't fair, but it was all too common. Lewis has been sued several times. Misdiagnosis of cauda equina is probably the most common one, where a delay in surgery can cause severe incontinence. This is often due to a large disc in the spine that has popped out and dangerously presses on the nerves to the bowel and bladder causing permanent incontinence. On one occasion, Lewis had no idea that the patient was even waiting in the emergency department for a scan. Nobody had warned him, you see. Once referred to him, Lewis removed the sizeable lumbar disc causing the compression as soon as he could. Nevertheless, the solicitors came after him on the grounds of negligent care as he was the consultant in charge.

"So, how exactly are you going to remove the tumour?" the patient asked. Lewis didn't think it was wise to go into the finer detail of the surgery.

"With skill and elegance!" he quipped.

With the platitudes exchanged, Lewis headed to change into his theatre scrubs. He kept a stock of them in his office —

woe betide if the infection control nurse knew. He was lucky he still had an office. It was far better than getting changed in the usual NHS changing rooms which always smelt of blocked drains and urine. After changing, he headed down to theatre to discuss the list.

Amal, Lewis's registrar, would normally be there briefing the team and checking the necessary equipment for theatre. This time, however, Lewis would have to do it all himself. This included the boring stuff too, such as marking the correct side of the patient, filling in the pathology form, positioning the patient and writing the operation note. When he got down to the theatre, two people were waiting there who he didn't recognise. It soon transpired that Lewis had been tasked to be a personal tutor for medical students.

One of them was a gangly bespectacled boy who looked much too young to be assisting in surgery. He wore an overly serious expression, perhaps to mask his nerves. His shirt was poorly tucked into his overly high-waisted trousers, causing the fabric to make a little ducktail behind him. The other student happened to be an extremely attractive young woman and looked like much more fun than her male companion. She stood alert, her ocean blue eyes calmly tracing her surroundings. Long, manicured fingers hung softly by her thighs, relaxed and motionless, totally at ease. The boy, in contrast, fidgeted impatiently, twiddling his thumbs in anticipation. Together, they made an almost comical duo. Lewis forgot about the email he responded to a month ago saying he was happy for a medical student to come to the theatre to shadow him. He didn't know Amal was not going to be there that day either, which threw a slight spanner in the works. It would take extra time and effort for him to talk to them instead of just getting on with the operation. He was equally surprised to see two students had turned up.

"Hi!" the boy chirped. "My name is Harry! But you can call me Firefly, that's my nickname!"

"Firefly… right… Nice to meet you," Christ alive. "I'll stick to Harry, I think. Little more professional." Lewis turned to look at the girl. "And you are?"

"I'm Deborah. No nickname," she said with a voice like honey.

"Deborah," Lewis repeated, "nice to make your acquaintance." He held her gaze for just a little too long, enamoured by her mesmerising eyes. He felt himself begin to blush.

"We're here to shadow you!" Bug boy interrupted, jolting Lewis back to the present.

"Right, of course! So, you two," Lewis announced. "What do you know about neurosurgery?"

They both stood there in the operating theatre, lit up by the large monitor showing the patient's scan. Harry, whose theatre trousers were tied so tight and high around his abdomen, eagerly and somewhat breathlessly spoke first.

"Well, Mr Thomas, I know this patient has a tumour, and from my understanding, it is vital to remove all the tumour without destroying eloquent areas." Lewis decided that his first impression was correct: Harry was not going to be much fun, but at least he was keen.

Deborah responded after. "Not very much, Mr Thomas. But we heard you are one of the best teachers in this field." Lewis allowed himself another cursory glance at her face as she spoke, not wanting to appear too moved by her beauty. She was a vision, a beautiful painting even. He'd never seen anyone wear a scrub cap so… perfectly. And she was flattering him. Shit. Every surgeon loves to hear that, especially from a fit medical student. Whether it was true or whether she was just buttering him up, Lewis didn't know, but he was lapping it up, nonetheless. Deborah was going to get special attention. He smiled and then quickly looked away, not wanting to blush again if she smiled back.

"Okay, Harry, how do we do that?"

"Well, I would have thought you have to remove the tumour while the patient is awake, and that way, you would know whether you are damaging an eloquent area of the brain?" — a typical response from an uber keen medical student, who has been watching too many brain surgery videos, on the internet.

"Not quite, Harry. In this case, fortunately, the tumour is not in an eloquent area, it's in the right frontal lobe. What does the right frontal lobe control?"

"Personality?"

"Yes, Harry!" Lewis suspected that Harry had an underdeveloped right frontal lobe. "Don't tell me you've watched an awake craniotomy on YouTube?"

"Yes, Mr Thomas. It was awesome! The patient was playing the guitar while having brain surgery."

"Well, we only do that when necessary." Lewis got irritated when anyone said the word 'awesome'.

"My registrar has to go on a fire safety lecture today, so I need an assistant. Okay, Deborah, you are going to get scrubbed up for this case, and Harry, you can do it next time."

Lewis knew that there wouldn't be a next time as they only get one chance to watch live neurosurgery in their training. He didn't have the patience to listen to Harry chirping

73

throughout the operation about how 'awesome' it is. Deborah's eyes lit up. "Thank you, Mr Thomas!" Lewis nodded to Patience, who was fortunately in his theatre today. "Patience, can you show young Deborah how to scrub up later please?"

"Yes, your majesty. Whatever Mr Thomas wants, Mr Thomas gets." She said in her thick, Afro-Caribbean accent.

There was always a bit of downtime while the anaesthetist did what anaesthetists do. Although Lewis didn't understand what they did, he knew he couldn't operate without them. Sometimes, he wished he could operate without them. Sometimes, he wished that patients had an 'on' and 'off' switch, so he didn't have to wait for all the... well, all the stuff they did.

He was a real wind-up merchant and came alive in the theatre environment. His naughty school-boy antics increased when he found new prey, such as the students or new doctors. There were the apparent jokes such as sending the student nurse to the renal ward to find a Bowman's capsule (which was a microfilament in the kidney) or asking the student operating theatre assistant to shout if anyone knew where 'Mike Hunt' is. Convincing the observers that the bone wax used to stop bleeding from the bone was the sterilised ear wax from the Mongolian sheep, which had unique properties to clot the blood. It amused him immensely and gave him momentary relief from the seriousness of what he was about to do.

In the meantime, Lewis had taken the medical students around the other theatres. He peeked through the small shutters of the different theatres making sure he knew who the surgeons were before making his grand entrance. He spotted Giles who he liked. They both shared a common mistrust of management.

"Ah, Giles, I have a couple of enthusiastic young surgeons

here wanting to know what this heart surgery lark is all about."

"Ah, well, heart surgery is the pinnacle of a surgical career. My colleague, Lewis, however, uses a spoon to scoop out bits of brain, and when the patient in question can no longer walk or talk, tells them it's a complete success. Isn't that right Lewis?" Giles grinned under his mask with a glint in his eye.

"Yes, that is correct, Giles. You guys can walk on water! Gosh, how amazing to be able to perform two different operations in your lifetime!"

"What do you mean?" Giles stopped operating.

"Well, you do a cabbage on people (Coronary Artery Bypass Graft — CABG — pronounced 'cabbage') and a valve operation. I bet you any money you're doing a CABG right now. Apart from transplant surgery, it must be pretty dull doing the same operation, every day?"

"Ah, that is where you're wrong. We are masters of our art; you guys just make it up as you go along. But yes, today you're correct. I am doing a CABG."

Giles had a point. There was a lot in neurosurgery that was beginning to come to light. It was just over 150 years ago that we thought the heart was where the soul sat rather than the mysterious blob inside our skull. Both surgeons enjoyed this sort of banter as both were comfortable in their respective specialities. If Lewis had said this to another surgeon, he would have gone off crying to the medical director and a letter of inappropriate behaviour would have been filed.

"You two stand where the anaesthetist is," said Giles. "You can see the beating heart in my hand. Look at that contraction, it sends blood throughout the body. Even to the jelly bit that Mr Thomas tries to heal! We are going to stop the heart, and we are going to plumb this bit of vein from the main artery into the artery of the heart and thus…" In a booming voice, added: "Resurrect this man from his sins and give him a second chance!" he paused. "Was that a bit dramatic, Lewis?" Giles asked.

"No, Giles. Completely in keeping with your phenomenal surgery." Lewis laughed.

"Cheers, matey." Giles replied.

Both the medical students were watching from the top of the operating table. It was quite an unreal sight for them. They could see the patient's face, asleep, behind a curtained drape. They glanced over to see the breastbone cut in half with a metallic retractor spreading the bone, exposing a large pulsating fist-sized lump of meat. It had big tubes coming out which went to a machine where a very bored looking technician was overlooking the monitors. The nurse assistant was harvesting a vein from the patient's leg which connects to the coronary vessels. It was a fantastic sight compared to the theory taught in their lectures.

"Right, I'm bored now. You two want to see some proper surgery?"

The medical students didn't know whether to say yes and offend the heart surgeon or say no and offend Mr Thomas.

"Don't worry, you don't need to see any more. If we came back in a year, Giles will still be doing the same two operations. No pushing back the frontiers of medicine here."

"Yes, bye arsehole, go create more vegetables. I may be doing a cabbage, but you create them."

"Touché." Lewis ushered the students away. "Right, let's see what those vascular surgeons are doing."

The two medical students trailed along with Lewis like

little ducklings behind a mother duck. He entere
and told the medical students to wait outside. T
surgeon who he thought was in there. It was a locu
surgeon, as his mate, having apparently ruptureu ᴵⁱⁱˢ ⁱ ⁻⁻⁻
tendon playing squash, was on sick leave. The poor bastard
was trying to relive his youth by playing as he did twenty years
prior... That will be a bit of a hit for his lucrative private
practice. He would be off work for the next six weeks. As
Lewis entered, he could feel the tension in the air. Everyone in
the theatre was on edge. There was complete silence apart
from the anaesthetic machine. Even the anaesthetist was
paying attention to the monitors and scribbling notes, which
was not a good sign. It transpired that the locum doctor had
amputated the wrong leg.

The patient was a smoker and a diabetic and had
developed narrowing of the arteries in both legs. The left leg,
however, was worse than the right. As per policy, he had seen
the patient before the surgery, but the patient was confused by
the foreign-sounding doctor. When asked which was the good
leg, he thought the locum doctor was asking which was the bad
leg. The patient had, therefore, pointed to the normal leg. The
surgeon diligently marked it with a permanent marker as per
hospital policy. When they made the checklist, the healthy leg
had the arrow on it. Halfway during the procedure, it was the
medical student who was present who eventually dared to
whisper to one of the nurses that he thought it was the right leg
that needed to come off. The nurse checked the notes and,
instead of calmly telling the surgeon, blurted out: "Everyone
stop! We're chopping off the wrong fucking leg!"

Lewis took stock of the situation and felt he best disappear
as soon as possible so as not to ruin his good karma. He picked

up the two medical students at the door outside, mumbling to himself. "Probably not the best way to inspire you two."

They began to make their way back to the sanctuary of Lewis' theatre. Harry was overcome with curiosity, though. So, dawdling behind, took his chances and peeked through the theatre door window. The locum surgeon was flapping his arms about, skidding over a puddle of blood on the floor around his feet from his botched operation. Harry noticed he was wearing a distinctive gold chain around his neck. He thought infection control probably wouldn't like that! Without further ado, he darted away to catch up with the others.

Back in Lewis' theatre, Lewis was washing his hands. He started with the usual chlorhexidine prep but lost patience and rushed through the process. It should have taken him at least three minutes, but he did it in about twenty seconds.

"Mr Thomas, you know we get into trouble if we don't tell you to wash your hands for longer." Patience said in her distinctive voice.

"Yes, I know, Patience. Just don't tell anyone." Lewis replied and winked at her.

When there was a breakout of unexplained infections a year ago, the management sent down an infection control nurse. She didn't tell anyone who she was. She just wandered around the theatre complex with a clipboard, writing silently, obviously to send a report back to the management to single out any naughty surgeons or theatre staff. She had stood behind Lewis, watching him as he scrubbed up. Lewis was aware of her standing there behind him and instantly put her in the enemy camp. After he had finished washing his hands, she had told him that she wasn't going to pass his 'Washing Hand Training Exercise' and that he would have to go for further training. Lewis could have just gone along with it and that would have been the end of it. But something inside him flipped. The last thing he needed was to have his surgical karma wrecked by this well-meaning fuckwit hanging about with a clipboard, especially before a complicated case.

Looking back, it was more the condescending way in which she spoke to him rather than what she said. He had been scrubbing up for twenty years and had one of the lowest post-surgical infection rates in his hospital. Lewis knew from his own experience that the length of washing his hands had little effect on his infection rates. There were so many more other factors.

"So, are you telling me that the paper by Nobski et al. published last year about excessive hand washing and increased infection rates means nothing to you?"

The infection control nurse replied that she wasn't aware of the paper. Lewis wasn't aware of it either as he had just made it up.

"Yes, you see if you scrub too much, it takes the good bacteria away from the hands and that leaves the deeper bad bacteria exposed on the surface." The nurse said she was just doing her job and that he would still have to go on the training. Lewis knew it was just another exercise to ensure that the hospital management could tick a box. "Wonderful. Can't wait. Sign me up, please." He heard nothing further from the handwashing police.

Patience was tying up Lewis's gown. "Mr T, you're getting bigger. I can hardly get this gown to tie up at the back."

"No Patience, the nurses always get me a large gown out, and I'm extra-large! How long have I been working here?"

79

"Sorry, doc. I will tell the other nurses."

"Why don't you tell them to look at that fucking board which has all our gown and glove sizes on?"

Lewis hated waste, especially in a public hospital. He wondered how many times around the country the wrong gowns and gloves were opened by staff who then threw them away. They couldn't be re-used or resealed once opened. It would probably save the NHS millions! It was good for the glove companies, though, Lewis would joke to himself. At least someone was profiting from this stupidity. Oh, to go back to the good old days. Lewis never thought he would miss those lovely, reusable emerald green cloth gowns. Or those white cloth masks that remind you of horror films, either. Everything was disposable these days. The drapes, the gowns, the masks and now pride.

Patience carried on. "Right, young lady. If this is your first time in theatre, I will go through this carefully. After putting your gloves on, do not touch anything other than your other glove. Resist the temptation to touch your face, mask, or anything else unless told to do so."

Deborah, who had appeared so cool and collected before, began to look uneasy. Lewis remembered how intimidated he was when he first scrubbed up and observed a real-life operation. He was ceremonially ejected from the theatre by the sister for wearing the wrong-coloured hat. In that hospital, surgeons wore blue caps and medical students wore yellow ones. For a laugh, one of his fellow medical students gave Lewis a blue hat on purpose and told him that if he wore the blue one, he would be allowed to scrub up. When he turned up in his blue hat and asked the theatre sister when to scrub up, she asked if he was a locum doctor. Lewis proudly said that he was a medical student. The theatre sister then grabbed Lewis by the scruff of his theatre scrubs and dragged him out of the theatre doors, screaming at him: "You never, ever wear a blue hat, you idiot! Get out of my theatre!" His colleague got his laugh, all right.

"Okay, Deborah. Keep your hands together until we prep the patient, and when we have all the sterile drapes on, you can keep your hands on the drapes. Don't be nervous."

Lewis started to prep the patient with aqueous iodine solution. He liked the contrast of the brown solution on the pale skin with the theatre lights beaming down. The rays reflected on the wet surface, accentuating the curves of the skull. Painting the patient like this gave him time to contemplate the operation. As he was imagining making the first cuts in the brain, avoiding the superficial cortical vessels, he was abruptly stopped by the operating department assistant or ODP, Terry. Terry was an ex-military, stout looking chap.

"Right, shall we do the WHO checklist?" Terry bellowed.

The checklist was a tried and tested method developed in the USA to reduce complications in surgery. It ensured the staff knew which was the correct side to operate on or whether the patient had any allergies, for example. This was important information to go over, of course, but it was a lengthy process and distracted Lewis from working out the operation in his mind.

Although the World Health Organisation (WHO) checklist had become another tick box exercise for a lot of staff, it clearly hadn't helped the vascular theatre a few doors down.

"Does everyone know each other?" Terry continued, ensuring the theatre team knew everyone's name in case of an emergency. Surprisingly frequently, people who had supposedly worked together for years had no idea what each other's names were. Due to chronic staff shortages, though, theatre nurses and the like were expected to help with whatever surgical procedure they were called for and thus were sent to different theatres without much warning. Long gone were the days where you had a tight theatre team with familiar faces and procedures. Now, you could be assisted by a nurse who had never seen a brain operation before. Lewis was lucky that he managed to keep his team close around him for most of his cases. It was something he felt really strongly about. As well as trying to maintain a relaxed atmosphere by being encouraging and playing music, he also often bought the whole team coffee and croissants. By the same token, if someone didn't fit in with the rest of the team, Lewis either ignored them or was particularly vindictive so they didn't want to work on his team again.

They went around the room introducing themselves. "Andrew, Anaesthetist."

"Patience, Senior Sister."

"Terry ODP and porn star. Just joking, I'm actually a stunt cock, just go in for those difficult scenes."

Patience gave him a look which suggested, despite him being a big lad, she could knock his block off at any time.

"Becky, Runner." A runner was a health care assistant who fetched things that were needed in theatre, helped connect the cautery machines, with suction and the like. She usually sat by the computer updating her Facebook status, but Lewis tolerated this. She was brilliant when help was needed quickly.

"Lewis, top Brain Surgeon. Not joking."

Everyone looked at Deborah waiting for her to introduce

herself, but she wasn't sure whether she was part of the team or not. After an uncomfortable pause, she realised that she had better say something.

"Deborah, Medical Student."

Harry, who was in the corner, piped up: "Harry, top Medical Student!"

Another uncomfortable pause, but much more awkward this time. Poor kid, Lewis thought.

God loves a trier, but… you're not funny.

Terry again continued. "What is the procedure we are doing?"

Lewis responded this time. "Right craniotomy and excision of right frontal lobe glioma." The checklist went on.

Terry: "Any unexpected events anticipated?"

Lewis: "How would we know if they are unexpected?"

Terry: "Ah, always expect the unexpected, just like the Spanish inquisition!"

Lewis: "Yeah, that's really helpful, Terry. Can we get on with the checklist?"

Terry: "Anticipated blood loss?"

Lewis: "Well, that depends on whether I tear the anterior cerebral artery. If so, there will be loads, if not, hopefully not much."

Terry: "So, what do I put down for anticipated blood loss?"

Lewis: "Make it up Terry. Just make sure there is some blood cross-matched in the fridge."

Terry: "Any good news the team want to share?" Pause. "I have some. I got laid last night."

Patience: "Good Terry, and how is ya pet cat this mornin'?"

Terry: "Ha, Patience, I know you want me. You're just jealous."

Terry was behind Patience grabbing her large waist. Patience grabbed his testicles. "With this little thin', I don't think so." Harry and Deborah were not expecting this sort of crude joviality in the theatre environment.

Lewis: "Andrew, can I start?"

Andrew: "Yep, thanks for letting me know."

Lewis: "Becky, what have we forgotten?"

Becky: "Music, sorry Mr T, what do you want on?"

Lewis: "You choose, or you can stick on my playlist."

Lewis couldn't operate without music. For some reason, whenever there wasn't music, something went wrong. It served two purposes: Firstly, he loved music, and secondly, it created a chilled atmosphere in the theatre. Becky put Queen on. 'Another One Bites the Dust' started pumping out of the Bose speakers Lewis had bought for his theatre.

Andrew: "Err... Can we choose another song?"

Becky put on Lewis's playlist. The first song that came up was 'Midnight Train to Georgia' by Gladys Knight and the Pips.

Lewis said "I love this song. Deborah, listen for the backing singers, best backing singing ever."

Lewis picked up the knife and made a firm and deliberate cut into the skin which briskly bled, while humming and singing the lyrics under his breath.

"Right Deborah, while I'm putting these clips onto the skin edges, I want you to press firmly on the other side. It helps control the bleeding." Deborah tentatively pressed her fingers onto the skin edge.

"Press harder, Deborah, that's it." Deborah got the hang

of it.

Out of the corner of the theatre, Harry could be heard saying "Awesome..." while still standing with his theatre trousers up by his abdomen. Terry had patted him on the back at some stage previously and stuck a piece of paper saying 'I love cock' on his back.

Like a well-oiled machine, the team worked in perfect unison together. Patience passed the instruments directly into Lewis's hands without him even asking, anticipating every move. She had done hundreds of these operations and knew precisely what he needed, when he needed it.

"Deborah, you need to suck when Mr T asks, okay."

Lewis and Patience looked at each other, Lewis grinned under his mask, glancing at Deborah to see if she got the double entendre. Luckily, he thought, she was innocent enough and used the suction with one hand to remove the blood coming from the bleeding edges of the wound. With her other hand, she pressed firmly on the skin edges.

"Magnificent Deborah, you're a natural," said Lewis. Deborah was concentrating too much to acknowledge the compliment.

"Drill, please." Before Lewis had even finished his words, Patience had already set up the electric drill. She had it in her hand, waiting to pass it to him.

The patient's skin and muscles now retracted back, exposing the creamy white surface of the skull. Lewis handed the drill to Deborah.

"Right Deborah, today you are going to drill into someone's head. Are you up for it?"

"Err, yes, Mr Thomas." She replied, wondering if he had lost his mind letting her do it.

"Hold the handpiece in your hand firmly and, when I say so, press the pedal and press firmly down."

Deborah did this, and the drill slipped off the curvature of the skull.

"STOP!" said Lewis in a loud voice. Deborah panicked, thinking that she had completely messed up the operation and any chance of drilling into someone's head. "Listen carefully..." Lewis whispered. "Can you hear the harmonies of the backing singers? It's amazing!" He gestured with his left-hand, mimicking pulling the horn of a steam train. The portable speakers in the corner of the theatre, despite their diminutive size, were pumping out the classic Gladys Knight and the Pips, Midnight Train to Georgia.

Deborah was still holding the drill in her hand. "Don't worry, we will try this again. This happens, and that's why you have to hold it firmly." Lewis said. Deborah was surprised that Lewis had let her have another go. She steadied the drill onto the skull and pressed the foot pedal. After a few seconds, the drill began to penetrate the skull, millimetre after millimetre. Bone dust collected around the whirring drill piece.

Lewis spoke in a higher-pitch, raising his voice over the noise: "Deborah, how do you know when to stop? What happens if the drill goes through the brain?"

Deborah's face was one of terror. How was she to know what to do? She hadn't been to an operating theatre before. Will the drill go into the brain and the patient die? The drill suddenly stopped, perfectly deep enough to penetrate the skull but not the covering layer of the dura.

"Well done!" Lewis said, as he rocked the drill bit out of the thick skull. "The drill has a clutch, so when there is no resistance, it stops automatically. Don't worry, I won't be letting you do anything that I'm not comfortable with."

Deborah's heart was racing. She could feel adrenaline pumping through her veins. The hairs on the back of her neck were erect and her pupils were dilated with excitement. She couldn't believe that she had just drilled into someone's skull.

"There's something quite exhilarating about drilling into someone's head." Deborah nodded. He could have said anything. She was still getting over the fact that she had not only performed her first operative procedure but that it was a neurosurgical one!

Harry, who was still in the corner, watched in silence. He had discovered the piece of paper that Terry had stuck on his back. Lewis sensed his dejection and turned around.

"Hey, Harry. Come over, stick a mask on and let's see how good your anatomy is." Harry smiled, put a mask on and came closer to the operative field.

"Not too close." Patience said with a kiss of her teeth, protecting her sterile field. "So, what are these?" Lewis said, pointing to the fine lines running along the skull.

"These are the cranial sutures. I can see the sagittal suture in the midline and part of the coronal suture," said Harry.

"Good, what's this tough layer of tissue covering the brain called?"

"That is called the dura." Harry was quick.

"And what does the dura mean?"

"Actually, I don't know."

"Okay, think of words that begin with dura…"

"What, like durable?"

"Yes, anything else?"

Deborah whispered to Harry. "Durex!" It was precisely

what Lewis was trying to get them to say. Everyone in the theatre stopped, Deborah blushed.

"Yes, good example!" Lewis said. "Dura means tough, and dura mater, which is the covering layer of the brain means, 'tough mother'. A bit like Patience, here." Despite Lewis initially wishing Amal was there with the medical students, he was beginning to enjoy their company. He had forgotten how much he liked teaching.

After the dura was open, it exposed the brain which pulsated and glistened in time with the heart-beat. The cortical surface was well-defined by the convoluted furrows forming the sulci and gyri. Lewis had brought in a large microscope which magnified and shone a light over the area of interest. The view was presented on a television monitor so everyone in the theatre could see. You need a steady hand for this; every movement the surgeon makes is magnified under the microscope.

"How do you get the deep tumour out without damaging the surface of the brain?" Deborah asked inquisitively.

"With skill and elegance," replied Lewis, repeating what he had told the patient earlier. "Suction down, please." He had a suction tip in his left hand and a bipolar cautery in his right. The bipolar was like a pair of forceps with small, fine metal tips. When Lewis pressed a foot pedal, an electric current passed between the ends, frying the brain tissue between them. This way, he could control the bleeding as he dissected the surface of the brain. "This is where the anatomy you learnt in your second year at medical school comes in handy. You don't want to go too far back. You want the shortest trajectory to the tumour," said Lewis.

"Are you using neuro-navigation?" asked Harry. Neuro-navigation is a system where the scans of the patient are integrated into a computer. These are aligned with the image captured by the microscope and displayed on a computer console. Using probes, you can then locate the exact position of the tumour. Prior to this, all neurosurgeons had been using was a mixture of experience and luck. It was clear to everyone else that Lewis wasn't using this navigation as the computer console was not in the theatre. Lewis stuck his right index finger in the air. "This is my navigation probe, Harry." Lewis trained to perform surgery in the days before navigation, using the anatomical structures on the skull as landmarks. He worried that there would be a whole generation of surgeons who would rely so much on technology that if there was a glitch in the computer, they would be utterly lost.

As Lewis was dissecting the cortical surface, Deborah's leg inadvertently touched his under the table. A tingle rushed up Lewis's spine and he paused for a moment.

"Everything all right, Mr T?" said Patience.

"Yes, all fine," replied Lewis. Lewis felt the tingle reach his groin area. The last thing he needed was to get an erection while operating. Firstly, because it would distract him, and secondly, it would be evident under the theatre gown and everyone would see. In his head, he repeated: mother on the toilet, mother on the toilet, mother on the toilet. It seemed to quell any erotic thoughts for the time being.

At last, he felt the firmer tissue of the tumour and slowly dissected this from around the normal brain tissue. Normal brain tissue has the consistency of poached egg white, while the capsule of the tumour is firmer. Fortunately, in this case, the difference was enough for Lewis to be sure that it was, indeed, a tumour. On occasions, it's impossible to differentiate between what is normal and what is abnormal tissue. That is where navigation is useful as is intraoperative MRI, where you operate while intermittently scanning the patient. The problem with the latter process is that everything needs to be MRI compatible. In other words, non-magnetic. Anything magnetic would fly off and stick to the large magnet in the scanner.

He knew he had to take his time while removing the tumour. He effortlessly dissected the tumour away from the normal brain tissue. Lewis was ambidextrous, which was a real advantage in neurosurgery and any other form of surgery for that matter. He switched hands with the suction, bipolar and micro-dissectors, and then adjusted the microscope several times to get every angle on the tumour. He proceeded to stop the small bleeding vessels on the brain, and to make sure the brain was kept moist with normal saline. Without the saline, the heat generated by the microscope light would dry the surface of the brain and make the instruments stick onto it. This would then snag on the vessels or cortical surface. Lewis spared a thought for how much he loved his job. It never failed to amaze him how his education was a total disaster, and yet surgery came so naturally to him. That's the education system for you, though.

Once, when he was a junior neurosurgical registrar, Lewis was assisting his boss at the time who kept on pausing and looking at the clock while operating. He presumed it was because he had to go to his private clinic in the afternoon in Harley Street. His boss was getting more anxious, huffing in between constant expletives. Suddenly, he turned around to the anaesthetist and said, "Tom, how old is this patient?"

"About 75 years." The anaesthetist replied.

"Right then, we better get a move on." He then proceeded

to stick his finger into the brain tissue, swirl it around and out popped the tumour. Brain tissue was still hanging off it. It was a dreadful sight.

"Right, everyone, the tumour is out. Lewis, are you okay to close up?" Lewis could not believe that after taking the time to expose the tumour, within a few seconds, the tumour was out due to sheer impatience. The patient woke up paralysed and could no longer speak. Lewis knew that if his boss had taken more care, the patient would have walked home after a few days in the hospital. One thing he took from his training was how not to operate.

Lewis took his time taking the tumour out, ensuring there was as little trauma as possible done to the underlying brain. Finally, he was glad to close up. Firstly, he sewed up the dura with continuous sutures. Then, he replaced the bone flap with small plates and screws. Lastly, he sewed up the skin, after removing the clips which stopped the highly vascular skin edges from bleeding. Neatly placed metal staples closed the superficial skin.

"Righty, I'll write the operation note. Why don't you two grab a coffee and we'll reconvene in ten minutes?" Lewis hated writing the operation note. He usually left this to someone else, usually Amal who wasn't there, so he had to do it himself. "Can someone log me onto the computer?" Everything was now computerised. There were so many systems for different things that Lewis couldn't remember the passwords. Since he rarely typed the operation note, he had to log in, and when Lewis did, it said the password had expired. He would need to choose another password. What a ball ache.

The patient woke up successfully and able to talk. In a post-operative haze, he'd even asked Lewis when the operation was going to be. As Lewis was just about to exit the building, Deborah approached him at the doors. She had waited until she was away from Harry to talk to him. She had taken her surgical scrub cap off and boy… was she beautiful, even more so than Lewis had originally thought. A cascade of luscious, blonde locks delicately framed her face.

"Mr Thomas, that was one of the best experiences of my life. Thank you so much for letting me perform the burr hole! Would you mind if I could help you again?"

"Not at all, Deborah, but you know, I also have training commitments with my registrars, and they have to come first." Lewis got that tingle down his spine again, especially as Deborah flicked her blonde hair and fluttered her long eyelashes. Her pupils, again, dilated as she spoke.

Lewis' head began to spin. She fancies me. She fancies ME! Or maybe she doesn't. Who would fancy an old fart like me? But she does! The truth is in her eyes! There was this ethical dilemma, though, that she was a young medical student, and he was her superior. Someone could accuse him of abusing his position of power. Damn right!

"Mr Thomas? Are you, all right?"

"Ah!" Lewis cleared his throat. You dimwit. "Sorry! I have, err… a lot on my mind. Hospital life. Saving lives. You know…"

"Well, I've jotted my email and phone number down for you. If you think there is an interesting case or a project I can help with, I would like to help!" He could think of plenty of ways she could be helpful. Mother on the toilet, mother on the toilet, mother on the toilet…

He cleared his throat, dragging his mind back to reality.

"Sure Deborah, it was nice to have you in theatre."

When Lewis arrived home later that evening, he opened a bottle of his favourite red, lit a cigarette and listened to loud rock music. He put Deborah in the 'Wank Bank' as his guilty pleasure and concluded that he had had a very good day.

CHAPTER 6

The weather was blistering in San Paulo. Professor Pedro Santos was chauffeur-driven to the Brazilian Brainionics lab. It was nothing like the main headquarters of Brainionics. It was not brain-shaped, for starters. The building was an extension of the original lab that Professor Santos had been working in, though now with updated equipment and a modernised interior. There was a clear divide where the old laboratory ended, and the new extension began. From the outside, it almost looked as if a fancy showroom had been stuck onto a former, colonial establishment.

Pedro entered the reception. It was, indeed, very fancy. The hot sweat covering his brow was immediately cooled by a frosty breeze. High-powered air conditioning whirred aggressively above him, while beneath him, the white marble floors appeared almost luminescent. Harsh white lights glared down from the ceiling. Bright, iridescent eye-like bulbs obtrusively spying on new arrivals. There was something brutally sterile about the location. The receptionist toddled over to him, her heels click-clacking on the marble, and greeted him with a glass of chilled water with lemon and ice.

"Boa Tarde!" She chirped. He drank the water, completely dismissed her and walked off to his office. His two bodyguards followed in quick succession. Pedro was rarely left unprotected. His sense of self-importance was fuelled by how indispensable he was to Brainionics to which he was a vital asset. Shares in Brainionics had rocketed since the launch of their battlefield intraoperative brain monitor RiPTIDE. RiPTIDE had been used extensively in recent wars. It had some commercial success as well with usage in large intensive care wards where severely brain-injured patients were treated. Local doctors could send the information wirelessly to neurosurgeons who were thousands of miles away for expert advice. If the pressures started to increase, the patients were transferred by ambulance or helicopter to the neurosurgical departments, saving a lot of money and unnecessary transportation. The fact that this particular device was biodegradable also meant that the implant didn't need removing at a later date. It merely dissolved over time thanks to the body's natural enzymes, leaving a tiny microchip in place which was inert and didn't seem to cause any problems.

Pedro was working on a bigger project than just brain regeneration though. He'd already championed that. He had a funding budget of $10 US million. His remit was to develop a neurostimulator which modulates the functions of the brain rather than regenerates the neurons. It had taken years to build a prototype. He had moved on from rat brains, many of which he fried, and progressed to living baboon models. Very few people knew that the baboons lived in the original part of the laboratory, for fear of animal rights activists attacking the building. Rather than sticking a wire through brain tissue, Pedro wanted to create a stimulation zone within the brain, so different areas of the brain could be stimulated either alone or in combination with other areas. The main problem was to target the deeper areas of the brain. More brain damage can occur the deeper the wire enters the brain.

He eventually came up with a triangulation technique. This involves placing three electrodes in the head apart from each other. By varying the currents of the three surface stimulators, he was able to target the different areas of the brain where the electrical signals intersected, causing a larger current to flow to the targeted area. It all sounded good in theory, but a lot of baboons were sacrificed in the name of the cause. Pedro realised, though, that putting three stimulators in the head would not only be expensive but would put off a lot of surgeons using it. It would also not be commercially viable. With the engineers and technicians of Brainionics, they developed a triangulation disc. It was a single disc that was able to triangulate the currents and achieve the same effect. It was another moment of genius. Whether it worked on humans or not, only time would tell.

He met his team of technicians in the laboratory. In a row of cages, there were baboons in various states of activity. One was slumped in the cell, inanimate. Its eyes, though they followed Pedro as he inspected the cages, were totally vacant. Another looked terrified, cowering in a corner as if it feared for its life. Some looked normal, bouncing around, scratching their bums and having a good old time. One, however, jumped towards Professor Santos, gnashing and baring his razor-sharp teeth. Pedro recoiled back in alarm. They all had shaved heads with small scars over the right frontal area of their heads.

Viktor was the chief laboratory technician. "Greetings Professor, so glad you could come.

Let me update you on developments."

"I'm expecting good things, Viktor. There's a lot at stake with this project. You remember what happened to Roberto?" he said in a slightly joking and yet menacing tone. Roberto was

Viktor's predecessor. He managed to kill three of the baboons during the operative procedure. Pedro thought he was incompetent and fired him. He suddenly disappeared. He didn't even stay to clear his office. All that was left behind was a desk picture of Roberto and his son, Avelino. The pictured gathered dust until Viktor took office. The other technicians were equally bemused as they were expecting Avelino to join the team as he had prodigious computer skills at such an early age. Though nobody liked to speculate, his colleagues knew Professor Santos had a lot of connections. It was true that people were afraid of him.

"Do not worry, Professor. We have had no baboon deaths so far. The project is right on track, even beyond!"

"Okay, Viktor. Show me some results."

In front of the cages were a set of controls corresponding to each of the pens. One by one, Viktor adjusted the dials. The dials controlled the electric current of the device in the baboons' brains. One dial was to turn it on and off. Another, to adjust the intensity of the stimulation. The final one was to increase the amount of tissue radially receiving the electricity.

Viktor started playing with the dials. The baboon which was previously slumped in the cage suddenly sprang into action.

Viktor commented. "Clarissa, who you will remember was artificially paralysed six months ago by occluding the internal carotid artery causing a massive stroke... Well, look at her now!"

Clarissa, the baboon, came to the front of the cage. She looked inquisitively at Pedro.

The baboon had several small electrodes sticking out of her shaved head. Viktor played with the dials again, causing

Clarissa to hold her hands up to her head. She then slumped back into the corner again.

"Remarkable." Declared Pedro. "Does it hurt them?"

"We have been remotely monitoring their blood pressure and heart rate, and there doesn't seem to be a significant increase when we stimulate. So, we are concluding that it doesn't hurt." Replied Viktor.

"Well done, Viktor. Finally, we are getting somewhere. Tell me, the baboon in cage ten, why is it so aggressive?"

"Professor, watch this." Viktor, once again, started adjusting some of the dials on the console. The grimacing baboon's face suddenly became calmer. "Why don't you say hello to Angelo, Professor?" said Viktor.

Pedro looked indignantly at Viktor and replied. "No. Why don't you say hello to Angelo?"

Viktor proceeded to walk to the cage and, stopping in front of the cell, stared directly into Angelo's eyes. Pedro suddenly forced Viktor's head into the bars of the cage and kept it there. Viktor instinctively started to struggle. The baboon's mouth came closer to Viktor's face. There was a pause. Both Viktor and Pedro prepared themselves for the baboon to tear into Viktor's flesh. Thankfully for Viktor, quite the opposite happened. The baboon gave a big sloppy kiss to Viktor's lips. Pedro let go of Viktor's face.

"You know I trust you, Viktor. Don't be angry. I have every faith in you." Viktor adjusted himself, wiped the sweat off his brow, the saliva off his lips and adjusted the controls. Angelo reverted to the aggressive baboon that he was before, now with even more intensity, shrieking and grabbing at the bars, hitting his head against the metal.

"This is something new, Viktor," said Pedro.

Viktor replied in a slightly more distressed tone. "Exactly, it seems that we can control Angelo's aggressiveness by a flick of a switch."

"This is a real breakthrough," Pedro concluded. "For the first time, we have something that can not only help paralysed victims but also potentially help those who commit murder, rape and grievous bodily harm. And all without permanently damaging their brains! Moniz would be proud. Outstanding work! We must move on to the next phase."

Viktor and the lab team looked at each other nervously. "Professor, we are really only in the early stages. We don't know the long-term effects."

"Typical! I have also worked in the lab like you, Viktor, and for many years at that! If I had the same attitude, you and I wouldn't be here today." Pedro came close to Viktor and whispered in his ear. "Please don't stand in the way of medical breakthroughs; they only become breakthroughs when the world knows about them." He then left the laboratory and was joined by his bodyguards who escorted him back to his silver Rolls-Royce which was parked outside.

In his car, Pedro called the CEO of Brainionics, Gad Dayan. "Gad, we must meet. I think we need to move onto human trials."

"How do we do that, Pedro?" asked Gad, curiously. "I have a few ideas. Let's meet to discuss."

CHAPTER 7

Once Lewis realised that he had to take medicine seriously, he didn't know what to specialise in. He had survived his junior house jobs without killing anyone and got through his probationary period as a junior house officer alive himself. Although he secretly loved the idea of being a surgeon, he didn't think he would make it with his past track record. It is often apparent at medical school which students are going to become surgeons and which are not, at least, that was what Lewis thought. Those that wanted to be surgeons tended to be confident characters, something Lewis certainly didn't used to be.

In the old days, you were able to do various jobs while training before settling into one speciality. Lewis taught anatomy, did a stint in A&E and, at one point, God forbid, was nearly going to consider cardiology. He came to a crossroads in his career: should he pursue a medical or a surgical career? He wasn't interested in being an anaesthetist, radiologist or family doctor. His boss at the time suggested that he should do a bit of neurosurgery as it combines elements of both careers. Lewis applied for a six-month post and became a senior house officer in neurosurgery in an ex-military South London hospital. The hospital had very long corridors with portacabins outside. There were lots of open doors on the wards too, so veterans could venture into the outdoors to get fresh air.

He loved it. He remembered the first time he saw a consultant neurosurgeon make a hole into a skull. They didn't have the electric drills that we have now. They used something called a 'Hudson Brace and Bit'. The skill was to exert enough pressure to drill through the hard skull bone and to know when to reduce the force so as not to penetrate through the brain below, causing death or disability. It was a defining moment in taking his first career steps. From that point onwards, he worked his arse off to become a neurosurgeon. There were only two other SHOs, Senior House Officers, and two registrars. It was a tight ship, but everyone worked hard. The main function of the job was taking blood, clerking the patients, writing the drug charts and seeing to the emergency admissions. It was not to assist in surgery, unless you were on call, in which case, you would go and help the registrar. It was during these moments that Lewis realised he had a natural ability to operate. He didn't know where it came from. In fact, he didn't expect it at all. Operations seemed to be easy for him though.

At the time, it was one of the few Neurosurgical Centres that had a CT and MRI scan. Nowadays, every hospital has them. We have now come to rely on modern imaging immensely. Back then though, patients had to travel from other hospitals to get a scan. It was Lewis' job to look at the scan and decide whether to keep them in — if they had a neurosurgical problem — or send them back to where they came from. Again, in those days, it was easy to transfer patients back once the neurosurgical episode was over. There was a standard agreement between hospitals that the neurosurgeons had to take their patients on quickly and therefore needed beds urgently. There were occasions, however, where beds weren't available.

Lewis remembers once walking onto the neurosurgical ward and seeing a visibly upset nurse taking a telephone call.

"Shall I take this?" Lewis mouthed to her, probably only because the nurse was attractive. The nurse mouthed back. "Yes, please," then whispered, "he's a consultant from another hospital. He wants to transfer a patient. I've told him that there are no beds at the moment, but he won't listen."

Lewis pumped his chest up and strode over, a knight prepared to do anything for his damsel in distress. "Don't worry, I've got this."

"Can I help you?" Lewis said into the phone, altering his voice slightly to sound much more senior than he actually was. "I understand you are trying to admit a patient."

The doctor on the phone spoke with a lisp. "Yes, that is correct. The patient is a private patient who has severe sciatica down the leg. I've just spoken with the neurosurgical consultant and he promised he would transfer the patient, but you're saying there are no beds."

Lewis replied without hesitation. "That is correct. As soon as we have a bed available, we will admit him, we promise, but we are waiting for some patients to transfer back."

A frustrated, whining voice reverberated down the line. "Well, that is not good enough."

Do you know who I am?" Lewis hated hearing that.

"No, err, I don't. Who you are?"

"Well, my name is Dr Wright, Consultant Rheumatologist." Lewis retorted. "Do you know who I am?"

"No, I don't."

After a pause, Lewis returned with: "Well, fuck off then!" And slammed the phone down.

The nurse was in shock. Lewis, however, left the ward feeling quite pleased with himself.

During his early neurosurgical career at that same hospital, Lewis became fascinated by neuromodulation, the ability to change the functions of the brain by destroying certain tracts and connections. His senior boss and mentor pioneered psychosurgery, which fell into disrepute after the film 'One Flew Over the Cuckoo's Nest' and the advent of psychotropic medication which virtually replaced surgical lobotomies. Modern medicine has come a long way since then. The pioneering work of Professor Pedro Santos has meant that surgeons no longer need to destroy parts of the brain to stop aberrant signals. It was these abnormal signals that caused a whole manner of brain disorders such as epilepsy and chemical imbalances leading to Parkinson's disease and psychosis. Once destroyed, it was virtually impossible to regain the function. However, modulating the brain by the use of electrical currents can be reversed. The technique was very controversial, and other surgeons in this field could not reproduce the results of Professor Santos. Lewis had been following the work of Professor Santos, reading his publications and watching his lectures online or at events. The professor attended numerous neurosurgical meetings as the Guest of Honour or a Keynote Speaker. Although he wasn't a particularly good orator, his work was of significant interest to the neurosurgical community.

Once, Lewis did get to meet the great Professor in person. It didn't exactly play out as Lewis had imagined it would though. It was the World Federation of Neurosurgeons congress in Morocco. Lewis, being a part of the Young Neurosurgeons Forum, along with another ambitious junior neurosurgeon Crispin Humphries, had been invited to present. Lewis was presenting his unit's series of cases that had specific surgical procedures. It was an honest study which looked at the outcome of operated patients who had had brain bleeds due to cerebral aneurysms. The results showed that 10% of the cases died. In most units in the UK, that was not a bad death rate. After his presentation, Professor Santos stood up and publicly castigated Lewis for presenting these terrible results. He concluded that his unit in London should stop operating immediately as the death rate was unacceptably high. No one knew what to say after that, so the room just fell silent. The only sound that could be heard was the uncomfortable shifting in seats; the audience knew that the results were similar to, if not better than, their own. Nobody would dare challenge the great Professor though, especially after that performance.

At these meetings, it is common for a certain number of prominent surgeons to broadcast how good they are. Some surgeons never have any complications, which they like to make a good ballyhoo about. All of their patients have fantastic outcomes, or so it seems. Of course, they never really follow up on them long-term. Lecture after lecture, there is the same conclusion: the results are promising, but further long-term studies are needed. Lewis never learnt anything new at these meetings, so they became more like a social gathering rather than a scientific one for him. To be publicly humiliated by the Professor, and as a junior neurosurgeon still in the embryonic stages of his career, was incredibly shameful. But despite being rejected like a perforated condom, Lewis was still in awe of the great Professor Santos.

Lewis managed to briefly speak to Professor Santos at one of these social events. "Professor, how do you get such great results?" Lewis asked expectantly.

"Well, my boy, I only select those patients who are likely to survive. Clearly in the UK, you operate on anyone. That is the secret of success in surgery."

"Thank you, Professor." Lewis, disheartened, walked away. He had felt rather cheated by the fact that Professor Santos didn't mention that fact after reprimanding Lewis on the public stage. In the UK, they didn't have the luxury of turning patients away. All patients were admitted whether they were going to die or not. That was the NHS way. Thus, the results always showed more considerable mortality than other countries and especially in comparison to expensive, private clinics. This didn't take away from Lewis' fascination with the Professor's work, though.

As he walked away, Crispin Humphries, one of his rival registrar trainees from London, barged past him. Lewis hadn't realised that he was attending the same conference. Crispin had trained at St Thomas's Hospital, was a public-school boy at heart and was absolutely in love with himself.

Lewis, naturally, wasn't thrilled to see him. He was making a beeline straight to Professor Santos. Intrigued by whatever rubbish Crispin could pull out his arse, Lewis hung back, concealed by the crowd, trying to listen to their conversation. He couldn't make out much of their interaction, but got the general gist.

"Dear Professor," he had begun, as if reciting from a letter, "my name is Dr Crispin, and I'm one of your greatest fans. I love the work that you are doing." It went on and on. Lewis had felt nauseous listening to Crispin delivering his ode to the professor. He did hear something strange though. Crispin was saying he wanted to bring the Professor's work to the UK, or at least, it certainly sounded like that. Lewis knew that Crispin wouldn't be able to do this until he was at least at consultant level, and that would not be for another two years. Regardless of Crispin's position, it would still have to go through the ethics committees.

Anyway, that was then. Crispin became a renowned Consultant Neurosurgeon at another London teaching hospital. He was at every meeting, always there on his high-horse presenting his incredible results. Crispin never failed to stand up at conferences. He unapologetically loved the sound of his own voice. With an oh-so British accent, he would say things like: "In my experience of this condition...", or, "My results are not in accordance with yours!" If you have been a consultant for over a decade, this level of self-promotion is an unwritten but accepted right. When you haven't even done one year, well, your colleagues will just think you are a knob. Crispin was a committed self-publicist though, so he didn't give two fucks about what his colleagues thought. He was always in the Daily Mail Health Column, commenting as a Neurosurgical Expert on some new technique or other.

His website was impressive and highly convincing. Even just at a glance, you can see why people want to throw money at him. You almost wanted to have an operation under him even if you were healthy. If you typed 'Brain Surgeon' into a search engine, he came up high on the front page. A picture of his round face, narrow eyes and balding head, wearing a smug smile in his scrubs came up. He was holding a mini placard with: VOTED BEST BRAIN SURGEON IN BRITAIN printed on it. Voted by one person, himself. Lewis felt somewhat wounded whenever he came across this image. It was hard to see such a fool get such credit and public attention in his own field, knowing how hard he himself worked and how much he cared.

There were, of course, patient testimonials to back up his supposed monumental level of expertise. "Mr Humphries is the most wonderful surgeon ever. As soon as I met him, I knew I could trust him." This person clearly needed more brain surgery. What the testimonials didn't cover, nor anywhere else on his website for that matter, was how half of the neurosurgical community had ended up sorting out one or more of his complications in the past. The 'Most Brilliant Surgical Mind' was actually responsible for many severe, post-operative difficulties. It seemed that as soon as you paid the money for the private surgery, patients could never contact him afterwards. Especially if they had a complication. Of course, it was never his fault, he just didn't see himself as accountable for the difficult stuff. Instead, he left the rest of us to clean up his mess. A lot of surgeons referred to him as 007. He thought it was because he was suave and had charisma. It was actually because he had a licence to kill — literally, a medical licence — which he abused beyond reason.

One day, when Lewis was particularly bored in his outpatient clinic, using an alias email he had typed false details into the referral box on Crispin's website.

Dear Mr Humphries, I have terrible headaches, and my doctor won't do anything about it. Can you help?

An automatic reply came back.

Mr Humphries is currently operating and saving lives but will come back to you as soon as possible.

After an hour, Lewis received another email.

Dear Gertrude, I am sorry you are having problems. Of course, I can help! Please contact my private secretary.

His secretary's phone number was then displayed before a large portrait picture of Mr Humphries flashed onto the screen, filling the monitor with his cheesy smile. A more reasonable pop-up would have been wheelchairs and walking sticks, as that's what his patients would need if they were going to have surgery with him. Or maybe even a coffin, Lewis scoffed to himself. Unexpectedly, the image of Mike Taylor popped up in his mind again.

CHAPTER 8

Crispin Humphries had an outstanding curriculum vitae. He had attended Eton, gained a medical school place at St Thomas's Hospital and did his surgical rotation in Cambridge. He was a straight-A student. He did a neurosurgical fellowship at the Cleveland Clinic in the US and became a Consultant Neurosurgeon in a large London teaching hospital. Despite all of this, he couldn't operate for toffee. No one knew how someone so good on paper was so useless in action. He was great at writing papers and had extensive publications which were, Lewis hated to admit, truly insightful reads. When he presented at scientific meetings, everyone knew about him and his work. For a period, he did work in an NHS hospital, but he hardly turned up. His juniors did most of the operating unsupervised. He spent most of his time doing research or rather getting someone else to do the research.

If you want an operation, don't go to a professor who spends all of his time in a laboratory. Go to the jobbing surgeon whose life is spent in the theatre. Crispin only specialised in functional neurosurgery. Although this was an exciting branch of neurosurgery, it didn't need much surgical skill. After all, it just entailed making a small hole in the skull and guiding a small wire to the appropriate part of the brain. Even a medical student with a bit of help could do it. If Crispin had to be in charge of an aneurysm clipping, tumour resection or spinal work, he would be punching well above his skill set. As a trainee, although his bosses didn't like him, no one gave him a bad reference for fear that he would complain to the postgraduate dean which would have disrupted their own lives. They would sign the necessary paperwork to offload him onto the next consultant, glad to be rid of him. He would only be with them for six months and during that period, when the consultant realised — and there were definitely no ifs — that Crispin couldn't operate, they did most of the work themselves. Even then, he used any excuse possible to get out of attending surgery. The clues were in his UK references: Mr Humphries has a wonderful research career ahead of him and Mr Humphries enjoys many activities outside the surgical theatre. None whatsoever mentioned his medical incompetence.

His junior colleagues had disliked him as much as the consultants. He had always been a bully. Someone at some stage should have had the courage to highlight this to the higher authorities and stop him from operating, but nobody did. It takes a lot to stop a trainee becoming a consultant once on a training scheme, whichever speciality they choose. Just forward a few years and here we have Mr Crispin Humphries, owner of a large private practice, still the star of the show but just as distrusted by professionals across the board. The public foolishly thought he was terrific though. It was his celebrity appearance, thanks to his glamorous clinic, exuberant website and the interest he received from the press that made him seem like he was a one-of-a-kind surgeon. As far as skill and expertise are concerned though, he's an absolute bonehead.

Having kept in close contact with Professor Santos over the years, Crispin Humphries learnt about the new developments of Brainionics long before the technology had hit the shores of the UK. He became a consultant for the company and would give international talks on behalf of Professor Santos. His lectures were well-rehearsed and dramatic. He knew how to create a buzz. The company loved this, as did the audience. He was a far better speaker than Pedro, but Pedro did not mind. This UK scholar gave his results more kudos than any of the work done in Brazil. The fact that Crispin didn't look like a malformed ugly duckling, unlike Santos, also helped. What's more, who wouldn't be impressed by a glowing reference from an international giant of neurosurgery?

At a neuromodulation conference in Miami, Pedro met with Crispin.

"Crispin, it is time for you to take this technology to the world. It will take some time for us to get FDA approval for this scientific know-how. We need to do some clinical studies. I am getting older, but you, you are the future!"

Crispin, of course, was flattered by this. "Professor, it would be an absolute honour for me to take this on. Do you think that..." he faltered mid-sentence, unsure of whether he should continue, "if I can perform this on my patients, do you think Brainionics would give me some shares in the company?"

"Leave it to me," Pedro said confidently.

It wasn't ethical, but the more success Brainionics had with their technology, the more chance it would be bought by a larger company. If Crispin had share options, he might get a large dividend if the company was sold. The potential wealth and fame were too much for him to resist.

The CEO of Brainionics was also in attendance. This

would be the first time that Crispin met Gad Dayan.

"Crispin, I've heard many great things about you from the Professor," said Dayan. Crispin and Dayan dwarfed the diminutive Santos. He carried on in a thick Israeli accent. "I am so glad we are going to be working together, correct?"

Crispin had felt like an overly excited groupie. Just hearing his name come out of Gad's mouth made him want to hop and skip. "Well, it's a pleasure to work with the great Professor, a real honour for me." He hesitated, remembering that the company will eventually make him a lot of money. "And of course, I have heard wonderful things about the company. I'm really looking forward to developing this technology around the world."

Dayan paused and looked sceptically at Crispin. He could read him like a book. He leant over and whispered in his ear. "Crispin, if we work together and bend the rules a little for the sake of science, I will make you a rich man. Do you understand?"

"Oh, yes Gad," Crispin responded, his eyes gleaming with delight. Big dollar signs flashed in his pupils. "I will do anything!" And then quickly added with a wink, "of course, in the name of science."

"It's Mr Dayan to you, Crispin, until we get to know each other. Understood?" Gad Dayan wanted to make sure that Crispin knew where he stood. Crispin took a step back, wounded. "Okay gentleman, I bid you well. Enjoy the rest of the congress." He swiftly turned on his heels with an air of finality and headed straight for the exit. Crispin took note. Now that is how you end a meeting.

Mr Walsh entered the luxurious entrance of Mr Humphries'

Harley Street clinic. One of the clinic concierge staff dressed in a starched white uniform pushed Mr Walsh's wheelchair for him.

"I've come to see Mr Humphries." A young, Latino receptionist wearing glasses and a headset looked up from behind the reception. She smiled in acknowledgment of Mr Walsh, flashing a set of pearly whites so bright they would have dazzled Mr Walsh were he not wearing sunglasses.

"Mr Walsh, I presume?"

"Yes." Mr Walsh was not a man of many words. He did not waste his breath on non-essential conversation.

"Wonderful, Mr Humphries is looking forward to meeting you. Would you like a drink?"

"A large bourbon." No please no thank you followed. Mr Walsh strongly believed that he was inherently deserving of life's privileges in reward for having served as a Major General in the British Army. Hence, you might say, his choosing of an extortionately priced clinic over typical NHS treatment. He would not have to re-mortgage his home to pay for the fees, as some people did, but the money his family would inherit from his will would be lowered — not that he planned to give much of what he owned away when he kicked the bucket. His sense of entitlement would accompany him to the grave and beyond. He was not a rude man by any means, simply sure of himself and his preferences. He did not waste time dilly-dallying with platitudes, he preferred to just get on with things.

The receptionist, expecting him to just say tea or coffee, was taken aback. She proceeded to whisper into the headset, waited, then nodded.

"Charlotte? Could you make Mr Walsh a large Jack

Daniels on the rocks?" she said into the microphone. "Please, take a seat, Mr Walsh." She smiled back at him.

He looked back at her blankly. She had failed to realise he was in a wheelchair. "Oh, I'm so sorry! It was a force of habit."

"No problem, I get it all the time," he replied politely. Mr Walsh was pushed to another waiting area where he received his favourite tipple. Newspaper clippings, various certificates and photographs were delicately framed and hung around the room.

Before long, another porter came over to assist Mr Walsh to Mr Humphries' office. "I'm going to take you to see Mr Humphries now, Sir. I hope you are comfortable."

"Right, go on then!" he said gruffly. He was used to being in charge, not being pushed around in a wheelchair.

As Mr Walsh entered the office, Mr Humphries stood up and rushed over to him. "Mr Walsh, how wonderful to see you. Thank you, Frank." Crispin dismissed the porter, shooing him away with his hand. Crispin positioned Mr Walsh in front of his immaculate, mahogany desk. He then returned to his leather chair, sighing as he interlaced his fingers behind the back of his head, sinking comfortably into his seat. There were candles lit on the windowsill, infusing the room with soft lavender and chamomile scents. The lighting was soft, as was the classical music playing overhead. It wasn't clear whether Crispin had just been receiving some kind of private spa treatment in there, or whether he had set this up to put Mr Walsh at ease.

Crispin proceeded. "I have reviewed the medical records from the stroke unit. It looks like this was out of the blue. The scans show…"

"Doc, I didn't come here to learn what I already know. I

came here to know whether you can help." Mr Walsh interrupted.

Mr Walsh was a wealthy man who, after retirement, to keep himself busy made money by buying luxury cars and renting them out. He purchased his first car 30 years ago for £50, did some work on it and rented it out to his friends. Within a month, Walsh got his money back. The plan worked well for him so he bought more cars. From cars, it progressed to small boats and then to yachts. He would rent one of his vessels for £25,000 per night. The fee included the staff, a chef and, of course, a captain. His turnover was a tidy £25 million per year, but he was no fool and was not going to waste time if Mr Humphries couldn't help.

"Right, yes. Let's not beat around the bush." Crispin understood that Mr Walsh wanted a straight-talking, no bullshit doctor and so adopted his patter suitably. "Mr Walsh, I can help. As you know, you had a large middle cerebral artery occlusion which blocked the blood supply to the motor cortex of the left hemisphere. This resulted in paralysis down your right side. We want to see the neurons regenerate, but we know that this takes time and the results from the stem cell trials have not shown great promise in this area. So, we have been using neurostimulation for strokes. I must stress, the results are experimental, but we are pleased with the results up to now. At least with the Brainionics implants, which is what I use these days." He paused to take a sip of his water. "The way it works is that we put a small hole just on the front of the head, and we insert the implant which is attached to a small wire. There is a risk to your life, a risk of further paralysis, infection, cerebrospinal fluid leak, and a chance it doesn't work. However, if I were in your shoes, you have very little to lose.

It works in two ways: by direct stimulation of the neurons, which gives the instant improvement, and by regenerating the neurons for long-term improvement. We monitor the whole process wirelessly by analysing the small changes to the voltage which happen when the neurons regenerate. Occasionally, we re-program the settings to get the optimal regenerative result. It is the only technology of its kind in the world." Crispin didn't actually know how it worked. He was regurgitating what Professor Santos had told him.

"And the disadvantages?" asked Mr Walsh. His face was unreadable.

"It is costly, it is experimental, and I cannot promise that you will be 100% cured. In other words, it may not work." This was a well-rehearsed speech. If he was overconfident, patients just thought he was in for the money and probably wouldn't believe him. If he were too negative, they wouldn't want the procedure done, and more importantly for him, they wouldn't pay.

Mr Walsh pondered for a while. He looked out of the window, sighed and looked back to Crispin Humphries. "Right, well. Good thing I'm not afraid of death. When can you do it?" he asked.

"Excellent!" Crispin clapped. "Let me just look at my diary." He already knew Mr Walsh would say yes, so he had booked him in for next Saturday in advance. "How does next Saturday sound?"

"The sooner, the better." Mr Walsh replied.

"Very good." Crispin scribbled in his diary and then pressed a buzzer. Within seconds, the porter returned to take Mr Walsh back to the reception area. The whole procedure would cost the amount of a small house, but this was disposable income for Mr Walsh. He wrote the cheque without a second thought with his non-paralysed hand, gave it to the receptionist, and then left the clinic.

Just as Mr Walsh was leaving his clinic room, Crispin received a call from Gad Dayan. "Crispin, you are going to be asked about a Mr Mike Taylor, a man who you operated on over a year ago. You will say you know nothing about him. This is very important. Your career depends on it. I will explain everything in due course." He then put the phone down before Crispin could respond.

"Well, nice to speak to you too." Crispin said to nobody. He didn't feel particularly comfortable with this, but there was no way he was going to argue with Dayan.

He couldn't remember who Dayan was talking about at first. Crispin fired up his computer and looked for the records. Surprisingly, he could not find any evidence of a Mr Taylor. He quickly picked up the phone and buzzed through to the reception.

"Lori, can you remember a Mr Mike Taylor?"

"Yes, he was the large American chap that Professor Santos referred to you. It was one of the first Brainionic implants you inserted about a year or so ago."

"Okay." He paused. "Just for the record, we don't know him. We didn't operate on him."

"Err, okay, Crispin. Is everything all right?" replied Lori She quickly searched for Mike Taylor on her computer system while Crispin was still on the line. "I've just looked at the computer files Crispin, and you are right, we never knew a Mr Taylor. It looks like someone has already deleted the file."

"Thanks, Lori. I must take you out for that drink I promised."

"Yes, Crispin, you must."

CHAPTER 9

Lewis had been summoned to a mandatory staff meeting organised by the dreaded management. He sat at the back twiddling his thumbs and playing with his phone. He was distracted and this was the last place he wanted to be. Just before, DS Smyth had called Lewis to ask him if he would still like to help with the investigation. The detectives were still trying to work out where the stimulator was and, more importantly, whether the stimulator had something to do with Mr Taylor's death. The pathologist's preliminary report raised questions about the dark staining in Mr Taylor's brain coating the wire's track. They had attempted to find the surgeon responsible for the implant but when they contacted Mr Taylor's family physician in the US, he had no details or medical notes about the operation nor the insertion of any device. They had drawn a total blank. They would need a neurosurgical expert to give a second opinion on the implant, hence requiring Lewis to be on standby. Strangely enough, DS Smyth had made several attempts to contact Mr Humphries, but each time had been put on hold by his receptionist. When questioned herself, the receptionist said that she had no recollection of any Mike Taylor being operated on. She then refused to comment further.

The meeting was, as expected, not as riveting as a police investigation. Today, the Director of Finance was harping on about initiatives to help the NHS Trust cut costs. He enjoyed making 'Executive Decisions', as he liked to refer to them, which hindered the work of well-to-do doctors, nurses and medical staff but improved cost-cutting targets. He had absolutely no idea what the medical staff actually did, not that he felt obliged to. His objective was to balance the books, justify his existence and his unfairly large salary. He was an unbalanced, egotistical man who, having failed at being an accountant, somehow managed to climb the ladder as a manager in the NHS. As unbalanced as his personality were his wonky eyes. When he spoke, you never knew which one to look at. He was awarded an OBE a few years prior for reasons not clear. Whoever decided that was a good idea naively contributed to his sense of self-importance. In line with his self-righteous persona, he also enjoyed picking on people in meetings to demonstrate his so-called superiority. Every so often, you would see pictures of him in the Trust newsletter with a group of hospital staff who no doubt hated his guts, showing how some initiative or other had increased productivity levels. Unfortunately, however, money levels had not increased. The Trust was in deep shit.

Lewis, more than ever, disagreed with the management staff. He now found any excuse to berate them. He didn't understand what they did, but then they made no effort to understand what he did either. Lewis knew that if he continued to argue with them, he would get into trouble. Over the years, though, the managers seemed to interact less and less with the clinical staff anyway. Even when the clinical staff had good ideas, the management ignored them. Instead of speaking to those at the heart of the NHS, the management spent millions of pounds of taxpayers' money on bringing in external companies to sort out their mess.

Ironically, they would post campaigns around the entire hospital; in the lifts, on the canteen walls, through emails and letters or via screensavers, asking staff to COME TELL US YOUR IDEAS. WE ARE READY TO LISTEN AND TO ACT. Well, Lewis thought, they might need to learn how to listen first before propagandizing such inclusivity. Their mantra was: TRANSFORM THE NHS. There were always new campaigns like this popping up, each time with a new Chief Executive appointed to run it and an extortionate accountancy firm organised at the publics' expense. A vicious cycle of money-wasting and pointless enterprises.

Lewis was trying to remain innocuous with his head down at the back. He really wasn't in the mood to be picked on today. The department's business manager introduced the proceedings. She was slightly overweight and wore an uncomfortably tight skirt. Her blouse, which she had miraculously managed to tuck in around her waist, bulged at the buttons. Her hair was swept back into a neat bun, aside from a few misbehaving strands that stuck to her greasy forehead. She spoke through plump, bright red, glossy lips.

"Thank you all for attending this exciting event. Our department has been specially selected for this initiative, which is excellent news! We all know that there have been some challenges in our department." As she said this, she glanced sideways and chuckled, trying to make light of the situation. "Unfortunately, our productivity is down. There are many factors contributing to that." Lewis imagined himself hurling a chair out the window. With the business manager sat on it. The reason productivity was down was because the management wouldn't let the medical staff do their jobs properly.

She continued. "We are delighted that the team from 'Transform Our NHS Life' have come to help us. I want to introduce Matt Wood who is leading the project."

"Hello everybody!" Matt Wood trumpeted excitedly. "Can we all hear me?"

Regrettably for everyone in the room, yes, Lewis thought. Matt looked like he had fallen into a fancy-dress cupboard and been attacked by a mob of flashy apparel. He was sporting a black pin-striped suit combined with a bright orange tie. The suit had green buttons on the pockets. His hair was slicked back with a gel that seemed to glow under the harsh artificial light. If he wasn't so tanned — no doubt from a recent, undeserved holiday to Bali — you might confuse him for a distant relative of the Adam's family. He was the sort to make exaggerated hand movements whenever he spoke — no doubt picked up in a 'How to Command your Audience' course — and to smile ingratiatingly at those close enough to him to make direct eye contact with.

"My name is Matt and today we are going to change any preconceptions you hold about life in the NHS." Lewis groaned under his breath. "This is a new beginning! But we need your help. If you trust us and work with us, we can help transform your working lives. We also want to help patients, which you can be a part of." Lewis was under the impression that he was already helping patients by saving their lives, but apparently not.

Lewis had brought a stack of paperwork with him to the meeting to distract himself. As usual, he had a load of admin to do that he'd let build up over several weeks. There were radiological reports, complaint letters, discharge summaries of patients for the general practitioners, and a whole bunch of referrals that he had to triage and place in priority order for clinics. He would label them: 'Urgent', 'Non-urgent' and 'Do NOT book into my clinic, please' respectively. In the background, Matt the Twat droned on about his revolutionary plans for the NHS. Lewis's mind started to wander. He imagined himself as Sherlock Holmes, catching bad guys and just being an all-round legend.

Matt had now produced a whiteboard and was going around the room asking people questions. "So, let's list the reasons why the unit productivity is going down. Where shall we start?" Everyone looked slightly bemused, some staring at the floor, some looking at each other whispering, some like Lewis, with his head buried in a pile of paperwork ignoring the compulsory proceedings. The hospital business manager looked around the room, silently prompting people with feigned encouragement. One of the matrons piped up.

"We need to get the patients down to theatre earlier and guarantee a bed so the list can start earlier."

"Great start! Love that! Thanks," said Matt, eagerly adding her words to his whiteboard. "We need to transfer our patients back to the regional hospitals so there are more beds available to admit patients." Another nurse shouted out. "Yes, love it! Great! Keep it coming, this is good."

"We need to keep the paperwork to a minimum so we can get on with the actual nursing."

"Good," said Matt, clearly not liking this one that much.

"You at the back there, what do you think?" Matt was looking at Lewis who was looking at his paperwork, totally unaware of what was going on around him. "Excuse me, you at the back." Lewis looked up. Everyone had turned in their seats to look at him.

"Sorry, what was the question?" asked Lewis.

Ignoring Lewis' question, Matt responded with his own. "What do you do in this unit?" Lewis pondered for a while. He wanted to stand up and tell Matt that he was a fucking brain surgeon and that he would like to be left alone to get on with his job. Lewis and his colleagues knew exactly how to increase productivity. They had plenty of solutions. In fact, they had written to management many times with their own initiatives but to no avail. Now this guy waltzes in dressed as Merry Andrew, showing off in front of Wonky Eyed Joe over there, and tries to make him feel like a worthless piece of shit under his clown shoe. Well, Lewis was not having it. He opened his mouth ready to commence verbal Armageddon but instead said: "My name is Lewis, and I'm one of the doctors here. When I arrived at this hospital, the Trust provided lunch for the theatre staff." He cleared his throat. Best not put his head above the parapet and make himself an easy target. On balance, despite this whole circus act, Lewis loved his job and would rather not put his position in jeopardy. "Everyone placed their order in the morning, and at a point during the day, in-between cases, we would all sit down together and have lunch. At some point, the management," Lewis said, trying to catch one of the finance manager's eyes, "decided not to provide lunch to save money. So now, the ODP, nurse and anaesthetist have a break to get sandwiches, but their breaks are at different times. Every time someone has a break, we have to stop the list. Then we have to change out of scrubs to go down to the canteen as per the new infection control policy. So," he said, in a moment of spontaneous genius, "I would propose to have the hospital organise the sandwiches for the staff, which would mean everyone could have their lunch at the same time. This would avoid stopping the theatre list and increase productivity." Boom.

Lewis waited for his colleagues to give him a standing ovation and for the finance manager to appoint Lewis as the next cost-cutting star for the NHS. Surprisingly, neither happened. The finance manager looked at Lewis. At least, one of his eyes did. After a pause, he said: "Mr Thomas, I have a better idea. Why don't you organise your staff to bring their own sandwiches in, and then eat them at lunchtime together?"

Lewis nearly let his mouth fall open. You've got to be kidding me. The tension between the surgeon and the finance manager was palpable. The front-line staff knew that Lewis had a point, but everyone was too afraid to defend him. Lewis tried to get a quip back but couldn't think of anything that was exceptionally clever or witty. He replied under his breath: "I bet you don't have any problems getting your lunchbreak in."

He was so angry with himself that the finance manager had got one over on him, and in public too. The business manager scowled at him. The finance manager just stared at him before starting to make some notes.

"We can't store our sandwiches anywhere when we bring them in." One of the theatre nurses said in a low voice.

Although Matt the Twat heard this, he chose to ignore the comment. It was a valid point, but everyone ignored her, actively or subconsciously, as everyone was worried that by speaking their mind, they would be a target for managerial bullying.

Matt responded. "And Sir, that is why you are the finance manager. Brilliant." Matt then wrote on his whiteboard. Staff to bring their own sandwiches and all staff to have lunch at the same time. "Thank you, you at the back, really positive." He concluded.

Lewis could not stand this any more. He texted Amal to call him with a fake emergency to get him out of the meeting. He answered his phone and, grabbing his belongings, proceeded to make his exit, semi-whispering on the phone.

"Really? Really, oh gosh. That's bad. I'd better come quick," as he passed the finance manager, he said, "Sorry, I have to go. Just saving some lives."

He regretted saying it as soon as the words escaped his mouth. That would definitely come back to bite him on the arse.

Lewis met Amal in the hospital deli. She was sat in her theatre blues with a steaming cup of coffee waiting for Lewis.

"Thanks, Amal, I really couldn't stand any more of that dreadful meeting. You wait till you're a consultant, it will be even worse by then."

"Thanks, Mr Thomas. I can't wait." She responded with a smile. Her navy-blue hijab was wrapped loosely around her head, highlighting her sweetheart-shaped face. Amal was a Muslim who had been born and raised in South East London. Her parents, also doctors, had emigrated from Pakistan before she was born and settled in the capital. Lewis had instantly taken to Amal when he first met her. He appreciated how calm and collected she was, even during the most stressful situations — of which there were many. Her technique was incredibly refined for someone so early on in their career too, which had astonished Lewis the first time they'd worked together. It wasn't easy for a female Muslim in a male-dominated speciality. Still, Amal was an exceptional trainee, and Lewis wanted to inspire and encourage her further to dispel the stereotypical neurosurgical type; male, aggressive and arrogant.

"So, Amal. How's it all going? Stamping out disease? Healing with steel?"

"Yeah, sort of. I'm losing a lot of operations since you guys are doing the simple cases in the private hospital. It's not so good for my logbook."

"I see, fair point. I'm afraid that if we didn't do it there, our waiting lists would be ridiculous. As you know, we can't even do some of the urgent cases here, let alone the routine ones. I'm happy for you to come over and help me, but you know you can't do the operations yourself in the private hospital until you're a consultant," Lewis looked at her apologetically, and then added chirpily, "but anyway, you know you're experienced enough to do the simple microdiscectomies, laminectomies and anterior neck fusions now! You're doing incredibly well!"

Amal looked down modestly as she spoke. She was always slightly embarrassed whenever anyone complimented her. "Thank you... I know, but I need to get the numbers in my book before I can get signed off by the postgraduate dean." She had carefully lined her almond-shaped eyes with black crayon, highlighting the length of her eyelashes with a subtle flick at the end of each eyelid.

Lewis thought about her response. "You know what's funny, Amal, when you get signed off, and you get your consultant post, it's probably the most dangerous time in your career. My advice is to stick with the everyday operations at first and build up trust with everybody. I know a lot of consultants who think that just because they have a consultant status they can suddenly do loads of complex operations, but it's just not the case. They get a bad reputation for causing complications. I know you won't do that, obviously, but it's something to be aware of. Anyway, how is your fellow registrar, David, doing?"

"Well, David, has…" she hesitated. "He has issues with several things."

"Go on, Amal, say it. David is a dick."

"Well, yes, he is. David bullies the juniors. He can't operate and he intimidates the nurses. To be honest, no one likes him. He is really disruptive to the team."

Lewis couldn't help but think of Crispin Humphries as Amal described David. This all sounded too familiar.

"Yeah, I suspected that. I have told my consultant colleagues about my concerns, but they are worried that if we take David to task, he will go to the postgraduate dean to complain and we will lose our training post. No one wants to stick their neck out… I'll try and talk to him though. I'm dreading him working for me on his six-month rotation."

There is a sort of chemistry between individual surgeons when they operate. It's completely non-definable, but when the chemistry is right, Lewis believed you could do the most complex of operations on the brain without any hiccups along the way. With some of the trainees, the chemistry is simply not right. Lewis could do the most routine procedure and be struck by disaster. He remembered one particular routine operation when his trainee, an unconfident young surgeon, the complete opposite of Amal, wanted to do a laminectomy. A laminectomy is an operation for people who have shooting pains down their legs, or sciatica.

As Lewis was watching her begin to make the necessary incisions, he felt a little uneasy. It isn't easy to be a surgical trainer. It's not like you can simply control the trainee's hands. There has to be some trust through guidance. Lewis was watching the slow, tedious motions of the trainee's hand while engaging with small talk with the nurse. As a trainer, he felt it was important to not watch every move the trainees made like a hawk as this could be really off-putting.

A gut instinct had made him turn around quickly; a pause in the noise between instrument and tissue, a little gasp from the trainee. As he turned back to the trainee, he caught the look in her eye. It said: Oh fuck.

"All okay?" he asked gently.

"Yes, Mr Thomas. All okay."

He knew she was lying but couldn't prove anything. No one else seemed to have noticed anything. They both carried on and completed the operation, seemingly without a hitch. Following the procedure, the pain down the patient's legs should have instantly improved.

On the ward round, not only did the patient feel severely weak down both legs but she could not stand. Worse still, she was incontinent of urine and faeces. That sensation of a full bladder or rectum that we usually get when we need to go to the bathroom was gone. It was very likely that the trainee slipped and plunged the metal instrument into the exposed dura, thereby damaging the sensitive sacral nerves and causing incontinence. There was no way to prove this, however. Any self-respecting surgeon would have admitted the truth, but she didn't.

Lewis had to apologise to the patient himself. He hoped it would improve with time and, fortunately, over the next few weeks it did. With help, she became continent again. The patient later sued Lewis for alleged negligence, though. The only silver lining was that Lewis later found out that the trainee gave up surgery and became a demonstrator in anatomy abroad. Thank goodness for that.

Unfortunately, he now had David to deal with. Another disaster of a surgeon in the making.

Later that evening, Lewis rather predictably ruminated over his day with a bottle of red, a cigarette and some rock music. Feeling sorry for himself, he dug out Deborah's mobile number and email. In his den of guilt, he lit another cigarette and conjured up several scenarios involving Deborah if he made contact.

Firstly, in the nobler one, Lewis meets her in a very public place. They have a perfectly normal chat about her aspirations and career ambitions. They both go to their separate homes. The end. Secondly, Lewis takes Deborah to a fancy restaurant, shares a bottle of wine with her, and then they have amazing sex at his home. The end. A difficult choice. It would probably be best not to contact her. You never know, maybe they would bump into each other randomly in a few years. But then again, why not meet her? She was enthusiastic and she wanted to learn. It wasn't like Lewis was going to force himself on her!

Lewis made up his mind. He would call her, gauge her reaction and take it from there. He continued to stare at the paper for a while. Finally, building up a bit of courage, he whipped his phone out, tapped in her phone number, stubbed his cigarette out and, with a deep breath, waited for the dialling tone.

"Hello, Deborah here."

Lewis, desperately trying to sound professional, said: "Deborah, hi! Sorry to cold call you, it's Mr Thomas, the neurosurgeon. I was very impressed with your enthusiasm the other day in theatre. We just had a management meeting today, and I think I have a project that you may be interested in so I thought I would ring you to chat about it." Having not realised he'd been holding his breath for the duration of the phone ringing, his speech gushed out of his mouth in a breathless avalanche of words.

Deborah paused. "Mr Thomas, gosh. It's an honour that you phoned. Yes, I would love to be involved." She answered excitedly.

Lewis, gaining confidence from her perceived interest, pressed on. "Well, I think we should have a meeting."

Deborah responded a little too quickly "Oh Mr Thomas, I would love that! The only problem is that I have lectures and work-based assessments during the day. Would it be okay to meet on an evening, I hope that doesn't sound too forward?"

Oh shit. Lewis could see how this was going to turn out. The age gap was twenty years. This could be disastrous. He could lose his job. He coul—, "Yes! Deborah. That would be lovely." He couldn't help himself. "While it's fresh in my mind, how about tonight?"

His heart was beating faster. Bloody hell. He felt like a schoolboy again.

"Why not, Mr Thomas?" she replied warmly. "Tonight, would be fine. Shall I bring Harry as well? Maybe we could do the project together?"

Bollocks. Disaster. Absolutely not. Lewis had to think fast. "Eh, good idea Deborah. But why don't we go over the bones of the project first and then once we have figured it out, let's get Harry involved."

"Of course, Mr Thomas. Where and when shall we meet?"

"How about the Dorchester?" It just came out. Fuck. Balls. Twat. Dammit. Now he'd really done it. Why the hell was he about to take a medical student to a three-star Michelin restaurant if it was not to impress her? Why was he trying to impress her if he didn't want to have sex with her? "Yes, I was given these vouchers to the Dorchester by a patient and to be honest, I haven't had time to use them. If I can get a table, I will text you. Otherwise, we may have to go somewhere really bad like… like, 'Le Gavroche'. Gosh, don't you hate it if you can only get into a two-star Michelin restaurant?" There was an awkward silence on the other end of the line. What the bloody hell am I saying? "Just joking, Deborah."

"Ah! Aha! Yes, funny," she humoured him.

"Anyway, I hope we can find some mutual areas of interest," he was digging an even bigger hole now and stumbling over his words. "I will let you know either way. I'll text you with where to meet."

"Great, Mr Thomas. Looking forward to it. See you later!" She hung up the phone.

"Fuck, fuck, fuck, fuck, fuck," Lewis shouted, slamming his fist down on the bar top. What was he doing? What had he done? From being just a bit bored and lonely to going on a date at a Michelin-restaurant. And, with a female medical student. A bloody gorgeous female medical student. He got straight on the phone to the Dorchester, praying that there were no tables available.

"Oh, hello, I'm just ringing on the off chance that you have a table tonight for two?"

"Well, Sir, we have just had a cancellation, so you're in

luck."

Fuck.

"What is your name?"

"Lewis Thomas."

"Excellent, Sir. The table will be available at nine p.m. Is that okay?"

"Oh, yes." Oh, God. I've really done it now.

"Fabulous. If I could take a deposit that would be wonderful."

While Lewis paid for the deposit, he knew he had every opportunity to cancel the reservation. For some reason or other, though, he simply couldn't. The temptation to meet Deborah again was simply too strong. She was like the forbidden fruit, and he had been well and truly lured by the sweet prospect of sinning.

Again, the onslaught of "Fuck, fuck, fuck, fuck, fuck" began. It was going to happen. Maybe she'll get cold feet, then I will have been worrying about nothing. He decided he better text her to confirm, just in case.

Deborah, we are on for tonight, meet in the reception of the Dorchester at 8.30 pm, that okay? Mr Thomas

Mr Thomas, how wonderfully exciting! See you then! X

Okay, she's put an x on the end. What does that mean? Lewis was frantically trying to decipher the messages in his head. Does she like me, or does she put an x on every text? Okay, don't read into it, go with the flow, be happy you have a date. Would it be okay to go out with her if she wasn't a medical student? Yeah, that's a good point. If she wasn't a medical student and I just happened to meet her in a bar, there would be nothing wrong in asking her for dinner, would there? But she is a medical student... am I abusing my power? Well, nothing is going to happen in any case, we will have a nice, civilised meal, a chat, that's all, and that will be that.

An email popped up, causing his phone to chime, startling Lewis out of his internal panic. It was from the Hospital Trust: 'Transform your NHS lives meeting today' was the subject line. He clicked on the email to read the full message.

Dear Mr Thomas,

The senior management were very disappointed by your actions in the meeting today. They felt you did not take the meeting seriously. I hope in the future you will show a better example to your colleagues.

Sandra,
Business Manager, Neuroscience Division.

"Oh, bollocks," he said.

CHAPTER 10

Mr Walsh entered the anaesthetic room at Crispin Humphries' clinic. There, standing with the anaesthetist, was Crispin himself. Mr Walsh, perhaps for the first time since the Army, felt like he was lacking cojones. He was nervous. For most of his adult life, he had been in control of everything he did, but now he was at the mercy of these two doctors.

"Ah, Mr Walsh! Welcome to the theatre of dreams," said Crispin, not noticing Mr Walsh's nervousness. "My colleague, Dr Vardy, will give you some powerful medicines to make you sleep, and before you know it, you'll be awake again, back in your room and feeling great." He didn't hang around to hear Mr Walsh's response. "See you soon."

Dr Vardy, the anaesthetist, spoke in a low monotonous tone. "Hello, Mr Walsh, my name is Dr Ralph Vardy. I'm going to put this needle into your arm, then inject a mixture of drugs that will make you very sleepy. Won't be long now." Mr Walsh was silent.

Crispin, meanwhile, was waiting impatiently in the theatre next door. He was thinking about whether he could do this genre of operation under local anaesthetic to dispense of the anaesthetist altogether in the future. Not only would this enable him to claim a larger surgical fee but it would... no, it would just make him more money. Reason enough. While the scrub nurse was preparing the equipment, Crispin checked his bank balance on his mobile phone. Blimey. That's a nice figure. In the excitement of seeing his bank balance, Crispin completely forgot which side of the head he needed to insert the stimulator.

"Hey, nurse, which side are we operating on?"

The nurse purposely didn't reply, offended that Crispin hadn't remembered her name. "Hey you, I'm talking to you! Which side is the stimulator going in?"

The nurse glanced up from her preparation and responded, "I don't get paid enough, doctor, to take responsibility for such a decision."

"Fine, fine. I will find out myself."

At this particular private hospital, there were not the routine checks like the ones that occurred in the NHS. They were slowly introducing the WHO checklist, but since the consultants brought in a large amount of money for the hospital, they could get away with a lot more. The managers would turn a blind eye. On this particular occasion, there were no scans nor notes. Crispin was desperately trying to remember which side was weak. He should have double-checked before Mr Walsh was put to sleep, but it was too late now. Dr Vardy thought he was weaker on his right side. He could wake him up and ask him, but this would be too embarrassing. He phoned the receptionist from his clinic.

"Hey, Lori, it's Crispin here. I know this sounds a little odd, but do you remember Mr Walsh who I saw last week?"

"Sure, Crispin."

"Can you remember if he signed the forms with his right or left hand?"

"I remember he couldn't sign the forms well and used his left hand."

"Great, thanks, Lori. I owe you one."

Crispin put the phone down and fist-pumped the air, proud that he had deduced that he should be operating on the left side of the head. Mr Walsh was using his left hand to sign his signature as his right hand did not work. As each half of the brain controls the other side of the body, he must have had the stroke in the left hemisphere and, therefore, he needs to insert the stimulator in the left side. What it was to be a patient of Mr Crispin Humphries.

After positioning the patient on the operating table and draping the head, Crispin made a small incision over the left side of Mr Walsh's head. Self-retaining retractors were used to stretch the skin. Crispin scraped the periosteum off the skull, a dense layer of vascular connective tissue enveloping the bone. He used the Brainionics electric burr kit to remove a disc of bone and then, after nicking the dura, placed a fragile platinum wire into the left side of the brain. At this time, Crispin was unaware of the latest stimulator developed by Brainionics. His hands were shaky, and his movements were cumbersome. The wire was attached to a voltage meter which varied according to the depth of the wire. It responded to the small electric voltage of the brain tissue. When the reading reached nearly zero, at about 5 cm into the brain tissue, Crispin stopped.

"This should be okay," he said flippantly. Once satisfied with the placement, he connected the battery and placed this in a subcutaneous pouch at the back of Mr Walsh's head. Staples closed the skin, marking the end of the procedure.

"Okay Ralph, all done here. See you next week, I think."

"No problem, Crispin. A pleasure to work with you, as always." That was a lie. Dr Vardy hated working with Crispin

Humphries.

Lewis was waiting in the reception of the Dorchester. He looked impeccable, sporting a navy-blue tailored three-piece suit; a perfectly ironed white shirt, Jeffrey West shoes and a black cravat with white skulls on it. Deborah pulled up in a taxi. As she walked towards Lewis, Lewis could not believe his luck. She looked stunning. He remarked how Deborah looked much more mature than a lot of, if not all, the medical students he had worked with. She wore a shin-length red dress that hugged her thighs and waist, elegantly accentuating her figure. Her blonde hair was loose and tousled around her shoulders, perfectly wind swept as if even the weather had meant for Deborah to tease Lewis with her exquisite appearance.

Lewis' heart throbbed. He felt more nervous than he did removing the most difficult tumours of his life. He gave himself a mental pat on the back for having booked a hotel room for after, just in case. Not that anything would happen. Of course, this was just a work meeting.

"Deborah, you look…" Lewis choked on his words. "Let me start again. You look wonderful. Did you have to travel far?"

"Mr Thomas, thank you! Not far, just Hammersmith."

"I've got the table booked. Aperitif at the bar?"

"Yes, good idea. Champagne for me." She winked.

Lewis liked her confidence. She didn't look like a student at all. She fitted in perfectly with her surroundings, almost as if she were a part of the charming, haute décor.

"A glass of champagne for the lady and a gin and tonic for me, lots of ice and lots of lime squeezed in please."

"Mr Thomas, how lucky a patient gave you some vouchers to eat here. I bet you get a lot of patients giving you gifts."

"What?" Lewis momentarily forgot that he had made up the story about the vouchers. "Ah yes, very lucky!" He quickly tried to change the subject. "Deborah, please, outside of the hospital, call me Lewis. Mr Thomas is a bit of a mouthful."

"Mr Thomas, it's tough for me to do that. I'll try. Please, call me Debbie."

Deborah flicked her hair. Her piercing blue eyes made direct contact with his. Lewis felt like he was watching the evening unravel in slow motion. The entire situation felt unreal to him. He couldn't decipher whether she was flirting, or whether this was just her natural personality.

"So, Mr Thomas, I mean Lewis." Deborah smiled, quickly correcting herself. "I am interested in what you are doing. Any project at this stage of my career would be so valuable. What did you have in mind?"

She then took a small black book and a pen out of her handbag, placing it on the bar expectantly.

"Well, err, I was thinking about looking at the results..." Lewis was thinking on his feet. He had been so carried away by the thrill of the evening that he hadn't even thought to think of what this special project was supposed to be. Bollocks galore. He started mumbling to himself "...it's a little top-secret and... it's, err, something I cannot do myself as I don't really have much time. Are you up for it?"

He could feel himself beginning to sweat.

"I'm up for anything!" Her eyes gleamed as she spoke. Deborah was even more attracted to Lewis because of his apparent humility and awkwardness around her. He bumbled through the conversation. Lewis, again, didn't know whether this was further flirtation or Deborah just being herself. He continued. "One of my colleagues from another hospital is doing some fascinating work, but I am not sure whether it's making any difference for the patients. I think it would be good to compare outcomes. Is that an avenue you would want to explore? The surgeon in question is Mr Crispin Humphries. We can work on it together but, because you're a medical student, he won't feel threatened by you visiting him. He wouldn't tell me anything, you see. He sees me as a rival." Lewis was listening to himself as he spoke. Was he really asking a medical student to spy on Crispin, just to prove he was a surgical crook?

Deborah looked concerned. Her facial expression lost its zeal as she tilted her head inquisitively to one side. Maybe this was too much of a task for a medical student, Lewis thought. He gulped.

"Lewis, I'm happy to do anything for you!" She giggled. Her beautiful smile returned. Lewis looked straight at her. Deborah met his gaze with her own. There was a pause that felt like an eternity.

"Lewis, I am going to get straight to the point. I find you adorable, and I wanted to kiss you the moment I saw you." Lewis spat out his drink. "Oh! I'm sorry... I didn't mean to alarm you!"

"No, no! Don't be sorry!" Lewis said, wiping his chin. "I'm... flattered. Really! I..." he trailed off, bedazzled by her eyes again and totally stunned by what was happening. He forgot about the conversation they had just had. He imagined them both in a 1950s black and white romantic movie; Lewis, a young Gregory Peck, wooing an innocent — but blonde and curvaceous - Audrey Hepburn. He could not believe that this goddess had just propositioned him. Lewis grabbed her hand. "Fuck dinner, follow me."

They half-walked, half-ran to the elevator and pressed the call button. Lewis could feel his stomach knotting with anticipation. They hopped in, and as soon as the elevator doors closed, Lewis moved towards Deborah. He grabbed her by the waist and pushed her against the side of the lift. His lips came crashing down onto hers, the scent of her sophisticated perfume filling his nostrils as they did so. Deborah wove her fingers into his hair and let out an involuntary moan, the pressure between her hips mounting. The elevator slowly ground to a halt. Lewis reluctantly took a step back from Deborah. They both let out a laugh in unison. He took her by the hand and led her down the long corridor to the room he had thankfully booked. He fumbled in his pocket for the key card, opened the door and, like a true gentleman, motioned for Deborah to go in first. As she walked ahead, he marvelled at the natural curves of her body through her skin-tight dress. Lewis couldn't wait any longer. He stepped into the room and let the door slam behind him. Lewis walked towards her and spun her around to face him. She kissed him with a hungry desperation. His throbbing bulge pressed up against her.

"Oh, Mr Thomas, you are a naughty supervisor."

Lewis threw Deborah onto the bed. He started to take off his clothes, mindlessly throwing his expensive suit into the corner. Deborah arched her back and slid off her underwear, a lacy red thong and bralette to match her dress. Lewis climbed on top of Deborah and started to kiss her neck. He ran his hands down her soft body, caressing every curve with his fingertips. As his hands reached her thighs, Lewis felt her slightly tense up in anticipation. He pressed his hand down in between her legs as his lips grazed her collar bone. The suspense was almost too much for him to handle. She wrapped her arms around him, brought her lips up to his ear and whispered: "Please, Mr Thomas, fuck me." Lewis gladly accepted! He slowly entered her as she wrapped her legs around his waist. It lasted about two minutes before he ejaculated.

After the initial mortal embarrassment, he wasn't so premature the next few rounds. Lewis told himself he had just been warming up. They spent the rest of the night talking. Lewis asked a lot of questions about her motivation to do medicine and about herself. She explained that she was a mature student, that she had entered medicine later in life and was only recently transferred to the medical school from another one as her mother was ill and she wanted to be near her. She had failed a lot of her exams and found it challenging to fit in. Lewis excitedly told her that it was the same for him.

"It's not where you start Deborah, it's where you finish." Lewis explained that he had been a failure early on and, although it was hard work, he eventually managed to become a neurosurgeon.

"You are so sweet, Lewis," she continued. "By the way, sorry to change the subject. Harry, the other medical student, was upset by his theatre experience. I think you should let him come in again."

"Firefly boy? Was he?" Lewis felt a pang of guilt. He knew he didn't want Harry to come into the operating theatre, but he equally didn't want to put Harry off surgery for life. Also, Deborah wanted him to come. Right now, Lewis would do anything to please her more. "Okay, I have an aneurysm clipping to do soon. Give me his number, and I will phone him and ask him to attend."

"That would be really kind of you. I know he would appreciate that." Then she changed the subject again.

"Do consultants check up on other consultant's results without them knowing?"

Lewis was slightly surprised that she remembered their earlier conversation. "Can I trust you, Deborah?"

"Of course, Lewis." She replied.

"Well, I visited a crime scene a couple of days ago. Two Americans had committed suicide. One of the patients had a stimulator inserted into his brain. The police and pathologist needed a neurosurgical expert which is why they contacted me. The night before I arrived, they think someone broke into the mortuary and stole the stimulator. Can you believe it? I mean, why would anyone want to do that?" Lewis was exaggerating the story to try to impress her. "I suspect the device was faulty as there was a lot of black staining in the brain when the pathologist showed me. Corporate espionage! Anyway, the reason why I wanted you to see this other surgeon was to see if he was the one who had put in the stimulator. We don't exactly see eye to eye, he certainly isn't going to tell me, but you could…" his voice came to a halt. Deborah did not look impressed. She sat up to face Lewis.

"Do you actually want to get involved in something like that? I don't think you should do it, Lewis. If you got found out, you could get into trouble. I'm sure we can find another project."

"I just don't trust him. I really think he has something to do with this." Lewis responded earnestly. When Lewis attended the mortuary to inspect the body, he saw that Mr Taylor's left-sided muscles were smaller than the right after such a long period of inactivity as a result of his stroke. From this, he had deduced that Mr Taylor had had a stroke on the right side. Lewis' gut was telling him that it had to be one of Humphries' patients because he was one of the only surgeons doing this kind of procedure for cerebrovascular patients in the UK. He couldn't prove anything, though, not without more evidence.

"Let it go! Let the detectives deal with all that." Deborah laughed again, trying to lift the mood. "Anyway, speaking of stimulators, I can think of something much more stimulating that we can do…" she said amorously. She let out a flirtatious growl and began to crawl across the bed towards Lewis. Case closed.

When Crispin Humphries inserted Mr Walsh's stimulator, a white light lit up on a large monitor displaying the map of the world at the Brainionics headquarters in Israel. It indicated that the device was implanted but not active. On the same monitor, there were hundreds of green lights designating the number of successfully activated implants. There were a few red lights too, which indicated faulty implants. Rather than recall them, the Brainionics team kept an eye on the devices and observed the behaviour of the patients whose stimulators were malfunctioning. Apart from Mike Taylor's suicide, no other adverse incidents had ever been reported.

The latest stimulators had been updated with a radio-navigation system. This enabled the technicians at Brainionics to monitor the exact position of each implant and, therefore, each patient, using a highly intelligent global positioning system. When a technician clicked on a light, the associated patient details, including the voltage of the device, were displayed. The technicians could also activate and control the parameters of the stimulators remotely. Indeed, patients assumed that it was the surgeon who programmed the stimulators post-implantation, but in actual fact, the surgeons had no idea how the stimulators worked. Surgeons were given a dummy box with a switch and a dial in it. By flicking the switch once they had inserted a stimulator, the surgeon alerted technicians at Brainionics to remotely activate the stimulator by causing the little white light to alight on their monitors. Beyond that, the surgeons had little to no power at all with regards to controlling the implants.

The technician on shift clicked on the new white light causing Mr Walsh's details to pop up on the screen. He then proceeded to activate Mr Walsh's implant, making his designated light turn green on the monitor.

Meanwhile, back in London, Mr Walsh was starting to wake up from the general anaesthetic. He didn't feel much pain. In fact, he didn't feel much at all. Suddenly, he detected a slight tingling sensation down his right arm and leg. A flicker of movement spontaneously occurred in his right hand. He smiled.

CHAPTER 11

Lewis got home in the early hours of the morning and woke up in his own bed. After his rather lustful night, Mr 'Come-Too-Early' Thomas felt quite the stud. It was his operating day and he quickly remembered to text Harry as requested by Deborah.

Harry, this is Mr Thomas here. It's your lucky day, if you would like, you can come to my theatre and watch a brain aneurysm. If you can make it, come at nine a.m. to Theatre ten.

He felt guilty that Harry had been upset about what had happened the other day and worried Harry would not even respond out of bitterness. Lewis need not have worried though, as he got an immediate text back from Harry. His mood instantly turned sour as he imagined Harry in the theatre saying things like, "that was rad" or "awesome" all day. Weird kid, Lewis thought. He felt there was something sad about Harry that he couldn't quite put his finger on. He would honour his vow to Deborah though.

Oh, sweet Deborah. Did my heart love till now? What a sight she had been. His mood yo-yoed back to elation as he texted Deborah to make sure she got home all right. It took him a worrying amount of effort to not weep at the fact she didn't reply with the same speed as Harry. Lewis looked at the clock. It said seven a.m. He needed to get his shit together. He didn't get drunk last night, but his body ached. He felt like an excitable, pubescent teenage boy.

He texted Amal and told her to set the patient up as he would be a little delayed. He then began to go through the operation in his head. As he always did, he visualised the patient who was due in for surgery, what equipment he would need and what he would do if the metaphorical shit hit the fan. An aneurysm is like a blister on one of the blood vessels in the brain. They can be in the brain for months, totally symptomless, before they suddenly burst. Even routine CT scans sometimes fail to detect them. If the blister bursts, blood rushes into the cranial cavity leading to life-threatening internal bleeding and dramatically increasing the intracranial pressure on the brain. Some people die instantly; those who survive are at risk of having a rebleed and, in a worst-case scenario, death. The symptoms are a sudden onset of headache with nausea and vomiting. It's often referred to as a thunderclap headache because it feels as if someone has given the back of your head a thunderous thwack. Anything from having sex to defaecating could precipitate a burst or rebleed by increasing the blood pressure.

Once, one of Lewis' colleagues had an unfortunate encounter with an aneurysm. This colleague was having an affair with one of the nurses. While engaging in you-know-what, she had a subarachnoid haemorrhage or bleed on the brain and fell unconscious. Not wanting anyone to find out about his illicit affair, Lewis' colleague phoned the ambulance and left her for the paramedics to sort. As he dashed from the scene to save his balls, he inadvertently left his wallet on the floor with all his details in it. To cut a long story short, he had a lot of explaining to do to his wife when the police turned up about it the following day. It's safe to say, escaping backfired. He just about avoided being neutered by his wife.

The patient Lewis was about to operate on was in her forties. She was found unconscious by her husband after complaining about a sudden headache. After being taken to hospital, she was put into a medically induced coma; it was too dangerous to do an emergency operation on her as the brain was too swollen. In these cases, it's best to wait for a few days for the swelling to settle. After ten days, the patient was brought out of the coma and clinically assessed for possible permanent brain damage.

There are primitive reflexes which we all have, and as we develop, more sophisticated reflexes override the primitive ones. Depending on the damage done to the brain; one can assess the level of brain injury by trying to elicit which reflexes are present by applying pain over the middle of the eyebrow. If the patient pushes the hand away, it's a good sign. If the response is a basic reflex, for example, twisting both arms inwards, called extension, the prognosis is bad. The patient Lewis was going to operate on, luckily, had a good prognosis. Lewis decided to perform surgery, find the aneurysm and put a metal clip across its base to prevent another bleed.

The relatives of aneurysm victims generally expect surgeons to operate immediately. You see, it's not like in TV dramas where, at the first strike of a headache, a surgeon is instantly transported to the scene to operate.

"Doctor, are you saying that you're not going to operate now to stop another bleed, and if you do perform surgery, she may not improve?" the husband had asked.

"No, unfortunately, she may not improve. The operation

is solely to stop another bleed, and we will do this once the swelling has settled."

It was the same conversation he always had. Lewis tried to remain objective and sympathetic. He understood that it was painful for family and friends to see their loved ones like this.

"So, you are saying she's made it to hospital but she may still have a bleed and die? And you're just going to watch her?"

Lewis once had a patient where exactly this had happened. While waiting for the swelling to reduce, they ill-fatedly had another catastrophic bleed which killed them. The relatives then tried to sue him on the grounds of negligence. In some cases, people can get pretty hostile towards the medical staff simply because they are the first people these feelings of angst and panic can be taken out on. Being in the firing line wasn't one of the perks of the job. Lewis found that the response was generally worse if there were a lot of guilt issues surrounding sick relatives. Take the daughter who never sees her mother, for example. When her mother becomes ill, the daughter is confronted with the fact that she never made enough effort to see her mother when she was well. In a pit of self-destructive guilt and denial, the daughter unleashes verbal hell on the staff about her mother's care because she feels bad about being a failure of a daughter. Lewis thought the husband was probably a wife beater. He looked the stereotype; shaved head, beer belly, tattoos with menacing monsters and quotes covering his skin. The woman, on the contrary, was a small, frail thing. What a pity, Lewis had thought, to be married to this thug of a husband.

"Sir, I could do the most technically perfect operation, and she still may die. I'm sorry, but these are the facts." Lewis replied calmly.

"I bet if I went private, she would get better treatment."
The husband sneered.

Lewis realised that there was no point in arguing with this brainless goon. "I wouldn't advise it, but you are free to explore that option."

He scowled. "Right doc, well you better get it right."

"I'll do my best."

Before heading to the hospital, Lewis' stomach got the better of him. He swung by a nearby delicatessen, located just one hundred yards from his house. He hardly ever went there, but felt like he wanted to treat himself today. He ordered his coffee and croissant and managed to get one of his favourite Pastel de Nata cakes too. The delicatessen bought them from a Portuguese patisserie just minutes around the corner and sold them at a much higher price — this was Notting Hill, after all. He took his spread to a table by the window where he sat, watching the world go by outside. His back was aching. Unsurprisingly, this made Lewis smile. He must have reawakened a few dormant muscles the night before.

Looking around at the newly decorated shop with its trendy young clients, chic interior and extortionately priced flat whites, Lewis let out an audible sigh. The place was thriving and obviously appealed to the local demographic, but Lewis couldn't help but shed an invisible tear for what it used to be. The café was once a greasy spoon. Back in the day, it was a great place to have a fry up after a long night of boozing. God, Lewis thought, I sound like a right old geezer. With a sip of his coffee, Lewis instinctively reached for his smokes and realised he was inside and couldn't. Another sigh escaped his lips. Maybe I am getting old...

He took a bite out of his croissant, allowing his attention to drift back to what the patient's husband had said to him the other week. It was just too easy for the public to abuse staff nowadays. If the tables were turned though, there would be a police investigation before you could say "what a load of codswallop!". Because of this, the staff just have to suck it up. Lewis remembered one particular occasion when he was a young casualty doctor at the Westminster Hospital. During the day, flocks of models, actors and politicians would walk through the hospital doors. During the night, though, the dark side of London invaded. From criminals to the homeless to delusional drug addicts, the wards would be teeming with the lost souls of the city.

One morning, a fairly attractive middle-aged woman had been sitting in the waiting room. There was a box kept at reception which contained all the registration cards of those waiting to be seen. The triage nurse would write what their ailment was on a card and then pop it into the box. This card just said, 'sprained ankle'. You didn't tend to get the 'foreign body stuck up the arse' until much later in the day. He called out the name on the card and the woman stood up with a big beaming smile on her face. Lewis had introduced himself before he earned the title of being a 'Mr' by passing his surgical examinations.

"Hello, my name is Dr Thomas. What seems to be the problem?"

"Oh, it's nothing really, Doctor, but I thought I'd just get it checked out. It's my ankle. It seems a bit swollen." Lewis guided the woman into a cubicle, pulled the curtains around them and knelt on the floor to examine her ankle. As he did so, the lady opened her legs widely. When Lewis looked up, he was met with the site of her crotch. He could practically see what she had had for breakfast. Lewis, as many a young man would be, stared in shock at her suspenders and lack of knickers.

"You can examine me now, Doctor." She had said, leaning forwards towards him. "Well… I, err…" his words caught in his throat. Funnily enough, advice on how to deal with streakers hadn't been included in any of his Oxford medical textbooks. Before he had had a chance to properly respond, the woman suddenly bolted. It seemed Dr Thomas had miraculously cured her swollen ankle. When the casualty sister had asked why the patient had run away, Lewis was too embarrassed to relay his encounter.

The converse situation arose at the same hospital but during a night shift when the not-so-glamorous of society grace the hospital floors. Lewis had been pottering around the department when he heard raised voices coming from reception, so he went to see what all the commotion was about. The triage nurse had been arguing with a patient who wanted to get his hands on some controlled drugs, such as the strong codeines or morphine. She was telling him that he had to go to see his family doctor and get a prescription, and that this was an emergency department for emergencies only.

Lewis had tried to pacify the situation by protectively stepping in front of the nurse and politely asking the man to leave. Typically, his good intentions boomeranged. The man unceremoniously hurtled over the reception desk and ran towards Lewis, causing an explosion of notebooks, phones and pens to fly this way and that. The triage nurse took a blow to the forehead from a rogue biro and the man skidded on a notepad that had found its way underneath his foot. Lewis froze as the man closed the distance between them. This was also a situation his training manuals had failed to include.

Without further ado, a comical wrestling match ensued. Lewis managed to swerve and miss the first punch. Lewis was many things, but he wasn't a fighter. He also knew that if he hit the patient, he could get into big trouble. He managed to wrestle the patient into the resuscitation room, which was empty, hit the patient in the stomach and then press the panic button to alert security. With the help of the triage nurse who chased after the bumbling man, they contained the patient on the ground until the police arrived a few minutes later. The police took the man away in handcuffs. That time, nobody had really been harmed. Sometimes, the staff aren't so lucky. A few weeks later, one of his colleagues was badly beaten up by an aggressive drunk patient. Somehow, the patient not only left the department without a scratch but also without any action taken against him. Wanker. Alas, these stories are not uncommon in the hospital world.

Lewis finished his coffee and got himself ready to leave. He hoped the aneurysm operation would all go smoothly, especially if he would have to face that ungrateful shit of a husband afterwards.

Later that day, a technician stumbled upon the missing stimulator at the hospital morgue. They alerted the pathologist, Dr Davies, to their discovery, who then went on to inform the police. What he didn't inform the police of, however, was that this stimulator looked different to the one he had removed from Mike Taylor's brain. Something wasn't right. Dr Davies couldn't understand how the stimulator had managed to fall onto the floor at the back of the refrigerated chamber. He also couldn't understand how the stimulator found on the floor was not the one he had placed on top of Mike Taylor. As he had been the only one to see the original disc, he couldn't prove anything. In his rush to get to the pub after the autopsy, he hadn't had time to photograph the original stimulator or study it in much detail which he should have done as a matter of course. Nevertheless, he clearly remembered that the logo and the shape had differed to the newly discovered disc. What could he do now though? He feared losing his job if he revealed he'd lied to the police, and the longer he left it, the greater the penalty might be too. Dr Davies desperately wanted to keep his privileged status as a police forensics expert and, therefore, sought out the quickest route possible to get the case closed. Rather than pursuing the mystery further, he chose to stick his head in the sand and lose himself in a pint at the pub.

CHAPTER 12

When Lewis arrived at the theatre, the patient with the brain aneurysm was already asleep in the anaesthetic room. Amal, his registrar, was in charge and seemed to be doing a good job. Lewis was surprised to see Harry hovering in the corner of the theatre, eagerly waiting for the surgery to commence. He had already forgotten that he had asked him to attend the operation that day. Harry grinned ecstatically at Lewis as he walked in. He was happier than a pig in shit.

Amal had transferred the patient across the table, placed the head so it was slightly turned to one side and secured it in the headpins. She then got out a small electric razor and trimmed a small line of hair over where the incision would be. Amal was going to carry out the operation under Lewis' supervision. She was a competent surgeon, excellent even, but this was an unpredictable procedure. You know the game 'Operation'? When you have to remove the tiny plastic bits without touching the sides? Well, it's kind of the same idea. Except, in this scenario, if you make a mistake, you won't hear a buzz but a potential flatline due to torrential bleeding.

After making the skin incision and retracting the soft tissues, Amal performed a craniotomy, removing a large piece of the patient's skull. Lewis was impressed by the ease with which Amal proceeded and proud that he was able to train her. One day, Amal would be as good as him. Maybe even better.

Amal opened the dura to expose a pulsating, swollen brain. Blood stained the surface. This next part was called a Sylvian fissure dissection where the surgeon has to separate two lobes of the brain and retract them without causing any damage. The main priority is to find the artery feeding the aneurysm so it can be secured if the aneurysm bursts. Out of the corner of Lewis' eye, he saw Deborah walk in. He hadn't heard from her since they had sex.

"Is it all right if I observe, Mr Thomas?" asked Deborah. She winked at him. How different she looked in scrubs.

"Yes, Deborah, nice to see you," Lewis responded with an awkward croak. He was struggling not to imagine what underwear she had on underneath her medical attire. Deborah also winked at Harry who was giving her a thumbs up. Harry knew very well that she had made this happen for him.

Lewis, trying not to be too distracted by Deborah's presence, nervously observed Amal as she slowly started to dissect the brain. As a surgeon in charge of a patient, one of the most challenging aspects of the job was to watch a trainee perform a complex operation where you're not directly in control. Amal hadn't quite seen the internal carotid artery, the one pumping into the aneurysm. Without warning, the view through the microscope magnified a large jet of shiny red blood which burst out from within the depths of the brain. There was a red out. Lewis asked Becky if she could turn down the music. He could have taken over, but he kept himself back to see how Amal handled the situation.

The aneurysm had burst. Bright red arterial blood was pumping in the field of view, obscuring the blister that had torn. Lewis looked on uneasily, ready to jump in if needed. With one hand, Amal endeavoured to suction the flow of blood that was pouring out of the patient's head, aiming to pinpoint the source of ejection. With her other hand, she held the forceps-like instrument which would be used to deploy the clip when she found the neck of the aneurysm. If she wasn't careful, she could accidentally clip a main artery, triggering a stroke.

The blood continued to flow. Red eclipsed their view. The anaesthetist informed them both that the blood pressure was decreasing. They began to pump transfused blood into the patient's arm to maintain the blood pressure, but this was only a temporary solution. They desperately needed to curb the flow of blood.

"Amal, are you okay? Do you want me to take over?"

If they were to switch, they would have to be quick about it. Amal didn't reply. Lewis trusted her, but the patient would die on the table if they didn't act fast. Everyone in the theatre was transfixed by the screen, watching the blood erupt from the crevice deep between the two lobes of the brain. Amal continued to focus on suctioning the profusion of blood flooding the fleshy canyon. She held her breath as she spotted a flimsy, vesicular pouch at the bleeding point. The aneurysm. Amal deployed the clip and the bleeding reduced instantly. An audible sigh of relief echoed throughout the theatre.

"Okay, well done, Amal. Are you happy with the position of the clip?" Lewis asked.

The bleeding was now but a trickle and she was able to inspect where the clip was. "I think the clip is also trapping the middle cerebral artery, so not good."

"Yes, I agree. What are you going to do now?"

This is what differentiates an average trainer from a good one. Most consultants at this stage would take over and redeploy the clip — a dangerous manoeuvre but potentially necessary to save the patient's life. If the clip is released, arterial bleeding will instantly flood the cavity again. "Okay, Mr Thomas, I am going to put a temporary clip on the middle cerebral, remove my clip and place it properly over the neck of the aneurysm."

"Very good. Go ahead," said Lewis calmly, careful not to distract Amal.

Amal had the suction tube in one hand and another clip in the other. She could practically feel her pulse drumming in her ears as the tension continued to rise. She managed to put the temporary new clip just under the previous clip. It was far more complicated now as the jaws of the new clip were against the first clip and wouldn't close properly. After a few moments, she managed to put the new temporary clip over the major artery supplying the middle part of the brain. Most of the bleeding had now been impeded. She then removed the first clip, which caused an initial rebleed, before swiftly repositioning it to prevent another bloodbath. The bleeding stopped. Everyone in the theatre took a deep breath. The aneurysm was now safely cut off by the clip and the main vessel providing the brain with blood was unhindered. As a final manoeuvre, Amal performed the removal of the temporary clip. Harry was practically drooling as he watched the microscope monitor. His jaw hung open in awe.

"Excellent, Amal. What a fantastic pair of hands! I'm very impressed!" applauded Lewis. He was honestly blown away by how well she had managed the burst aneurysm and resulting blood loss. Amal, however, looked drained. She slowly looked up to meet Lewis' eyes with her own and coerced her face into a passably appreciative smile. Lewis understood. This was a significant moment in Amal's career, one that she would never forget.

"Thank you, Mr Thomas, for believing in me."

"Ah, well, how else would we produce great surgeons? One day, when you eventually train registrars too, I hope that you will do the same."

"Of course, Mr Thomas. Of course," she humbly acquiesced.

"Bravo, Amal. Truly. Are you okay to crack on and close up? I just need to speak to this medical student about a project."

"Sure, Mr Thomas."

"Harry, come with me." On hearing his name called, Harry looked as if he had just won the lottery. Surely, this day couldn't get any better.

Lewis took Harry to one side. He knew Deborah didn't want to get involved with snooping around Crispin Humphries but, having technically just done Harry a favour by letting him watch the operation, Lewis thought he might be able to persuade him to get involved instead.

"Harry, what did you think of that then?"

As predicted, Harry replied, "I thought that was awesome, Mr Thomas! I want to be a brain surgeon."

"Okay, Harry," Lewis laughed. We'll see about that. "Would you like to see more neurosurgery?"

"Absolutely, Mr Thomas."

"Grand. I want you to see if you can email a colleague of mine, a Mr Humphries." It came out as more of an order than a request, but Harry's exultation did not appear to falter. Lewis was pleased to see that Harry had been sufficiently buttered up. "I'll give you his details. Tell him that you heard that he is the best neurosurgeon in the world. That should get his attention. I believe he is doing some ground-breaking brain surgery in epilepsy patients. In all honesty, I think you'll benefit from seeing it for yourself."

"Wait, let me get this straight. You want me to spy on him?"

Deborah, overhearing the conversation, was trying to tell Harry not to get involved by shaking her head and waving her hands behind Lewis.

"I think spying is a strong word, Harry. I was thinking more about remote research. How good are you with computers?" Lewis asked.

"Well, actually, I'm pretty good." Harry was being modest. He was a computer genius. It helped that his lack of social life gave him a little too much time to practice coding and, on the odd occasion, hacking too.

"In that case, why don't you find out as much as you can online in the first instance and then report back to me. If you get nowhere, then you follow this up with an email to Mr Humphries. Yeah?"

It was not unusual for Lewis to receive emails from medical students and doctors requesting to visit or shadow him in hospital. For the most part, it was just too time-consuming to fill out the application form and submit it to HR for approval.

"Count me in, Mr Thomas. I would so love to do this." Harry had already convinced himself that this might be his first step to becoming a neurosurgeon. He couldn't say no.

"Good. Well, start by seeing if you can do any background work and let me know what you find. You have my number."

Lewis sensed Deborah behind him. She looked furious

when he finally turned around. "Ah, Deborah. How are you?" Perhaps annoyingly for Deborah, she looked even more sexy when she was angry.

"I'm excellent, Mr Thomas," Deborah said through gritted teeth. "That was a tricky case. I was very impressed with your teaching technique. I hope one day, I might have the opportunity to be trained by someone like you." She looked him directly in the eyes. Again, Lewis struggled to stop imagining Deborah in her underwear. How scandalous it would be for them to have a quick shag in the theatre right there and then... Mother on the toilet, mother on the toilet, mother on the toilet!

"Deborah," Lewis cleared his throat. "Why don't we, err, go up to my office so we can have a chat about another project?" Deborah nodded silently, the corners of her mouth turning up mischievously. "Harry, I'm going to have a chat with Deborah in my office about a separate matter. Do keep in touch and, err, get that email sent off to Mr Humphries!" Lewis dismissed Harry and walked off in a hurry with Deborah.

In Lewis' office, Deborah scolded him for involving Harry in his schemes. "I can't believe you're getting Harry involved in this!" she said scornfully.

"Why are you so worried about it, Deborah?"

"I just think it's too dangerous. Harry is vulnerable. He's too impressionable. He calls himself Firefly... I mean, that says it all."

"Look, he's an enthusiastic student. If he emails Crispin and the show-off agrees, Harry could watch him do some procedures. What's wrong with that? I just don't trust him. If he really is putting dodgy stimulators into people's heads, someone should know! Harry is a big boy. He will be fine."

"I'm still not happy about it."

Lewis couldn't understand why she was so concerned about Harry. He was about to reassure her again when Deborah stopped him from opening his lips by planting a kiss on them. Lewis was starting to detect a pattern. Whenever he seemed to mention anything about the stimulator, or Crispin for that matter, she turned into a nymphomaniac. He wasn't going to argue though. He was a horny man, after all, and she was a devilishly beautiful woman.

Lewis locked his office door, and they began to take off their scrubs. Deborah slowly got down on her knees, pushing Lewis back against his office door. Probably best, since his secretary had a key to his office as well. He caught sight of them both in the mirror; her blonde hair rhythmically bobbing up and down, his cheeks blushing furiously. Lewis didn't know what he'd done in a past life to deserve this kind of special treatment, but it seemed to be paying off now. What made it even more exhilarating was that it was a disciplinary offence to have sex on the premises. He gazed at the city skyline through the window, wondering if anyone was able to see what was going on. Sunlight shimmered and danced off the skyrises in the distance, reflecting prismatic rays of light back into his office. A small flock of birds flew by and, intermingled with them, what appeared to be some kind of silver drone. Lewis chuckled to himself. Whoever's flying that thing will get a shock if they can see into my office, he thought. Looking out over the city, Lewis came quickly with a grunt. It felt as if he had been flying.

"Wow, saving a life and getting a blow job all in the space of an hour. What could be better?"

Detecting the sound of footsteps walking by his office door, they quickly made themselves more respectable. Deborah wiped her mouth. Lewis futilely rubbed the damp patch that had formed at the front of his scrubs where his penis had tented the light blue fabric. They both giggled.

People have sex all the time in the hospital environment. It was more common than not. Working closely in a high-pressured environment is hard and what better way to relieve the tension than a quick bonking session in the store cupboard? The secretary and the surgeon are a popular duo, always shagging between ops like rabbits. But then there are also stories about scrub nurses, ward nurses and even cleaners getting funky from time to time. Junior doctors also often take the opportunity to have sex with each other when on call. Surgeons were by far the worst, though. Lewis believed it was because they were probably the most stressed, and therefore, the horniest.

Occasionally, when Lewis was a junior doctor, he would get the odd nurse knocking on his door with some excuse or other, trying to seduce him. He, of course, wasn't entirely innocent. He had also done his fair share of wooing various student nurses in his time too. A hospital which had a nurses' home attached was a real bonus for even the ugliest of junior doctors. It was less common now as most of the old accommodation rooms were taken over by hospital managers. Ah, yet another case of those half-witted hospital managers spoiling all the fun. The extent of sex in the hospital was exposed when engineers came around to install new wall-hanging telephones in theatres. They were set up in an odd position at about hip-height on the walls. This meant that you had to bend over to pick up the handpiece. Initially, none of them worked. It was supposedly because of cabling issues which were to be resolved in due course. They were present in theatres for about a year and then, suddenly, one day, they vanished. It later transpired that they were not telephones at all. There were actually hidden cameras within the telephone casing. The National Crime Agency had been called to find someone who had apparently been tampering with the anaesthetic machines. They did not find the culprit. What they did find, however, was that hospital staff were having sex out of hours on the operating tables. Glorious! Thank goodness the tables are scrubbed down in the morning before the cases started.

Lewis was shaken out of his post-coital reverie by his telephone chiming. DS Smyth was calling.

"Lewis, DS Smyth here, sorry to trouble you. Are you free to talk?"

"It's good timing, actually. I'm just in my office doing some..." he paused. "Some hands-on training. It's called a transoral approach, but that probably won't mean much to you." He smiled and winked at Deborah. "What's the news?"

"They have found the stimulator. Don't ask me how, but the stimulator was found at the bottom of the refrigerator floor. It was lodged in a crevice. The forensic team only found it on the second sweep. No one is taking responsibility, but the pathologist again has asked me to apologise to you. He swears he put it in Mike Taylor's shroud. We have the make and the model of the stimulator, and we are making further enquiries. Nothing is pointing to the fact that Mr Humphries put it in. He still alleges that he has never heard of a Mr Taylor."

"Ah, I see. How peculiar."

"Peculiar, indeed. The stimulator we found is actually not available in the UK, so we are presuming Mike Taylor had the procedure done secretly over here. Once we have made our enquiries, I suspect the coroner will release the bodies back to their family in America. I just wanted to thank you again for your time. It's unlikely we'll be needing your services any more."

"Oh, well, thank you for letting me know. I guess it was fun to get involved in something a little different to what I'm used to doing. I've never come across a stimulator with that strange logo before."

"Sorry?" replied the detective.

"Dr Davies mentioned something about a strange logo on the battery to the stimulator, didn't he? He must have made some enquiries and found out that it was made in the US."

"Right, well, we'll chase it up. Anyway, if we need any more information, I will get back in contact with you. Until then, thanks for all your help. I know how busy you are."

"My pleasure, detective. All the best to you… Goodbye." Lewis hung up.

"What was that about?" Deborah asked.

"They have found the so-called missing stimulator."

"Is it still suspicious?"

"Why are you bothered, my sweet?" Lewis smiled and sidled up to Deborah, stroking her hair.

"Well, I had a bad feeling about it. Do you still need to be involved?"

"Not any more. They're saying that it can't be one that Humphries uses. I'm not entirely sure how they know. I'm a bit confused about the whole thing, to be honest. I still don't trust Crispin."

"Let it go, Lewis!" Deborah smiled and stroked Lewis' hair in return.

"Yeah, I guess you're right. Fancy coming to mine for dinner tonight?" asked Lewis hopefully, after a pause.

"Can you cook?"

"No, but that doesn't mean I can't invite you around for dinner." Lewis hardly ever cooked, unless you count toast and marmalade in the morning.

"I would love that, Lewis!" Deborah replied excitedly.

"Right," Lewis looked at the clock. Time sure does fly when you're having fun. "I must see how the patient from this morning is doing." He gave Deborah a long passionate kiss farewell, still finding it hard to believe that this — Deborah and he — were... a thing. It all felt like a dream.

He slowly unlocked the door and, after checking the coast was clear, Deborah sneaked away. After a minute or so, he went into the adjoining secretary's office hoping nobody in there had noticed anything. He held some paperwork ready in his hand as an excuse. He placed the papers down on his secretary's desk. "Here's some discharge summaries that need sending. All okay?"

"Yes, Lewis, all okay." She had clocked the young woman leaving his office but chose to exert the origin of her title and keep it a secret. Lewis was naively satisfied that his secretary hadn't noticed anything out of the ordinary. She was usually quite blunt and would tell him straight when she had an issue with him. "You received this." She said, passing him a letter.

It was an invitation to give a lecture at the Royal College of Surgeons of England in Holborn. The invitation proposed he prepare for a debate regarding robotic-assisted surgery replacing human surgeons. He would argue against, and his opposition, none other than Mr sodding Crispin Humphries of all people, would argue for. He didn't really want to think much about it there and then, so shoved the letter into his pocket for later.

"It's just an invitation for a conference debate thing. Thanks. Well, I'm just going down to recovery to see my patient." As Lewis turned to go back into his office, his secretary called him back.

"Lewis!" she paused "You may want to change your scrubs." Lewis looked down. He still had a wet patch around his groin.

"Shit!"

When Lewis arrived in the recovery ward, Amal was already there watching over the patient. The patient's chest slowly expanded and softened as she breathed. All was silent except for the monitor's beeping and the gentle, oceanic sound of her breath. It had been Amal's first time dealing with a potential death on the table and so she had taken an active interest in her patient's recovery.

"How are you feeling, Amal?" Lewis asked quietly.

"Well, I'm still coming down from the adrenaline rush. I'm just hoping she does okay."

"I'm sure she will, Amal. You did well today."

"Thanks to you, Mr Thomas."

CHAPTER 13

Although Crispin was pleased with Mr Walsh's progress, he didn't feel wholly able to celebrate the success of his procedure. Being told not to discuss one of his patients with the police had left a sour taste in his mouth. Crispin had desperately wanted in on Brainionics, but he hadn't considered the potentiality of being in a prison cell for them if he got caught. He decided to phone Gad Dayan to express his dissatisfaction. After a few rings, Gad picked up his phone.

"Mr Dayan, it's Crispin Humphries here."

"Hello Crispin, how can I help you?" Gad answered flatly.

"It's about that patient you asked me to deny all knowledge of the other day."

"I don't know what you're talking about, Crispin," responded Gad. His voice was unadorned by any detectable emotion, making it impossible for Crispin to decipher Gad's reaction to his call.

"You know, the—" Crispin was abruptly cut off.

"I'll phone you in an hour." Gad ended the call.

Crispin waited in his office, marvelling at the artefacts he kept in his cabinet. He traced his awards with his fingertips and smiled an egregious smile as he looked out his window onto Harley Street, fantasising about being a millionaire. He truly loved himself and his success.

After a short while, his phone rang. It was Gad Dayan, as

promised.

"Crispin, please remember who is in control of your neurosurgical career. Remember who is directing patients to you, who is paying you and who could end your career with a flick of a switch. It is sometimes better for you not to know the finer details of our business. I am trying to protect you." He continued in his thick Israeli accent. "I will only tell you this once. You are not the only neurosurgeon we are working with. We can easily find someone to replace you."

Crispin knew he had overstepped the mark. He tried to backtrack. "Yes! I'm so sorry! I should not have asked any questions." He stuttered.

"Do not grovel to me, Crispin. It's pitiful."

He feared the sudden curtailing of his lucrative consultancy payments. He had no idea that Brainionics had other surgeons involved in their products apart from himself and Professor Santos. "I was just concerned that if I lied to the police, I would get into trouble! I would never do anything to jeopardise you or Brainionics!" Crispin pleaded tearfully.

Gad let out a tired sigh. "Do you remember Mr Taylor?" he asked, bored of Crispin's fawning.

"The fat American?"

"Ah, always the caring professional," Dayan let out a sinister chuckle. This was why Crispin had been such an attractive candidate to him — he didn't care about anyone but himself, his fame and his money. "Yes, he was, as you call him, the 'fat American'. Do you know what happened to him?"

"Did he do fantastically well?" Crispin replied, a little bit too cockily and somewhat recovered from his infantile meltdown a few seconds prior.

"He killed himself. And his wife."

There was a pause as the information sunk in for Crispin. He did not feel any guilt nor mercy for this loss but, instead, an almost immediate primitive need to defend his honour and his reputation.

"Well, that's not my fault, Gad! A lot of patients become depressed after the trauma of surgery. Nobody can blame me for that!"

Gad chose to ignore Crispin's comments and continued. "There have been a few problems with some of the older stimulators, Crispin. Without going into too much detail, as a company, we had to investigate this without bringing too much attention to ourselves."

"I programmed him myself," said Crispin, ignoring Gad.

Dayan was losing his patience. "Don't be stupid, Crispin, we gave you a dummy box. We program the patients you operate on."

"Well, thanks a lot. I thought it was me that was making the patients better—"

"If someone finds out that the stimulator belonged to us," Gad broke Crispin off again, "It will come back to you. We will say that you have been implanting them without our knowledge and off-licence. You will be disgraced; your career will be over, and you will never work again." To add further fuel to the fire, Gad quickly added to close: "And you won't receive a dime more." There was a short, theatrical gasp at the other end of the line. "However, Crispin, if you keep your mouth shut and continue to put the stimulators in under our supervision, we will support you." He waited for Crispin to respond. Crispin remained silent, breathing heavily into the mouthpiece. "You will have whatever you need at your disposal. You will be rich and famous. Your legacy will continue forever more. Do you understand, Crispin?"

"Yes." Crispin squeaked, only able to muster one word.

"Good. You will find a special payment in your account shortly. Let's call it a loyalty payment."

"And, if the police contact me again?"

"They won't. It's sorted Crispin. As I said, we are here to protect you. One more thing. Don't ever phone me directly again. I will text you a separate number if you need to speak to me." At that, the phone call ended.

Crispin stood still listening to the dialling tone, unable to put the phone back down. His face had turned a ghostly white. He chewed on the inside of his mouth nervously as the colour slowly returned to his face. It dawned on him that he had no choice but to go along with Gad's orders if he truly wanted fame and fortune. If it meant he was to be a prisoner to Gad Dayan, then so be it.

Lewis was sitting in his makeshift office at home. He had set it up in his spare bedroom, better described as a box room because of its petite size. It wasn't very glamorous; a hodgepodge of files and papers sprawled all over the place, and his computer. Lewis was adept at shuffling his papers around, but utterly inept at actually filing them and tidying them away. His folder of urgent things to do was massive and had remained untouched for several months. He looked around at the various stacks and decided he would have a think about what to do with them all. But first, he would need a coffee. And a cigarette. As he settled down into his usual window spot with a smoke and a cup of coffee, his phone buzzed in his pocket. It was a text from Harry.

I've got some interesting information about Mr Humphries, when should I discuss it with you, Mr Thomas?

Wow, already! Lewis thought. Maybe Harry wasn't such a nuisance after all.

Excellent. Give me a call.

Harry phoned just seconds after Lewis had clicked send. Harry explained that he had been able to examine the records of the patients on whom Crispin Humphries had previously performed surgery in his private hospital.

"But… How?" replied Lewis, awestruck. "I have my ways, Mr Thomas."

Harry was a living and breathing cliché of a geek. He had never had a girlfriend, was terrible at sports and nearly always ate his lunch by himself. He was, however, president of the Computer Club, an achievement which he used to console himself whenever he felt lonely, which was rare. He preferred the company of computers, anyway. When he was younger, Harry and his friends were the first students to build computer programs at school. He had developed a knack of understanding binary code and would make silly computer games in his free time. While this did gain him a handful of also geeky friends, he spent most of his time being bullied for his spotty skin and oversized clothes.

Harry was an introvert at heart and preferred to be by himself. He had been fostered, and though he was grateful for the relationship he had had with his carers, they had never understood his introversion and had taken great efforts to try and coax out a more confident, normal side to him. He rarely saw or spoke to them now. They spent most of their time taking care of their latest, more suited foster child. He didn't mind. He also didn't feel any inclination to discover the identity of his real birth parents. He kind of liked the feeling that it was him against the world. In his mind, he was all the family he needed. As a teenager, he had spent most of his evenings in his bedroom exploring the world through his computer screen. This was partly what made him decide to call himself 'Firefly', as he was primarily active at night and would reflect the glow of his computer screen as he worked in the dark. Lit up like twilight, he wandered alone through cyber space. He felt the name more fitting than Harry. Harry was too... normal-sounding.

With the advent of social media, he had quickly learned how to hack into some of the bullies' accounts and humiliated them with false postings. Revenge was sweet. It gave him an immense feeling of power. This soon advanced to hacking into school computers before entire systems. He loved it! It was his secret life. One of the reasons he wanted to be a neurosurgeon was because, to him, the brain was like another computer he could hack into, fix and put back together again. It suited the way his brain seemed to work.

On the phone, Harry told Lewis that Mr Humphries was using stimulators manufactured by a company called Brainionics. Lewis asked whether a Mike Taylor had been among the patient files, but Harry didn't recall coming across anyone by that name. He had planned to get more information on the company, but it was proving a little harder than expected. He was confident that over the next few days he could get more information to Lewis, though. Lewis told Harry that he didn't want to know how he got the information, but if he found a connection with Crispin and Mr Taylor, he would be sure to speak to DS Smyth on Harry's behalf. He, of course, didn't want to get Harry into any trouble.

"Thank you, Harry. Truly. I really appreciate it," said Lewis.

"You're welcome. I'll let you know what else I find... just one question. Why the interest in this Mike Taylor?"

"Ah... no reason, really. He sadly died not too long ago, and we found a stimulator inserted in his brain. I just wanted to know who had implanted it." Lewis was careful to not reveal too many details. Not that Harry wouldn't be able to find them out for himself. It appeared he was smarter than Lewis had originally thought.

"Right, well. Awesome. Speak soon, Mr Thomas." Harry hung up.

Lewis looked at the clock and realised it wouldn't be long until Deborah turned up for dinner that evening and began preparing for their date. This entailed popping to M&S for the ultimate, ready-made meal selection.

Later that evening, Deborah rang the doorbell at Lewis's home in Notting Hill. He had tried to mask the smell of stale cigarettes with scented candles. Somehow, he didn't think that Eau De Fumer would be that appealing to a classy, young lady like Deborah. The candles were labelled Evening Romance which seemed appropriate if not a little cheesy.

Lewis opened the door to greet Deborah.

"Hello, gorgeous," he said warmly. He had dressed down for the evening, wearing jeans and a plain white shirt. She didn't wrinkle her nose when he ushered her inside, which he took as a good sign.

"Very nice, Mr Thomas." He guided her into the kitchen which he had thoroughly fumigated and polished within an inch of his life a few hours before. She carefully surveyed the room before sitting down at the little island. Lewis poured her a glass of wine.

"So, you're a smoker as well as a good lover?"

"How do you know I'm a smoker?" Lewis said. Dammit. Busted.

"Only a smoker can't tell when a place stinks of cigarettes." She laughed.

"I'm not proud of it, I've tried everything to stop."

"You should try Yoga if you want to zone out, it's good for you too, especially since you're an old man now." She laughed again.

"Funnily enough, I was thinking about doing that."

"I'll organise for my Yoga instructor to come around if you want."

An image of a Kamasutra-style threesome quickly flashed across his mind. "Okay, deal."

Lewis began to prepare the dinner. In other words, he took out the food he had already removed from its Marks and Spencer's packaging and placed it neatly onto some white dishes.

"That looks interesting. What is it?" Deborah asked, peering over his shoulder. Lewis could feel her warm breath on the back of his neck which tingled with pleasure.

"Just something I knocked up earlier. Some pasta. I didn't ask you what you don't eat…"

"I eat anything, particularly dishy neurosurgeons." She replied coyly.

Lewis turned around to face her, looking down at her

174

perfectly manicured, lotioned hands. He interlaced his fingers with hers and, without looking up, said quietly: "Yeah, about that. Are you cool with err... us?"

"Of course, Lewis. I wouldn't be here if I wasn't." When he didn't look up immediately, she lifted his chin up with her finger and gazed into his eyes. "I promise. It's a bit complicated, but I'm okay with it. It's going to be fine." She reassured him.

Lewis felt like a vulnerable school kid about to get his heart broken. He hadn't felt so exposed in... well, ever. "Well, good. If it doesn't bother you, it doesn't bother me either."

The smell of burning wafted up Deborah's nose. She let out a snort and got up to assess the damage. Lewis was attempting to scrape burnt pasta off the bottom of the pan.

"Yikes! Listen, Lewis. I think I can help."

She giddily ran to fetch her bag and quickly returned. Like a magician, she pulled out the bag some fresh pappardelle pasta, truffle, olive oil and a bottle of chianti. "Tada! Somehow, I didn't think you were able to cook. Sit down Lewis and let me prepare something."

Without giving Lewis the chance to argue, she took his pan to the bin and began to scrape the insides out. She chose not to comment on the Marks & Spencer's packaging she spotted sitting in the bottom.

Lewis couldn't believe it. Not only was she beautiful and smart, but she could cook too. She was by no means a one-trick pony, she was a bloody unicorn. Deborah took over at the hob, gently pushing Lewis out of the way.

"So, Lewis, tell me the news. How did the aneurysm patient do?"

"I think she's going to be okay. Thanks for asking!" he

answered, pouring her another glass of wine. Unlike girlfriends he had had before, Deborah seemed to understand the stresses of what a neurosurgeon must go through. Previous girlfriends initially liked the glamour of going out with a brain surgeon, but soon got fed up with the gruelling on-call rotas, midnight operations, poor to non-existent social life and everything else that was restricted by hospital duties. He liked how compassionate she was.

As he was watching her, a fly flew into the kitchen. With one fell swoop of the tea towel, the fly was dead on the kitchen floor. She didn't even look up from what she was doing.

"Harry loved being in theatre with you today, thank you for letting him go, he really appreciated it." Is this woman a robot? Lewis stared at her as she cooked. She was simply too good to be true.

"How do you know Harry?" asked Lewis.

"I don't really know him that well. But I know he's not that popular at medical school."

"Why? Because he's a geek and says awesome all the time?" He tried to do a Harry-sounding voice when he said 'awesome'.

"That's so unfair. He's a sweet guy. I hope he's not involved in any of your spying missions." Deborah turned to give Lewis a stern stare.

"Well… He may be doing a bit of work for me. I know you're not happy about it though, so I didn't want to bring it up."

"Lewis, you need to stop this nonsense. Please don't get Harry involved in this, it will only end in trouble." Her voice became slightly terser. End of the unicorn theory, Lewis thought.

"Okay, okay, look let's not ruin the evening. I'll tell him that there is no case to follow up and to drop it."

"Promise?" she said, tilting her head to one side like a little puppy. "Yes, I promise. Let's not mention it again, you promise?"

"Cross my heart."

CHAPTER 14

Harry also didn't know Deborah that well either. The first time he met her was actually in the theatre when he first met Mr Thomas. He didn't know her from medical school. After being acquainted with her, out of habit he had tried a little background research on her. Just little facts like where she was schooled, where she lived, who her friends were. He only wanted the information for himself. In a way, this was the closest he got to having a conversation with people sometimes. Interestingly, he found very little about her. A Facebook page, a couple of Instagram photos, but nothing much else. Rather than look too much into it, as was his tendency as a compulsive hacker, he chose to assume she was a secretive person who didn't share much of her life online.

Harry's flat was just as cold and bare as Deborah's cyber-footprint. A little bed, a sink and his tech station by the window was all it contained, spare a small collection of clothes he folded neatly and kept in a cardboard box which he used as a wardrobe. He had medical textbooks scattered on the floor, hand-drawn anatomical drawings pinned up in his small kitchen and a collection of notes dotted around the landscape of his basic surroundings.

Harry had spent all night scouring Crispin Humphries' website, fuelled by his endless supply of Lucozade and Skittles which he kept stashed underneath his bed. He had looked at the private hospital website too. It didn't take him long to hack both of them. Harry had developed a series of his own programmes to break through the security walls and encryptions allegedly protecting our privacy on the web. Perhaps a perk of his poor-socialisation, Harry's little master-mind had learnt how to spin his own complex web of intricate digital pathways, trapping even the most advanced antivirus software like flies in his labyrinthian cyber mesh. Despite his ease of accessing them, the process was still long due to Harry's obsessive, perfectionist nature. He left no code, no number, no link unturned. More than anything, he desperately wanted to please Mr Thomas. Harry felt truly inspired by him and, deep down, he thought that if he got this research right, they could even be friends in the future. Neurosurgeon pals, he fantasised.

Although he could see all the electronic records on both websites, most of the details, unfortunately, had been left blank. He could see the names of the patients, the date of their operations and their reason for surgery. Moreover, he could see the name of which implants Humphries was using which is how he found out about the Brainionic implants. It looked like Humphries had switched to using these implants about a year before. Harry made a note of this, wondering why. He then started to look into the Brainionics website. His initial assessment was that it was pretty poor for a medical device company. There were a few anomalies but after one hour or so, he was able to hack into the mainframe website. He found a hidden area at the back of the website, though not hidden enough for Harry. "Wow," he exclaimed. Streams of information flooded his computer screen. He quickly tried to download as much information as he could; employee reports, computer-aided design drawings, clinical studies and even further encrypted data. Suddenly, a skull and crossbones sign appeared on his laptop.

"Shit!" he slammed his laptop shut. Someone in Brainionics has caught him snooping on their website. He sat for a moment, slightly shaken. He would have to update his Virtual Private Network software. Nobody had ever discovered him in action before.

He grabbed his phone and sent a text to Mr Thomas to inform him of his findings. He had a weird, unfamiliar feeling in the pit of his stomach, telling him that something wasn't right. He couldn't quite put his finger on it though. He spent the next few hours laying wide awake in bed, contemplating what had just happened, before eventually falling asleep.

When Lewis got into his office, there was an email from his business manager waiting for him.

Urgent, please see me was the subject line. He phoned her office. "Hi, Sandra, it's Lewis Thomas here. What's up?"

"Are you in your office?" she responded plainly.

"Yes." Lewis, getting a bit paranoid, wondered whether someone had seen Deborah performing a lewd act on him?

"Okay, I'll come around." She replied in an authoritative tone.

"Okay..." Lewis felt that familiar naughty schoolboy feeling. What a way to ruin his good mood. He had spent the morning attempting yoga for the first time with Deborah. Balancing on one leg was, apparently, very difficult. He had provided Deborah with an unintentional pantomime-like performance as he hopped around his living room trying not to fall. Deborah found this absolutely hilarious, of course. Well, you can't be good at everything. Although the yoga didn't feel particularly meditative, just being in her presence made him feel light and content. The business manager knocked on his office door a few moments later.

"Thank you, Mr Thomas, may I sit down."

"Sure." Lewis said, anticipating the worse.

"I've had to compile a list of doctors who haven't completed their mandatory training. I'm afraid you haven't attended any of the training sessions over the last two years."

"Is that it? Is there anything else you've come here to speak to me about?" Lewis was relieved.

"It is dire, Mr Thomas. If we don't get over 90% of our doctors to complete the mandatory training, we get fined by the commissioning groups. The Trust simply cannot afford to lose money right now."

"Well, Sandra, what can I say? I have found it difficult to attend the fire lecture, it always occurs when I'm either in theatre or in clinic. Do you want me to cancel my clinical duties to attend?"

"I would expect you to attend them in your own time actually and not cancel either, there are plenty of sessions throughout the year."

"Well, I'm not going to. I have a life outside of surgery." Up until very recently, this would have been a lie. But now, what with seeing Deborah more frequently, doing his research into Crispin and fighting crime… well, he just wouldn't have the time.

"I will have to report you to the clinical manager. He has the authority to start disciplinary proceedings."

"You are joking!" Lewis couldn't believe what he was hearing.

"Nope, this is not a joking matter. It's crucial."

"It's not! What is serious is the gross mismanagement of our department. We are losing nursing staff, there are no beds and we get no support from you lot. What is serious is a cancer patient waiting in agony for a bed because it is blocked by a patient who has a bit of backache. They get sent to our ward because they may breach the stupid four-hour target. What are you going to do about that?" Lewis was tiring of the hypocrisy of the administrators.

Sandra was breathing heavily. Clearly, she had not emotionally prepared for Lewis to retaliate. "You will have to take this up with the clinical director." Her voice broke slightly as she spoke. It looked like she was either about to cry or to hyperventilate. Or both.

Lewis obliviously continued his tirade. "Okay, tell me about my figures. Do you know what my performance is like? My readmission rates? My infection rates? Or my mortality rate?"

"Mr Thomas, please don't raise your voice. I'm just doing my job." Her bottom lip wobbled. When did hospital life get so bloody operatic? Lewis thought.

"Fine. Right, tell me when the next training days are, and I will attend. Happy now?"

"There is no need to be so aggressive, Mr Thomas! I'll have to refer you to the Anger Management course too!"

Lewis laughed. "I'm not being aggressive. I was saying that I will do the mandatory training sessions to ensure that the Trust is compliant." He could see she was getting upset. There was simply no point in arguing. He couldn't win. He would have to attend the stupid meetings and work with more stupid people if he wanted to keep his job. His voice changed to that of a sympathetic one, sensing that the business manager was on the verge of tears. "I apologise, Sandra, for reacting so abruptly."

"It's your tone. I don't care much for it." Sandra spat back, a hint of malice in her voice.

She stood up with tears in her eyes and stormed out, slamming the door behind her.

"Bloody hell." Lewis rubbed his face with his hands and pretended to scream at the closed door. He hated the management, even more so now because Sandra had made him feel bad. He didn't want to upset anybody, he just wanted to be left alone to do his job properly. Some in the hospital only cared about the corporate side of things; they didn't give a toss about making a difference for the patients. With this thought, he decided to go and do what he believed was important: see to his patients.

Lewis made his way to the neurosurgical ward. As he entered, he heard the familiar banter of the junior doctors and nurses. The health care assistants were gossiping and eating a box of chocolates. Lewis would often overhear them chatting about being overweight. You wonder why.

"Hello, Mr Thomas, fancy a finger of fudge?" one said. They both giggled.

Lewis didn't mind the girls directing jokes at him. He was glad that he didn't seem unapproachable like some of the other doctors. Lewis sensed David approaching before he heard him. He wrinkled his nose as if a bad smell had wafted up his nostrils.

"Mr Thomas, we weren't expecting a ward round, but I'm happy to tell you about your patients! Amal isn't around, not sure where she is actually." Ever the irritating registrar trying to one up the other trainees.

"No problem, David. How's my aneurysm patient?"

"She's doing okay — her husband's more of a problem than she is. The nursing staff are frightened of going near her. He's a bit of a gorilla, isn't he?"

Gorillas would be offended to hear that. Lewis thought.

"Apart from that, she has the typical memory problems and headaches, but she's getting better. Hopefully, she will be discharged next week."

"That is good to hear." Lewis said. He then turned to the nursing sister on shift. "Sister, what's the deal with Mrs Stringer's husband?"

The nursing sister stopped what she was doing on the ward and, in a low voice, whispered. "He is such a pain in the arse. Every time we go to take her observations, he keeps telling us that we are not looking after her properly. And then other ridiculous things such as telling us that we have to plump up her pillows or that the medication is not given precisely on time. It's making us very nervous."

"Do you want me to get involved or will that make it worse?" Lewis asked.

"We would all be grateful. Both David and Amal have tried to speak to him, but he just tells them to fuck off."

"Okay, I'll speak to him, but I will need you to back me up."

The sister, David and Lewis marched over to Mrs Stringer. She had a bandage around her head and her eyes were still closed due to the postoperative swelling. Her husband was looking through the nursing notes and pharmacy chart at the end of the bed.

"Oh, look who it is, love! It's that fancy surgeon who cut your head open," he said condescendingly.

Lewis took a deep breath in. "Mr Stringer, your wife is recovering well. Is there a problem?"

"Problem? Who said there is a problem? Have you got a problem?" Mr Stringer pumped up his chest in a bid to make himself seem larger and more intimidating than he actually was.

"Well, yes, as a matter of fact, I do have a problem. We have done our best to look after your wife and, as you know, she is not the only patient on the ward. The nurses work really hard to give the utmost attention to all our patients. However, due to staff shortages, they simply don't have the time to give your wife special treatment."

"Special treatment, my arse! I've barely seen any treatment around here. It's not my problem if you've not got enough staff! You lot have a duty to look after her, mate. I've read the patient's charter and it says that you lot have to do your job properly. I mean, look at her, she's a right mess! She can't even remember what day it is. What are you going to do about it? I mean, I can't look after her like this."

Lewis was trying to remain calm. Mr Stringer didn't care about his wife. He was just thinking about how this would impact on himself. He wished that it was Mr Stringer that had the subarachnoid haemorrhage and not his wife. "Well, Mr Stringer, if you carry on with this behaviour, I am going to have to tell security not to allow you onto the ward because I do believe it is interfering with your wife's care."

Mr Stringer walked forwards and pressed his nose up against Lewis'. Lewis was forced to crane his neck backwards as Mr Stringer leaned into him. Up close, Lewis could see that he was a real nasty piece of work. His skin was porous and stained from years of smoking and alcohol. His teeth were yellow and crooked like the discoloured, veiny whites of his eyes. His breath smelt like bile. "Really? Is that so?" he spat out at Lewis like a slavering dog.

Lewis took a step back and wiped a droplet of slaver of his cheek. "Yes." He responded, standing his ground. He could feel his heart rate beginning to rise with the pressure of confronting this hound. He hoped it didn't show on his face.

"You can't do that, mate. I know my rights. If you do, I'll sue you!"

"Right, I've had enough. As her consultant, and in her best interests, you are banned from the ward until your behaviour improves."

Mr Stringer took one look at Lewis and then stormed off the ward, barging into him as he did so. Everyone paused, still half expecting Mr Stringer to run back and wage war on the three of them. Lewis, regaining his composure, leaned over Mrs Stringer's bed to speak to her.

"Mrs Stringer, you are doing well. I know you still have headaches, but as the blood is reabsorbing, they will improve." Mrs Stringer just nodded. They all left the nursing bay believing it best to give Mrs Stringer some peace and quiet. The nursing sister took it upon herself to inform security that Mr Stringer was to be banned from the ward.

Lewis left the ward and headed back to his office. No sooner was he in his office did the phone ring. It was the business manager and, worryingly, she sounded slightly gleeful.

"Mr Thomas, Sandra here. We have received a complaint from a Mr Stringer. He phoned the Chief Executive's office who have asked me to look into it. You have been accused of being aggressive to one of your patient's relatives. I'm afraid we will need to investigate this." That was quick. "Please can you make yourself available when we arrange a panel meeting. I'm afraid we will also need to look into the fact that you are not up to date with your mandatory training too. I will send you some dates once we have finalised the panel."

Lewis didn't bother to defend himself. He knew that the management had it in for him. "Right, do whatever you have to do." Lewis slammed the phone down. He stared at his computer screen in silence. The new screen saver was: 'Are you up to date with your mandatory training?' He imagined smashing the computer monitor to smithereens, and delivering the broken pieces on Sandra's fucking desk. 'Stick that in your mandatory training file.' Lewis could feel himself getting a tension headache. His eye began to twitch as if to confirm the onset. The whole situation was utterly ridiculous. He had saved Mrs Stringer's life, for Christ's sake. He had been trying to help the staff deal with Mrs Stringer's relentless, bullying husband and now the dithering idiots were going to make him attend a potential disciplinary hearing. More so, it gave the stupid business manager one over him. He was royally fucked off. No doubt the hospital trust would support the bully rather than him and the only person who would be on his side will be the nursing sister. He knew he couldn't trust David, and Amal hadn't been there to be a witness.

Lewis lamented how things had changed over the years. There had been a complete erosion of power for consultants, to the point that they didn't have any real influence over anything, including their patients. The only reason the older consultants hung around was for their pension. Lewis had at least another fifteen to twenty years to go, before he could think of retiring.

To take his mind off of things, he turned his attention to the debate against Crispin Humphries and started to draft his talk for the upcoming conference.

CHAPTER 15

Harry was fast asleep when someone entered his room, jolting him awake. He couldn't see anything in the dark and, for a moment, thought he had imagined the creak of the door opening. His uncertainty was instantly cleared up when, as he stared into the darkness, two hands dragged him from the bed onto the ground, taped his mouth and pulled fabric over his head. He desperately tried to scream and break free as he thrashed around on the floor.

"Shut up you little shit!" There was a loud crack as the intruder, or one of them, he couldn't be sure how many people surrounded him, stamped down on his chest. Pain exploded around his ribs. Harry convulsed in agony on the floor. He tried to open his mouth to cry out for help but the tape tore at his lips. There was another thunderous crack as Harry's head made contact with a blunt object, knocking him out instantly. He was dragged from his flat and bundled into the boot of a car. With a screech of the tyres, the car sped away.

Back at the hospital, Lewis had become distracted for the umpteenth time. He sat with his laptop open, still seething at the way he was being treated by the hospital management. Part of him felt totally defeated. Maybe they were right. Maybe he was just too cocky. Would he be happier if he just… let go and accepted whatever the management threw at him? Many of his colleagues seemed to have no problem with how things were run. But then how could he stop being the patients' advocate? He wasn't rebelling just for the sake of being a nuisance, but for the benefit of those who genuinely needed good help and care. Augh. He shook his head as if he could physically shake the thoughts out of his mind. Another thing that was bothering him was a text he had received from Harry last night. Harry had said he had some new intel about Brainionics. Lewis wanted to call Harry, but he needed to concentrate and knew he would get carried away with the investigation if he called him. He had to get back to preparing for the debate.

Crispin Humphries. Now, here is someone who actually trumps how wanky the hospital management are. This was his chance to challenge and defeat the charlatan for good. The debate was timely and would no doubt cause a buzz at the conference. Lewis felt strongly that robots should not and would not replace surgeons in the future. That said, robotics was already being used in theatres and beyond to a certain extent. In some technologically advanced hospitals — in other words, in hospitals with an insane budget — surgeons were already being navigated by computers and Artificial Intelligence, telling them where to place things.

The history of medicine always fascinated Lewis. Even in the last decade, medical science has advanced and developed dramatically. One of Lewis's heroes happened to be the fastest surgeon in the 19th Century, Dr Robert Liston. He could amputate a leg in two and a half minutes. Lewis couldn't imagine him working in the current NHS. There was a notable case where Liston was so fast, he amputated not only the patient's leg but the patient's testicles too. He also managed to sever the fingers of his assistant in his haste and splash blood on one of the spectators who, poor sod, had a heart attack and died. Both the patient and the assistant also subsequently died of infection. His mortality rate for this case was 300%!

Perhaps thankfully, surgeons don't have to be superhuman quick any more. Evidentiality, you still can't traipse about — if you are a slick and safe surgeon, your patient is more likely to have a positive outcome than if you are a slow and clumsy surgeon. Nowadays, survival is less of an issue though. Not too long ago, before the advent of antibiotics in the 1930s, you probably would have died of some horrendous infection even if you only had a quick operation. In those days, no one wanted surgery unless it was a question of life or death. Jump ahead to the present day and you can have surgery for anything and everything. You name it; facelifts, face transplants, penile enlargements, penile transplants, designer vaginas and, for those with body dysmorphia, even amputation of limbs! All you need to do is go online and find an unscrupulous surgeon who would be prepared to do it. At a cost, of course. Take Crispin Humphries, for example. He'd be more than happy to enlarge your penis and take off your arm for a bit of extra dosh.

In all reality though, at the pace medical technology is progressing, it probably won't be that long before robots take over surgeons. Lewis didn't want to admit it though. He would not lose against Crispin without a fight. This wasn't going to be a battle of scientific knowledge; it was to be a battle of the egos.

When Harry eventually came to, he was sitting on a chair with his hands tied behind his back. One of the abductors took off the hood covering Harry's face. The fabric had stuck to the side of his head where the blood had congealed. As the material was torn away, the wound was painfully re-opened. His head throbbed with a vengeance. It felt as if his very brain were trying to hack its way out of his head. Harry couldn't see clearly. His vision wavered and his head lolled this way and that. He felt too weak, too disorientated to hold it still. Harry ran his tongue along his bottom lip. It was dry and cracked from the tape. He could taste blood in his mouth.

A single bulb hung from the ceiling spotlighting Harry beneath it. The room was damp and humid, the moisture in the air prickling Harry's skin. There was the sound of shuffling and muffled voices. Harry couldn't work out whether they were speaking a foreign language or whether his brain just wasn't capable of making sense of words any more. The dizziness slowly began to subside and he saw, clearly enough, that the two figures were bearded and slightly tanned. Before he had a chance to take in any more detail, they departed, turning off the single light as they left. Harry began to cry.

He did not know how much time had passed when the door flew open again. Minutes? Hours? Days? He couldn't think properly. A flashlight was shone into Harry's face, blinding him. He gasped and squinted, trying to make out the figures beyond the glare of light. He felt, before he saw, one of the figures release his hands from behind him. The release for his wrists and shoulders was instant. He took his time placing them on the armrests, afraid of making any sudden movement.

"Harry," one of the figures began. He tutted like a parent would to a disobedient child. "What have you been getting up to? Hiding behind your computer? Couldn't just look at porn, could you? Like normal kids?" the voice laughed. Harry couldn't quite work out where the accent was from. Possibly Spanish? Maybe Middle-Eastern? He couldn't concentrate.

"I haven't been looking at anything." Harry's voice sounded dry and hoarse. "I swear!" The other figure in the room came towards Harry and flashed a knife, tormenting him.

The knife's edge glinted hypnotizingly in the dim light. Suddenly, Harry felt a severe stabbing pain in the back of his right hand. He hadn't even noticed the attacker move. Harry silently turned his face downwards towards his hand where the knife was now embedded, nailing his palm into the armrest. He let out a terrifying, ear-piercing scream.

"I will repeat it, Harry, what have you been looking at?"

Harry sobbed in disbelief. This couldn't be happening. It had to be a dream. When he didn't respond, the knifeman twisted the knife in his hand. Harry let out a deafening wail. Urine dribbled down the side of his leg. A steaming puddle formed around his feet.

The voice spoke again from the darkness. "Harry, please don't make this worse. We know that you hacked into the Brainionics website which, I have to say, we were all very impressed with. What have you been looking at and why?"

The knifeman went to twist the weapon again when Harry cried out in surrender. "Okay," Harry whimpered. "I was just doing some research. I'm a medical student; it was for a project for one of the surgeons."

"Which one?"

Harry hesitated. The knife went in deeper. Harry let out a fresh, blood-curdling scream. "Okay, okay. It was under the instructions of... Lewis Thomas."

"That's better, Harry. What were you looking at?"

"We were trying to find out which patients had been operated on by Crispin Humphries. Mr Thomas wanted to know which stimulators he was using. I stumbled across your website. I'm so sorry." Harry was stuttering and slurring his words.

"We thought so, Harry. We are so happy that you can help us with this."

"Can you let me go now? I promise I won't tell anyone about this!"

"I'm sorry, Harry, that is not going to happen."

"Please!" He begged.

The hood went back on, choking him on his tears. The door closed and Harry was left once more in the darkness.

Lewis arrived at the Royal College of Surgeons in Lincoln's Inn Fields. He walked into the reception where he saw a plaster bust of William Harvey, one of the great pioneers of medicine, atop the marble pillar. Everyone looked very distinguished in their suits and ties. Lewis recognised most of them from previous conferences and gatherings. He spotted Crispin Humphries holding court in the distance. He was wearing a three-piece suit with golden cufflinks. His hair, or what little was left of it, was combed to one side. From a distance, his hair looked plastic from the amount of hairspray he had no doubt drenched it in. A crowd was beginning to form around him. Crispin looked at Lewis and pointed a long finger at him. He beckoned him over. What a creep.

"Ah, look who it is: my challenger."

"Hi Crispin, how are you?" Lewis said, unwillingly wandering over.

"Lewis, I'm fantastic. Looking forward to the debate? How can you possibly say we humans could be better at performing surgery than robots? We are the 'walking unemployed'." All the surgeons around Crispin started laughing.

"I'm looking forward to it too, Crispin. See you soon." Lewis chose to save his energy for the real debate.

Everyone started to take their seats in the auditorium. A general chitter-chatter commenced as the audience exchanged platitudes. Lewis's phone vibrated in his pocket. It was a text from Deborah.

Haven't seen Harry, have you? Hope you haven't got him in trouble. D x

Lewis felt uneasy. He still hadn't had a chance to get back to Harry yet about his text. He tried to brush aside his angst. What could have possibly happened? Deborah was overreacting.

I'm sure he's okay, relax. Just about to give my presentation, I'll call later.

There was no reply from Deborah.

The President of the College of Surgeons introduced the agenda for the meeting which was entitled 'Surgery for the 21st Century'. There were to be talks led by a range of UK-based and international speakers from a variety of surgical specialities including plastic, gastro, neuro and orthopaedic. The debate between Lewis and Crispin was second on the programme.

"Good morning everyone and welcome. Surgery is going through a dramatic change. Patients expect better. Technology is improving and, as a group of surgeons, we must stay in control and on top of what technology has to offer us. We have a fabulous set of speakers, and we hope everyone can participate in a lively discussion." Lewis was bored already. The President went on to discuss the usual housekeeping points before finishing with the obligatory joke that there is no fire alarm test so if it goes off, just run for the door.

"I would like to introduce the first speaker, Professor Arnold Cuthbert, who is going to talk about the current ethical status of using artificial intelligence in surgical operations. Professor Cuthbert is a world expert with over 300 peer-reviewed publications, the author of several textbooks and is on the International Advisory Board for the WHO Government Policy... Professor Cuthbert." A half-hearted round of applause took place as a white-haired gentleman in his early 60s got up and proceeded to the podium. He then looked around for the clicker to advance his slides but, seeing there wasn't one, had to then shout at the AV technicians.

"First slide, please. Excuse me! The first slide please!" The first slide was already on behind him. Awkward. Nobody said anything. He eventually figured it out and commenced his talk. Lewis didn't pay much attention to his speech. It was wordy and full of speculation with no take-home message. It was a relief when he finally wound down to his conclusion.

"Professor Cuthbert, a fascinating and brilliant insight into the future of surgery," said the President.

"Thank you, Professor. Now, I would like to start the grand debate. We have two feisty neurosurgeons, both from London, to debate whether robots will replace humans as surgeons. To start, can we have a show of hands: who thinks robots will replace humans as surgeons in fifteen years?"

About half the audience put their hands up.

"Thank you. I would now like to introduce Crispin

Humphries who is going to tell us why robots will replace humans in fifteen years. Mr Humphries…"

Crispin gallantly walked up to the podium and stood silently, eyeing up the audience. He dramatically burst into speech, addressing the room. "Ladies and gentleman, we cannot stand in the way of progress! Where would we be if we did? Can you imagine the days without antibiotics? Or anaesthetic? If we had refused to accept these innovations, well… half of you would probably be dead."

Crispin reeled off statistic after statistic about how many bad outcomes are due to human error and how many preventable mistakes could be reduced by having robots perform surgery. He went on to say how surgical training is suffering and that surgeons of the future will not be as experienced as they are now.

"Look at technology now. We cannot imagine where it will take us in fifteen years. I can guarantee Mr Thomas will want his surgery performed by robots rather than an inexperienced surgeon of the future." His argument was sound and presented with flair. When he finished, the President asked for a show of hands again. Virtually the whole audience put their hands up in agreement that robots will replace surgeons. Crispin had convinced them. Fucker.

"And now, for the argument that robots will never replace human surgeons, I would like to present Mr Lewis Thomas, a neurosurgeon also from London. Mr Thomas…"

Lewis, like Crispin, came to the podium and paused before speaking. His first slide was a picture of Metal Mickey. Metal Mickey was a television character from the 1980s.

"Yes, I know a little extreme but don't let Crispin lead you to believe that robots are the only way forward in fifteen years.

Robots are still mechanical devices. All mechanical devices, like humans, will fail. Humans maintain themselves; they talk to each other, they are by definition, humane, and have empathy. What would a robot do if, or rather, when there is unexpected sudden blood loss? Or, for instance, the surgeon accidentally tears the dura, leading to a leak of cerebrospinal fluid? Or indeed, what would happen if the robot broke during an operation? Who would save the day then?"

Lewis went on to explain that there was little evidence to suggest that robotic surgery will be better than human surgery. He did openly accept that these technologies do need to progress and the landscape in fifteen years will be a lot different.

"However, ladies and gentlemen, I would like to put forward another perspective. Surgeons are relatively cheap. Currently, robots can cost about a million pounds! And then you have the maintenance to cost in, too. The question is, who is going to buy them? The NHS is already cash-strapped! Are taxpayers going to fund them? Unlikely. Are we going to be at the beck and call of the companies? Undesirable. If a company invests millions into this technology, they will want their pound of flesh back sooner or later. Robots may one day be better, but we, as a medical community, will not be in charge of them. It will be the company controlling the technology. Surgeons will lose their ability to operate in the best interests of the patient. The companies may even limit which patients are robotically operated on to ensure their target outcomes are maintained! So, I suppose, yes, robots may replace humans as surgeons in fifteen years... but at what cost? Therefore, I stand by my argument. Robots, for the sake of patients, should never replace humans." Lewis left the podium to applause and sat down.

The President replaced Lewis at the podium. "Well, well, well. What a fiery response! I thank you both, speakers! Let us put the vote to the audience! Please, those who vote for the motion that robots will replace humans in fifteen years, put your hand up." The majority of the audience put their hands up. "Mr Humphries, it appears that you are the winner!" The audience clapped. Crispin stood up and joined in the applause of himself. He looked over at Lewis with a smug, punch-able expression on his face. "If it is true, I suggest we all start looking at another occupation! I would now like to introduce the next speaker..." Lewis zoned out the President's drone. What a joke. What happened to empathy? To being human? Lewis spent the entirety of the next speech worrying about the mental state of the surgeons operating on patients today if that was the kind of attitude they had.

During the break, Crispin approached Lewis. Lewis spoke first. "Congratulations, Crispin. It was a good debate. What are you up to these days?"

"Ah, well. At least you're not a sore loser, eh?" he winked. "Nowadays? Well, you know what it's like. A bit of NHS, a bit of private, a bit of consultancy work."

"Which company do you consult for?"

"Various companies, Lewis. They pay well. You should get into it. I can introduce you if you want." Crispin had no intention of introducing Lewis to anybody.

"Do you do any work for Brainionics?" Lewis pushed on.

Crispin seemed cagey. "Eh, not much any more." It was obvious to Lewis that he was lying.

He was dying to ask him about the stimulators. He couldn't hold himself back.

"Are you still inserting stimulators for stroke patients?" He regretted saying the words as soon as they left his mouth.

"How do you know about that Lewis? And anyway, what does it matter? You're not interested in this work. Someone has to do it. The results are fantastic."

"Fantastic? No complications?" asked Lewis.

Crispin was getting irritated. "Lewis, you ask a lot of questions about things you know nothing about. I don't have complications. We evaluate all the results, and so far, it is going amazingly well. I don't need your condescending remarks. What are you implying?"

"Hey, Crispin, don't get stressed out about it. I was just asking. I have loads of complications. Just part of the job." Lewis didn't have many complications at all but thought it might get Crispin to open up a bit more. Humphries' brow started to look a little moist. It didn't take long for the conversation to turn juvenile.

"Listen to you, loser. I know you're jealous. I'm a surgical pioneer; I have my own private practice and I won the debate. I pity you." As Humphries' monologue gained momentum, a few strands of his hair began to unravel and rise away from his scalp as if charged by static electricity, giving Crispin the look of a true, mad scientist. Lewis imagined himself patronisingly patting Humphries' hair down to flatten it again, but then thought better of touching his greasy head. Lewis laughed internally to himself. He empathised with Humphries' hair; he, too, desperately wanted to escape his presence. "Listen, Lewis, I would be pissed off as well. I mean, look at you. What have you really got going for you now? You've already peaked in your career, and it was an uneventful peak at that. What's next? Retirement and death. What a life! Anyway, if you want to continue the debate another time, I'll happily kick your arse again..."

Lewis observed Crispin, unsure of how to respond.

"And again!" Crispin quickly added, ever in need of the last word. Feathers evidently ruffled by what Lewis had asked, he fluttered off like a startled hen with an air of finality.

Lewis stood glued to the spot, so stunned was he by how immature Crispin had been. He looked around to see if anyone else had witnessed this absurd egotistical display, but it seemed nobody had been taking any notice of them. It was true that Crispin was incredibly successful, though Lewis would never understand how he had managed it. Or rather, he could understand how but did not want to believe that surgeons could be so corrupt and get away with it. Crispin was so full of shit, but he could talk the talk. He had everyone fooled. Lewis left the conference early. He lit a cigarette on the steps of the institute but was promptly told to move on by one of the security guards. He did as he was told and, as luck would have it, found himself outside the cancer institute a few yards along. Genial.

Crispin Humphries made a phone call to Gad Dayan after the conference.

"I think Lewis Thomas knows about my patients. He was asking some questions. I thought you should know."

"Crispin, relax. We are aware of the situation. We are dealing with it."

"How? What happens if he finds out about the complications?"

"Crispin, the situation has been contained. Please concentrate on recruiting more patients and leave this to us.

Mr Thomas will not be stopping the programme. We continue as usual."

"Fine, but I thought you'd better know."

"Thank you, Crispin. Goodbye."

CHAPTER 16

Harry was awoken by the sound of the door to his cell opening again. His hood was pulled off and Harry squinted as his eyes readjusted to the lighting. A distinct putrid smell of urine sticking to his skin. The two abductors had taken their balaclavas off. Harry had seen enough police dramas to know that this was not a good sign. He began to panic, whimpering and crying and repeating that he would do anything to make things right again. His eyes like soulless wells overflowed with water. Tears fused with snot, sweat and grime as they rolled down his broken and hysterical face. "Shh, shh… Harry, don't worry. You are going to make things right. We know…" one of the abductor's spoke softly. Harry was so petrified that he couldn't see straight. He tried to identify the man's face, but it multiplied into several floating heads which seemed to swirl around like a cloud of smoke in front of him. A solid gold chain dangled around his neck. As he lent forward, it swayed from side to side like a pendulum; some kind of cruel allusion to a time bomb. The other abductor grabbed Harry and forced him to stretch out his arm.

"Hold still!" He barked, before he injected something into his arm. The injection had its desired effect almost immediately. Harry's head lolled forward. Darkness encroached. He felt as if he were being sucked into a black hole. Just before he fell unconscious, he could have sworn he heard a strange, undulating voice say something about prepping him for surgery. The words seemed to merge into deep, whale-like moans. Harry was engulfed by the howls and the shadows. His mind came to a halt and then there was nothing.

Harry was taken to a mobile operating theatre. It was small and unremarkable from the outside, attached to a cab at the front where medical gases were stored. Within, however, the theatre was equipped with state-of-the-art medical technology. There was an anaesthetic machine on one side and a dedicated area for the patient to recover on the other. The only people required are a surgeon, and a patient, of course. The surgeon would just need to insert an endotracheal tube connected to the anaesthetic machine into the patient, used to inflate the lungs with oxygen. The anaesthetic machine calculated all the necessary variables of the patient such as body weight, height and length of surgery through artificial intelligence. Once connected to the patient, the machine's monitoring system would then continually react to their changing physiology. Perfect for an illegal operation. Drug cartels have been using these mobile operating theatres for some time. They are ideal for helping their most essential, non-disposable gang members. Gangs use them for reconstructive plastic surgery of the face on the most wanted criminals, for abortions, for female genital mutilation, and occasionally, for trauma, such as removing a bullet or debris from a wound.

On this occasion, someone was using it for brain surgery.

Harry was asleep. The endotracheal tube had been inserted into his trachea and a tiny portion of his hair had been removed from his right frontal area. The surgeon made a small skin incision about an inch long. He stopped the bleeding with a small self-retaining retractor, used to generate pressure on the wound edges. Harry was a lucky boy. The first-ever Brainionic 'Twist Drill Electric Stimulator' was going to be used on him. It was their latest development. The Superstim Version 1, they called it. The project in which Harry had found himself was called 'Live Human Testing'. The surgeon pressed the device into Harry's skull and delivered the stimulation disc, placing it perfectly on the surface of his brain. The surgeon finally closed the wound with metal staples. Harry was transferred under sedation to a hotel room to recover rather than being left in the mobile theatre. His captors chained his arms and legs to the bed. This wasn't entirely necessary - this little weakling wasn't going anywhere. The surgeon just wanted to. He thought it might give him a little more standing in the company if the experiment was successful. He liked to flex his power too.

It took a couple of days for Harry's system to be fully free of the sedatives. Harry drifted in and out of consciousness for some time before being able to maintain any level of alertness. He gathered he was in some sort of hotel apartment but couldn't see any clues pointing to his actual whereabouts. He heard car horns beeping and a general city clamour and ruckus in the distance. The curtains were drawn closed. His body felt stiff, his spine solid like a block of wood beneath him. He tried to lift his head, but it triggered a shooting pain around the top right of his head. He instinctively tried to raise his hands to caress the area, but his wrists snagged on handcuffs. The cuffs had been secured so tightly that they were cutting into his flesh. On moving his hands, another pain throbbed in his right fist. The memory of being stabbed in the back of his hand came rushing back to him. Harry wanted to cry but the tears wouldn't come. He was so dehydrated, so drained. The thought crossed his mind that he wanted to die. He wanted to give up.

Harry managed to lift his head high enough to look down the length of his body towards the end of the bed. He had been given a urinary catheter which was attached to a urine bag. The balloon of the catheter was inflated and fast becoming another source of unbearable pain. Harry knew that these balloons are used to stop the catheter from being displaced out of the bladder. He had put these things into older men's bladders in his first urology placement as a medical student. He realised what the problem was and feebly asked the now masked assailant if he could have a syringe to deflate the balloon and remove the catheter. The pressure of the inflated balloon made him feel like he desperately needed to urinate. The insertion of a urinary catheter is one of the most rewarding actions any doctor can perform on a man when he is writhing around in agony with urinary retention due to a large prostate gland.

The assailant pointed a gun at his head and put a finger to his mouth, signalling for Harry to shut up. Harry curled back into himself. The assailant picked up his walkie-talkie and left the room briefly. He soon returned with a small syringe and threw it at Harry. The assailant uncuffed Harry long enough to let him attach the syringe to the port of the catheter and withdraw the saline that was inflating the balloon. There was a bit of a sting, but he managed to remove the catheter. Urine dribbled out of the end of his penis. It felt much better. He was swiftly re-cuffed.

As Harry drifted back off to sleep, he thought about his recent paid work placement. He worked as a nursing assistant in a care home for ex-servicemen to earn some money. He never told anyone that he was studying to be a doctor to try to blend in. Harry was always the one on sluice duties. The sluice was the place where you emptied all the effluents from the patients. No one wanted to do this job, so it always fell to the temporary personnel. One time, he was helping one of the stroke patients who was paralysed down one side of his body and couldn't speak. The man just grunted.

One of the other nurses pointed out that he needed to urinate and asked if Harry could get him on a commode. A commode is a chair with a hole in the seating area. You remove the plastic pull-out tray in the middle when the patient has finished their business. Harry fetched the commode and managed to manoeuvre the man into position by standing him up, pulling his trousers down and sitting him on the commode so he could urinate into it. When he was done, Harry tried to remove the plastic tray underneath, but it was catching on something. The old man was grunting every time Harry tried to remove it. After the fourth attempt, Harry realised that the reason he couldn't remove the tray was that the poor old man's testicles had been dangling down into the tray and getting caught. Harry should have stood him up first before removing the tray but instead, he was smashing his testicles against it. This man had survived two world wars, only to have his balls battered by Harry. Harry was mortally devastated. What he had just experienced felt like some kind of karmic, rough justice.

The door opened. Another figure came in wearing black with two lightning bolt symbols on the lapel. He was also wearing a black fabric hood to mask his face. Harry figured it must be someone from Brainionics. "Harry, you're a clever boy." He spoke. "Unfortunately, too clever. What's it like being involved in one of the most exciting experiments in the history of medicine?"

The man held a smartphone in his hand. He typed something into the device and within a few seconds there seemed to be a faint buzz in Harry's ear. It felt like a switch had been flicked on. The figure signalled to the guard who then proceeded to remove the handcuffs.

"Harry, I want you to get on all fours and bark like a dog," said the man.

Harry looked at him blankly unsure of what to do. Were they really going to make him act like a dog at gunpoint? This couldn't be real. Suddenly, there was an intense searing pain behind the back of his eyes which swept down his neck. The pain continued down through his torso into his testicles and then back up to the centre of the head. Harry screamed for it to stop, cupping his head in his hands and falling to his knees on the floor. It stopped. The man laughed.

"Harry, I want you to get on all fours and bark like a dog."

Poor Harry, still reeling from the pain he had experienced, got on all fours and started to bark like a dog.

"Thank you. Now stop. I want you to lick the boots of that man over there." He pointed to the guard. It felt as if someone had poured acid over Harry's body. A rancid, acidic smell filled his nostrils, and he suddenly felt the need to either vomit or have diarrhoea. Harry crawled over to the guard and began to lick his boots. The guard hovered over Harry, shaking his head. He kicked Harry away, lifting his boot and giving his shoulder a forceful shove. The man with the device lifted his phone, meeting Harry's gaze as he did so.

"Please, no! What do you want me to do? Whatever I did, I'm sorry!" Harry cried out, terrified to be inflicted with the same pain again. He would rather be stabbed in the back of his hand again, over and over, than experience whatever that device was capable of. The man touched a button on his phone. The putrid smell returned. It made Harry think of rotting corpses. There was a pause. And then, pain. Harry's entire body convulsed in agony; a splitting, tearing, burning, stabbing, aching pain all at once. Harry thought he might die. He wished for it. This sadistic, uniformed monster had only just begun.

When Lewis arrived home later that evening, the door of his house was unlatched. He prodded the door with his finger and it slowly creaked open, revealing a dark empty hallway. He stood in the doorway, trying to see if he could hear anything or anyone in the building. His heartrate rocketed in his chest; the rhythmic pounding reverberating throughout his body. He took a step inside, waiting another moment there to listen. Lewis could throw a good punch but if there was an armed intruder, he'd be fucked. He debated calling the police.

"Hello?" he called out, half-expecting someone to shout back from within the darkness. He must have been stood in the entrance for about ten minutes when he finally decided there was no threat. He switched the hallway light on and hung up his coat. He'd been spending too much time thinking about detective mysteries and murders that he'd scared himself silly. He had probably just forgotten to lock the door before leaving that morning.

He made his way to the kitchen where he stopped short. There, on the kitchen table, was a picture of him in his office with Deborah on her knees, giving him a blow job. It had a note made from cut out newspaper graphics on the front. Two sentences read: 'STOP NOW BEFORE ITS TOO LATE. WE

KNOW ABOUT EVERYTHING.'

"Fuck!"

Someone had been in his house. Someone knew about him and Deborah. He didn't know which was worse. His gut was urgently telling him that Humphries' last conversation with him had something to do with this. Deborah had repeatedly tried to stop him from interfering. Did she have something to do with this? But then, why put a picture of herself giving him a blow job? It would incriminate her too, wouldn't it? He realised there must be a hidden camera in his office, and someone must be watching him. Was his phone bugged too? It must be Crispin and his connections, he concluded. He still hadn't spoken to Harry about the message he received from him late the night before. He wanted to call him back but feared someone may still be watching him. He went down to his basement and lit a cigarette to think. After three cigarettes and an espresso, he left his phone at the house, picked up the photograph, put on his motorbike gear and headed to Notting Hill Gate Police Station. He had to do something.

Lewis spoke to the Duty Officer about the break-in and was eventually put through to DS Smyth. DS Smyth told Lewis to calm down and that he would look into it. Lewis still felt incredibly anxious. He was just about to call Harry in the safety of the Police Station when a text came through from him.

I've got some information on Crispin. He is not using Brainionic implants. Will catch up soon, hope all is well. Nothing else interesting here, I'm afraid. Harry.

Oh, well, at least Harry is all right. He thought.

Harry was still in the hotel room. He was now unchained. This was more representative of his lack of freedom than being less restricted. He wouldn't dare do anything now he knew the kind of pain they could inflict on him.

"Harry, you have some work to do for us to repay the damage you have caused by hacking our site and interfering with Crispin. Did you think we wouldn't find you? It's straightforward. If you don't do what we ask, then Hell will feel like paradise compared to the pain you will endure. Do you understand?"

"Yes."

"Do you have any questions?" Harry's spirit was broken.

"No."

"Oh, Harry. This won't do, would you like to feel happiness?"

Harry didn't know what to do or say. "Yes?" he replied tentatively.

The figure tapped on his smartphone. Harry experienced the most hilarious sensory overload and couldn't help but burst out laughing. He looked at the guard and laughed even louder.

"You like it? Harry?"

Harry laughed so much it started to hurt his sides; he was finding it difficult to breathe. The figure tapped his phone again. Excruciating pain jolted through his entire being; tears of laughter turned to tears of extreme pain. Harry was screaming again. The figure was puppeteering Harry, now their little plaything. Harry realised that these fuckers had got him and there was nothing he could do. Was this to be his life forever?

"So, Harry. This is the deal." The figure continued to

explain Harry's new responsibilities. "I think we have convinced you that we can turn on the pain you have experienced everywhere in your body from anywhere in the world. We will be watching and listening to you. When you sleep, eat, shit, talk, fuck… we will know. If you make a mistake, we will hurt you. If you betray us, we will hurt you more. Not enough to kill you though, just enough to make you wish you were dead."

Harry completely understood. The fear and anxiousness about getting another shot of pain started the Pavlov dog response. He was pre-empting the pain and broke out in a sweat. He just nodded his head. The man handed him a baseball cap.

"Wear this until the scar has healed." Harry put the cap on. "Back to medical school tomorrow, Harry! We will be giving you instructions in due course. When people ask you where you have been, you will say you have been working on a project for Mr Thomas. Here are some documents that have most of Mr Humphries' patients on. Give it to Mr Thomas, understood?" Harry nodded again. "Okay, Harry. Just one more thing." Harry stopped to look at the figure. The man removed his mask. A gold chain swung loose around his neck and glinted. Harry looked at the man's face and instantly recognised him. He let his mouth fall open as it dawned on him who he was.

"You're the—" His words were cut short. Pain ripped through his body. "Don't forget, Harry." The pain ceased.

The guards escorted Harry blindfolded into a car and took him back to his flat. When they had gone, Harry collapsed in a heap on the floor surrounded by the smashed-up, shattered remnants of his previous life.

DS Smyth travelled to meet Lewis. The police had already come to inspect the alleged break-in and make a statement. Lewis had given a policeman the warning note but kept the picture of him and Deborah tucked into his pocket. The police officers had briefed DS Smyth about the break-in but confessed that, since there was not any real evidence suggesting an act of intrusion, there wasn't anything further they could do. DS Smyth suggested that Lewis and he meet back at the police station the next day. They both sat down with a cup of tea.

"Lewis, what's the problem?"

"As you know, there's been an intruder in my home and, apart from the warning note, there was some, err..." Lewis hesitated. "Well, a picture of a medical student giving me a blow job in my office at work."

DS Smyth spluttered on his tea. "Wow, that's not good. Have you any idea who you think may have done this?"

"Well, it might be a coincidence, but I was at a conference with Mr Crispin Humphries earlier today. I told him that I knew he was putting in stimulators for stroke patients. He didn't take it well. The next thing I know, I get that warning note." He continued. "I trust you, and that's why I wanted to see you. I know the Taylor case is closed, but there is something not quite right about any of this. Harry has uncovered a company called Brainionics based in Israel. He emailed me some information about Crispin and Brainionics the night before last and then, out of the blue, went back on himself and said that Crispin wasn't involved with them. Do you not think that's suspicious? I haven't managed to speak to him since."

DS Smyth put a finger to his mouth and then started chatting to him about work. "So, how is saving lives and making people walk again going?" Lewis, bemused, watched as DS Smyth began to pat him down, checking around his neck and inspecting his jacket and trousers. "All clear. I was just making sure you haven't got any bugging devices on you."

"It's okay. I left my phone at home." Lewis was chuffed with himself. He nearly smashed his phone like they did in the movies to avoid being tracked by GPS, but then panicked that he wouldn't be able to get hold of Deborah.

"Who is Harry?" asked DS Smyth.

"Well, that's another thing. Harry is a medical student. I asked him to do some digging for me. He sent me a text giving me some information about Crispin and a company called Brainionics—"

"Lewis, there are other ways to track someone other than just with their phone." DS Smyth interrupted. "If they are serious, they will know you are speaking to me right now. What I want to know is why the hell you thought spying on someone was a good idea? Can you leave the investigations to us, please? Where is this, Harry? We may need to talk to him."

"Yes, I know. I'm sorry. I just… I just don't trust Crispin," Lewis replied, disappointed that DS Smyth didn't acknowledge his detective skills. "I haven't heard from Harry. I only know his first name but I'm sure I can find out about him from the medical school."

"I understand how you feel about Crispin, but we don't have enough evidence to challenge him at the moment. Look Lewis, I think we can probably take things from here. I'll need to talk to the Chief Inspector about getting some surveillance on you for the time being, just to be safe."

Lewis pressed on relentlessly. "I just thought it was strange that the mortuary lost the stimulator and suddenly found it. Don't you?"

DS Smyth sighed in agreement. "I did too, Lewis. Last time we spoke you mentioned something about a strange logo on the stimulator from Mike Taylor's implant? Well, I spoke to Dr Davies and he said he doesn't recall mentioning any strange logo on the stimulator to you at all."

"He's lying! He definitely mentioned the stimulator had a lightning strike on it." Lewis demonstrated.

"Lewis, that is impossible. Dr Davies is a trusted and well experienced pathologist, there must just be some confusion. There is no reason why he would hide this information. Now we have found the stimulator, we can confirm, it is only implanted in America, so Humphries isn't your man."

"I'm not being overly suspicious, but there is something odd going on, I know it. Someone is trying to stop me finding out what's really going on."

DS Smyth continued. "As you say, although we can't be certain, someone may be trying to stop you from investigating this. It may help if you use your phone to let someone know that you are no longer looking into this. Hopefully, that will throw them off the scent and the threats will stop. Let us do the rest."

"Who do you suggest I phone?" asked Lewis.

"I would start with this girl in the picture. Whoever took this," he said, pointing to the image, "is likely to have been involved in scaring you off."

"Right. Yes, good shout."

"Also, Lewis, one last thing. Please stay out of trouble."

"I'll try." Lewis left the police station.

As he was walking, Lewis felt increasingly paranoid. Everyone walking by seemed to be looking at him suspiciously. The market sellers on Portobello Road, the beggars on the street, even the jolly tourists suddenly looked mistrustful. A Japanese man stepped in front of him and took Lewis's picture.

"Back off, you fucker!" Lewis shouted, putting his hands up in front of his face.

The man looked shocked and confused. He gestured for Lewis to move as he was in the way of one of the antique shops. The confused tourist only wanted to take a picture of the shopfront. Lewis realised how ridiculous he was being and apologised to the man. He continued to walk back to his house with his head down.

When he got home, he made a phone call to Deborah as advised by the DS Smyth.

"Hi, Debs, I just had to go to the police station as there was a break-in at home. They've said that there's been a spate of burglaries in the neighbourhood. They're in the process of investigating them."

Deborah was quiet on the phone. "Right." She eventually replied, thinking Lewis was speaking in a strange tone to her.

"Listen, I think it's best that we just keep it cool for a while. I've got a lot going on at the moment and you were right about the Crispin thing. I was foolish to get involved. I don't think we can go down that route any more. I won't be involved any more."

"Hang on, Lewis. I'm confused. Are you dumping me?" He had already told her that he was giving up on the Crispin connection, that much she knew. But wanting to keep things casual was news to her and came as a harsh slap in the face.

"No, Deborah. I'm just saying that I don't want to get you into trouble. I mean, with medical school and all that…" Lewis was rambling. He was making a complete mess of his first chance at a solid relationship in years. Typical. He didn't want to tell her that someone had taken a photograph of them together. He was trying to let whoever was bugging him — if indeed they were bugging or tracking him — think that he was off the Crispin connection.

"Fine. You know what, Lewis? You're a twat. Go fuck yourself." Deborah hung up.

That went well, Lewis thought to himself. He didn't expect that reaction but, then again, he didn't expect any of this to happen. Hopefully, someday soon, he would be able to explain everything properly to her.

CHAPTER 17

At the Brainionic's headquarters in Israel, Gad Dayan received a phone call. The voice on the phone informed him that the first Superstim had been implanted successfully in a human subject. Apparently, it was a complete success. Dayan was furious. The heat was still on in the UK. As one case closed, another one could open up.

"Who put this in?" he demanded.

A low voice on the phone replied. "It was Agent 14."

"That man needs to be stopped! How dare he do this without my permission? Right. Keep a close eye on the subject and make sure no one knows about this. We will track and monitor him from the headquarters."

He was fully aware of the implications of neuromodulation and how it could impact society. The company needed more clinical studies. It was the beginning of what could be one of the greatest advances in medicine. Dayan had convinced the investors that their returns would be generous once the technology had been proven successful. He had given Professor Santos free rein with medical resources and finances to explore behavioural neuromodulation by whatever means he felt appropriate. Professor Santos' already dwindling morality was no match for the potential personal gain offered by this new technology.

Professor Santos was, incidentally, also aware of the

news. After all, unbeknown to Dayan, it was Santos himself that had ordered Agent 14 to put the stimulator into Harry. Everything had gone according to plan, but the stimulator still needed to be perfected. It could modulate pain, but it needed to modulate other functions of the brain too. He would need some expert help from someone he could trust. He would also need someone who shared similar ambitions to himself. He made an unannounced visit to London to meet with Crispin Humphries.

As Lori entered the room with Professor Santos, Crispin was shocked to see the Professor in his clinic.

"Pedro!" He exclaimed and went over to hug him. "Lori, thanks. Can you bring us some coffee please?"

After the usual pleasantries, Santos got down to business. "Crispin, I have some excellent news. We have had our first successful behavioural neuromodulation case! I am going to persuade the Brainionics board to give the go-ahead for more patients. I want you to come to Brazil and work with me for a few months."

Crispin was dumbfounded. He was simultaneously flattered and disquieted by the offer. "But Professor, I can't simply leave my position here. My practice will flounder! I would also have to speak to my NHS managers."

"Crispin, I'm not talking about forever, it would just be for a few months. You can ask for a sabbatical for two to three months, that would suffice. Regarding your practice, once you have worked with me, it will be even bigger! Crispin, this is going to be an amazing opportunity for you."

Santos could see that Crispin was apprehensive and would need some convincing. Santos was no stranger to blackmail.

219

He licked his lips. "I don't want to beg you, Crispin, but after all the support I have given you, I am now asking for you to help me."

Crispin was trying to make sense of the logistics in his head. He knew that, ultimately, he didn't have much choice. Santos knew too much about him. He could ruin his career with just a click of his fingers. It wasn't necessarily that he had that much power at Brainionics, but that he knew enough people to smite Crispin if he so wished.

"Okay, Professor," Crispin assented. "I guess I will set the wheels in motion. I need to give a few weeks' notice to the hospital unless I can find a replacement for my NHS work."

"Okay, Crispin. I think I have just the person." Santos handed him the name of a surgeon he knew on a piece of paper. "I hope to hear from you soon. I will make the arrangements for your arrival in San Paulo. I'm sorry I can't stay longer. I have some unfinished business to attend to. I bid you farewell." With that, Santos left.

Crispin felt uncomfortable at the prospect of leaving everything behind and going off to work in San Paulo. However, if behavioural neuromodulation really could be developed, it would be Nobel Prize-winning work! Regardless of procuring the biggest scientific award on the planet, there would be a pot of gold at the end of it all too. Of course, he didn't need the money. He sure liked it, though. Not only would he get a hefty cash prize from his share in Brainionics if the project paid off, but patients would kill to be treated by him. He almost drooled at the possibility. Crispin caught his reflection in the window and smiled. He began to pace up and down his office, imagining what he would say when receiving his Nobel Prize.

"Thank you, thank you!" he said to an imaginary audience. "Please, oh… a standing ovation? Oh! And roses too? My, my!"

It took him a few moments to notice that Lori was stood in the doorway watching him. Crispin jumped back, covering himself as if he'd been caught
in the nude. "Lori! You must knock first!"

"Sorry, Mr Humphries. I was just bringing the coffee in…"

"Ah, yes. Of course. He already left."

"Oh, I see. Well, I'll just… be on my way."

"Yes. Please. Thank you."

Lori awkwardly closed the door behind her. Crispin composed himself. He unfolded the piece of paper that Santos had pressed into his hand. He knew he would have to convince his NHS employers that the sabbatical was necessary. Crispin then wondered what unfinished business Santos had to sort in the UK. Was he recruiting other surgeons for the company? Hopefully not. Crispin laughed out loud. Bah, nobody could replace me anyway…

Professor Santos was actually on his way to the hospital where Lewis worked. He had an appointment with someone who worked there.

Harry, as promised, went back to medical school. He turned up to his statistics lecture wearing his baseball cap. He spotted Deborah sat in the front row. He had never seen her attend a lecture before. While she was pleased to see him, anger was written across her face.

"Where the fuck have you been, Harry!?" Deborah asked protectively but in a hushed voice.

Before Harry could muster his response, the lecturer began the session. "Now, I know you all think statistics is boring! But, let me tell you that every ground-breaking clinical study needs them." The lecturer had a tendency to emphasise random words in his sentence to reinforce his point. It didn't work. It just made him sound ridiculous. "I want you, young medics, to be able to look at the evidence critically, and for that, you need a knowledge of statistics!" he droned on, telling the students how his subject was for the most intelligent amongst them implying that those who "didn't get it" were lacking the required brain cells.

Every specialist thinks his clinical area is the most important whether you are a gastroenterologist, neurologist, surgeon or gynaecologist. There is an unspoken hierarchy in medicine; hospital doctors claim to be more superior than family doctors while surgeons claim to be more important than medics.

Deborah nudged Harry in the ribs and asked again. "Don't ignore me, Harry. What happened to you?"

"I got some information on Crispin Humphries. I had to go undercover for a while, I'm sorry."

"Undercover? You're kidding me. Is that why you look like dog shit?"

"Yep, thanks for that."

"I cannot believe you got yourself involved in such a thing. Bloody Lewis Thomas." She scowled.

The statistics lecturer could see them chatting and became a little agitated. "Ah, you two! At the back there! Do you have something you would like to share? Tell me, which clinical paper has made an impact on you?"

Deborah responded without hesitation. "Sorry, Sir, we

were just discussing the clinical impact of the Nobski et al. paper."

The lecturer looked slightly confused. "Eh? Not sure I know that one."

Deborah spoke with confidence. "Oh, really? It's a well-known paper about the length of scrubbing up and the number of bacteria on the hands." Lewis had told her the story about the infection control police and what he said to the nurse. Lewis said to her that if people keep quoting it, the fictional Nobski paper will be ingrained in hearsay.

"Right, well there you go. I hope there are some good statistics in that study and if there aren't, it's not worth the paper it's written on."

The two refrained from talking for the remainder of the lecture. When it was over, Deborah grabbed Harry's frail wrist and led him outside to the university courtyard, worried he would try and escape before talking to her.

"Harry, I want you to drop this Crispin thing. It's not right that this Mr Thomas has got you involved. I don't know who he thinks he is. I want you to stop it immediately!"

Harry was looking at the floor, nudging a dropped pen with his shoe.

"What is it, Harry? Do you want to tell me something? Has someone done something to you?"

"No, Deborah. It's okay. I got the impression that you and Mr Thomas were very close, I know it was you who got me to watch the aneurysm operation. You know… I thought that I would be the only one doing a neurosurgical placement. I hadn't been informed that I'd need to share the experience with anyone else."

"Oh? Well, lots of placements are shared. Maybe there

was an admin error or something."

"Maybe." Harry went silent. He felt uneasy talking to Deborah. He felt like any wrong move or word could end in excruciating pain. "Well, Lewis dumped me anyway. It's over."

"I'm sorry about that, Debs."

Deborah was touched. It was the first time she had heard Harry call her Debs. He looked so sad, so unsettled. She wanted to reach out and hug him. Harry desperately wanted to tell Deborah about his ordeal, but he knew that if he did, he would pay for it later. He kept having flashbacks about the pain and the darkness, the putrid smell and the humiliation. He felt nauseous.

"Yeah, I'm okay about it. It was sweet while it lasted. It was partly my fault anyway... I shouldn't have got involved in the first place. Anyway, Harry. This is coming from my heart. My advice is to give that damn file back to Mr Thomas and to put a lid on this thing." As Deborah was talking, Harry became distracted. This was the first time he had properly looked at Deborah's face. She looked familiar, like he had seen her recently or, at least, somewhere outside of Med School and the hospital. "Harry... Harry?"

"Wait, what?"

"I said, what happened to your hand?"

"Oh..." Harry looked down at the bandage. "I cut it by accident. Silly me. Listen, Deborah, I've got to go. Thanks for the advice." Harry walked away, hunching his shoulders as if trying to disappear into himself. He shoved his bandaged hand into his pocket, out of sight.

"But... wait, Harry!" Deborah called after him. A few other students stopped and looked at her, curious to know what the fuss was about. Deborah watched Harry disappear into the crowd of students.

Crispin Humphries had made an appointment with one of the clinical directors at his hospital. In reality, he hardly worked there. The management offices were in an old nurses' home. In the heyday of the NHS, student nurses and medical students had their accommodation paid for. They worked hard and probably shagged harder. Since the massive increase in hospital managers, the nursing accommodation has slowly transformed into management offices. He walked past a long line of rooms: Performance Management Suite, Human Resources, Risk Management, Compliance Officer, Mandatory Training Office, Organisational Development, Facilities Manager, Appraisals Team, Workforce Officer… there was a position for everything. Crispin, like most doctors, didn't know what they all did, but he thought that they must be important as they all had their own chilled water containers. Funnily enough, they looked like the ones that had been taken from the wards and general medical staff rooms.

Crispin eventually found the Executive Office Suite. This was where the top dog managers lived. The door to the Executive Suite was locked, and he had to phone one of the PAs to let him in. He knocked on the clinical director's door and entered. He was sat behind an even larger mahogany desk than Crispin had in his private clinic. Crispin was a little envious. The director was an anaesthetist but, due to his managerial duties, hardly ever went to anaesthetise patients any more. Rumour had it that it wasn't unusual for some of his patients to start moving during surgery. It was even rumoured that a couple of his patients had even been aware of the whole procedure. The senior managers liked him though, so they had essentially groomed him to be a clinical manager and then a clinical director.

"Crispin, great to meet you. I see you're doing some great work," said the director. Of course, he had no idea what Crispin Humphries did. When looking at their staff, all most managers saw was a report sheet showing the number of breaches they had made from the government targets. Crispin knew that he would look good on paper. He had given his NHS secretary his login details. It was her that completed his mandatory training, so his reports were sparkling.

"Lovely to meet you, Dr McPherson. Thank you for your kind words. I do try my best. The reason I am here is that I need to ask you a big favour. Do you think I could have a sabbatical for two to three months?"

"I'm sure we can work something out. What do you plan to do about your clinics and waiting list? You know this will be a non-paid sabbatical?"

"I'm aware of this, yes. I would like to gain some more experience with the world-renowned neurosurgeon Professor Santos in San Paulo. I think the research that he is doing has great potential. If I could spend some time learning about his work, I think I could get better results for this hospital, and in turn, improve its profile…" Crispin watched the director's face. "And your profile too!" he quickly added. Crispin knew how to turn on the charm. "I will organise a locum to cover my clinical duties; in fact, I will happily pay for the locum to ensure the clinics and waiting lists are covered."

"Well, that is a compelling case, Crispin." A clinician who not only wants to save the Trust money but wants to improve the hospital with his ground-breaking research? This man must be a superhero in disguise, he thought to himself. "Okay, Crispin, you're on. I will give you permission providing you can find a locum to replace you for the three months and pay for it."

"Many thanks, Dr McPherson. You have my word. I will be in touch soon."

Crispin left the office and instantly phoned the man Professor Santos had suggested during their meeting.

"Hello?" Mr Afghani answered with a thick, middle-eastern accent. "Mr Afghani? This is Mr Crispin Humphries."

"Mr Humphries! The one and only! How are you? How did you get my number?" replied Afghani.

"Yes, fantastic! I hope you are well too. I actually received your number from Professor Santos. I believe you know him? I need a locum and he suggested I contact you." Locums are doctors who do not have a permanent post at any particular clinic or hospital. Some doctors are happy with locum work as their hourly rates are dramatically more than their permanent colleague counterparts'. They don't have any real responsibility though; they come in, do a shift, submit their timesheet, get paid and then leave. The downside for them is that they have to move from one department to another, often around the country too, so they never have a workplace to call home. They are nomads of the medical world, so to speak. "How about a locum in neurosurgery at my hospital for three months?" Crispin couldn't be bothered to beat around the bush.

"Depends on the pay." said Afghani. Crispin liked his transparency.

"I'll ensure you have £50,000 for the three months if you can start within the next two weeks."

"Make it £60,000 and I'm in. I have to give two weeks' notice on my current job, you see, and they wanted me to carry on for another month." He lied. He wasn't currently employed by another hospital. He had just finished a locum position in general surgery at the same hospital that Lewis worked at across the Thames.

"Okay, deal." Crispin wasn't worried about the money at all. Although it appeared as if it was coming from his account, the payment would come from Brainionics. "If you get your references and documents together, I will inform HR. We will need to go through a formal interview process which I can set up next week. Of course, there won't be any other candidates…"

"Excellent. I look forward to working for you."

CHAPTER 18

Brainionics had installed a tracking system on Harry's phone. Harry received a text message from an anonymous number.

Keep the camera on the phone exposed at all times.

Harry was still half in denial about everything that had happened to him. Part of him wanted to believe it was all a bad dream or that he'd fallen and cut his hand and head. Maybe he had been concussed? Or there had been some other head trauma that was making him remember weird things that had never really happened? He couldn't live in fear for the rest of his life. He put the phone in the fridge with shaking hands in the hope that it would dampen the phone signals. Maybe, just maybe, it wasn't real.

He went to make himself a cup of tea in the kitchenette. As he flicked the kettle on, something within him switched on too. Within moments, Harry was crippled by that same searing pain that scored through his body; the burning of his skin, the acrid smell, the deep, stabbing sensation in every sinew of his body. Harry spontaneously defaecated and urinated. The whole experience lasted less than 5 seconds, but it felt like an eternity of the most horrific torture. He retrieved the phone from the fridge. The screen displayed the very same image of skull and crossbones that his computer had when he was caught hacking into the Brainionics system.

Once, Harry had visited a torture museum where he saw some of the most unimaginably horrendous pieces of equipment. There was the thumbscrew, for example, which penetrated slowly and deeply into the thumbnail and the flesh beneath with every turn; the rack, which dislocated the limbs of the body, tearing the muscles and ligaments apart. One device in particular caught his attention. The victim was placed in a crouched position over a pyramid-like contraption with a sharp spike at the top. As their hands and legs were tied together, if the victim faltered from the position, the sharp end would slice their rectum. As they were chained all day and all night, when fatigue arose, they had no choice but to impale themselves on the sharp spike. The torturers could claim that they had not inflicted the injuries because, technically, they hadn't forced the victim to sit down. They would say that it was God's will. At the time, Harry had tried to imagine what it would be like to experience such pain. Now, he understood.

Harry obediently turned the phone on and put a few tissues at the base of his shirt pocket so that the camera of the smartphone was exposed.

"That's a good boy." A computerised voice spoke out from his phone. The phone was now the eyes and ears of Harry's thoughts.

Harry had just about recovered from the assault on his senses. The burnt flesh-like smell in the air was exchanged by the stench of faecal matter wafting up from his trousers.

"Harry, we are here to help you. Listen to us and all will be fine." The computerised voice spoke again. It was a cold and mechanical inhumane voice. Harry thought for a moment that the voice may have just been in his head. There was nobody else there, so how could he be sure that the phone had actually spoken? He felt like he was losing his mind. Harry was a prisoner in his own body.

Things seemed to have returned to normal for Lewis. Although the police were still keeping an eye on him, he was doing pretty well. He had been working hard to curb his late-night drinking when he was on call and had started to do yoga most evenings. By yoga, that meant two minutes of stretching and a meditative wank before bed. His mobile phone rang. It was Harry.

"Mr Thomas, I wonder if we could meet? I have some information about Mr Humphries."

"Harry, are you alright? No one knew where you were. I've had a few problems myself. You don't sound okay, are you?"

Harry ignored Lewis' questions. "Can I give you a file that I completed?"

Lewis thought Harry might be dealing with other issues and didn't push his interrogation further. "Sure, head on over to my house this evening. I'll phone if I need to go into the hospital as I'm on-call." As he said that, a No ID caller came through. It was usually the hospital.

"Harry, I've got another call coming through. I think it's the hospital calling. I'm going to hang up, but I will text you later if we can meet. If not, I can see you at the hospital if I have to go in?"

"Okay, thanks, Mr Thomas."

"You're welcome."

Lewis accepted the call on his phone. "Mr Thomas, it's David here. Are you on call tonight?"

Lewis, wanted to say: "Yes, of course I'm on call, you twat. That's why you're calling me." But, instead, replied more civilly with: "Yes, I'm on call, David. What's the problem?"

"Well, it's been a particularly busy day and a forty-three-year-old female solicitor who is married with three children suddenly lost her sight and—"

"David!" Lewis snapped. "Get to the point! What does the bloody scan show?" David, as always, was trying to be some great orator. It would seem that he often forgot he was living in real life, not in some TV hospital drama.

"I was getting to that, Mr Thomas. She's had a CT scan, but it's normal. I spoke to the radiology registrar to suggest an MRI scan, but they refuse to do it."

It was not uncommon for the radiologists to refuse scans. Scans cost a lot of money. If a junior doctor has no idea why their patient might need a scan, a radiologist is not going to give them the green light. Another reason, however, is that radiologists simply don't want to have to come in at night. That was probably the case on this occasion.

"Okay. Have you got the number of the radiology registrar?" Lewis asked. David reeled off the number, but Lewis didn't have a pen. "Actually, David, can you text it to me? I agree she needs an MRI scan."

After an angry phone call from Lewis to the radiology registrar, the patient was booked in for an MRI scan that night. However, David, being David, decided that he could not wait for the porters to transfer the patient for her scan. At the hospital, David asked a nurse to urgently locate the porters.

"They will be on their way. I have called them." The nurse replied calmly.

"Ridiculous. They're taking too long. I may as well take

the patient down myself." The nurse wanted to object. She had only called the porters moments before and they were nearly always on time, if not a little early in her experience. She didn't have the energy to argue with David, though. It was too late at night and he was too ruthless.

David grabbed a trolley and rolled it towards the patient's bedside. David and the nurse transferred the woman onto the trolley and then proceeded to wheel her down the hospital corridor to the ground level where the radiology department was located. When they arrived, no one was at the reception, so David decided to get the patient on the machine himself to save time. As he entered the MRI scanner, he felt a force pulling him towards the MRI machine.

"Stop pushing the trolley!" he ordered the nurse.

"I'm not even holding it!" she replied.

With accelerating force, the trolley crashed into the MRI machine with a loud clang. David, in his ignorance, should have customarily transferred the patient to a special non-magnetic trolley before scanning. Unfortunately, David had brought a steel-framed trolley from the ward to an enormous powerful magnet. In between yells from the patient asking what the hell was going on, the nurse and David frantically fought to lever the trolley off the machine. Thank God the patient was blind. After about five minutes of huffing and puffing, they finally managed to drag the trolley and the patient away from the scanner, just in time to bump into the radiographer outside.

"What in the devil..." She began. She looked at David and the nurse, then at the trolley, and then back at the two of them again. "This is for the urgent MRI of the brain, right?" asked the radiographer.

The nurse and David nodded sheepishly. The patient was still demanding to know what all the noise and banging was about. David signed to the radiographer that she was a little crazy, rotating his index finger around the side of his head.

"Best be still, dear! We need to transfer you onto this trolley. Then don't move until we have done the scan, do you understand?" he said condescendingly slowly, as if explaining the process to a young child.

"I'm blind, not stupid!" she barked.

The scan showed that there was swelling around the back of the brain due to a blocked vein. It was causing a build-up of pressure and thus impacting the blood supply to the occipital lobe where the visual centres are. David phoned Lewis.

"Hi, Mr Thomas. Nothing neurosurgical here. I will transfer her to the neurology team to see if they will take her."

"Okay, David. All else quiet?"

"All quiet apart from the usual cauda equina patients queuing up in casualty, you know, the usual Googlers."

Google-ology seems to be a new branch of medicine where you don't need doctors, instead, you self-diagnose. Millions of people every year convince themselves they are seriously ill or even dying after using the internet to Google symptoms. Nine times out of ten, it's just a common cold or some back pain. Google-itis is the condition.

"Right. Well, keep it quiet if you can, David. Call me if you need me."

"Okay, will do." He replied.

After getting off of the phone to David, Lewis phoned Harry back.

"Harry, come around to my house. All is quiet on call. See

you here in about an hour?"

"Yes, Mr Thomas. Thank you."

When Harry arrived, he was wearing his baseball cap. He looked subdued and dishevelled. "Harry, you look like shit."

"I've been told."

"Everything okay?

"Yes, honestly. All good. This is the document I've compiled about Mr Humphries." Harry handed Lewis a typed manuscript about the patients and their outcomes. Lewis studied it. It all seemed reasonable. There was some documentation about outcome data. There didn't seem to be any complications.

"Where did you get this information, Harry?"

"I stole it from the Brainionics data system that I hacked."

"Harry, you have to stop this. Someone broke into my house yesterday." Harry could only guess who this may have been. "The project is over. I will hand this over to the police, but I'm pretty sure Mr Humphries was not the surgeon involved in the case of Mr Taylor." He continued. "Look, it's my fault, Harry, I shouldn't have got you involved in this at all."

Harry didn't want to accidentally say something he shouldn't. He wanted to leave as quickly as possible. "Well, I better be off now." He said with a vacant expression. Lewis could see that Harry's mind was elsewhere.

"Hang on a sec, Harry." Lewis wrote on a piece of paper and held it out to Harry with a pen to respond with.

Is everything okay? Are you being watched? I can help you.

Harry just looked at the paper. His eyes were vacuous, devoid of any warmth or emotion. "I'm fine, Mr Thomas. Just a bit tired. I fell off my bike, injuring my hand." He held his bandaged fist out in front of Lewis. "See? All good."

As Lewis was taller than Harry, he couldn't see his face as he spoke. Lewis intuitively whipped the baseball cap off of Harry's head, as if Harry were hiding answers beneath it. Although Lewis didn't know it then, how right he had been! Harry quickly snapped it back off of him and replaced it. He wasn't quite quick enough, though. Lewis clocked the small scar and bruising encompassing it. He wanted to assume it was from the biking accident, but he couldn't help but doubt Harry's story.

"I'm fine! Mr Thomas, really. I'm fine. Look, I need to go. Thank you."

"No thank you, Harry. I'm sorry I got you involved in this. Let's consider the project closed, okay? I'm happy to support you, and you can come to theatre at any time you want."

"I'm just doing my bit. Thanks for that."

Lewis watched Harry as he rode away on his bicycle. He went back into his flat and opened a bottle of red. Brain juice, he told himself. He needed to think.

CHAPTER 19

As Crispin Humphries was landing in San Paulo, his replacement, Mr Afghani, entered the operating theatre in the NHS hospital that Crispin worked at. There was a female neurosurgical registrar scrubbed up trying to be pleasant with him.

"Hello, Dr Afghani. My name is Rebecca, I'm one of the ST 8's." ST stood for Surgical Trainee, and she was in her eighth and final year, so fairly senior.

Afghani did not respect female surgeons. Women from his motherland were only allowed to be nurses; they were not encouraged to become doctors, let alone surgeons.

"What are you doing?" he asked abruptly, feeling no inclination to introduce himself in return. Rebecca tried to avoid looking at the dark chest hair sprouting out of the top of his scrubs. "It's one of Mr Humphries' long waiters, just a lumbar laminectomy." Rebecca responded coldly, reflecting Afghani's frosty demeanour back at him. She was used to Mr Humphries being an arrogant noodle, but he never spoke to her aggressively.

"Oh, I better get properly scrubbed in."

"I've nearly finished actually, but thank you!"

Crispin had made sure that only simple cases would be listed on Mr Afghani's surgical list. All of the more complex cases were to be transferred to another consultant's waiting list which, naturally, they were not happy about as they already had enough to do. They would also have to deal with a mob of outraged patients demanding to know why they were no longer going to be treated by Crispin the Great. Why isn't Mr Humphries doing my operation any more? They would ask. Because he doesn't give a shit about you and has fucked off to Brazil to make lots of money. The consultants dreamt of responding.

"It's okay." Afghani responded assertively. "I'm in charge of the patient, I better make sure this is done properly."

Mr Afghani started to scrub up. It took him so long that the scrub nurses began to wonder what he was doing. Mr Afghani, for some reason, had a noticeably high infection rate and he didn't want to give anyone the excuse that it was because of his scrubbing technique. Eventually, he made it back to the operating table.

"Excuse me, my dear. Let me take a look." He pushed the registrar out of the way, took the suction out of her hands and began to inspect her work.

"The nerves are still compressed." He spoke crisply. "We need to decompress them adequately or the patient will still have sciatica."

"Nurse, get me a drill." Some surgeons use a high-speed drill to remove the bone, especially hard bone, as decompressing it with normal rongeurs can cause blisters on the surgeons' hands. A rongeur is an instrument used for gouging out the bone. The circulating nurse went to find the drill and set it up. The drill was composed of a handpiece with a small 4mm burr attached to the end. Afghani lifted the drill and pressed the foot pedal to test it. It started whirring around at high speed. "Ah, now we are talking." Rebecca could not help but detect a sinister look in his eye as he held the device out in front of him. She wanted to remind him that the drill wasn't a toy, but held her tongue due to his seniority. Instead, she said, "I've never been allowed to use a drill on a laminectomy before. To be honest, Mr Afghani, it scares me using it next to the dura."

"Don't be silly, my girl." He responded obnoxiously. Hearing herself called my girl by Mr Afghani made Rebecca shudder. "I will show you how to use the drill."

Afghani started to drill into the bone near the exposed, soft water-filled sac of the spinal dura containing the nerve roots. Small bits of bone from the drill bit started to collect. He had the suction in his other hand. One would usually ask the assistant to suck the blood and bone while the operator of the drill used both hands to steady the drill near delicate structures.

"Do you want me to do the suction for you?" asked Rebecca. "No, no, not necessary."

Just as he said this, the drill jumped from his hand and careered into the dura, the covering layer of the nerve roots. The dura tore into shreds. Copious amounts of cerebrospinal fluid gushed from the torn dura. The delicate nerve roots were then wrapped around the high-speed drill like spaghetti on a fork.

"I told you I didn't need your help!" he shouted at the registrar. "Now look at what you made me do."

They both knew that Mr Afghani had paralysed the patient. There was no doubt about it.

The scrub nurse stood open-mouthed. Rebecca felt sick to her stomach. She wanted to cry.

The anaesthetist piped up behind them. "Have you nearly finished?"

"Just a small tear in the dura." He called back to the anaesthetist while looking directly at Rebecca with scorn. "I will need to put some glue on it and then we can close up. Rebecca," Mr Afghani pronounced Rebecca's name as if it tasted sour in his mouth. "Did you consent this patient for paralysis?"

"Yes," she stuttered. Tears were beginning to form in her eyes. She could not believe what she had just witnessed. "We always do." What she wanted to say was: "You complete cock! What have you done?! You will have ruined her life!" but, again, held her tongue. She was afraid of Mr Afghani.

"What shall I tell the patient?"

"Tell the patient that there was a tear in the dura, which is a known complication, and tell her that there may have been some nerve damage, but it should get better with time."

"But it won't get better…"

"That is not for you to say. I don't want to hear another thing about it. I will speak to the patient myself. Now, close up and let me know when the patient is on the ward." Afghani left Rebecca to repair the dura and clean up his mess. She had to carefully put the shredded nerves back into the defect and attempt to close it. As she sealed the incision, Rebecca was shaking like a leaf. The nurse who had prepared the drill stood behind her and placed a hand on her shoulder in solidarity. They silently agreed that the next few months were going to be dire working alongside this monster of a surgeon.

When the patient eventually came to a little while later, she instantly panicked at not being able to feel her legs. Crying could be heard on the ward. "Doctor, why can't I move my legs? I am completely numb down below." She had had a urinary catheter inserted and the poor woman had soiled the bed.

"Don't worry, my dear. It is normal with such a complex procedure. I am afraid that the registrar tore the covering layer of the nerves and may have damaged them. I came in to repair them. It may take a bit of time, but it will get better." Mr Afghani would be long gone by the time she came to sue the hospital.

As he walked away, Mr Afghani was joined by a young woman who fell into step beside him. Afghani was visibly repelled by her presence. Without turning to face her, he broke the silence.

"What do you want? What is your name today?" His tone was displeased. He wasn't happy to see her. The woman was wearing a short white lab coat. Her dark brown hair was tied into a neat bun at the nape of her neck. A few strands were left loose, softly framing her face. She reached out and tucked the strands behind her ears revealing perfectly polished, manicured hands. She kept looking forwards as she spoke under her breath.

"Don't worry about that. Can I have a quick word with you?"

She led him to a quiet part of the ward. He looked at her name badge.

"Oh, Jasmine, what a lovely name. I heard it was Deborah last week. I also heard through the grapevine that you were getting a lot of hands-on neurosurgical teaching." He laughed. "You are going to be in a lot of trouble, my dear."

The woman grabbed his arm and dug her nails into his bicep, pulling him to one side. "This time, you fucker, you have gone too far." She hissed. "I've just found out what you did."

241

"Yes, my dear, but you haven't exactly been a good little girl either. have you?" He laughed again, a deep snarling laugh, and yanked his arm out of her grasp. "I would keep your mouth shut, you little tramp, and your hands to yourself. This is nothing to do with you." He paused. "Let's just say, if you're not careful, your lover will be next."

CHAPTER 20

Meanwhile in San Paulo, Crispin Humphries was greeted at the airport as he disembarked the jet. He was then escorted through the airport, fast-tracked through immigration and whisked to the hotel in a limousine. He marvelled at the no-expense-spared treatment. There was a beautiful Brazilian maid in his apartment who greeted him with a dazzling smile. She started to unpack his suitcases for him.

"Mr Humphries," she said. "The car will be arriving in one hour to take you to the laboratory. Professor Santos is looking forward to meeting you."

It was hot. Crispin was wearing a white suit with a purple tie. He could feel the fabric sticking to his back and armpits. He was relieved when his transportation arrived. He hopped into the air-conditioned limousine with glee. Professor Santos greeted him in the reception at the cool air-conditioned Brainionics Lab.

"Crispin, welcome to San Paulo! I trust the hotel and service is satisfactory?"

"Amazing, Pedro. Thank you." He then added with a wink and a whisper. "Even the maid is of a high standard."

Pedro laughed. "Right, come on. Let me show you around."

Pedro led Crispin to the laboratory. It was spotless. There was not a speck of dust in sight. The lab was made up of various workstations, all with sparkling white surfaces and all supplied with the most advanced medical technology and resources. A distinct smell of disinfectant lingered in the air. There was a glass display cabinet in one corner of the lab. As Crispin walked over to it to inspect what was inside, his shoes squeaked on the whiter than white tiles beneath him.

"What's that?" Crispin asked while peering through the glass at a small device exhibited within the cabinet.

"This was the very first stimulator we trialled. The wire is relatively thick, and the battery pack is enormous, but it worked. We trialled it in baboons. It was the first time we were able to show the regenerative power of electricity in a human-like subject."

"Good god…" Crispin said. His eyes gleamed with delight at the knowledge of working somewhere where such advances were taking place.

Crispin was led past some administrative offices and into another part of the building. "This was the first laboratory we had before we expanded the building. It's much smaller, but this is where the real breakthrough occurred." Pedro's phone began to ring. Pedro motioned to Crispin that he needed to take the call and disappeared out of earshot.

Crispin took his time wandering around the laboratory, curiously picking up artefacts and putting them back down in the wrong place. This laboratory was nothing like the previous one he had just been in. It was dusty and didn't contain any of the expensive equipment displayed in the new laboratory. The room had more of a musty smell than one of disinfectant and was much darker, void of the harsh white lights which lit up the other lab. Crispin felt like he was walking through an old scientific museum. There were plaques on the wall with

Professor Santos' name engraved on and old medical contraptions dotted around the various stations. He noticed that one of the large cabinets had been left slightly ajar from the wall. On closer inspection, he could see that there was a door frame behind it. He looked around to see if anyone was watching him. With Pedro still out of sight, Crispin quickly shoved the cabinet slightly further along. A door handle was exposed. This had obviously been preventing the cabinet from being entirely pushed back against the wall. He gave the handle a wiggle, but it was locked. He shoved the cabinet further still along the wall to find that, in the middle of the door, there was a small window. A dim light shone through from the other side. Crispin pushed his nose up against it to try and see through. His breath condensed against the window pane.

"Crispin," Crispin jumped out of his skin. Pedro had silently returned and was standing behind him. "Do you want to know what is behind that door?"

Pedro reached for his phone again and started dialling. Crispin became anxious. Pedro held the phone to his ear and, looking into Crispin's eyes, said in a quiet voice. "Do not disturb us, we will be some time." Pedro ended the call and spoke frankly to Crispin. "This is your opportunity to carry on with your good work without any ethical compromise. However, once we enter the door, there will be no turning back. I've had to make some difficult choices Crispin, but I believe it is the right decision for the good of humankind. If you want to know what is behind the door, I will show you, but this is the time to choose."

Crispin pressed his lips together. Without much hesitation, he gave his answer. "Yes, Pedro, I want to know what is behind the door."

"Very well. Follow me, Crispin." Pedro moved the cabinet aside so the door was fully exposed. He took out a key and inserted it into the door before looking back to Crispin.

"No return," he said. The door opened.

They descended down the steps on the other side of the door. A damp odour permeated the air. Six doors stood in a row at the bottom of the stairs. Each had a small square window towards the top with metal bars covering the window. Prison cells, Crispin thought. Pedro nodded at Crispin, giving him his consent to go ahead. Crispin paused before walking up to the first door. At first, he didn't see anything. It just looked like an empty cell. Crispin lifted himself up onto his toes to get a better look, interlacing his fingers around the metal bars to hold himself up. A mutilated face slowly eclipsed the glass panel and started to repeatedly headbutt the frame. Blood splattered onto the glass. Crispin reeled backwards in fright, almost falling as he did so. He jumped when Pedro placed his hand on Crispin's shoulder.

"These are the chambers of the lost souls, Crispin."

"What in God's name is going on?" Crispin yelled. "What happened to these people? Why are they down here?"

The ghoulish being continued to smash his head with inhuman force, obscuring the window with a layer of thick red gore. Pedro spoke over the unabating thuds.

"All of these people have had implants inserted. They were all violent prisoners, rapists, serial killers, the worst of humankind. The government are struggling to house the ever-increasing number of violent criminals in prison; the cost to isolate them, look after them, pay the workforce needed is becoming an unsupportable burden. We offered to help by taking some of these… offenders, off their hands." Pedro was careful not to say lab rats, but the words did cross his mind.

Crispin noticed that the thudding had stopped. There was a muted clunk, the sound of body and bones contacting hard earth, and then silence. There was a slight pause as the two of them looked at the prison cell door. Crispin, frightfully, and Pedro, blankly.

"Don't worry. He does that. He'll be fine," said Pedro unsympathetically before restarting his spiel. "We gave them an opportunity to make things right by dedicating themselves to advancing medical science. We said we could modify their behaviour by inserting the stimulator, which we had managed to do with the baboons. All the patients consented. Of course, they knew it was all experimental. They were promised that if it worked, they would be given special privileges… good money too if they ever got out of prison. In return, the prison would be able to integrate the most violent prisoners back into the normal prison blocks. It was signed off by the highest authority. Initially, it all seemed to go well. The implants were inserted a year ago. Their behaviour changed for the better. They were calmer, more friendly and more talkative than ever before. The implanted prisoners were, therefore, integrated with the other prisoners. It was a great success. Everyone was happy. Over the next few months, however, they slowed in speech and movement. It appeared they had developed dementia. The most hardened criminals were now like babies. The government felt that although they were no longer a risk to society, they couldn't keep them in prison. Brainionics took full responsibility and made a deal that, providing the results were kept secret, they would look after the prisoners." Crispin needed some time to take this in.

"What, like animals in a cage? This is awful Pedro."

"Not quite. We removed the implants and found that a metallic iron compound had accumulated in high doses. The iron was part of the wire component. We have since removed it from the device completely. We are confident that this will never happen again. I'm afraid this is the reality of experimental science." He could see the angst on Crispin's face. "Crispin, I know this looks terrible, but we had no way of predicting it. They seemed to be doing so well. It was just a… glitch. Collateral damage."

"So, what happens to this lot now?" Crispin peered through another window panel.

Inside was a young-looking man covered in faeces, smelling it on his hand.

"We have a duty to look after them. We report back to the government as often as we can. But no one knows about them. They don't have families or friends. The government has all but abandoned them."

It suddenly dawned on Crispin that maybe the stimulators he had implanted were faulty too. "Pedro, have you had any problems with the implants that I put in?"

Pedro hesitated. "Yes."

"What do you mean?" asked Crispin. Deep down, however, he knew the truth. An image of Mike Taylor flickered across his mind.

"You remember that American patient, Mike Taylor." Pedro sighed. "It was the first implant you put in for us."

"Jesus, Pedro!" Crispin exclaimed. "So, this can be traced back to me? That's why you asked me to deny all knowledge of him? I lied to the pathologist as well!"

"No, Crispin. Brainionics have protected you and will continue to do so. Our organisation is very loyal to those that see the good that the stimulators can do for humanity." He continued. "Yes, it is sad, but Mike Taylor had a wire made out of the same material. We knew he was becoming demented, but we just thought he would be admitted to a nursing home. We foolishly ignored the problem. We had no idea he would try to kill himself and his wife. You have to understand. We had to keep this completely confidential. If we were investigated, our top investors might have pulled out and the dream over. It would have been a disaster. After the police got involved in your country, we had to intervene. But by the by, Crispin, we are confident with our latest version. Without the deep brain wire, this will never happen again."

Although Pedro was incredibly convincing, Crispin understood that now he had seen these prisoners and what had been done to them by Brainionics, he didn't really have much choice in the matter. Who knows how they would try to keep him silent after? They might cut off his money supply, for starters. He didn't fancy a life of blackmail and bargains.

"Crispin, please join me on this journey. There is so much more to do."

Crispin took a deep breath and exhaled. "Okay Professor, I will join you." They smiled at each other and shook hands.

"Let's be getting back to the new lab." Pedro said, finalising their discussion.

As they walked past the cells on their way out, Crispin spotted a label on one of the six doors with the occupant's name written on it. ROBERTO. It was one of Professor Santo's old technicians. Pedro had been right. There was no return for Crispin now.

CHAPTER 21

Only a week had passed since Lewis had met Harry. The police surveillance on him had stopped. As no further evidence had been found at the mortuary to suggest any suspicious activity, DS Smyth's chief had told him to close the case. The coroner had released both bodies back to the US where the Taylor family had them cremated. The pathologist, Dr Davies, reported the company who made the newly found stimulator to the regulatory bodies, the FDA and MHRA, for further investigation. There were no threatening letters or any other incidents. He never heard back from Harry, and Deborah never returned any of his texts. He had tried calling, but her number must have been blocked. He felt terrible about what had happened between them. He understood now more than ever that his feelings for her had been real. It wasn't just about the sex or being with a younger woman. She had understood him and his quirky ways. She just got him. But like all his relationships, it had come to a bitter end.

Heartbreak aside, he was genuinely worried about Harry. It was as if both of them had just vanished off the face of the earth. Lewis took it upon himself to go to their medical school and hunt down the undergraduate department. He explained to the Dean's receptionist that he was concerned for the safety of two undergraduate students who had done a neurosurgical block with him. Interestingly, they had a Harry Tindall on their books but there was no record of any Deborah being enrolled that year. Both parties were confused. Lewis knew that there were things that he didn't know about Deborah but, surely, she didn't go by another name? He didn't understand. It also transpired that Harry had not been in attendance for the last week of school.

He thought he'd better update DS Smyth with what was going on. He was aware that Crispin had left for Brazil for three months and that Harry Tindall was missing. The timing was too much of a coincidence. He phoned DS Smyth straight away.

"Lewis, how can I help?"

"Sorry to bother you, Steven. I am a little concerned about Harry Tindall, one of the medical students who I mentioned before. Harry hasn't turned up to any of his medical school placements and is missing. I feel it is my fault and I wonder if the police could at least see if he is okay?"

"Well, Lewis, I'm not sure we can get involved. Students go missing all the time and then turn up again. They're stressed. It happens."

"Please, Steven." Lewis pleaded. "I'm really worried about him. He's a good kid." DS Smyth sighed. "I will see what I can do. Have you had any more incidents?"

"No, I took your advice and made out that I was dropping any interest in the Crispin affair."

"Sounds like it worked then."

"Well, not exactly. The girl in the photograph hasn't responded to me either."

DS Smyth paused. "Lewis, I hope you don't mind me asking this, but how well do you know this girl?"

"Good question." Lewis was ashamed to say he didn't even know Deborah's surname. "Well, I thought she was a medical student. She turned up to theatre one day with Harry and said she was, so I just never questioned it. We got on and one thing led to another. I'm embarrassed to say that I've checked with the medical school and I don't think she is a medical student after all. I have no idea who she is, and her mobile number doesn't connect any more."

"Do you think she was there to keep an eye on you, Lewis?" asked the DS, tension rising in his voice.

"I never thought about it. Do you think she set me up?" asked Lewis nervously. "I don't know. I was just asking myself the same question."

"Well, I'm not sure what she got out of it apart from me cooking her terrible pasta. I mean… my house key has been missing since the break-in, but nothing unusual has happened since… it's also not unusual for me to lose my keys anyway." It dawned on Lewis that he must seem like an absolute fool to DS Smyth. What kind of mess had he got himself into? "By the way, the last time I saw Harry, he gave me a file about all the private patients that Crispin has performed surgery on. According to the document, the stimulators are manufactured in America like the one they found in the mortuary. I've skimmed through it and there's not much of interest, but I suppose you better have it."

"Okay, Lewis. Try not to worry. Thanks for filling me in. I'll try and get that file at some point soon."

"Okay… But anyway, the main reason I called was about Harry. Can you please keep an eye on him, for my sake?"

"Yes, I already said that I'll see what I can do. I will keep you updated myself. I have to say, Lewis, I just wish you had told us about him before. Do you know where he lives?"

"Sorry, I don't. The medical school should have his details."

"Okay, I'll be in touch." DS Smyth stared down at his desk after he put the phone down. The Taylor case had just been closed but, in his mind's eye, he knew it should be reopened. This was beginning to get a lot more complicated; an apparent double suicide, a missing brain stimulator, two fighting neurosurgeons, a mystery girl and an absent medical student. There were too many coincidences. He decided to pass the information onto his chief and MI5. The only action they sanctioned was to keep surveillance on Harry Tindall — if they could find him. The rest of it sounded like something from a novel.

Lewis realised that he was no detective. He should never have got involved in the case and just stuck to what he was good at — being a surgeon. He needed a big case, something that would test his surgical skills and make him feel better about himself. He needed a distraction. Back in his office, he looked through his computerised waiting list. He found what he was looking for: a massive calcified thoracic disc. This should do. Lewis sent a couple of emails to the management and the theatre scheduler to put the patient on his next list. She had only been waiting for two months.

Lewis phoned the patient and told her that there was a space available. If the patient wanted surgery, he explained that he could book her in in a couple of days. The patient was going off her legs. This is a term used for someone who is starting to trip up due to spinal cord compression. The patient gladly accepted. Lewis informed her that someone would be in touch. He then proceeded to call Amal to see if she would be available to help.

"Amal, are you around the day after tomorrow to help me with a particularly big case?"

"I can be, Mr Thomas. What is it?"

"It's a massive calcified disc causing severe compression on the spinal cord. I'm going to do the case, but it would be great if you could help me."

"I'm there. Can I do the exposure?"

"Sure, Amal. If you could consent the patient and tell them about the risks of paralysis and death etc., that would be good. See you soon. I'll need you there first thing."

"No problem, thank you. See you then."

Lewis then went onto look through a trail of emails to and from the management about thoracic discs. He wanted to purchase an ultrasonic curette. This is a device that cuts through bone like butter but bounces off soft surfaces. It would have been perfect for this genre of delicate operation but at a cost of £30,000, the NHS Trust certainly wouldn't bite. There is money in the NHS, but it is not always directed at the right places. He had been told to write a business case for the curette, which he reluctantly did, only for it to be rejected. The irony was that if the patient was paralysed and sued the NHS for millions, it would come from a different budget — the NHS litigation authority. This meant that middle managers of the Trust were simply not that interested in buying new equipment on the hearsay of one surgeon, and even if they were, it was down to some low paid administrator to authorise it. Occasionally, hospitals will rent the equipment rather than buy it. Stupidly, the rental costs end up being more than double the cost of buying the equipment outright. Just another anomaly in this so-called brilliant health service, Lewis thought to himself. When Lewis got home later that night, rather than popping open a bottle of red, he treated himself to some herbal tea. I'm a changed man, he said to himself. Well, slightly changed. He still couldn't help but feel compelled to text Deborah.

Deborah, sorry for the abruptness of our last encounter, hope you will understand x

A few hours passed. Still no response. He kept checking his phone at regular intervals, willing for a reply to appear. He eventually fell asleep gripping his phone to his chest.

The next day flew by in a blur. Before Lewis knew it, it was time for the big operation. What the two of them were about to do is probably one of the most complex operations a neurosurgeon can do. The cause of compression is a rock of bone sticking into the spinal cord. No one yet knows why it starts to grow into the neural tissue. Any extra pressure from surgery on the already compressed spinal cord could leave the patient completely paralysed. Most surgeons try to pass these cases onto someone else for fear it may ruin their surgical results. Lewis was confident that he could operate on the patient and get good results, however. He texted Amal as soon as he arrived at the hospital to meet him on the ward and then changed into his theatre scrubs.

Once on the ward, he found Amal. David was also there and, despite being uninvited to the discussion, he unabashedly joined them. They both looked at the CT and MRI scans on the computer. The screensaver popped up and Lewis aggressively waggled the mouse. Lewis wondered how many computer mice, or monitors for that matter, had nearly been thrown out of the window in angry retaliation at the hospital screensavers.

"Okay, Amal, how are you going to approach this?"

David broke in, bulldozing through Amal's answer. "Mr Thomas, I would probably remove the bone at the back first to give more room for the spinal cord during the manipulation."

"Thank you, David, I am aware that some surgeons may do this, but any manipulation of the spinal cord would be a disaster. Amal?"

Amal replied patiently, seemingly unaffected by David's interjection, she was used to it, "I would remove the calcified disc from the front which means, in the thoracic spine, you have to go through the chest. This way, there would be no manipulation of the spinal cord at all."

"Yes, Amal. It's more difficult but safer for the patient. Right, let's talk this through with the patient."

David scowled plainly in front of them, uninterested in concealing his disdain at Amal's suggestion being chosen over his. They asked one of the nurses to accompany them and made their way to Mrs Johnson's bed. They closed the curtains around the patient and gathered around her. She looked up at them all, petrified. Amal gave Mrs Johnson a reassuring smile which seemed to calm her nerves.

"Mrs Johnson, I'm Lewis Thomas and this is my team. You're in safe hands. I know we talked about this in clinic but today we are going to do the surgery. You will be taken down to the theatre complex and the anaesthetist will put you to sleep. Once asleep, we will position you on your side. I'm going to make an incision on the left side of the chest—" Lewis was interrupted by Mrs Johnson.

"Hang on, what do you mean you're going through my

chest? I thought this disc was in my spine?" The colour drained from her face.

"I'm sorry, Mrs Johnson, I thought we explained this in the outpatient clinic." Lewis knew that he had explained all of this in the clinic, but many patients completely forget the outpatient consultation as soon as they leave the room. He was understanding though. It's an awful lot of information to retain, on top of the justifiable anxiety triggered by major surgery. Lewis continued. "I'm afraid it's the only way to remove this safely."

"How many of these have you done before?" she asked dubiously.

"Well, it's not a very common operation. The best way to look at this is to imagine if you didn't have surgery. You will, over time, become paralysed. The risks of the operation do include a chance of death, paralysis, infection, but then there's also the high chance of a full recovery. Without surgery, the only outcome is paralysis."

"Have you ever paralysed a patient, Mr Thomas?"

"Not yet, Mrs Johnson, and I don't intend to start doing that now."

"Okay, Mr Thomas, I'm in your hands. I trust you." She smiled nervously.

"I'll look after you, Mrs Johnson. I promise." Lewis said with utmost sincerity. "Okay, we will see you in theatre."

Lewis and Amal left to go and carry out a theatre brief. They had to ensure the theatre team knew exactly which instruments to get ready. Once they did this, they queued up in the hospital deli for a coffee. There used to be a fast track for staff who didn't normally have the luxury of time, but that had long gone. They had to queue up with everyone else who happened to frequent the hospital for various reasons; patients, relatives, people that simply have nowhere else to be, and the myriad medical staff on shift. Eventually, they got their coffee and sat down with another surgical team.

"Have you heard?" one of the junior doctors gushed. "Apparently, one of the consultants is shagging a medical student!" she laughed out loud.

"Ah! Really!?" Lewis said. He wanted the ground beneath him to swallow him up. "Where did you hear that?"

"Oh, just rumours. Why, do you know something else?" she pressed on excitedly. Not a moment too soon did Amal's bleep go off. Thank fuck for that.

"Mr Thomas, it's theatre. I think the patient is ready."

"Great, let's go."

As they both walked away, Lewis looked back over his shoulder at the gang of staff. All of them were watching him. The doctor who had asked if he knew more was sniggering with her hand over her mouth. There's nothing better than hospital gossip. That is, until it's about you.

The patient was anaesthetised. The endotracheal tube was sticking out of her mouth. The theatre team gathered around her and then slid her onto the theatre table.

"1-2-3 slide," Terry shouted. "So, you're going through her chest, Mr Thomas? Nice one. I haven't seen a thoracotomy for a while." Terry continued in a jovial fashion. "Let me get this straight, you're a neurosurgeon and yet you go through the head cavity, the chest cavity, the abdominal cavity and all the other bloody cavities to get through to the spine? Is there any cavity you don't enter?"

"The pelvic cavity, Terry," said Lewis.

"Apart from on the weekends, heh!" Terry laughed out loud.

"Not funny," responded Lewis, trying to ignore the sexual connotation.

They positioned the patient with the left side up and strapped the patient to the table. Patience was getting her instruments ready, music was playing softly around them, Becky was checking her Facebook status and Terry was in the process of connecting tubes and various bits of monitoring equipment to the patient. All was well, for the time being.

Lewis and Amal proceeded to scrub up. They all stopped before draping the patient to confirm the details of the patient and the operation. Lewis hadn't done a thoracic disc for a while. He was gathering his thoughts while the WHO checklist was being performed. Once finished, they started to drape the patient with the sterile blue drapes exposing a square foot of flesh where the incision was going to be. Lewis took the knife and asked the anaesthetist if it was okay to start.

Andrew, the anaesthetist, who Lewis trusted wholeheartedly nodded. Lewis swiftly took the blade and purposefully made an incision on the left side of the patient's chest wall.

Amal used the bipolar cautery to stop the bleeding as the operation progressed. A rib was exposed. Lewis stripped the muscle off of the rib. Underneath, he could see the lung tissue inflating and deflating.

"Is she a smoker, Amal?"

"Yes, Mr Thomas."

Lewis could see multiple black dots peppered over her pink lung tissue. He wondered what his own lungs would look like, then quickly dismissed the thought. He asked the anaesthetist to stop the ventilation. They didn't have long. The patient would have enough oxygen to circulate the body for a few minutes without the support, provided the anaesthetist had done a good job. They used metal retractors to spread the ribs, exposing the hump of the thoracic spine that ran down the body. The thorax gaped open; a fleshy, volcanic crater heaving and surging as the aorta, the largest artery in the body, thumped aggressively. When the patient had been sufficiently opened up, ventilation recommenced and the microscope was brought in. The operation was displayed for all the theatre team to see.

The clock ticked. Lewis used a drill to take some of the vertebral body away. It was hard. Thick beads of sweat rolled down his face. Hours passed. They eventually got to the large rocky, disc. Lewis found the normal dura and then followed this down to the disc. The disc was suffocating the spinal cord. He knew he had to be extremely careful with the dissection. Amal was assisting him; under the microscope, she had the suction close to the disc and dura. Their fingers danced over the body with unfaltering grace; the intertwining of hands, the slick gliding of utensils and the steady, controlled rhythm of their breath was like a perfectly orchestrated spectacle. He knew any minor slip would be a disaster for the patient.

"You're brave, Mr Thomas," said Amal.

"Or stupid," Lewis replied.

As he was drilling, Lewis imagined the drill slipping from his hand and tearing into the spinal cord. He saw the drill ripping into the aorta and then a catastrophic eruption of bloody lava spraying out of the body, boiling over onto the table. All the dozens of mistakes he could make circulated through his subconsciousness. Fortunately, none of these things happened. Four hours had passed. There was just a small fragment of hard disc left on the spinal cord. Once he removed it, the operation would be finished.

Unexpectedly, the neuromonitoring technician let the anaesthetist know that there was a subtle change in the electrical signal of the spinal cord. The anaesthetist whispered to Lewis.

"Lewis, the technician has detected a change."

Lewis turned to the technician, "Everything okay?"

"There has been a decrease in the evoked potentials down the left side," replied the technician.

"Nothing has changed here. Blood pressure okay?" he asked Andrew, knowing a change in blood pressure could decrease the blood supply to the spinal cord. This risks paralysis in the same way having a stroke does.

Andrew replied. "No change here, either."

Lewis stopped operating and decided to take a break rather than continue to carry on and cause potential damage.

"I'll be back in ten minutes." He announced and then turned to Amal. "Amal, let's just see if the potentials return, keep everything steady." Amal remained scrubbed while Lewis took his theatre gown off and went outside to the hospital smoking shelter.

"Excuse me, madam, can I steal a cigarette off of you?" he asked an elderly patient. The patient was sat in an electric wheelchair and dressed in a hospital gown. Lewis hadn't properly looked at her before asking for a cigarette and instantly regretted his request. Both of her legs and one of her arms had been amputated, presumably from years of heavy smoking causing vascular disease. He didn't much fancy a quick smoke any more.

"Course you can, doc." She shoved the cigarette in her mouth that she had been holding with her one remaining hand and managed to get another cigarette out and pass it to Lewis. "Need a light?"

"Eh? Oh, no. I'll get into trouble if I smoke here, but thanks very much! What are you in for? If you don't mind me asking," Lewis asked.

"They're going to chop this hand off tomorrow. I'll be completely 'armless after that!" she cackled to herself and then started to cough uncontrollably. Jesus Christ. Lewis patted her on the back.

"Thanks for the smoke. Good luck with everything!" he said, disappearing back inside. He got the lift to the top floor and then proceeded up the back stairs to the helicopter deck. He opened an AUTHORISED ONLY PERSONNEL door and admired the view from the top of the hospital. He cupped the end of the cigarette with one hand, shielding it from the wind, and lit it with his other hand. He took one long drag, held it, and exhaled. Lewis gazed out over the city and breathed in the scene. A soft din resounded from the world below and around him. He suddenly had an intense feeling of being alone. He tried to focus on Mrs Johnson's case and why the monitoring signals had deteriorated, but Deborah's face kept flashing before his eyes. He missed everything about her. Her soft, gentle hands, her mesmerising eyes and her playful sense of humour. He loved how she always giggled to lighten the mood whenever anything became too serious. Lewis remembered the sound of her laughter, sweet and melodious. It echoed through his mind, crystal clear, like a song that had got stuck in his head. He didn't want it to end. Just as he was stubbing the cigarette out, the exit door flew open. Out came the

Hospital Fire Officer. Lewis then realised that four cameras had been pointing at him the entire time and that security had not doubt alerted the fire officer that someone was smoking on the helicopter pad.

"Doc, you're not allowed to smoke here. I'll have to report you, I'm afraid."

"Sorry, mate. I've just got a challenging case on the table and needed a bit of a breather."

"Sorry, doc, that's not going to wash with me. What's your name?"

Lewis put his hand over his ID badge. "It's Crispin Humphries, gynaecologist. I'd better get back to operating." He quickly scuttled past the fire officer and made his way back down to the theatre complex, laughing quietly to himself.

The theatre was quiet. Lewis washed his hands again but a bit longer this time to get rid of the smell of smoke on his fingers. Becky had already put a new theatre gown and gloves out. She tried to tie it around his neck, almost strangling Lewis.

"Becky, for fuck's sake, this is a small gown. Can you get an extra-large one out?"

"Sorry, Mr T. Will do," she said, throwing the gown in the bin. She opened a new XL gown for Lewis.

Amal was sitting on a theatre stool, clasping her hands together to keep them sterile. "Right, Amal, I'm feeling better. Any change in the monitoring?"

"I'm afraid not, Mr Thomas."

"Okay, let's get the final fragment out and get out of here."

Lewis continued to drill the last fragment of the disc. The spinal cord was now free from its grasp, completely reducing the compression. Apart from the unexpected loss of monitoring, the operation had gone exceptionally well. He proceeded to remove the swabs, put in a chest drain and sew up the wound. He watched the collapsed lung expand as the anaesthetist pumped air back into it. He instructed Amal to write the operation note while he closed the skin with fine dissolvable sutures. The wound was an elegant fine line. There would be minimal scarring. Damn, I'm good. Lewis thought. At least there was one thing he wasn't failing at in his life.

"It will be about thirty minutes for the paralysing agents to wear off. Then we can assess her leg function," said Andrew. There was nothing more that Lewis or Amal could do for her at this stage. Although the operation was a technical success, only time would tell whether Mrs Johnson would be okay.

Amal and Lewis decided to head back down to the hospital deli again to pick up some over-priced cardboard-tasting sandwiches. They needed to refuel after the lengthy operation. Lewis hoped they wouldn't bump into any of the staff who had been talking about him and Deborah before. They stood in a long queue. Amal could see that Lewis was distracted.

"Mr Thomas, don't beat yourself up if she isn't okay."

"Who?" Lewis was paranoid that Amal was now talking about Deborah too.

"The patient... Mrs Johnson?"

"Oh, right. Thanks, Amal, but you know I will."

"I've only seen two of these operations in the past, and both didn't end up well."

Lewis didn't respond. They presented their sandwiches to the cashier. "I'll get these, Amal."

"Would you like a muffin with this?" said the cashier.

"No, thanks," replied Lewis.

"It works out cheaper with a muffin," said the cashier.

"What do you mean?"

"Well, it's on a deal today: with the muffin it's £3.50, without the muffin, it's £4."

"But I don't want the muffin, I just want the sandwich."

"Well, that's £8 in total then," she replied in all earnest.

"Do you know how ridiculous this is?" Lewis was beginning to lose his temper.

"It's okay, I'll sort it," Amal quickly got her card out and paid contactless before Lewis lost it completely, smiling apologetically at the cashier. She understood that Lewis was worked up because of the operation and not because of the cashier trying to get impressionable punters to buy unhealthy muffins. Amal led Lewis away and they found somewhere quiet to sit down. They both tore into their sandwiches. Lewis was starving.

"Mr Thomas, how did the operation go?" Lewis spun around to see an older man sitting behind him. The man smiled compassionately, his eyes friendly, warm and wrinkled around the edges as he grinned. He registered Lewis' lack of recollection through his large, thick-rimmed spectacles. "It's Mr Johnson," he let out a low, humble chuckle. "Not a very memorable face, I know. I met you in the clinic with my wife."

Oh, shit. This does not look good. Lewis really didn't want to be in this position. Of all the places he could bump into Mr Johnson, it had to be in the hospital deli after his wife's op, stuffing his face with shitty sandwiches. Not that he had much choice where he did his stuffing; the management closed the consultant dining room years ago for being too elitist. Lewis swallowed and wiped his mouth with the back of his hand.

"I presume it all went well," Mr Johnson continued. "I mean, I doubt you'd be here if she was paralysed." He chuckled again. His belly wobbled as he laughed.

Lewis and Amal stood up simultaneously. "We better go and see how's she's doing, actually, I will find you on the ward once I've assessed her!"

"Fuck, fuck, fuck, fuck..." whispered Lewis under his breath as he walked away. They both hastily made their way to the recovery room. In their haste, however, they forgot to discard their sandwiches. As they walked in, a paunchy middle-aged nurse barked at them.

"Oi! You two. No food in here. Oh, and you are supposed to get changed out of your scrubs if you leave the department." She tutted audibly. Lewis took one look at her and knew that enough was enough. He walked right up to her and looked her in the eye.

"Listen, you condescending cow!" Lewis exploded. Years of hatred and disappointment and guilt caused by the management surfaced and spilled over and out of him in a stream of exasperation. The theatre receptionist winced. Amal put her head in her hands. "I've just performed one of the most difficult operations of my life. I have no idea if the patient is paralysed or not. I haven't eaten for twelve hours. I've been overcharged for these crappy sandwiches. And I may have to face telling the husband of the patient that his wife may never walk again. I have no idea who you are or why you have to be so belligerent but it's certainly clear that you don't have a problem finding food. Let me do my fucking job, saving lives, and get back to your petty admin work sucking the soul dry out of this hospital, all right?!" Lewis obviously didn't think any of the work the receptionists or nurses did was petty or soul-destroying. They were of paramount importance to the hospital. It couldn't function without them. He had simply finally been pushed over the edge which meant that this churlish, overweight nurse had found herself staring down the barrel of Lewis' verbal gun. She was aghast. Lewis was breathless. As soon as he finished talking, he knew he was going to get into big trouble. The nurse demanded to know who he was, but Lewis just walked away, ignoring her.

Amal ran to catch up with Lewis. She didn't say anything. They both entered the recovery area where the patients were coming out of anaesthesia. They found Mrs Johnson who was still sleepy.

"Hello, Mrs Johnson. The operation went very well. How are you doing? Can you wiggle your toes?"

Mrs Johnson couldn't lift her head up from the pillow.

"Are they wiggling now?" she asked tiredly.

It was evident that there was no movement at all in either foot. Lewis tried to remain positive. "The spinal cord is very sensitive, let's give it some time, and we will assess it later. Rest well and see you soon." As Lewis walked away, he turned to face Amal.

"Bollocks, Amal. I'm not sure I could have done anything any differently. Let's get an urgent MRI scan on her. If there is nothing on the scan, we will be having a tough conversation with her and her husband."

"Of course, Mr T, you did your absolute best."

"Thanks, Amal, but that doesn't help right now." This time, her usually pacifying smile didn't ease the pressure he felt.

The anaesthetist came to the bed. "All stable from my point of view, Lewis. I'll review her later too."

Before leaving, Andrew put his arm on Lewis' shoulder and added with a whisper, "Sorry, mate."

It was Lewis's worst nightmare. Despite the complexity of the operation, the guilt a surgeon is left with after unintentionally paralysing someone is sickening. Lewis felt like a complete failure. Everything in his life seemed to be falling apart. He'd fucked it up for one of his patients, fucked up his relationship with Deborah, potentially fucked up with Harry as the poor kid had vanished, and now his job was probably on the line because of his meltdown with the nurse earlier. As he walked out of the theatre complex to his office, the same oafish nurse roared irascibly after him.

"I know who you are, Mr Thomas. I will be reporting you! I have witnesses! You are a very rude gentleman." Lewis thought about apologising but just walked past her, dejected. At that moment in time, he didn't care if he was reported or not.

He eventually went back to the ward after Mrs Johnson had woken up completely and explained to her and her husband that despite the operation going well, they lost monitoring of the spinal function. He explained that he didn't know whether she would regain power in her legs. He thought he'd better give them the worst-case scenario so they could get used to the potential idea of complete paralysis for the rest of their lives. After all, it wasn't just Mrs Johnson's life that would be changed but that of her husband and three children too. He documented the events in the medical notes and left the hospital. The last words Mrs Johnson said to him before the operation, I trust you, Mr Thomas, rang in his ears. He got back to his house and opened a bottle of red, smoked furiously, then hit the Japanese whiskey. By the time Lewis got into bed, his head was spinning in an inebriated haze. He missed Deborah.

CHAPTER 22

Pedro and Crispin had been pretty busy. Pedro had introduced Crispin to the Brainionics staff in San Paulo. They greeted him with kindness and respect. After all, he could be the key to taking their products to a global market. A UK based surgeon, to outsiders, was an important asset to the company. Crispin was still upset from seeing the caged prisoners hidden deep in the underbelly of the building. Pedro had explained that they had tried to put the new stimulators in them, but it had been like putting a new battery into a broken transistor radio. The stimulators worked, but all they did was power up a clogged neural pathway. It made them worse. Pedro reassured Crispin that they were like zombies, sometimes aggressive, sometimes passive, but basically just insane.

"The good news, Crispin, is that today, I'm going to take you to one of the most notorious prisons in San Paulo. A couple of years ago, there was a riot. The two gangs went crazy, beheading and mutilating each other. The government never want a repeat of this and have asked us to help them again. Those who have nothing to lose, the worst of the worse, have been allowed to have a new stimulator. We have taken several opposing gang members and inserted stimulators into their heads. After a bit of programming, they are now the best of friends!"

After arriving at the prison with their armed bodyguards,

both went through the security checks. Their mobile phones were confiscated, and they were both searched as they entered a secure area. Two prisoners from opposing gangs were sitting playing cards. Pedro explained that they had had their stimulators inserted about a month ago. Unlike the earlier stimulators which could regulate and regenerate different areas of the brain, these were even more sophisticated. There was a piano and guitar in the corner of the cell. Pedro explained that neither was able to play the piano or guitar before coming into prison nor ever had access to them. The Brainionics team in San Paulo were able to programme information from the electrical impulses of musicians, decode them and upload them to the stimulators. The only side effects were that the prisoners did not just inherit the musical capacity but the personality of the musicians too. The prisoners also had no short-term memory because the stimulators affected the hippocampus, the part of the brain which processes short-term memory. But how they played! Think Tchaikovsky, Beethoven or Mozart symphonising in the middle of a prison. It was extraordinary.

The director of the prison came to meet Professor Santos and Crispin. "Pedro, Crispin, thank you for coming by. It's all going very well so far. Everyone is happy, particularly the prison guards."

"How many have been implanted?" asked Crispin.

'Four, currently," replied the Director proudly.

"I did them all myself, Crispin," said Pedro. "The programming still needs to be slightly tweaked though. Look what happens when we turn the stimulators off." Pedro gestured towards the prisoners. The director asked them to play some music which they obediently did. As they were playing, the director took out a smart device and pressed a button. Their harmonious melody suddenly turned into an ear-splitting cacophony. The prisoners dropped their instruments, looked at each other in slight bewilderment and then lunged at each other. Crispin jumped back in horror, using one of the armed bodyguards as a human shield. As soon as the stimulators were turned back on, the prisoners separated and returned to their instruments. One started playing 'Superstitious' by Stevie Wonder on the guitar, and the other followed in complete harmony on the piano.

"Impossible…" Crispin couldn't believe what he was witnessing.

"Who knows? One day, we may even release them back into society. It's unlikely, but it's something we can aspire to," said the director.

Crispin and Pedro were led outside back to their vehicle. In the back of the car, Pedro cooed over how magnificent the stimulators were. He was practically shaking with anticipation. "Crispin, can you imagine? Picture it! People wanting to learn any skill whatsoever, be it the piano, the guitar, water skiing, a new language, ten new languages! It's all in the realm of reality and we can control it all." Pedro had a devilish look in his eye. Crispin wasn't really listening to him though. He was imagining counting all the money he was going to get from the invention.

"Crispin," Pedro continued, unrelenting. "I want us to work on the devices with the lab team and perfect the ultimate stimulator. I want us to create something that will make men into… Gods."

The two sat in silence, basking in their shared vision of glory and power.

"Yes, Pedro, I want to be a part of this." Crispin now understood the sacrifices that Pedro had made.

"Crispin, there is one thing I am concerned about," Pedro said in a grave voice, snapping Crispin out of his fantasy. "I am worried about our leader. I think he may have other plans for the stimulator. Military plans, I mean. Remember, we must ensure that we implant the Superstim for the right reasons." This feigned benevolence did not seem consistent with the look on the Professor's face as he was speaking about power and Gods just before, but Crispin chose not to question it. He just nodded and then reverted back to thinking about the fame and prestige that awaited him.

Back in Israel, Gad Dayan was still livid about the stimulator being transplanted into a medical student without his permission. It was causing unnecessary attention. He couldn't understand how this had gone under the radar as Brainionics had one of the best security divisions in the world. They were all ex-military and had been trained to an exceptionally high level. Dayan could deploy them anywhere in the world if he wanted to. He hadn't even had time to relax after the Mike Taylor case was closed before a new spanner was thrown into the works. His security operatives had informed him that the police had organised surveillance on the student. The last thing he needed was anyone finding out Harry Tindall had a stimulator inserted. If the company got embroiled in a media frenzy, if the truth ever got out, the business would go down taking the billions of dollars of investment money with it.

More so, the military had a vested interest in the stimulators. They had gambled on the possibility of controlling people in battle and thus spent millions on funding Brainionics research. Dayan could justify anything in the name of progress. To him, it was akin to making the nuclear bomb and hailing it as a peace-making device. The stimulators could be the global peacemaker the world has been looking for, but they could also instigate worldwide oppression if they fell into the wrong hands.

The arrival of Crispin Humphries in San Paulo had given kudos and a morale boost to the company. Crispin's belief in the success of the company was all-encompassing. He accepted that there had to be some casualties on the way. Unfortunately, Harry was just going to have to be one of them. Once the early results had been made public (at least the good ones), the share prices would soar. Gad Dayan would be the new technology mogul; the face of the next stage in the evolution of the human race. Gad just had to figure out how to get this Harry out of the picture without the Superstim device being discovered. They would have to dispose of the body somewhere where he, and his stimulator, would never be found. There had to be a way to eliminate him and destroy any evidence at the same time. The complicated part was that the police now had surveillance on Harry. But, then again, Gad knew this wouldn't pose much of a threat to his security division, especially now that they were on high alert. The surgical operative who messed up in the first place would need to make amends. Dayan made a phone call.

Back in London, Harry was sitting in his flat. He was too scared to do anything. Brainionics technicians, in combination with their security, were continually monitoring him and now, unbeknownst to Harry, the Greater London constabulary were too. All he wanted to do was to help people, but now he couldn't even help himself. He heard that familiar buzzing sound and then a surge of pain sliced through him. It only lasted a second, but it was enough to make him keel over in agony. His phone chimed.

You are being followed by the police, do not try anything stupid. Write down these instructions.

Harry wrote them down and did as he was told. He created a new Facebook and Twitter page and uploaded the images he had been provided with. He had no choice.

At first blush of the following day, a bright Saturday morning, Harry got dressed, read his instructions again, got on his bicycle and headed towards King's Cross Railway Station. An unmarked police car was following Harry. It didn't take long for Harry to realise he was being trailed so he began to peddle faster. He manoeuvred his bike through a pedestrian zone, looking back at the car. The police had radioed in to say their cover was blown. Instructions came through to continue the pursuit. Alerts on Harry Tindall by MI5 revealed that Harry Tindall was a Jihadist sympathiser. They had uncovered cryptic tweets and Facebook statuses about how he was planning to do something significant this very Saturday morning. Although unlikely, MI5 and the police had to take this seriously. Harry was pedalling faster and faster. The wind took his cap off. It blew away into the distance behind him. Another police car had appeared and tried to cut him off, but Harry swerved into a housing estate and disappeared out of sight. They radioed in to say that they had lost him but, again, were told to press on. The police helicopter was yet to be sent out. Harry breathlessly and frantically cycled away. Part of him wanted to turn his bike around and run back into their path, to explain everything to them. The pain he would experience even if he just changed the course of his bike was enough to force him to keep pedalling on, harder and faster than he had ever in his life. He was just as terrified to follow the instructions as he was to breach them. He weaved between roads and alleys until, eventually, he reached his first destination. In a dank, hidden backstreet not too far from Camden Town, Harry paused to catch his breath and dismounted his bike. A figure placed a rucksack onto Harry's back, patted him on his shoulder and sent him on his way. With not a minute to lose, Harry shot off in the opposite direction. He emerged through another part of the housing estate, cycling furiously towards his final destination. The police helicopter had now been deployed. It didn't take long for it to identify Harry.

All units had been radioed in. Suspect with a suspicious rucksack at Camden Lock heading towards King's Cross. The chase intensified. Harry was making headway, cycling madly away from the police cars. He rode on the pavements, through the grassy verges parallel to Arlington Road, his eyes like those of a hawk guiding him forth. He zigzagged between pedestrians, pillars and other blocks and bricks barricading his way, his legs snagging on protruding obstacles as he zoomed ahead. The pursuit lengthened. Harry could hear the helicopter nearing, but he was indefatigable. He couldn't slow now, even if he tried.

Harry stopped just outside the Jewish Military Museum and dismounted his bicycle. The loudspeaker on the helicopter blared out above him: STOP NOW AND REMOVE THE RUCKSACK. NO HARM WILL COME TO YOU.

Oh, how wrong you are, Harry thought to himself. His eyes watered.

He stared up at the helicopter hovering above. How had he got here? Why me?

Armed police officers gathered around the scene. He was surrounded. Harry took the rucksack off of his back and replaced it on his front. With quivering hands, he removed a detonator from within the bag. The speaker ordered Harry to be still and to drop his weapon. DO NOT MOVE. It bellowed. WE ARE HERE TO HELP, LET'S JUST TALK THIS THROUGH. Harry felt the buzzing in his head followed by the familiar acrid smell. He knew what he had to do. Tears ran like a river down his face. His whole body began to shake uncontrollably. This time, he couldn't tell whether it was his nerves or the stimulator causing him to convulse.

He cried out in defeat; his voice unrecognisable amidst the sobs and the sirens. "I'm sorry!" The explosion drowned out the rest of the world. Harry's body exploded like a firework; a kaleidoscopic display of blood, flesh, tears and bones rained down on the vicinity amid sparks, like fireflies, fluttering nervously away from the scene. A mound of smouldering debris remained where he had stood just moments before. His body had disintegrated. A small metal fragment had been blown away from the blast. It clattered to the ground and bounced one, two, three times before finding its way into a drain. The stimulator buzzed, burrowing deeper into its newfound home. On the street, chaos ensued.

Lewis shot up in bed as if awoken from a bad dream. His head pounded. He felt terrible and his breath stank. He hadn't drunk so much for a long time. He had several missed calls on his phone. No caller ID. It was ten a.m. He would normally have been up a lot earlier to go in and see his post-operative patients. A breaking news alert appeared on his phone from the BBC app.

MAJOR TERRORIST ATTACK IN LONDON. ONE DEATH AND SEVERAL CASUALTIES.

Fuck, Lewis thought, and then rolled back over in bed. He rubbed his eyes with his hands then picked his phone back up. He listened through the multiple voice messages on the phone. It was the medical director of the hospital wanting to meet him urgently. Lewis thought he better have a coffee and cigarette before phoning.

He phoned the hospital switchboard. It was an automated voice recognition system.

If you know the extension you want, type it in now and press hash. It was a computerised female voice. If you don't know the extension, say the name of the department you want after you hear the tone. Lewis waited for the tone sound and then said: "Medical Director's Office."

I'm sorry. Did you say Estates Office? Say yes, if you want to be put through to the Estates office, say no, if you want another department.

"No," replied Lewis.

Please say the name of the department you wish to speak to after you hear the tone.

Lewis spoke more firmly the second time. "Medical Director's Office."

I'm sorry. Did you say Estates Office? Say yes, if you want to be put through to the Estates office, say no, if you want another department.

"For fuck's sake!" Lewis shouted down the phone. "Just put me through to the operator."

You are being transferred to the operator.

After a few seconds, Lewis was transferred to the operator who put him through to the medical director's PA.

"Hello, can I help?" asked the PA.

"Yes, it's Lewis Thomas, I received a message from the medical director. He said he needed to talk to me urgently."

"Ah yes, Mr Thomas, I will put you through."

A few moments passed and then the medical director's voice came on the line. "Lewis, I would like to see you urgently please." He said solemnly.

"Sure, is there a problem?" replied Lewis.

"I would rather see you in person today, and I have to warn you, our representative from Human Resources will be there."

"Oh, right." Lewis was a bit taken aback. "I can make it at midday?"

"Yes, I will see you in my office at twelve thirty."

The phoneline went dead.

Oh fuck, fuck, fuckeroo. Lewis threw his phone across the room. It landed with a soft thud on the floor. He had been waiting for that call for some time. Why am I such a shit human being? He counted the number of things he knew he had done recently to upset the management and the people in his life. Jesus. I am a shit human. I mean, that fat nurse deserved what I said, but apart from that...

Lewis toyed with the idea of leaving his flat, going to the airport, hopping on a plane to Bali and never coming back. I'm sure they need consultants in Bali...

Lewis sprang up. "Well, as they say, let's face the music

and dance. No time like the present to lose your fucking job."
He had a shower, shaved and shot off to the hospital.

He went straight to the ward to see Mrs Johnson, still carrying his motorcycle jacket and helmet. He would usually put them in his office first. Mrs Johnson was lying in bed. She had a urinary catheter inserted and was crying. Lewis came over to the bedside and sat down on the edge of it.

"Mrs Johnson, I'm sorry that this has happened to you. I know it won't mean much to you, but the operation did go really well. I really don't know why this has happened."

Mrs Johnson wiped her eyes. "Yes, your lovely registrar Amal came around earlier and said the same thing. Will it ever get better?" she asked, her bottom lip wobbling.

"I don't know."

Lewis explained that during the operation, the monitoring signal down the spinal cord reduced and that this could have been due to lots of reasons. He explained that the post-operative MRI scan looked good and that there was no more pressure on the spinal cord. There was still a possibility of recovery, but it could take many weeks, even months. He wished he could do more, but he couldn't. He left Mrs Johnson and reminded himself that surgery can have catastrophic consequences on people's lives. He knew this well, but it didn't stop him from getting too emotionally invested in his cases sometimes. He passed David, the other registrar, in the corridor. "Mr Thomas, I was just thinking about the thoracic disc case. Do you think it may have been better if she had had a laminectomy first?"

Lewis knew that this was a subtle dig at him. Although David knew better than to disrespect a consultant, he wanted

Lewis to know that his previous suggestion was not as stupid as Lewis had made out.

"Maybe, David." Replied Lewis dismissively. He did not stop to talk.

Although paralysis was a risk, in this day and age, it was still a rare outcome. He knew the rest of the staff and his colleagues would know about it. Humiliatingly, some of them may even be pleased about it. Some surgeons, as with many other professions, feel reassured about their own practice when other surgeons experience complications. Unfortunately, it is an ego thing. So much for doing a big heroic operation. Pride does come before a fall, as they say, Lewis thought. His old boss used to tell him that if he had a post-operative complication, the best thing to do is to perform the same operation as soon as possible. Otherwise, you could be put off doing surgery ever again.

After dropping off his things at his own office, he made his way to the medical director's office. He was asked to wait in the plush managerial suite like some guilty felon. The suite looked expensive with its pretentious velvet cushions perfectly plumped and placed on a pretentious-looking sofa. Lewis scowled and perched on the end of the sofa which was royal purple to match the cushions. The seating area was more like an Ikea showroom than a hospital waiting room.

He was called in by the HR representative. A young, friendly looking woman whose warm voice matched her maternal expression.

"Mr Thomas, thank you so much for coming in," she said apologetically, understanding that he wasn't here for fun. "If you would like to follow me." With a voice like that, he thought, she would make an excellent cancer bereavement councillor. Lewis followed her in and sat down in front of the medical director's desk while another HR member, a gentleman, sat by the side, making notes.

"Mr Thomas," the director started. Lewis interrupted. "Lewis, please."

"Mr Thomas," he insisted with a sigh. "We have concerns about your behaviour. This is a formal meeting, and this will be put in your file. Firstly, we are aware that you have failed to complete your mandatory training despite being asked to do so several times. Secondly, we are concerned that you have been abusive to one of our staff members. It has come to our attention that you have been rude on a previous occasion to a patient's relative as well. This is against the trust policy. Do you understand? You will now be under investigation for harassment and bullying. Do you have anything you wish to say?"

Lewis felt like he could do without the hassle, and yet it simply wasn't in his nature to take things lying down.

"I had a bad day yesterday, and yes, I agree I was rude to one of the nursing staff. For the record, I apologise." Lewis knew it wasn't about this. Hundreds of staff are rude, all the time. Lewis had been shouted at and sworn at by members of staff a million and one times but never reported it to HR because he understood that people have bad days and that it's simply not a big deal. He chose not to mention this, though. Some people, it seems, feel that if they have been aggrieved in any way these days that they have to take it further. It was the medical director's call, however, whether to take this further or not. It would have been much easier for the director to simply let Lewis know that he was rude and then for Lewis to make an official apology. But no, they had to go down this formal disciplinary route. It was a way of shutting up loudmouth clinicians like Lewis. A way to control them. The trust couldn't let nasty consultants like Lewis talk to poor innocent handmaiden nurses in the wrong way, even if she was the size of a small barn and rude. The pendulum had swung the other way. Consultants were now managerial fodder. They no doubt knew about the disagreement he had had with the finance manager at the 'Transform your NHS life' meeting too.

Lewis continued. "So, why the need for an investigation? I admit being rude and I will gladly apologise. I will complete the mandatory training without question. I'm sorry it has taken me so long. But what is the point of an investigation? Surely, it's just going to be more work for you and everyone else involved."

"We take these matters very seriously, Mr Thomas, and we do have the power to suspend you pending further investigation."

"Fine, suspend me."

The medical director couldn't believe the arrogance of Lewis and just stared at him for a few seconds. Lewis had shocked himself!

"Very well then, you are suspended pending further investigation."

Lewis couldn't believe the stupidity of it all. He wasn't sure if he wanted to work in an environment of fuckwits who sit in their ivory towers fire-fighting the mess they have often created by ridiculous rules and policies. He left without another word and slammed the medical director's office door. On his way out the building, he phoned Amal and asked if she could keep an eye on Mrs Johnson as he would be away until further notice. He also called his secretary and told her what had happened but to keep it confidential. He asked her to cancel all his clinics and surgery. They can deal with the waiting list, he thought.

He wondered how long the whole process was going to take. He had heard about colleagues who had been suspended for months for some innocuous, alleged wrongdoing. They were suspended on full pay, but the money isn't really the issue. The psychological impact can be devastating. How do you ruin a quality consultant's career? Just send in a few narcissistic, psychopathic managers. It won't take long. Just as Lewis was walking out of the hospital, he received a phone call from DS Smyth.

"Lewis, I have some news."

"What is it?"

"It's Harry. He's dead."

When the coast was deemed clear and there was no further threat, the forensic team swept the area. The few burnt parts of what remained of Harry's body were contained. Remnants of the rucksack and metal shrapnel were also collected to be sorted and tested later. A police officer in the cordoned-off area noticed something gleaming down the drain he was standing over. He alerted the forensics team. The drain lid was lifted, and a small metal disc was recovered. It was obviously part of the detonator mechanism and duly placed in a secure bag and labelled.

The next day, the press went to town on Harry. All the papers claimed the medical student had been groomed by an extremist, Jihadi group in London. Some even stated he had gone to a training camp in Afghanistan. He had supposedly attempted to blow up the Jewish Museum, which was thankfully only partly damaged. Lewis spent the entire day at home in shock, smoking like a chimney and drinking wine as if it was water. He knew that Harry was not a Jihadist. He also knew that there was someone corrupt behind this fake news story. It had to have something to do with the stimulator. It was undeniable. The disappearance of Deborah, Harry's death, Crispin buggering off to Brazil… it must all be connected. He wanted to believe that DS Smyth and his team would follow it up, but he wasn't confident. If they had looked into the original case with Mike Taylor more, maybe none of this would have happened. Maybe Harry would be still alive. Poor, poor Harry.

Meanwhile, Crispin Humphries and Pedro Santos had made exceptional progress in San Paolo. With help from specialist engineers, they had been able to freely experiment on prisoners without any recourse. They were in sight of making a super stimulator even better than the Superstim. They had engineered a disc that could be inserted under local anaesthetic and used to modify the recipient's behaviour and capabilities, both physical and mental. The new stimulator had also been developed to no longer impact short-term memory, so the new abilities uploaded to the stimulator could remain to be lifelong skills. While they were confident that the new device was safe, they equally had no idea what the long-term effects could be. They would need to do more human trials. As with any device, it needed FDA approval to grant this, though. This usually takes years. Luckily, thanks to a generous educational grant donated by Gad Dayan to the honourable committee members, the trials were approved. In fact, all members were unanimous. The human trials were due to commence within a couple of weeks. After the human trials, provided there were no adverse complications, Brainionics would be free to market the device to doctors and patients alike. Everything was falling back into place. Gad Dayan had also been informed that his little problem in England had been sorted. The only thing left for Gad to decide was what to do with the English consultant.

CHAPTER 23

DS Smyth and Lewis met for a coffee at a café in Notting Hill. Lewis slurped his coffee. It tasted strong and bitter. He liked the feeling of the hot liquid in his belly. He hadn't eaten for days.

"Lewis, you look like you haven't slept in months. Everything okay?" DS Smyth said, concerned.

"I've been suspended for calling a nurse fat."

DS Smyth raised his eyebrows. "I thought I said to keep a low-profile Lewis?"

"Yeah, I know. Well," Lewis sighed. "It couldn't be helped; I'd had a bad day in the hospital."

"Right… well, you need to take care of yourself, Lewis."

"I can't act normal when I know that Harry may have died because of me and that Deborah might also have disappeared because of something I started."

"Lewis, I know this doesn't all add up, but you can't blame yourself. None of this is your fault."

Lewis didn't respond. He didn't have the energy to argue. They both took a sip of their coffee.

"Confidentially," DS Smyth broke the silence. "If you have a bit more time on your hands, we could still use you. My suspicion is that the stimulator put in Mike Taylor's brain was faulty. Maybe the company are trying to cover it up. Maybe Dr Davies was lying? If so, this is going to be a bigger job than you and me Lewis. So far, we have no evidence that Crispin put the stimulator in Mr Taylor and secondly, we can't find a connection between the stimulator and his death if Dr Davies was telling the truth. We need more proof. We know from the pathologist's report that there was some staining in the brain, which makes me think someone was trying to switch the original stimulator. We need a man inside, and with your expertise as a neurosurgeon, I can't think of anyone better. What do you say, Lewis?"

"How?" Asked Lewis.

"Well, you know Crispin, right? Why don't you try to contact him and say that you want to work with him?"

"Are you joking? He hates me and I hate him. Why would he trust me?"

"Well, we need to work it out, but we will find a way."

"I'll have a think."

Back at Crispin Humphries' NHS hospital, Humphries' replacement Mr Afghani was causing disaster after disaster. When he first arrived, he took it upon himself to interrupt any and every operation and take over and then, more often than not, cause some complication or other. The junior doctors and the nursing staff were then left to look after the wound infections, cerebrospinal fluid leaks, and patients who should have been discharged after a couple of days, but instead, were taking weeks to go home due to pain or another preventable issue. After two weeks on the job, however, he went from being an obsessive tyrant to disappearing for hours at a time. His presence initially weighed down on the staff like a tonne of bricks, but he'd since become an elusive figure never to be found on site. The staff preferred it like that. Most of the work was now being left for the junior staff to sort out. His name just became a token consultant that management could tag to patients. Mr Afghani was always on his phone, either texting or speaking. He never made eye contact, laughed or tried to integrate with the other staff. What was the point? Why make friends with people he was never going to see again? When he wasn't in the UK, he would be doing clinics in Qatar, UAE, Dubai and Saudi Arabia. He used his UK work experience to convince others that he was a well-qualified respected doctor, essentially polishing up his CV. He didn't care for the patients or where the work was based. He was simply prepared to do any job which would pay well.

Crispin was nearing the end of his tenure with Professor Santos. It was his last night in San Paulo, and Crispin was out for dinner with Pedro. At last, they had begun the clinical trials with the new Superstim, Superstim 2. Soon, Professor Santos would be marketing the device to potential patients, and at a phenomenal cost too. It would probably take years to get this through the Medicines and Healthcare Products Regulatory Agency (MHRA) in the UK, but he was prepared to wait. He knew that he was well on his way to becoming one of the richest consultants on the planet. He would be able to implant the Superstim in clinics around the world. He had plans to go to the Middle East where there was a growing appetite for quick-fix surgery and patients willing to pay a lot of money. The marketing team at Brainionics had already started to put together programmed packages perfect for even the most demanding clientele.

Need to lose weight? Easy. Superstim will suppress your appetite. Need to quit smoking? Easy. Superstim will stop the cravings. Desperate to impress your musician lover? Learn to play the cello. Whatever your dreams are, the Superstim can make them come true. How about the playboy package? It will enable you to have a great body, speak Italian, learn jazz piano and enhance your sexual ability. Or, the classic scholar package? It programmes Latin and a comprehensive knowledge of the arts and literature. The possibilities were endless. There was still only so much that could be programmed into the stimulators, but further downloads would be available eventually. It was only a matter of time.

At the dinner table, Lori, Crispin's PA, phoned him on his Brazilian mobile. "Excuse me, Pedro," said Crispin. "I should take this."

He accepted the call. "Hola! Mr Humphries!" said Lori. "Gosh, we missed you, Crispin!

How are you?"

"Magnificent, Lori. Missing you guys too," he lied. "I'm looking forward to coming home.

How is everything?"

"Well… when you left, we had a mass revolt. We had to field all the patients that were phoning for an appointment with you. It has tailed off, thankfully. People know you're due back soon though, so please expect to be busy!"

"Lori, I can't begin to tell you how busy we are going to be. It's been a real learning curve here, but it will be nice to get back to some normality."

"Crispin, the real reason I am phoning you is to let you know that you have some competition."

"Competition?!"

"Yes, Crispin. Lewis Thomas is setting up his own neurostimulation clinic. He asked me to be his PA."

"What?!" Crispin was gobsmacked. "That little shit knows nothing about neurostimulation. He's taken advantage of me being away. What did you say to him?"

"I said I wasn't interested! My loyalty is with you, Crispin. I thought I'd better let you know, though."

"Thank you, Lori. You're a diamond. Let's catch up when I'm back. I'll take you out somewhere nice to celebrate my new talents."

"Oh, Mr Humphries!" she said flirtatiously. "I'm going to take you up on that, Crispin!"

"What was that about?" Pedro asked when Crispin ended the call.

"Pedro, I need some advice." Crispin was visibly affected by what Lori had just told him.

"Anything, Crispin," Pedro replied in a fatherly manner.

"One of my, well, let's say a competitor, wants to start putting in stimulators. I know Brainionics will want to expand but I don't want him involved. What would you do?"

"Crispin, first of all, you need to relax. You are in the inner sanctum of Brainionics and they love you. You are going to be rich. My advice is... why not let him help?"

"Really?" replied Crispin, surprised by Pedro's advice. He didn't like the idea of Lewis getting in on the fun.

"Yes, let him help. Invite him to watch. You have a large practice, and it will get bigger. Brainionics will look after you. When I've retired, you will be the face of the company. You can't do it all yourself. Embrace it, Crispin, encourage it, but control it." Pedro said with a stern stare. "You need to make the decisions and make the money, but let him do the work."

"Thank you, Pedro. Good idea. I'll contact him when I'm back."

They both toasted to their new venture and future. "Here is to the next generation of humankind," Pedro said as they clinked glasses.

Surprisingly, Lewis was actually enjoying being suspended. Lewis now had the opportunity to travel more and spend time doing what he wanted. He received a letter through the post from human resources which stated the claims of the disciplinary: failing to comply with trust policy regarding his mandatory training, bullying and harassment. The timescale stated that the investigation had to be completed within six months. Suspension for six months on full pay... incredible! He thought. He knew the news of his suspension would go around the hospital like wildfire, but he wasn't bothered. Of course, it wasn't all sunshine and rainbows. He could see why some doctors become psychologically distressed when such things happened to them. The hospital management forbid suspended doctors from seeking legal counsel, for one, or making the reason for their suspension public. This means that, essentially, they have nobody to talk to. It can be incredibly isolating. Ironically, this was basically bullying and harassment by the NHS Trust. You could spend months not knowing the future of your job. Despite the fact that six months of paid free time, so to speak, sounded inviting, the hospital trust could and would sacrifice a doctors' career at the drop of a hat if it means that they are seen to be doing the right thing. There have been too many hospital scandals for them not to be risk averse. Take Dr Harold Shipman, Stafford Hospitals, the Bristol heart deaths, Morecambe Bay or Gosport War Memorial Hospital. Obviously, these are extreme cases, but Lewis wasn't ignorant to the fact that he was utterly helpless now. There would also not be any help available for him if or when he gets reinstated. If it all blows over, there will be no apology, no support, nada. Lewis will just be expected to carry on working as if nothing ever happened.

Lewis took his newfound free time to develop his own website to promote his private clinic and advertised that he was going to venture into neurostimulation. He paid someone to make it all fancy, of course. He needed a good website for his ploy to be convincing. He had called Lori, Humphries' receptionist, asking her to be his new receptionist too. He was proud of his cunning idea. Almost as soon as his website was relaunched, Lewis received a phone call from his neurosurgical nemesis.

"Lewis, my friend, how are you?" asked Crispin. "Really good, Crispin, how was Brazil?"

"Amazing, Lewis! I learnt a tonne. I just got back. What are you up to these days?"

"Having a bit of time off, actually. I was going to call you as a matter of fact. Since you have been away, I've had a lot of patients ask about neurostimulation for strokes. I thought you might help me get set up?"

"Yes, I understand you spoke to Lori."

"Yes, I hope you didn't mind! But she is faithful to you, Crispin. So, what do you say? Will you help me set a service up in the private sector?"

"It would be my pleasure, Lewis. We should meet up. Let us meet in my private clinic tomorrow, say about ten a.m.?"

"Great, see you then. Thanks, Crispin." Too easy.

The board of Brainionics had decided that they would need to train new surgeons to insert Superstim 2 when the clinical trials ended. Training the new surgeons would be straightforward. They only needed to drill a hole in the skull, and this is one of the first things any trainee neurosurgeon learns to do. They set up a training lab in San Paulo where Professor Santos could show neurosurgeons how to insert the stimulator. It cost the company a significant amount to train each surgeon. They paid for business class flights, hotel accommodation and various other expenses for the trainee. The surgeons were hand-picked from across the world by Professor Santos himself. He chose surgeons from a variety of specialities so that the Superstim 2 could be inserted for all different health concerns and desires. All accepted the invitation. Professor Santos had also been busy selecting patients who had enough money to pay for the procedure. The company knew the investors were getting anxious, so they needed to recoup the millions of dollars of investment that had been put into the Superstim project. Each patient chosen had paid thousands and thousands of dollars for the operation. This covered all the expenses. The company had been careful to make the process as cheap as possible; as it was a day case procedure, there were no inpatient hospital costs and, as the Superstim 2 was implanted under local anaesthetic, they didn't even need to pay an anaesthetist either.

The first patient was a grossly overweight businessman in his 50s. He had tried the usual diets. They failed. He had had a gastric band. This also failed. His final and most recent effort was to have his jaws wired together. This also didn't work. His diet of sugary drinks, chocolate and fatty foods were too much for him to give up. When his jaws were wired together, he blended chocolate bars so he could drink them instead. Professor Santos promised him that he would be able to program his brain with the Superstim 2 to stop these cravings. The second patient was a twenty-eight-year-old son of a politician. He was a heroin addict. He had rebelled against being the 'good boy' all the time and had been in and out of rehabilitation for most of his twenties. His father was worried that his son being an addict would affect his political career. Pedro had craftily reduced his surgical fee in return for political help, should he ever need it in the future. The third patient had epilepsy. She was going to have a stimulator put in by another surgeon but came to Santos for a second opinion. One of her dreams was being able to learn to play the violin. When Santos mentioned that the Superstim 2 could upload skills, she jumped at the chance to have the device inserted. The final patient was an Israeli soldier sent by Gad Dayan. The soldier was tall, muscular and had different coloured eyes, one hazel and the other blue. He also had the Hebrew star of David tattooed on his left arm. No questions were asked. Despite Pedro not wanting to get involved with military affairs, it was apparent that Dayan had other plans. Pedro went ahead anyway and had the Superstim inserted in the name of science.

Throughout the morning, the patients were led into the operating room. Pedro did all three patients while the other surgeons watched. He injected the local anaesthetic with adrenaline to reduce the bleeding and prepped the skin with an alcoholic solution to make it sterile. Santos made a small, inch long incision over the right frontal area of the skull. The disposable drill mechanism which housed the stimulator was delivered and sat on the cortex of the brain surface. Pressing another button on the device deployed the stimulator. Once this was on the surface of the brain, he could remove the drill mechanism. The whole thing looked like a hand-held Magimix device. He then stapled the wound, and the operation was over. The visiting surgeons were amazed by how fast the procedure was. In total, ten minutes to be precise. Professor Santos then explained that the programming would be done centrally by Brainionics after one or two days to give the wound time to heal first. All the patients looked fine and were discharged by late afternoon the same day. All the other surgeons then went to the lab where they practised inserting the stimulator into cadaver heads. It was easy. They enjoyed a wonderful meal and received a training certificate to certify that they were Brainionic trained Superstim surgeons.

Now qualified, they could start inserting the stimulators in patients, provided their country allowed it. Even then, Brainionics provided mobile operating units for patients who wished to remain anonymous so the insertion could be done remotely and undetected. Crispin Humphries was to expand the traineeships and mentor surgeons in London and so had been sent a large batch of Superstim 2 to his Harley Street clinic. They arrived on the morning of his meeting with Lewis. Crispin endeavoured to tidy them away before their encounter but had fallen short on time. He pushed them into a corner in his office, just out of sight.

Lewis entered Crispin Humphries' private clinic. He was blown away by how grand the reception was. He wondered how much the chandelier cost and decided he best not touch anything, just in case. He didn't really fancy replacing something the same price as his salary.

"Hello, Mr Thomas! Welcome."

"Thanks, Lori," Lewis said.

"Can I get you anything to drink? Tea? Coffee?

Something stronger?"

Lewis really wanted a whiskey but thought he best stick with soft drinks. "Just water, thanks."

"Of course. I'll take you up to see Crispin. He's been waiting for you, he's very excited that you will be working together."

"Me too!" Lewis said in a high-pitched voice through gritted teeth. He thought he sounded a little too enthusiastic. He also thought he might vomit if Crispin was too chummy with him.

Crispin gave Lewis a warm welcome. He nearly hugged him but then quickly put his hand out for a firm handshake. They both sat down. Lewis sank into the chaise longue, his feet almost lifting off the ground as he disappeared into the fabric. He had a sudden image of it swallowing patients whole like a fly trap.

"Comfy, isn't it?" Crispin pointed out.

"Very." Lewis scooted to the edge of the chair and placed his hands awkwardly in his lap.

"Lewis, Brainionics are recruiting surgeons to put in their stimulators and, although you should go to one of the training centres, I'm happy to take you through the procedure. It's elementary!" Crispin was off on one. Lewis was amazed at how easily the information poured out of him. He hadn't even asked any questions yet. "Once you put the stimulator in, they do all the programming remotely, so you don't even have to worry. If you are satisfied, I'm happy for you to perform the surgery under my supervision, and until your practice increases, we split the fee. How does that sound?" He looked at Lewis expectantly, almost panting from the excitement of his speech.

"Crispin, that sounds great. I appreciate that."

"Well, it's the least I can do for an old friend. I have a list on Friday, why don't we do the first patients together?"

"Sounds like a good plan!" Lewis wanted to laugh when Crispin called him an old friend, but he knew he had to gain his trust. This all seemed a little too good, too easy, to be true. Lewis looked around Crispin's office, trying to guess where he could find some more information about Brainionics or, better still, some incriminating evidence against Crispin. There was the computer which sat on his large, mahogany desk. He knew there would be information about patients who had had previous stimulators inserted somewhere on his system. He suspected Harry may have found information from Crispin's computer in any case, but it was one potential target. He also saw a bunch of boxes tidied away in the corner of the room. One had been left open, and he thought he could see a sterile packed package poking out of the top. Could it be a stimulator?

"By the way Crispin," Lewis paused. "Sorry I was a bit of an arse at the Royal College meeting. I'd just had a bad week. I was genuinely curious about the work you were doing. Why were you so adamant you weren't working with Brainionics?"

"To be honest, I don't know why I acted the way I did. I suppose I just thought you were prying, and I didn't like it at the time. I'm sorry Lewis. But I'm excited that at last we're going to be friends. Let's shake on it!" They both shook hands. Lewis made a mental note to disinfect his hand after.

As soon as he left the clinic, he got out his phone and dialled DS Smyth's number. As it rang, he checked behind him to see if anyone was following him. He was alone.

"Lewis?" he answered.

"I just met with Crispin. It worked." Lewis recapitulated what Crispin had said about the stimulators and that he would be shadowing Crispin on Friday. DS Smyth was impressed by how seamless it had been but equally concerned for Lewis's safety.

"I think it would be best for you to wear a wire-tap and camera when you go back on Friday, then we can track you."

"Do you not think that's a bit... over the top?"

"Lewis, look what happened to Harry. Don't be a fool. I don't think either of us know who we are dealing with."

"Yes, but—"

"Listen, I shouldn't be telling you this, but forensics found a metal disc in a drain after Harry blew himself up, we don't really know what it is. It was covered in blood and the DNA match confirms the blood was Harry's."

"It could be part of a DBS stimulator." Lewis said excitedly. The pieces of the puzzle looked like they were finally being put together.

"What? Are you saying Harry Tindall had a brain stimulator inserted?"

"I don't know, maybe."

"Well, forensics think it's part of the detonator. If it is part of the stimulator and we can connect it to the stimulator that Crispin is using, we have a connection to Brainionics. Then it's over to MI5. They will take it from there. For fucks sake, Lewis, keep this strictly confidential, I don't want to lose my job over your suspicions."

"Right... I think I know where Crispin is keeping the stimulators in his office. At least, from what I just saw. He might have moved them by Friday. Can you send me a picture of the one they found?"

"Listen, Lewis. I know what you're thinking. Don't steal anything; otherwise, the evidence would not be admissible in court."

Lewis sighed. "Why don't you just go over and demand one from Crispin? You're a police officer, for Christ's sake!"

"Lewis, for starters, I'm a detective, and secondly, can you imagine what would happen if the police raided a hospital, took confidential information on patients and equipment and got it wrong? We'd get our arses sued right off! Anyway, I would need a warrant. As I mentioned before, we have a closed case with Harry. The newspapers have managed to get a hold of his social media pages. They show him dressed as a Jihadist. And anyway, why would an Israeli company like Brainionics decide to blow him up outside a Jewish Military Museum? It wouldn't make sense."

"Because it's a set up! A red herring! They're trying to throw us off the scent."

"Look, we need more evidence before I can invest any more time in this. I'm sorry, Lewis, but the Chief has already given me a warning. If there is no evidence to link this up, we have to shut the file."

"Okay, I'll see what information I can get. Can you get me set up with the tap and camera in time for the cases on Friday?"

"Sure."

"But wait… Maybe it's not a good idea to be wired up the first time. What if he spots it when I'm changing into my scrubs? Let me scope it out first, then I'll get wired next time."

"Okay, Lewis, but be careful. Just let me know exactly where you are."

"Roger that."

Lewis received an image of the device within moments of

ending the call. Wow, Lewis thought. He couldn't wait to take Crispin down.

Crispin returned to his NHS teaching hospital and met up with Mr Afghani for his handover.

"Crispin, nice to see you. All has been well here. There are one or two patients that are problematic and waiting for rehabilitation beds but, otherwise, we have kept the waiting lists down." He gave him a list of the current inpatients. "The junior staff need to show a little more… respect. I have tried to help them where I can, but they need a lot more training, I'm afraid."

"Yes, Firas. You are right. Thank you for your help. What are you going to be doing now?"

"A bit of this, a bit of that, you know." Crispin didn't really care; he had served his purpose and got well paid for it.

"Well, I wish you all the best, and I'm sure we'll catch up somewhere around the world."

I hope not, Crispin thought. They shook hands and then Mr Afghani was gone.

Crispin saw a huge mound of unopened letters in the corner of his hospital office and thought he'd better get on with some paperwork. A lot of the letters were addressed to Firas Afghani. It was clear that doing paperwork wasn't something Afghani excelled at. As he started opening and reading the letters, he realised that pretty much all of them were complaints. Letters from family members, patients and general practitioners detailing the terrible experiences they had had with Afghani. There were pathology results showing cancerous biopsy findings and radiology reports indicating the increased growth of tumours which were under surveillance.

Crispin didn't know whether any of these reports had been acted upon or not. He didn't feel any responsibility either, though. He was moving onto bigger and better things. He thought he better pay a visit to the ward, though, to keep up appearances.

For the first time, the staff and junior doctors were pleased to see him. "Mr Humphries, welcome back! Boy, are we glad to see you!"

"Thank you," he paused. He couldn't remember the name of this junior doctor. She had been in the hospital for years, but he had never bothered to ask for her name. Fortunately, he caught a glance of her hospital identity badge. "Rebecca." He finished.

"Do you have time to do a ward round?" asked Rebecca, a hint of pleading detectable in her voice.

"Yes, please! Can we?" Crispin wasn't used to doing NHS ward rounds but since he had been away, it felt like a bit of a novelty for him. Rebecca guided him to the first patient.

"This is Mrs Jones. This is one of the first patients who Mr Afghani and I operated on. Unfortunately, she had a dural tear and a severe neurological deficit."

Crispin asked in surprise. "Are you saying she's been here for three months?"

"Well, unfortunately, her wound got infected as she had a cerebrospinal fluid leak. We had to take her back to theatre several times to wash the wound out. We can't send her for rehab until the wound has completely healed. She then developed an infection in the vertebral bodies, and she's on long term antibiotics."

"Great," sighed Crispin. "Who's next?"

The sound of muted crying could be heard from beyond

the curtain. The patient had obviously overheard their conversation.

"Would you be able to have a word with her?" Rebecca whispered. "Sorry, Rebecca, I don't want to." Crispin answered curtly.

"Well, then—" Crispin walked towards the next bed before Rebecca could finish her sentence.

"Who is this?" he pestered. He was bored already.

"This is Mrs Carmichael. She had hydrocephalus and underwent an external ventricular drain. She didn't wake up well from the operation."

"Who did it?" Crispin asked.

"Mr Afghani." said Rebecca. "Who else?" she muttered under her breath so Crispin couldn't hear.

They both went to the imaging console. As they looked through the pre- and post-operative scans, Crispin suddenly spoke.

"That's the reason! Look! I can see on the postoperative scans that the catheter has been stuck into the brainstem, then on the next one it has been withdrawn into the right place."

"Well Mr Humphries, we were aware of that. When she didn't wake up, I asked Dr Afghani's permission to rescan her, but he refused. I rescanned her anyway, and when I saw where the catheter was, I took her to theatre myself and got another scan to ensure it was in the right place. I was too afraid to tell Mr Afghani; he didn't like me very much I'm afraid."

"Right, any more problems?"

"These are the only inpatients but there…" She was interrupted mid-sentence. Mrs Jones, from the previous bed, shouted from behind the curtain, "Is that Mr Humphries? Is that Mr Humphries?" in a rising crescendo. Crispin popped his head around the curtain.

"Yes, I'm Mr Humphries," he said with a hint of annoyance.

"Mr Humphries, I've been here for three months. I heard you were back, and I have been waiting for someone to help me. How long do you think I will be here for?" she beseeched.

"I'll have to look through your notes, dear, you're not called patients for nothing." He turned to look at Rebecca and winked before walking away. He had no intention of going through her notes. He had far more exciting things to do.

"Rebecca, I'm going to leave you in charge. I don't think there is much for me to do here. Are you happy?"

Rebecca wasn't happy but she didn't feel she could communicate this to Crispin, and even if poor Rebecca did, she knew he wouldn't be bothered anyway.

"Yes, Mr Humphries. Thank you." She clenched her fist behind her back as she said this, angry at herself for not having the courage to challenge him. As Crispin walked off the ward, she kicked the wall and let out a shallow, whispered scream. She had suffered three months of an incompetent consultant locum and now had a slightly more competent one who didn't give a shit. Crispin, oblivious to the damage he had prolonged, made his way back to his private clinic.

He had only had one half day back in the NHS and he was already tired of it. It was more of a hindrance being in the NHS, but it was good for his kudos being in a teaching hospital. He liked having the title of Senior Lecturer, University of London, and the regular pay and pension scheme were welcome benefits too. His real priority was making a name for himself on an international level, though. Money wasn't going to be a problem; power and the adoration of his peers was now his goal. And anyway, one of his rivals, Lewis Thomas, was coming to visit him. After all these years! The rivalry they had had from being trainees to consultant level had been intense. In Crispin's mind, the fact Lewis was coming to see him operate reinforced his belief that he was the bigwig, the overlord, the ruler in the London neurosurgical scene. The fact that he was going to get Lewis to work for him was even better.

Crispin greeted Lewis at his private clinic as soon as he arrived. They got straight to business. Crispin couldn't wait a second longer to flex his big, neurosurgical muscles in front of Lewis. They were both discussing the patient's scans in Humphries' office.

"This patient, Lewis, has had a left hemispheric stroke. We are going to put in a new device called the Superstim 2. It not only regenerates neurons but can program various functions into the patient." Lewis was aware of how stimulators for epilepsy and Parkinson's disease work, but thought it was best if he claimed ignorance. As Crispin took the stimulator out of the packaging, Lewis at last saw what he was expecting. The disc had a distinctive logo of a lightning strike with the letter 'B' background. He knew it! His instincts had been right all this time. Dr Davies, the pathologist, has some explaining to do. He had to focus and hide his emotions of anger and excitement.

"How does it work, Crispin?" Lewis asked, trying to keep his cool.

A demonstration model was showing how the device worked on a plastic skull and brain.

Crispin proceeded to explain.

"This is top secret Lewis, don't tell anyone. The inserter

has a burr drill which firstly removes a disc of bone. This blade lacerates the dura, and the stimulator device is placed on the cortex. The stimulator has an inbuilt rechargeable battery, a wireless microchip and a GPS device all built into this disc."

"I see that Crispin, but how does it actually work?" Lewis smiled encouragingly, trying to get Crispin to reveal more.

"Oh, bloody Hell, to be honest Lewis, I don't actually know. That is too technical for me." No surprise there, Lewis thought. "The engineers in Brainionics keep the technology a guarded secret. I just put them in."

Lewis held the stimulator. He ran his thumb over the logo, inspecting it in more detail. "Interesting. Have you had any complications up till now?"

"None at all." Crispin said, fumbling with the plastic skull and avoiding eye contact with Lewis. Lewis knew he was lying. "It's pretty safe. The best bit is that the aftercare and programming are done remotely, the people at Brainionics monitor the response."

Lewis was astounded that this was allowed to happen unregulated. It then occurred to him that Crispin must not have told the relevant authorities that he was putting in these experimental devices. Either that, or Brainionics had dangled some big money in front of them. Whether it was bribery or withholding information, there was something seriously corrupt going on. Lewis instantly regretted not wearing the wire as this was pretty incriminating intel. He couldn't wait to tell DS Smyth. He hoped that he would believe him. They both proceeded to the theatre where the patient was ready and prepped by the nurse. Lewis introduced himself to the patient and Crispin then injected the local anaesthetic. The entire procedure took about fifteen minutes. Lewis observed the roughness of Crispin with the tissues. The procedure seemed to go well, despite his careless movements. The patient tolerated the drilling noise and discomfort without any complaints.

"All done!" Crispin declared satisfactorily. He had been right. Any old fool with the right tools could do it. This made it all the more alarming.

After the procedure, Lewis and Crispin returned to his office. Lewis professed false admiration for Crispin's many certificates framed on the wall. There were pictures of him alongside world-famous scientists, a previous US President — God knows why — and even some magazine covers had been dishonoured with his weedy, smug face. A scientific journal had an enlarged, unsavoury image of Crispin grinning villainously with Top Ten Best Neurosurgeons; Voted by Neurosurgeons printed beneath him. I sure as hell didn't vote for the bastard, Lewis thought to himself. Having just observed Crispin's indecorous operating technique, Lewis felt even more uncomfortable reading the accolade than he would have before. It was as if he were sawing into a plank of wood, not into a poor person's head. He wondered how much Crispin had paid for the title or whether he had photoshopped the commendation.

He turned to Crispin and said, "you have a pretty impressive collection here." He then moved onto perusing his cabinet of antique neurosurgical tools. There was a Gigli saw, an old Hudson brace and an ancient compendium of surgical advances.

"Yes, it's my special collection. That book there is a first edition." He said, pointing to the antique anthology book Lewis had been looking at. Crispin then went onto talk about each of his antique instruments in great detail; how he had got a hold of them, how much they were worth, how many people had tried to buy them off of him, but no, no, no, he would not bargain. While Crispin performed his soliloquy, Lewis took his chance and lifted the demonstration Superstim inserter and placed it inside his bag. Crispin didn't seem to notice anything, so delighted was he by the sound of his own voice. As Lewis was closing the bag, Crispin quickly turned around to face him.

"Lewis," he said.

Shit. Lewis thought. His heart stopped. He had been caught. That was it. They were going to make cat food out of him.

"Look at this, my friend." He was gesturing towards a surgical instrument in the cabinet. "Do you know what it is?" Crispin asked joyously.

"Err, no, Crispin, what is it?" His heart returned to its normal rhythm. Thank goodness Crispin was such a braggart.

"This is an original Hey's Saw used by the original William Hey in 1776, probably similar to the saws you use in your hospital now." Crispin laughed to himself, proud of his bad joke. Lewis just nodded, still nervous about his theft.

"Well, Crispin, I have learned a lot from today. I really appreciate it."

"I can see you're a fairly quick learner, Lewis." Crispin said, somewhat condescendingly but enthusiastically all the same. "Would you like to start doing some procedures yourself? I mean, they will be my patients, but I'm happy for you to do them for a standard surgical fee. Under my supervision, of course."

A standard surgical fee? Not bad, Lewis thought. For a

ten-minute day case procedure, Crispin must be making an absolute fortune. If he could offer Lewis money too, he must be making even more than Lewis had previously believed.

"That is very kind of you. It would be an honour and pleasure to work with you."

"The pleasure is all mine! I will let Brainionics know that you are on the team."

"Thank you, Crispin. Really, you're doing me such a massive favour." Crispin, of course, was unaware of the extent to which he had helped Lewis, and indirectly, waded into mortally deep shit himself.

Lewis left the building with the evidence in his bag.

Job done, he thought.

Lewis immediately contacted DS Smyth and asked for them to meet urgently. They met at another café in Notting Hill. Lewis didn't wait for DS Smyth to say anything before pulling out the inserter from his bag. A couple at the next table were staring at them, intrigued by what Lewis had just placed on the table.

"This is a demonstration model but… I think it actually works. I think this is an actual device." Lewis started dismantling the model and removed a shiny disc.

"Jesus, Lewis, I told you not to steal anything!" DS Smyth sighed. "Hang on a minute." The detective took out his smartphone and compared the image of the implant recovered from Harry Tindall with the one Lewis had just brought in. "Bingo. It wasn't a detonator, after all. It was a brain stimulator."

"Exactly. This means that someone put a stimulator in Harry. Crispin was telling me how the new stimulators can control how the brain functions. The bastard! He fucked Harry up!" Lewis jumped up in anger. His chair legs scraped along the floor, screeching like nails on a chalkboard. The couple next to them continued to stare, all the more intrigued by Lewis' outburst. All they needed was some popcorn to go with the show.

"Hang on, cowboy! Hold your horses. What are you going to do? Eh? Go over and arrest Crispin for the murder of Harry Tindall? I don't think so." Lewis sat back down and tried to remain calm. "And keep your voice down. You're causing a scene." DS Smyth waited a moment before speaking again. Lewis looked down at his hands on the table, visibly unsettled. "I think we have something here, Lewis. I'm going to talk to my superiors. I think we'll need another team on this. This is bigger than just you and me. Are you sure he didn't notice you take it?"

"Yes, pretty sure. He was preoccupied."

"OK. Well, the hardest part will be putting it back. Remember it's void if they find out you stole it. You need to keep this," he said sliding the device across the table and pushing it into Lewis' hands, "and put it back in his clinic. I will organise a search warrant once it is back and then we can take things further." DS Smyth was painfully aware of how unorthodox this was going to be. Unfortunately, it was the critical piece that enabled him to make sense of it all.

"I don't need to be told twice."

Back at his home, Lewis sifted through a mountain of mail that had begun to form at the foot of his door. There was the usual rubbish. He opened a letter from the HR department of the hospital detailing the charges against him and stating a date for his disciplinary. It was a month away. That didn't seem too long to wait. He decided to give Amal a ring.

"Amal, it's Lewis! How's Mrs Johnson?"

"Oh, hello Mr T. She's started to wiggle her feet."

"Ah, really? God, that's such a relief to hear." I guess I'm not such a failure after all. "That's great news. Can you keep her well hydrated?"

"Of course. How are you? What's going on? Is there anything I can do to help? Is it because you called that nurse a cow?"

"Ha, all the questions! Listen, I'm not supposed to talk about it but... between you and I, it is partly due to that, yes. Thanks for asking, Amal. Hopefully, it will all blow over soon enough. Let me know if there is a problem with any of my patients."

"I will do, Mr T. If it's any consolation, I think that nurse is a cow too. None of us here have the balls to say it like you do, though." She let out a chuckle. "We all miss you, it's not the same without you."

Lewis didn't want to admit that he wasn't missing life at the hospital. At least, not yet. It's rare for a surgeon to have time away from life as a doctor. Not to be overly pessimistic, but you qualify, you work, you maybe have a few holidays, work again, potentially have some kids, and then you retire and die. At least, that was normally the case.

"Thanks, Amal. Stay in touch, yeah?"

"Of course, Mr T. Speak soon." The call ended.

Lewis placed the stolen stimulator on the table in front of him, wishing he could turn back time. It was too late for Harry, but hopefully, justice isn't too far off. As soon as DS Smyth connects Mike Taylor's death with Brainionics and, of course, Crispin Humphries, this whole mess can be put to rest. He would be personally challenging Dr Davies who lied from the beginning.

In the meantime, what better way to spend all his newfound extra time than by learning an excellent new skill? Or even better, bingeing on Netflix? Lewis threw himself into a police drama on the sofa, guzzling down a bottle of red and eventually, dozing off into a blissful sleep.

In his haste to start this new, temporary life of on-demand tv, take-aways and wine, he had failed to discover a note that had been left on his bathroom mirror. In dark, blood red lipstick, the message read:

LEWIS, STOP BEFORE IT'S TOO LATE — FINAL WARNING!

Lewis awoke at two a.m. to find himself hanging halfway off of the sofa, empty wine bottle knocked over on the floor. He peeled himself off the sofa in a haze. He felt hot and sweaty, and his mouth was dry. He also desperately needed to urinate. With his bladder ready to burst, he got up to go to the toilet. The whole house was in darkness. He dragged himself up the stairs to his bathroom, flicked the light on and used the toilet. His shoulders ached. It was only when he'd finished that he lifted his head to see the message on his mirror.

"What the fuck?" he gasped.

Strangely, he was not the only man reflected in the mirror. Stood behind him were two masked men dressed entirely in black.

"Hello, Mr T!" said one of them in a foreign accent.

Lewis, without thinking, swung around and lunged forwards in an attempt to push the men out of the way and escape. One of the men punched him in the stomach. He collapsed in a winded heap on the floor. A hood was thrust over his head. Lewis was punched again and again until he could hardly breathe; all the air had been forced out of him. The hood was lifted, and a cloth was shoved into his mouth, causing him to nearly choke. Unable to see where his attackers were, he thrashed his arms and legs around in an attempt to do damage. A blunt object smacked him on the back of the head and then there was darkness.

CHAPTER 24

Gad Dayan had come to learn from his operatives that Crispin Humphries had let Lewis Thomas watch a Superstim procedure. He was forced to make another call. Overseas, Crispin looked at his phone. An unknown number came up.

He answered. "Hello, who is this?"

"Crispin, you are an idiot." Crispin recognised his voice.

"Hello, Gad. I'm sorry, what's the problem?" Crispin was confused. Why would Dayan be angry at him?

"What the hell are you doing letting Lewis Thomas get involved in the Superstim project?"

"Relax, Gad. It's fine. Yes, he was one of my rivals, but he now wants to learn how to put the device in. He wants to be one of us. Pedro thought it would be good to get him on our side—"

Gad cut him off. "Both of you should have spoken to me first! Lewis Thomas is the one who has been feeding information to the police. You have put the company in jeopardy, Crispin. We installed a camera in your office. Not to spy on you," he added defensively, "but to record your consultations. I imagine you did not notice your good friend, Mr Thomas, steal one of our implants?"

Crispin hesitated on the phone.

"Well?" Dayan continued. "No, you didn't. You idiot! Now the implant will end up with the police.

It's only a matter of time before it's traced back to us."

"Gad, I'm really sorry. The sly dog. I'll kill him." He was enraged. The whites of his eyes turned red and bloodshot. Lewis had made a fool out of him.

"It's too late for that, Crispin. This is on your head."

"I… I" Crispin stuttered, unable to speak.

"Shut up." Gad snarled. Crispin had never heard Gad speak with such venom in his voice. "Listen, we have a way to make sure the pig cooperates with us. I'll deal with you later." In his usual manner, Gad Dayan hung up.

Lewis could not tell whether he had regained consciousness or not. He felt awake and could feel a dull pain in his stomach and head, but all he could see was black. The hood was still covering his head. The room smelt damp and humid. The moisture in the air made the hood stick to Lewis' face and neck, almost suffocating him. In an adjacent room, another figure was watching a monitor of the interrogation very closely.

"Mr Thomas, time to wake up!" The voice startled Lewis. He shook and shivered, unable to lift his arms. "Do not struggle. You cannot get away. You have been very naughty, my dear." The voice said derogatively.

"'Who the fuck are you?" Lewis tried to yell, but his voice was muffled by the hood. Lewis was slapped around the back of his head. Luckily, it didn't hurt much. Lewis figured it was not a professional hit. He guessed that this wasn't one of the men who had attacked him in his home.

"I'm afraid you have crossed a line. You were warned not to interfere and yet, you still did. You're very stubborn, Mr Thomas. We will have to… persuade you differently." Said the voice. Lewis heard the sound of leather creaking as the figure came closer, boots landing with a heavy thud on the earth as the steps approached him. Lewis's hood was removed. It took a moment for his eyes to readjust. Stood in front of him was a tall figure dressed in black wearing a mask, just like his abductors. He leant over Lewis, peering into his eyes through the slits in his mask. His breath felt hot and prickly against Lewis' skin. A gold chain swung from his neck, glinting in the light.

"We can do this the easy way or the hard way. You are going to have a stimulator inserted. It won't hurt. And then, you can go about your business. If you don't, it's elementary, my dear." He laughed. "We kill you."

Lewis did not say a word. He breathed heavily. His eyes darted to the chain which twirled tantalisingly, swaying from side to side in a slow, rhythmic dance. He tried to remember where he had seen it before.

"What is the big neurosurgeon going to do now? No more Sherlock Holmes for you."

Although he had his hands tied behind his back, Lewis knew that he would be able to fight the man. He just had to figure out how to get his hands free.

"Okay, go ahead. I'll have the stimulator in if it means I'll survive. I'm not afraid."

"Oh, you will be."

There was a table set up beside him with a variety of surgical instruments all neatly placed in order. The shiny instruments looked strangely beautiful with the background of the sterile green cloth. The figure took a syringe filled with local anaesthetic and started to inject it into Lewis's head. Lewis took his chance. He tried to stand up and, in doing so, headbutted the unsuspecting perpetrator, sending him flying backwards. He crashed to the floor. Lewis attempted to kick the masked man while he was down but as he stood up, his blood pressure dropped, and his head began to spin. He lost his footing and fell, hitting the side of his head on the concrete floor. The figure charged like an angry bull at Lewis. He punched him in the face several times, this time with much more force. Lewis had underestimated the strength of his opponent. His head was rhythmically pounded over and over again against the hard ground. His skin began to tear, blood bursting from his cheeks, forehead and nose. The man breathlessly ran to fetch the Superstim inserter. He came back and attempted to hold Lewis' head still. Lewis jerked his head frantically from side to side, trying to dodge the drill before it made its way into his skull.

"Argh!" the man cried out. "I'm getting too old for this." He kicked Lewis one final time on the floor and then pressed a button on the wall, calling for back up. "I have a surprise for you, Lewis."

Lewis squirmed on the floor like a tipped over turtle, unable to right himself. He was still tied to the chair. The door opened. In came a shorter figure, also dressed in black and wearing a balaclava. As the person came in, the taller figure gestured towards them.

"Ah, very good. I need some help here. He is proving to be a little… irritating. Thank you for coming comrade."

The smaller figure removed the balaclava. It was Deborah. "Deborah, what are you doing? What the fuck?"

It couldn't be. He must be hallucinating.

"Well done, agent 14," Deborah spoke. Her voice sounded different. It was cold and harsh, nothing like the honeyed sound Lewis had missed. Her blue eyes were no longer deep and inviting, but dark and hateful. "I will give you a hand. Give me the inserter." The man gave her the device. "You hold his head," she demanded. Lewis noticed that she had three lightning strikes on her lapel.

Lewis went limp. He couldn't handle this. Not Deborah. Please, not Deborah too.

"Oh, you're surprised now?" The man let out a low, sinister laugh. "You thought your little lover was going to help you?" This made him laugh even harder. He gripped Lewis's head, digging his fingers into his scalp. The inserter was edging ever closer to his face. Deborah held the scalpel in her other hand, ready to make the incision. How could she do this to him? Lewis looked her directly in the eyes and whispered, almost sobbing, please... Her expression was unreadable. The scalpel made contact with his skin. A tiny, teardrop of blood dribbled down the side of Lewis' head. The man smiled with evil delight like a shark inhaling the sweet scent of blood.

Just as she was about to make the full incision, Deborah stopped. Within a second, she assessed the situation and ripped the mask off of her so-called comrade. With all her prowess, she shoved the inserter into his left eye. He let out a shrill, penetrating scream. The inserter ripped his eyeball to shreds as Deborah pushed it harder into his eye socket. He fell limply to the floor. Lewis recognised him. It was the locum surgeon who nearly amputated the wrong leg from a patient. That's where he had seen the gold chain before.

Deborah started to untie Lewis. "Lewis, we don't have much time, I need to get you out of here. I'll explain everything later."

Just as they were getting up, Afghani grabbed Deborah's

leg. His bloodied hand wrapped around her calf and dragged her to the floor. She struggled to crawl away, kicking her foot backwards into his face. Afghani no longer looked human; the stimulator disc lodged in his eye like some sort of gruesome, robotic antenna.

"Deborah!" Lewis cried out helplessly, his hands still half tied behind his back.

She managed to grab the scalpel which was lying on the floor and slash it into Afghani's neck. It severed his trachea. He gasped and gurgled as blood poured from his mouth and neck, slowly asphyxiating him. Deborah and Lewis watched in horror as he spasmed, tried to catch his breath, drowning in a pool of his own blood. His movements began to slow until, at last, he took his final breath. A deathly silence followed.

Lewis broke the silence first. "Fuck!"

"His name is Abdulmalik, otherwise known as Mr Afghani," said Deborah. "He was the one that killed Harry. He made him carry the bomb."

"I recognise him, he was chopping off the wrong leg in my hospital."

"He works for Brainionics. He is…" she corrected herself while untying Lewis for the second time, "was, one of their mercenary surgeons. He would do absolutely anything for money." Lewis rubbed his newly freed hands. The skin felt burnt and swollen where the rope had strangled his wrists. "Listen, we need to get out of here. The entire place is surrounded by guards. Put that mask on and put your hands behind your back." Afghani's bloodied mask had fallen to the floor when they had fought. He slowly lent down to pick it up. "Hurry, put it on!" Deborah pressed. Lewis did as he was told. She removed a phone from her back pocket. "This is yours,

Lewis, let's go."

Deborah hurriedly led Lewis out through the door into the corridor which was lit with fluorescent lighting. Together, they climbed some stairs at the end of the hallway, trying not to make any sound. Lewis could barely breath with his mask on. Two guards at the top of the stairs stared at her as she appeared with Lewis.

Deborah snapped at them domineeringly. "The prisoner's location has been compromised; I need to get him out of here." There was an awkward silence. "What are you waiting for? She took the mask off Lewis's face, revealing the blood and swelling from his previous beating. "Unlock these doors." The guards were still unsure and remained silent. Deborah snapped again. "Unlock these doors now. That's an order."

One of the guards took a security pass from his belt and was about to hold it to a panel on the door. The other guard grabbed his hand. "Sorry, agent, but we need to get authorisation first." He reached for his walkie-talkie.

Within milliseconds, Deborah had whipped her gun from her holster and shot both the guards through the head. "Shit, we need to get out of here. NOW!"

Deborah raced towards the entrance, launching Lewis along with her. The building looked like some sort of disused garage or warehouse, but Lewis couldn't be sure. The entrance was locked. Deborah shot at the lock and Lewis opened the sliding garage door. More guards appeared and began shooting at them. Lewis felt the wind from the force of a stray bullet fly past his ear. He ducked for cover. Deborah picked them off, one by one, with pinpoint accuracy.

"Come on!" she yelled at Lewis. A bullet grazed past his arm. Blood instantly saturated his sleeve. Deborah fired back, killing two further guards. Bullets were still being fired but they couldn't figure out where from. One of the guards was hiding behind a pillar.

"Look Lewis, you see the bike over there," Deborah nodded her head to the right. There was a motorcycle parked up just a few meters away from them.

"Here's the key to the bike, get it started while I hold these guards off."

Lewis smiled at her and fired up the bike, waiting for Deborah to stave off the guards.

She rushed over to the bike, still firing her gun.

"I'm riding, get on the back." Deborah ordered.

Lewis did not argue. He manoeuvred himself onto the back as Deborah grabbed the handlebars and straddled the bike. More guards appeared like a colony of wasps signalled to an attack. They sped off, bullets hailing down on them.

One of the remaining guards radioed Gad Dayan at the Brainionics HQ in Tel Aviv. "Agent 42 has double-crossed us. She has escaped with the prisoner."

"That's fine," Gad didn't sound alarmed in the slightest. "They won't get very far." He said calmly. Dayan signalled to one of the operatives. The operative pressed a sequence of buttons on his console. A large display screen showed both of them riding through London at high speed from a distance. The images got larger and larger as the drones got closer and closer.

The motorbike roared as they zoomed away.

"Where are we going, Deborah?" asked Lewis. His voice smothered by the wind and the roar.

"We need to go to your hospital." Deborah shouted. "I'll explain when we get there." Lewis heard a strange buzzing sound overhead. He looked up.

"Drones!" he yelled! A single, warning bullet ricocheted off the bike's number plate.

"Fuckers." Deborah hissed.

The heavens opened. It rained lead. Drone after drone appeared. Lewis felt like they were caught in a game of space invaders. Deborah dodged them as best as she could as they flew through the streets of London. Thinking fast, Deborah made a detour to the one-way Strand underpass. She overtook a car and waved a gun at the driver of a Fiat 500 to slow down.

The operative back at Brainionics HQ watched the chase unfold. "We may lose the signal in the tunnel, sir."

"Okay, look out for them when they come out the other side." Gad responded.

The drones did not enter the underpass. Two of them swooped ahead and hovered above the exit, waiting for the bike to reappear.

In the tunnel, Deborah and Lewis dismounted the bike. The Fiat driver was forced out of his car at gunpoint. He held his hands up in fear. Deborah and Lewis quickly got in. Deborah rammed the Fiat 500 into gear and floored it. The poor driver could have sworn he heard a man's voice echoing SORRY out of the window as the car drove away. They pulled the sun-blinds down so their faces were obscured before exiting the underpass. They kept driving.

The operatives watched the display monitors. When the motorbike did not reappear, Gad Dayan slammed his fist down on the console.

"Clever bastards," he yelled. He left the control centre and walked down one of the corridors. Using his pass, he entered a small room which had two guards at the door. They stood to attention and saluted. Gad Dayan entered the room and used his access card to open a panel which was on the wall. He entered a code and turned a key. A white light turned on and started to flash. It had the number 42 underneath it.

Deborah and Lewis kept their eyes on the road. "Who are you?" Lewis blurted out. "This is insane!"

Deborah laughed. "It's a long story."

"I've bloody missed you, Deborah."

"I've missed you too, but just to let you know, my name isn't Deborah."

"I gathered as much." Lewis said.

"It's Viktoria. And, as you also probably gathered, I'm not a medical student. I work for Brainionics."

"Please don't tell me you were involved in Harry's death too?"

"No, Lewis, I promise. Listen, we need to get to your hospital, and you need to get this thing out of my head."

"What do you mean?"

"I mean, I have a stimulator in my brain and if we don't get it out, I will die." Lewis went silent. He couldn't handle the thought of Deborah dying. It was too much for him to bear. Deborah explained the situation in more detail. "All the agents of Brainionics have stimulators inserted. I've got one of the earlier versions. It was supposed to be for our protection. With the stimulators in, we could be tracked if we got into trouble. They can monitor our vital signs remotely. We were promised they would only be used in an emergency. Only Gad Dayan, the CEO, can activate them. A wearable one would just be confiscated if we were captured, but an implantable one, wouldn't be."

"What?! Why are you even working for them?" Lewis

asked, exasperated.

"It's complicated, Lewis. Brainionics have the technology to help so many people. I wanted to be a part of that, but the company spiralled out of control. They don't want to help people any more; they want to control them. My job was to put you off the scent of Mike and Beverley Taylor's death. It was me who sent the warning messages to you. Once I found out what they had done to Harry, I realised I couldn't be a part of it any more. I tried to warn you, Lewis."

"Did you really need to put that picture of me and you with the warning?"

"Yes, only so you didn't think it was me who was trying to warn you. It was given to me by one of the Brainionics security guards. They took the picture with a drone flying outside your office. I had no idea about it at the time, honestly, Lewis. I thought I may as well use it to my advantage though. I didn't want you to get hurt." She continued. "It was me and that psychopath Afghani who were supposed to switch the Brainionics stimulator when Mike Taylor was in the morgue, so it couldn't be traced back to the company. We needed a surgeon in case it was still implanted in Taylor's head. As it happened, the pathologist had already removed it. Everything was in order until you started interfering."

"And what about Crispin Humphries?"

"He's one of Brainionics biggest champions in the UK. I was following him too. He won't last too long."

"What do you mean being one of them?" asked Lewis

"There's another surgeon involved but I don't know who it is. They've already been putting the Superstim implants into patients. Only Dayan knows who it is." She looked angry and her eyes watered as she spoke.

"I hate Afghani! What he did to Harry was terrible, poor kid."

"Listen, Lewis. I promise I can explain everything in more detail later, but I need you to help me."

"Just tell me what to do."

"You need to get the stimulator out of my head, otherwise they will activate it to locate us.

Then they'll kill me and probably you too, or worse."

"I'll do whatever I can." Lewis promised.

"Phone your detective friend and get a theatre team organised pronto."

Dutifully, Lewis phoned DS Smyth. He answered immediately. "Lewis?"

"DS, I can explain everything later, but we have some drones trying to kill us. We are heading over to my hospital now an—"

"Drones trying to kill you? What on earth?!"

"Listen! Please! I need your help. We're on our way to my hospital now and we're being shot at. We're going to need some serious back up."

"I don't understand, Lewis. Who is we? Who is sh—"

"Sorry, I have to go! Just get back up to the hospital, ASAP! Thank you." He then dialled the hospital. If you know the extension you want, type it in now and press hash. "Oh, for fucks sake! Operator please!"

Lewis was put through to the operator. "Operator, get me the neurosurgical registrar on call. Now, please!" There was silence as Lewis was put on hold. "Please pick up, please pick up, please pick up…" he repeated anxiously.

"Lewis?" Amal answered.

"Amal! Thank fuck! I have an emergency. Where are

you?"

"I'm on call, boss. What's the problem?"

"I need you to get the theatre set up. I urgently need to take a stimulator out of someone's brain. Can you get an anaesthetist and pull a team together, pronto?" pleaded Lewis as Viktoria attempted to negotiate the London traffic.

"A stimulator?" Amal sounded puzzled. "What's going on? Are you okay?"

"No, I'm not. But I need your help. Can I trust you?"

"Yes, Mr T,"

"Thank you. Please, do as I say. I'll explain later."

"Consider it done!" Lewis ended the call.

Viktoria exhaled loudly. "Good work. I need to create some interference." She switched the radio on full blast. It was Gladys Knight and the Pips playing. *I'd rather live in his world than live without him in mine...* played out on the radio. Viktoria turned to smile at Lewis. He smiled back at her. A moment of calm before the storm. Her smile slowly disappeared and was replaced by a frown. The car swerved suddenly, jolting Lewis into the side of the car. Car horns beeped at them from either side.

"Deborah? Vik, Vik!" Lewis yelled. He grabbed the handbrake. The car shuddered and came to an abrupt stop. Viktoria was convulsing. Her eyes rolled into the back of her head as her whole body tremored and shook. Viktoria's stimulator had been activated. Lewis managed to haul her into the passenger's seat so he could drive. It was down to him now. He drove as fast as he could to his hospital. He had to get the stimulator out of her brain.

The technicians at the Tel Aviv building were sending impulses to Viktoria's brain, similar to the ones they had used to control Harry. Viktoria's implant wasn't as complex as the one Harry had had, and therefore, the sensory overload was not as intense. It merely produced seizures. However, if the seizures continued, they would starve her brain of oxygen and kill her.

When he arrived at the hospital, he lifted Viktoria out of the car. Lewis, carrying her slumped in his arms, rushed through the emergency department. He made his way to the lifts which they took up to the top floor theatre suite. Viktoria was convulsing in his arms. Lewis protectively cupped her head to his chest. He wasn't prepared to lose her. When he got to the theatre, his team had assembled as requested. They looked at Lewis quizzically, eager to know what the emergency was. It was so good to see their faces, despite the circumstances.

"Right, Andrew, get her to sleep! Amal, you get her positioned! Patience, we need to be fast. Can you be ready? This stimulator is going to fry her brain."

"Holy moly, Mr Thomas! Your arm! It's bleeding heavily." Amal shouted in horror. Lewis had forgotten about the bullet wound.

"Ah, shit. It's nothing." He'd deal with that later.

"Mr Thomas, isn't this the medical student?" Patience blurted out. Everyone turned to look at Lewis.

"Please, don't ask questions. We don't have the time. I'll explain later."

Lewis tore off his clothes down to his underwear, grabbed an extra-large gown and scrubbed up. Viktoria was positioned on the table. Amal had started to prep the head, but it was proving difficult. The spasms continued, despite her being anaesthetised. They had not yet been able to administer a

326

neuromuscular blocker to prevent her movements. Fearing the worst, they pressed on without it, not wanting to waste any precious time. Lewis came towards the operating table where Patience handed him the scalpel. It was like trying to hit a moving target. Amal, giving up on the pins, was trying to hold Viktoria's head still with her hands. Lewis attempted the first incision but accidentally cut into Amal's index finger instead. She squealed.

"Fuck, sorry! Amal!" Blood spurted out from the wound.

"Carry on, Mr T," she proclaimed. "It's fine, I'll manage."

Lewis finally made the incision on Viktoria's head. Patience pressed on the wound edges. Seconds passed. The Brainionics disc was uncovered; it seemed to gleam satanically from within the flesh. The convulsions started to decrease. The anaesthetic seemed to be working. They all breathed a sigh of relief. Lewis carefully dissected the disc from the surrounding tissues and managed to lever it from the skull. Very, very slowly, he began removing the lead that had been implanted deep in the brain. As he pulled it out, Viktoria suddenly shook uncontrollably. The convulsions resurged with a vengeance. Lewis let go, worried that he was going to cause more damage. Time was certainly not on his side. The longer the device was stimulating the brain, the longer the seizures would last. His hands began to shake, and he dropped the scalpel.

"I can't fucking do this!" he cried out in defeat.

Patience and Amal looked at each other worriedly. They had never seen Mr Thomas like this.

"Right, Amal. It's down to us, now." Patience grabbed Viktoria's convulsing head. "Lewis, step aside. Amal... take over."

Amal, in time with the tremors, was slowly able to withdraw the stimulator wire from Viktoria's head. "Nearly there, nearly there... it's out!"

Lewis put his hands to his head and took a deep breath. They'd done it.

"Patience, give me the staples." Amal said. Patience, unsurprisingly, already had them in her hand. Amal proceeded to close the wound. Andrew had started to fiddle with the anaesthetic machine when he noticed a red spot hovering on his chest.

"Hey..." he said, trying to catch the little red laser like a cat pawing after a buzzing fly. "What the...?"

The team turned to look at Andrew.

"What's the matter, Andrew?" Patience asked. Andrew looked up from the red spot on his chest and directed his gaze to the source of the ominous glow. Mirroring him, everyone turned to look at the window.

"That's odd." He pointed to the origin of the laser beam. "How unusual to see car brake lights so large from here."

"Those aren't car lights. Everyone! GET DOWN!" The drones had finally tracked them down. A meteoric shower of bullets filled the theatre. Lewis and Amal managed to drag Viktoria off of the table onto the floor. Patience was frozen in shock.

"Mr T!" she cried out. A bullet pierced her forehead and she immediately fell to the floor.

She was killed instantly.

"Patience!" Lewis screamed. He crawled to her side. He desperately checked her pulse and looked into her eyes. Both pupils were fixed and dilated. The drone ceased fire. There was silence. Amal, Andrew and Lewis huddled together on the floor. Patience's head rolled to the side, so she was no longer facing them; her dead eyes fixed on the door.

"Do you think it's gone?" Amal asked nobody in particular, shivering with fright.

"I don't know…" Andrew blubbered. "What the heck just happened? Patience… she's gone…?" His words came out as a question, but he already knew the answer. He swallowed, unable to take his eyes off of his now deceased, dear friend. Lewis pulled Viktoria into his lap and held her close to him in his arms. Calm descended in the theatre complex. Viktoria had her eyes open. She had no idea who or where she was. Amal, Andrew and Lewis just looked at each other panting and confused.

"Lewis," Andrew demanded again with a croak. "What the fuck just happened?!" All the colour had drained from his face.

Just then, an armed combat unit engulfed the scene. They were surrounded. DS Smyth appeared amidst the troops. He signalled for the soldiers to lower their weapons which were aimed at the quartet pressed together protectively on the floor.

"Better bloody late than never!" Lewis said.

"Lewis, Jesus. Can't leave you alone for a minute, can I?" DS Smyth responded.

"They've killed Patience." The words tumbled out, each syllable heavier and more painful than the last as the truth sunk in.

"Is everyone else, okay? Anyone else harmed?" DS Smyth said.

"I think we're okay… luckily, we're in the right place."

Amal and Andrew were still in shock. They had no idea what Lewis had been through before arriving at the hospital.

This was just the icing on the cake.

"We are going to take you down to the station once you've been checked over. You will be safe there." Amal and Andrew were led away by the armed police. "I presume you are Deborah?" Lewis looked down at Viktoria. She was staring directly at DS Smyth. Her expression instantly turned to one of alarm and fright. She leaped upwards as if to punch the detective in the face. Lewis held her back. She struggled initially, fighting against him, and then eventually calmed down. The seizures had wiped her memory.

"She's just in shock..." Lewis said, stroking Viktoria's cheek.

"Well, I'm glad you're both okay. You were right about Crispin Humphries. He did operate on Mike Taylor. We got an anonymous tip-off. Someone sent us a video recording of the consultation. Unfortunately, he's gone missing. As for you," DS Smyth looked sympathetically at Lewis and then at Viktoria. "Thanks for your help. As soon as I found out about Humphries' involvement with Mike Taylor, I knew you would be in grave danger..." he continued. "You were right about tracking your phone, Lewis, we traced it to the last known location but lost the signal until you called us again. Look... Let's get you patched up and for the time being, you will be staying in a safe house for your own protection."

"There's still more, though." Lewis replied agitatedly "I need to tell you about Harry. He was framed by Afghani... he works for Brainionics."

"Do you know where he is now?"

"He's dead."

"Right..." DS Smyth thought for a moment. "Let's not talk here. You're a mess. You've been through a lot. The guys will take you to the safe house and we can talk there. There are still a lot of unanswered questions."

"I'm kind of getting used to that." Lewis said.

"You'd make a good detective, Lewis." DS Smyth replied.

In the background, police helicopters could be heard surveying the vicinity. A white sheet was placed over Patience.

Crispin Humphries woke up alone, strapped to an operating table in his own private hospital.

"Hello, Mr Humphries. You don't know me." A masked figure loomed over Crispin. He wore a fully blacked out face shield which had two small slits for the eyes.

"Huh? What? Who are you? What are you doing?" He struggled to lift his hands and feet from the table. He shook them frantically and cried out for help. "Help! HELP!"

"Nobody will hear you. You are alone. Mr Dayan has asked me to give you a present. I'm the other surgeon."

"Who? A what? A present? What are you talking about? HELP! HEL—"

The figure sliced straight into the top of Crispin's head with a scalpel. No anaesthetic had been used. Crispin's scream was as raw as the newly formed gash on his head. He tried to shake his head from side to side but to no avail. His head had been tightly secured in a head clamp.

"HELP!" he cried out. His pleas seemed to reverberate off the walls and echo back to him, a diabolical confirmation of how alone he truly was.

"It won't take long." The masked figure spoke. "You should know." He shoved the Superstim device into Crispin's brain. He pressed hard on the skull until the device lodged tight.

"That wasn't so bad, was it?" Crispin was now whimpering. "This might be, though." He grabbed the metal staples and, with brutal force, closed the skin on Crispin's head, sealing his fate.

EPILOGUE

DS Smyth reopened the Mike and Beverley Taylor investigation, but it didn't take long for it to be reclosed. Crispin fully confessed to inserting the stimulator off-licence. Brainionics made a statement that the first generation of stimulators should only ever have been used for epilepsy, and never for strokes. It was with deep regret that Mr Crispin Humphries, once one of their most prized surgeons, had been profiting from vulnerable patients. They severed all connections with him. Well, not all. At midday, every day, an electrical discharge was fired to Humphries' stimulator. He would watch the clock nervously, sat at his kitchen table. Waiting. One day, not too long ago, he was found hanging in his mansion.

No further evidence was found to prove the involvement of Brainionics with Harry's death — Gad Dayan had disposed of Afghani's body and the only other witness to support his connection to Brainionics had lost her memory — he and his company were, for the time being, off the hook. Despite the setbacks, Gad Dayan was looking forward to a profitable year. The new Superstim devices seemed to have been an absolute success for the initial cohort of paid customers. The recipients were delighted, especially the pugnacious ex-soldier. His physical abilities had evolved beyond his and Brainionic's wildest dreams. The company continued to train surgeons across the globe unhindered by any political or military body. The plan was to ramp up the insertion of Superstims around the world.

After a period of recovery in the hospital, Deborah, otherwise known as Viktoria Ivanov, had not regained her memory. She moved into the safehouse with Lewis where he cared for her. Over several weeks, she slowly started to regain her strength. Only time would tell what sinister truths still lurked in her subconscious.

SIX MONTHS LATER...

A large monitor displaying a map of the world was covered in thousands of little white and green lights. The monitor showed the location of all the Superstim implants around the world. A white light indicated that the device was implanted but not active, a green light indicated a successfully activated implant. A technician in the engineering room was inspecting the global Superstim panel when one of the stimulation lights turned red. He mumbled to himself in Hebrew and hit the board. It turned green again. When he left the room, it flickered back to red, so did another. And another.

THE END

Printed in Great Britain
by Amazon

76052053R00199